· ANGEL'S WAR ·

· ANGEL'S WAR ·

C.W. REED

ROBERT HALE · LONDON

ISBN 0 7090 5491 2

Robert Hale Limited
Clerkenwell House
Clerkenwell Green
London EC1R 0HT

Photoset in North Wales by
Derek Doyle & Associates, Mold, Clwyd.
Printed in Great Britain by
St Edmundsbury Press Ltd, Bury St Edmunds, Suffolk.
Bound by WBC Ltd, Bridgend, Mid-Glamorgan.

One

It isn't there any more. Did it ever really exist, that fabled, mucky bit of land, with fabled giants who, too, are gone? Do their heirs, their descendants, live somewhere in the great brick and glass-balconied towers that mark the spot? New and ugly, not old and cosy and dirty and ugly, like The Street. They buried the name as well.

The soot brick, tiny houses went overnight, gaping windows, flowered wallpapers, unsteady floorboards, swept away with a disdainful swipe from a machine. And the little roads themselves, with their brown kerbs and grey gutters and mossy, mottled, crack-patterned pavements, still intersected symmetrically and forlornly, great patches of black level nightmare waste – a Chrysalids Badlands of emptiness.

Perhaps the ghosts still hung about then. Perhaps, for it was quite a while before the new world came in, churning, mixing, soaring. And no more doorsteps, no more fanlights, no more Sutherland Street.

To start with, it was *the* street, no doubt. In that mucky little town on the edge of the land, social and economic status were clearly defined; the wealthy, and therefore virtuous, lived around the Park, that large area donated by a rich councillor, whose posthumous reward was a stern statue of himself in that same park, atop a pedestal, clutching a scroll, frowning, righteous, and, maybe, just a mite perturbed, for there are no flies on his trousers. Then houses grew closer. They lost names, and had only numbers; streets were narrower, until, at the bottom of the scale, glorious in its infamy, magnificent in its general disregard for the values of other, more pretentious parts, stood Sutherland Street. Twin rows of terraced houses, facing each other, door to paired door, fanlights dim with ancient dirt, sacred almost. To clean the fanlight would be to go against the code. Like whitening the step. Or swilling the yard. Oh yes, Troutbeck, Lansdowne, only two streets and a few yards away, might do those sort of things. But not here. The line was clearly drawn. Here was different.

There was the legend that Sutherland Street itself had seen 'better' days. Days of shiny brass door-knockers, lace curtains, and scrubbed steps, when tradesmen and sea captains (for some strange reason an occupation associated with respectability) had resided there. But that was ancient history, in the closing days of another century. True, the street still had one captain; at least, that was the courtesy title he claimed and was given. Old Jonson everyone called him (actually Johansen), Ellis's grandfather-in-law.

This old man, bent, with white, brown-stained walrus moustache and beautifully white hair, still had his much battered seaman's chest, his knife, and an odd assortment of relics from his career. He had served under sail, could tell wonderful stories of high adventure if he could find an audience, which was not easy, for most of his acquaintance had heard them many times, and, besides, to the inhabitants of the street, the world was a very small, comfortable place. They did not venture far, unless they were forced to, and Old Jonson's tales of the Cape, or brawling in Hong Kong, were beyond their limited imaginative horizons. Some kindly, some not, they shut him up or escaped.

But now the street was in its heyday, in its glory. Its name figured almost daily in the local newspaper. Usually under Magistrates' Courts. Petty thieving, drunk and disorderly, disturbance of the peace. They were champions, like Arsenal, proud of their fame, basking justly in it. Not many of the men worked. Not at regular jobs, that is. They were regular only on Thursdays, at the Labour Exchange, where they drew their dole. The rest of the time, they did 'odd jobs' as and when the need or inclination arose. To some, careful study of the form of horses, dogs, and football teams, absorbed all their workaday energies.

There were exceptions, of course. Like Tojo, the chimney sweep. Every morning, his wizened, monkey-like figure could be seen riding on his high bicycle off to work, dressed in top hat and tailed coat, his brushes and bucket strapped to the rear. But he was odd anyway, a recluse, and he *did* live in the end house. Only one of his neighbours claimed to have been inside.

Proudly, those who could read would regale their fellows with the choicest epithets bestowed on them by the authorities. 'An eyesore', 'a blight on the town's fair name', 'a den of infamy'. Well might their chests swell, their hearts throb. They walked with fame, were part of it.

There were two main social centres of gathering, apart from the clustered, door-to-door gatherings of the street itself, which was limited climatically to spring (occasionally) and summer (less occasionally). Old Jonson described the area's climate fairly accurately when he said, as he too often did, 'Here you have vinter, and two months of very bad veather.'

The first was naturally the pub. It was not, technically, part of the street, for its building lay on the other side of the broader and longer thoroughfare, off which Sutherland Street ran. But it faced, almost directly, the end of Sutherland Street, and was very definitely regarded as their pub. It bore the splendid name of The Cleveland Arms, but if you had mentioned this name to one of the inhabitants of the street when seeking directions, he or she would probably have gazed at you blankly. After a few seconds, recognition might have dawned in the eyes of the more intelligent. 'Ah! You mean the Pothouse!' Who named it thus, why, and how the name came to stick, must remain unexplained. The fact is that, despite the dark lettering across the front above the windows, everyone knew it as the Pothouse.

The building blended beautifully with its surroundings. The first four foot six inches up from the grimy pavement was covered in shiny, brown, oblong tiles, of the public convenience type; then came the frosted windows (glass and dirt in almost equal thicknesses), patterned here and there with vague, rushlike fronds. All the exterior woodwork was green and flaking. The brickwork above the bar windows lapsed into the normal sooty red-black of the area, punctuated by the narrow spacing of the two further windows of the upstairs private quarters.

The interior was equally homely. Through the one entrance, you turned left for the bar, and right for the best room. If you carried straight on, you stood in a dark, narrow passageway by the stairs, which was the off sales department. This trade consisted chiefly of kids bearing large jugs which their parent(s) wished to be filled with the draught bitter – Ordinary.

The bar was brown – brown varnished wallpaper, brown counter, brown chairs and tables, all chipped, scratched and generally rubbed with time. Even the mirror's reflection gave a brown tint, like those early photographs. On the wall opposite the door, there was a dartboard. The three round tables were for the domino schools. The rest of the narrow space was for standing and drinking.

The best room had more tables and chairs, and upholstered benches around its walls. It had a gas fire, two pictures, and a calendar. Women were allowed to drink there.

Mrs Foster was the landlady. Dyed blonde, brassy, bosomy – yes, that's her. With a real Woodbine voice, the rasp of a file, and a cough that made you want to spit in sympathy. There were five spittoons at strategic points in the bar. None, of course, in the best room. There was a Mr Foster, too. He was short, stooping; his dark hair was sparse on top, so that his temples gleamed palely. He had a grizzling moustache and still favoured a bowler hat on Sundays. He was seen regularly behind the bar, serving, washing glasses, humping crates, disappearing to the cellars to tap new barrels. Yet though Mrs Foster was the landlady, no one regarded Mr Foster, Alf, as the landlord. Not even himself.

The other social centre was literally next door to the Pothouse. Much smaller, one room really, with a tiny space out back. That was Sam's, the fish shop. Not fresh. Good old fish and chips, the staple diet of the street. Sam opened every lunch-time (dinner-time in the language of the region) and every evening, except Sundays. Always there was a fair-sized queue around the four greasy walls in the hot, steamy room, where vapours eddied and lifted, to make vision uncertain.

Sam stood behind the high counter, his bald, freckled head shining, red face invariably smiling as he tossed baskets of sputtering chips, flipped over the cod or the haddock, or, always fascinating for the kids, and there were many of them, chipped potatoes into the large bucket, with a rhythm that was poetry. Pick up with the left hand, toss across, and down on the handle with the right. And out shot the chips through the grilled squares of the chipper. Toss, crump, toss, crump, a beautiful motion, at bewildering speed, a juggler who never dropped his ball. So Sam darted about, ceaselessly talking and working. His silent wife was usually in the dim recess out back, peeling, filleting, flouring, doing some dull but necessary chore out of the limelight.

Sam's had two ventilators, high on the street wall, no windows, so that the atmosphere was that of a well-lit cave, of a shelter sealed off from the world outside. Sam served alone, therefore his customers spent a considerable time edging in good order from the door round the three walls until they reached the counter. Once you made that turn from wall to elbow on counter, you knew you were almost home. Five minutes at the most, unless Sam had to put in a fresh batch of chips.

Here it was, often, that the choicest titbits of gossip were worried back and forth by the women, scarf tied turban fashion against the smoke from the Woodbine that bobbed ceaselessly from their lips, arms folded tightly across their old coats, or mackintoshes, or pinnies if the weather was warm enough, feet comfortably spread in old felt slippers or sand shoes. Sometimes, if they were busy, or if the weather was too inclement, they sent their kids, and shivering youngsters could be seen jogging through the rain, their lips moving as in prayer, repeating the complicated order, lest they should forget. 'Fish an' two four times an' a fish, an' a patty an' scraps.' But often as not, the women liked to come themselves and shuffle along the walls, chatting amiably or acrimoniously, free from restraint, crude, jolly, foul mouthed. Sam heard it all.

'Eh, Doris, me ole man was after us again last night. Ah told 'im, if 'e's put me up the spout again ah'll bloody kill 'im.'

'Ye'll 'af ter sew it up, kidder.'

''Alf a crown, Sam! Bloody 'ell! Eh, you pop round our 'ouse wi' me, son. Ah've got summat worth more than any 'alf a crown!' The pails out back would clatter extra loudly. Mrs Sam had little sense of humour.

At each end, the street opened on to wider, more respectable thoroughfares. Over a hundred yards away from the Pothouse and Sam's, a hundred dirty yards lined by two continuous rows of dwellings, cockroach, blackbeetle, mouse, rat and human infested, was, simply, the School. As grimly sooted as the surroundings over which its three storeys lowered, high bricked-walls, green railinged, the legends BOYS and GIRLS carved at a distance which determined that, if it lay at all within the powers of the town's education authority, never the twain should meet, it sucked in the young inhabitants of the area at the tender age of five, and endeavoured to keep them there sporadically until the day deemed by the government to mark the end of the minimum period of education Britons required.

It was run, not quite single-handedly, by Bruiser, a five foot six and a half inch man who, to generations of urchins, was a seven-foot, bowler-hatted fiend, propelled to work on a stately, six-foot bicycle. His fists were the size of footballs and clumps of black hair sprouted from his knuckles, matching those which lurked terrifyingly round the edge of his cavernous nostrils. Famous for his kidney punch, which could transport an unwary child ten feet horizontally while lifting him a foot clear of the ground, he ruled with his two hands and a rod of bamboo, and it was rumoured that even the female staff had been known to retire to the misty world of the nervous breakdown through dread of him. He, of course, dwelt a mile-and-a-half world away from the street, in a neat, front-gardened semi where he hopelessly endured a reign of terror from a fat shrew of a wife.

One windy July morning, the last day of the school year, which Bruiser was resolved should not be marred by any anticipatory pleasures of the freedom of the long holiday about to come, a stocky figure with dazzling, white-blond hair which neither the most persistent head louse nor clinging muck could dull, swung dextrously over the spiked railings from the school yard and dropped to the freedom of the pavement. A sole flapping from his ancient boots, he cheerfully flung a V sign at the padlocked gates before he sprinted across the road and into the narrow confines of the street.

Half-way down, playing with some objects in the filth of the gutter, was a tiny individual with a similar thatch, who looked up in pleased surprise. 'Eh! Our Elisha! What ye doin' outa school?'

Little Jimmy rose to his diminutive height. He was wearing a stained, brown, high-collared jersey. And nothing else. His legs from the knees down were almost uniformly black, except for the paler, suspicious rivulets. His penis and ball bag were looking blue in the unseasonably chilly weather.

'Listen, our kid,' Elisha hissed urgently, with a hurried glance round the deserted street. 'You 'aven't seen us. All right?' But this was too subtle for Little Jimmy, who smeared the snot absent-mindedly across his face as he began to argue.

Elisha ignored him, keeping a wary eye out for onlookers. Every door was closed. The street had a strangely tranquil look, as though everyone was out for the day. Then, with relief, he remembered. It was Rent Day. The grown-ups wouldn't risk appearing in the street even if the houses all caught fire. Not until the mackintoshed figure with the big bag had rat-tatted his bring-out-your-dead way along his route: Inkerman Street, Sevastopol, Balaclava – every one a battle he had little hope of winning.

Elisha decided on a simpler approach. 'Don' tell on us, will yer? An' ah'll bring yer a stick o' Spanish.' Hurriedly, he turned up the hem of his own greasy jumper, and Little Jimmy caught a fleeting glimpse of some gleaming yellow, wooden rulers. 'Ah'm goin' down the market ter flog these,' he announced proudly. 'Ah nicked 'em out the store.' He jerked his blond head in the direction of the school.

'Ah wanna come,' Little Jimmy cried in a wailing tone, anticipating, correctly, a firm refusal.

'Piss off!' Elisha cuffed him across his tousled locks and ran. Picking at his bottom, Little Jimmy stood watching him, while a tear channelled its way through the dirt on his pinched, already resigned face.

The houses were back-to-back with Inkerman Street and Balaclava Street (how Sutherland had squeezed into the middle of the Boer War was a mystery as great as Councillor Ward's flyless trousers) – only two streets further up did the elevated status of tiny back yards and cobbled back lanes make itself apparent – and Little Jimmy had to bawl through the letter-box on the flaking front door before it was whisked open with conjurer speed, an arm dragged him in, and it slammed shut again. 'Ah've jus' seen our Elisha,' he bawled, in the vain hope of averting the wrath which seemed to fall perpetually upon his young frame from the other members of the family. All bigger than him. Except the baby. But unfortunately the baby never shouted at him. Or at anyone. It just lay and gurgled. And smelt.

His mam was pulling at him in her bad-tempered way, the cigarette jumping at her lip. 'Yer little bugger! Ah've told ye not ter come bangin' on the door on rent day. Why don't ye bloody well stop out?' A final shove sent him stumbling over the ragged clippie mat and the black fender, on which were resting his father's sea-booted legs. This individual stirred irritably from his place of honour before the fire, which was banked high in the grate and glowed redly.

The Sea Coal Man flung a careless oath at his young son and scratched his scalp under his cap, whose check showed but faintly beneath its coating of grime. A striped, collarless shirt covered his upper torso, and his thick flannel trousers were supported by grubby white canvas braces and a wide leather belt. The latter he was threatening to 'take off to' Little Jimmy, a threat put into sufficient practice to make the child retire wisely to a peeling, damp-marked wall and blend with the drabness around him.

At a table covered with torn oil cloth, an adolescent girl sat painting her nails. She had rich, fair hair, like her brothers, hanging straight and long down her back at the moment. She was thin, and unhealthily pale, her sharply pretty face shaped already with the street's cunning look of survival, a sixteen-year-old adult who knew a lot. 'But Dad,' she whined, 'ye can get good money. And it's a job fer life.'

'Angela,' he said, the rarity of using her name marking the solemnity of the occasion, 'yer not goin' in the bloody p'lice, ah've tell't ye!' Shocked to the core, he muttered to himself, 'Women p'licemen. Ah don' know what we're comin' to!'

That it should come from his own flesh and blood, his oldest child, his own Angela Victoria. The police! Part of Them, the obscure but very real forces against which life decreed they should battle. The Sea Coal Man could not express even in his own mind his sense of betrayal. He started to heave himself out of his chair in his agitation before he recalled that it was rent day. Steady the Buffs! He sank back, reflecting on the ungratefulness of youth.

He lined up his family mentally and inspected them: Angela, Elisha, Terence – couldn't really count him, poor bairn. Ten years old but with the brains of a two year old – never come to owt, that one – Little Jimmy, and Edgar the baby. And there was the one after Elisha, the little girl, Roberta – she'd died of whooping cough, or some other fancy name the doctor had come out with, but it was the whooping cough that had been the start of it.

None of them gave a thought to him. He quivered in the delight of self-pity. Slaving away, racking body and brains to feed them and keep a roof over their heads, an old man at thirty-five. The jobs he'd had. All right, he was out of work just now, had been for a few months, but the dole money wasn't enough to keep flesh and bone together. No, he had to go down on that bloody freezing beach, scraping the sands, collecting the coal the sea didn't want. Pushing the great, wet, heavy sacks of it round the town on his old bike, doffing his cap and yes-sir-no-sir to all the silly old toffs and their bitches with enough in their purses to make it worthwhile.

'Gerrus another pot o' tea,' he growled, and his wife clicked her tongue disapprovingly. Aye, even Doris, he reflected, didn't appreciate him. He watched her thin figure in the shapeless pinny, the turban round her mouse brown, thin hair, her white limbs with the giraffe pattern of her 'fire legs'. Always a bloody fag in her gob, always moaning. He reached for his own cigarettes, took the last Woodbine out of the soft five packet, and tossed the crumpled scrap of paper on the fire.

One thing about sea coal: it didn't flame but it was bloody hot. He smelt the burning rubber and winced as the heat burned through the hole in his sock when he moved his feet. He slurped his tea, listening to Ange's rebellious mutterings. Kids are too clever by half these days. Reading adverts about the police, going away to training school. Bloody nonsense. He couldn't read properly, and it hadn't done him any harm. *His* head wasn't full of bloody nonsense. Too soft, he was. That was his trouble. Too easy going.

'Ah'll tek me belt off ter ye, if ye don' shut yer mouth!' he growled. 'Never 'eard such bloody tripe! The's plenty ter do at 'ome without buggerin' away somewhere. An' there's yer job at the market, isn' there? What the 'ell d'yer want?'

Angela felt the prick of tears. 'Oh aye! Sellin' bloody fruit all day. Workin' till seven on a Sat'dy night. And all Sund'y mornin' an' all. Some bloody life!'

'Well ye not there now, are ye?' he snapped. Her absence from work was another sore point. 'Ye won't 'ave the bloody job if ye tek any more time off. The'll dock yer pay, ye know. Women's troubles!' He echoed the phrase his wife had used to excuse her daughter's staying at home. His voice was thick with bitter scorn.

Angela's pale face flooded with crimson. Her tone was equally biting with sarcasm. 'That's right! Doesn't matter if ah'm dyin', musn' miss a day's wages to 'and over, must ah? So's others round 'ere can sit around on their be'inds till openin' time!'

'You watch yer lip, me lass. Don' think yer too old to 'ave yer arse tanned, ye monkey.'

She glowered but lapsed into pouting silence. He just might. She wouldn't put it past him. Oh, what's the use? The shabby room danced through the tears. How she longed to get away. To be smart, have nice new clothes. Have a bathroom, for Christ's sake! Instead of having to heat pans of water and use that tin thing in the back kitchen. With Dad or Elisha crashing in half the time, just to get a glance at her nakedness. Their eyes dropping out nearly if they caught her before she had time to cover herself.

If only she could meet a nice lad. But not from round here. A decent lad. The lads round here only wanted one thing. And they made no secret of it. Well, she wasn't going to get caught like that. Up the spout and having to get wed. Six kids by the time you're thirty. No thanks. She studied her scarlet nails and dreamed.

Things were always tense on rent day, while they waited, trapped in the insanitary walls, for the knock. When it came they jumped, as they always did, but there was a feeling of relief. This was it. A few seconds and it would be over. Doris glanced warningly at Little Jimmy. She had picked up the baby from its box, and was half hugging, half stifling it. The knock was repeated, louder, then again, thundering through the cardboard-thin rooms.

'E'll knock the bloody 'ouse down, the silly bastard,' the Sea

Coal Man muttered uneasily, disturbed at this tenacious change in routine. Crash!

'Come on! Open up! This is the police. We know ye're in there.' The Sea Coal Man glared at the wide-eyed Angela as though her ridiculous idea was somehow responsible for the law belting down their door. Little Jimmy crawled determinedly into the dusty boards under the table. Doris was frozen, even the Woodbine smoke carved on the air.

'Answer it, man!' her husband hissed, his mind working furiously. It was more than a year since he'd had owt to do with law-breaking. Then it was only loading that lorry with Blackie. He didn't know what was in them bloody boxes. And the gaffer had been a posh sort of bloke, with a funny, poofy accent. But that had been twenty miles and fourteen months away. Oh Jesus effing Christ! If he flung himself at that bloody no-good wall, he'd probably go straight into Balaclava Street, covered in shit and plaster.

'It's about our Elisha,' Doris said, and he wriggled with guilty relief. He recognized the bobby, a young lad who was a regular. And at his side was Bruiser, his thick nose and lips pulled back as though the stench might rot his bowler.

'Come in!' said the Sea Coal Man with biting wit. All wasted.

The bobby spoke ponderously, with the weight of his uniformed, official boots. 'Mr Adcombe called us in. There's been a theft at the school, an' 'e suspects Elisha Thompson. Your son,' he added by way of identification.

Attack being undoubtedly the best form of defence, the Sea Coal Man struck. 'Oh aye? 'E does, does 'e? Well, suspectin's one thing, provin' it's another, me bonny lad. An' ye can do yer suspectin' elsewhere's. Fuck off out of it!'

Bruiser's florid complexion darkened and swelled until his bowler cut into his large brow. 'Where's your lad?' he boomed accusingly.

"Ow the bloody 'ell should ah know? You're the one's supposed ter be lookin' after 'im now, like. Lost 'im, 'ave ye?'

Doris fluttered in nervously, waving her chapped hands and removing the Woodbine in her agitation. 'Now, 'Arry,' she cautioned. She smiled craftily. 'What's 'e supposed to 'ave done then, mister?'

Bruiser growled under his white collar. 'There's a lot of

supposing going on around here. But not in my mind. Your son is missing, madam. So are two dozen brand new rulers and a box of erasers.'

Christ, what's them when they're at home, the Sea Coal Man thought, and Bruiser, seeing the fleeting look of worried incomprehension, added nastily, 'Rubbers, Mr. Thompson.'

'Aye, aye,' snapped the Sea Coal Man. And up yours. And your white mice. But Doris's cunning was at work already. She was quick, the Sea Coal Man thought admiringly, and forgot his uncharitable thoughts of that morning. One thing you've got to say for the family. In a crisis, they stick together. Unite against Them.

'Oh, that's right,' she was saying ingratiatingly. 'Ah remember now. Ah told 'im ter go down ter King Ossy Street this mornin' ter collect summink fer me from 'is gran. That's right, our Angela, isn' it?'

The blonde girl had left school nearly two years ago but Bruiser still carried the authority of the classroom. If the bobby had been on his own, she'd have made mincemeat of him. 'Yeah, Mam,' she answered diffidently.

Bruiser's disbelief was expressed through his black nostrils. 'Constable, we're bringing proceedings. Mark my words, that boy will hang. He'll hang!' He turned on his steel-tipped heel with a final sniff and sought the open air.

The young bobby glanced at the hostile faces. 'Ye'd best bring 'im ter the station,' he advised heavily. 'Otherwise, we'll be back.' Solid, dark and large, he followed Bruiser.

The Sea Coal Man waited until he was safely into the street then pranced round the room, throwing a few punches. 'The bastards!' he exclaimed. 'The bastards. Ah'll do 'im. Poke 'is nose in 'ere again an' ah'll kill 'im, the bastard. No right. No bloody right at all. Man's 'ome!' He clattered over a chair and murderously cut the air.

Little Jimmy's head appeared between the table legs. ''E pinched 'em,' he announced simply, stopping the Sea Coal Man in his tracks and starting him off on a new one.

'Where is 'e?' he threatened. The bobby's life was safe. 'Where is the little bastard? Ah'll murder 'im. Bringin' the bobbies round. The thievin' git!'

At the first resigned knock, he sprang to the door and swung it open, to find himself staring from a distance of six inches into the equally startled face of the rent man. ' 'Effin' 'ell!'

Two

Old Jonson didn't mind facing the rent man. In fact, there wasn't much the eighty-one-year-old ex-mariner *did* mind facing. Beached in this dirty street in this dirty sea port, as old as the street itself, he nevertheless remained its most exotic flotsam. Even his accent was excitingly foreign. Walking slowly, for he could walk no other way, he urged on his serge-clad legs, watching the bobby and the teacher leaving his neighbour's. Maybe Peggy, his granddaughter, had got up against the wall and heard. His heart quickened. Yesus, those criminals next door. His rheumatic red knuckles rattled the knocker. 'Hey, Peggy, open!' he yelled, coughing a little. 'Come on, you bluddy voman,' he muttered, chewing at the yellowish strands of his stained moustache.

A plump blonde girl with a youthful, red face, let him in. 'D'you 'ave a nice walk, Grandad?' she asked, pleasantly enough. 'Rent man's been.'

'Valk? Rent man? Nyach!' He pulled off his donkey jacket and unwound the blue woollen muffler. 'Vod happen next door, den? I comin' down de road, and I see a policeman comin' out de Sea Coal Man's, ya, and wid de schoolteacher, too. Dat boy, ya. He up to no good. Vod you hear, Peg?'

'Ooh, Grandad!' She scooped up his discarded clothing, and moved to the row of hooks behind the door. 'Ah've got better things ter do than listen ter that lot. Come in. Kettle's on.'

He made an indeterminate sound to express both his irritability at her lack of interest and his delight at the thought of trouble to his vociferous neighbours. 'Dey get it dis time,' he wheezed. 'Must be dat Elisha. He go to yail for sure.'

'Eeh, Grandad!' She shook her head and went into the small, dark kitchen. The kettle was beginning to sing on the top of the black-leaded stove. He eased his stiff, aching bones into the high-backed rocker, which was strategically placed at a comfortably close angle to the glowing fire in the small grate. He studied the amply curving form of his granddaughter with tender, nostalgic regret as she busied herself warming the pot and getting the mugs ready. His blood stirred with muted passion at the memories she evoked.

She was so like her mother, his daughter, Mary, who had died three years ago, just a few weeks after the Abdication. He found himself staring at the dark bronze plaque on the wall, above the prettily inscribed parchment dated 1918, neatly framed, which stated how gloriously Bob Rowe had achieved immortal fame by getting his lung pierced with shrapnel. 'What was me da like?' Peggy had asked, over and over. What could he say? He had known him for a fortnight. A rather soft young fellow who doted on her mother and didn't assert himself enough. A most reluctant hero. But worth ten – no, a hundred – of the spineless, shiftless, snivelling wastrels like the misbegotten pimple on the arse of humanity Peggy had had the bad sense to hitch up with. 'Where's Ellis?' he grunted.

His granddaughter's voice came out defensively. "E wasn't feelin' too good. 'E's not up. His chest—'

'His chest,' he mimicked scornfully. 'What's wrong? Someone offer him a yob to get him so upset, ya? Dat husband of yours de most lazy, good for nothing—'

'Stoppit, Grandad!' Peggy protested. 'You know Ellis 'as alwus been bad. Ever since 'e was a bairn, 'e's been delicate. 'E's lucky—'

'Delicate! Hah! De boy's got de constitution of an ox, so vell he looks after himself. Delicate! Too damn delicate to go to vork, ya! But he beat me down to de Pothouse ven he got de shilling in de pocket. I get him out of de bed.'

'Grandad! Leave him!' But Old Jonson was already stomping in his polished boots up the tiny stairs off the dim lobby. The flowery clumps of the once white, now brown, wallpaper showed faintly in the gloom. A small, creaking landing allowed one to squeeze into either of the two bedrooms: the back one, windowless, and poky, his; the other, the front, into which he turned, almost filled with the solid, old, double bed mother and daughter had shared. In the centre, propped on pillows, sat a thin, balding young man with a pasty face, whose most interesting feature was the thick, dark-framed, twinkling glasses, like the shining bottoms of two bottles.

Ellis spoke with a soft, nasal twang which his enemies, among whom his grandfather-in-law loomed large, would describe as a whine. Over the eiderdown was spread a newspaper, several old comics and women's magazines. The spectacles beamed on to the old man. Their owner gave a sickly smile and a small, sample cough.

'Oh, 'ello Grandad.' Old Jonson walked through the blue Woodbine fug, round the bed to the window and struggled with the warped wooden frame and rotten sash cord, until he succeeded in opening it a few inches. Ellis glared malevolently at the aged back, but was smiling when Old Jonson turned round, panting with satisfaction.

'Dey tell me dis mornin' dat Stewart's is takin' on some men,' he said without preamble. Every day, unless it was raining or snowing with special force, Old Jonson walked a mile and a half through the town to the docks, where he would chat to fishermen, longshoremen and loafers, and, when he had money, which was most days, he would have two halves in The Grapes, beside the dock gates, and smoke a pipe of his pungent plug tobacco, telling yarns with his cronies of better days. Days before he had to share his roof with this measly sea cook of an idle grandson-in-law, who hated a day's work more than an all-over, strip-to-the-buff wash.

And so many like him among the young men. Complaining all the time, belly ache belly ache, no work no work. But when work came, they ran. There was going to be a war, my God yes, this Adolph, the crazy German, he was ready now. Then they'd have a job all right. There'd be no dole queues then. They'd work all right, for half a crown a day. Including his precious grandson-in-law, with his delicate chest. It was worth a war, just to see him in uniform. He chortled.

Ellis was lying back now on the pillow, trying to look delicate. The thick, grubby, striped pyjama jacket was fastened at the top button, hiding most of the scrawny, unwashed neck. He didn't bother to answer Old Jonson's remark about Stewart's. It was not worthy of reply. Old Jonson was tempted to take out his baccy, just for the pleasure of seeing Ellis's face, but he remembered grumpily Peggy's complaints. He limited himself nowadays to two pipes when he was in the house: one after dinner, and a last one after tea. It was something to look forward to. And God knows there wasn't much for an old man in this heathen land – this heathen town, peopled by savages. Ignorant, lazy know-nothings. Never been past The Street, most of them.

'Goin' to be a var,' he observed, silhouetted against the window. How he enjoyed baiting his grandson-in-law. One of the few pleasures left to an old man. 'Dey putting in dem sandbags by de Custom House. Dey got stuff on de vindows for ven de bombs smash de glass.' He relished the look of revulsion which flitted across Ellis's features.

Ellis gave a superior snigger. 'Naw, Grandad.' The bedclothes rippled as he warmed to his theme, an informed observer, our Sutherland Street correspondent. ' 'Itler's not after us. Now we know where we stand. That's one thing about Chamberlain.' He would never have voiced these sentiments in the Pothouse. In there he inclined towards the colour red. But Old Jonson was just an ignorant Scandiwegian. He didn't know his arse from his elbow, politically speaking. 'Aye,' Ellis went on. 'These Tories can 'andle the old foreign affairs, like. Know 'ow ter go on, see. Yer bloody Clem Atlees wouldn' know which bloody fork ter pick up. Breedin'. That's what counts. Old 'Itler knows now. That's it. As far as 'e can go. No, the blokes 'e's after is them Trotskies. 'E'll 'ave them Russian bastards an' good luck to 'im.'

'Vod about vot he do to dem Yewes?' Old Jonson argued, interested in spite of himself. 'He puttin' dem all into prison camps. Dey show de pictures at de bioscope. I seen it.'

Bioscope! Ellis smirked. What a Swede-bashing peasant! Bioscope! The smirk became a snicker from his nostrils. He pushed at his glasses. 'They livin' better in them camps than in their own 'omes. Bloody filthy some o' their places! An' yer've got to admit, there's a lot in what 'e sez. The've got all the money, 'aven' they? Look at ould Marky.'

Marcus Blaum had a shop three streets away. A lot of business came his way from the street. Clocks. Best suits. But he was a bugger. Lousy prices. And if you lost your ticket there was hell to pay. The fact that Marky was in the shop from dawn to dusk, ready at all hours to make a living, did not endear him to Ellis. Bloody Jews!

'Seems to me you all scared of dis Hitler. You like de ostrich in de sand. But he not gonna stop where he is, nossir. He goin' to keep comin' so dat you British gotta fight one day. Better do it now while you gotta chance, ya!'

You British! Cheeky bastard; Ellis seethed under his blankets. Bloody lived here for the last fifty years at least, and he still talks like a foreigner. And if the Nazis come, he'll be out there heil Hitlering and telling 'em, no, not me. I'm not British, mate. Up the Kaiser and three cheers for the Huns. Always on about a war.

Ellis couldn't help shivering in the warmth of the bed. He was frightened. Twenty-six. All this talk about conscription. They'd call him up, and have him marching and shooting and bayonetting and all that. Well, we'd see. Surely they'd see at the medical that he just wasn't fit for the military life? Trouble was, it was his nerves that was bad mostly, and that was harder to find. Especially those army doctors. Just looking for cannon fodder, they were. They'd be like Old Jonson, with his 'there's nothing wrong with you' touch.

But then they did say that nobody would be safe this time, even in England. These bomber planes. Hitler had hundreds of them, and he could flatten half of England in a week. He drew his knees up in plaintive self-pity. What a life! The world gone mad. But surely not *that* mad? What's the point of blowing everybody up? No, old Hitler wasn't so daft. Let him knock shit out of the Jews and the Reds, and good luck to him. Those planes. And those tanks in his parades. All cardboard, the lot of them.

Oh no! Old Jonson was off about the last lot again. How I won The Great War. Taking bloody coal across to the Frogs or summat.

'I tell you, we slept on de deck. Even in de snow. Dem submarines. One second you all right, den boom! In de vater, if you not dead. An' de Nord Sea in vinter. Hey, man. Five minutes an' you froze to death. I seen it many times, ya. Terrible!'

Ellis squirmed irritably. Why didn't the old bugger go away somewhere?

'Ya, you try to go in de army. Not on de sea. You got more chance in de army.'

For God's sake! Ellis was suddenly thirsty. A nice hot mug of tea would go down well. But he was afraid to shout to Peg with Old Jonson stood there. Why do folk always go on about war? Ma was just the same. Her favourite tale was of the bombardment. The only thing that had ever happened to the town to hear her talk. He could tell the tale word for word, chorusing with her.

'Ee, it was jus' before Christmas. We 'ad all the cards up. Bitter cold, it was. Yer pa 'ad just gone off ter Stewart's.'

1914, Ellis reflected, amused. The First Hundred Thousand, White Feathers, and all that crap. Elsewhere, men might be flocking to serve King and country, but not here. His pa had stayed home until Parliament dragged him in for the last year. Never volunteer. They should have carved that over the Town Hall steps.

'The bairns were passin' on the way ter school when the' was this terrible screamin' kind o' whistle. Like a railway engine. Then bang! We thought it was the end of the world. Ah was out 'ere wi' you an' Emmy in the pram. Ah ran in just me pinny – pushed the pram all the way ter the tunnel. An' there was 'undreds there. Women an' men an' bairns. Some of 'em got on the' knees. Everybody was wailin'.'

Aye, thought Ellis sardonically. And the German cruiser had stood off the port for half an hour shelling the town with nobody lifting a finger, because the battery had been sited behind the lighthouse and couldn't fire a shot in reply. Damn' clever, these Huns.

That was nasty but at least you could run away from a ship. Get on your bike and bugger off. Westward Ho! But where could you run from those dive bomber planes? Hundreds of miles an hour, those buggers went. Definitely not like the last lot.

Ma told about the Zeppelin. A notice put on the door of the Town Hall. Everybody had twelve hours' notice to trek up behind the Park and camp there for the night. And then the bloody contraption had caught fire over the coast coming in and landed in the waves at the sea's edge. Out came three poor Huns, half burned and half dead, shouting *kamerad, kamerad*. To be met by a hundred or more of the brave local citizenry, armed with pitchforks or shovels, who promptly despatched the enemy. Chopped them up into smallish sized mincemeat and were congratulated for it by the Bishop of Durham.

Fortunes of war! Bugger that for a game of soldiers. And there was Old Jonson telling him to go in the army. Better get shot than drown.

Oh well, better get up. Otherwise the old sod will stay up here forever. Maybe get a shilling out of him for a couple of gills at the Pothouse. Ellis gave his martyr's sigh. What a life!

Three

At No. 42, the house next to Tojo the sweep's, young Ginge Clay stared disconsolately at his bright red waves and the freckles filling his pale face. His head looked too large for his squat body, the stunted frame of the region. He contemplated putting on a collar; he had two clean in the drawer upstairs, but was afraid of his father's scorn. A collar and tie on a weekday!

At least, he thought rebelliously, he was earning money. Shift work was a bit of a nuisance, especially now that he was on nights, but it was cushy at Stewart's on nights. Most of the men played cards in the boiler room, and all he had to do was watch out for the gaffer, and help the lad to make the tea. At seventeen, Ginge was very conscious of his seniority.

But not where Angela Thompson was concerned. He moved sadly away from the spotted mirror over the kitchen sink. Ever since he had met her coming home one night from the late show at the Lex, and she had walked along with him, and they had talked, he had been more and more aware of the place she was occupying in his thoughts. He wished there was someone he could confide in. He wanted to tell someone how he felt, how beautiful she was moving down the street, but there was no one. His mother and father, his brothers and sisters? That was a laugh! He was the eldest at home, now that Maureen was married, and Geoff had gone into the Merchant Navy.

And his mates. He couldn't bear to hear them mention Angela, so crude were they. And worst of all, he was just as bad. So afraid to be different, he was as lewd as any of them, as he screwed his eyes against the bitter Woodbine, or pretended to pull eagerly at the flat beer. Little did he know how close in thought to her he was, as he dreamed of escape.

Picking her up in his Bentley. Driving miles, away past

Bonington, to that posh pub for a meal. Tennis at the club by the Park. White flannels and a house with a garden. Fat chance! Once a Sutherland Streeter....

He should get away, like Geoff. Geoff had already been to the States and all over. He was like a creature from another planet when he came home. Everyone stared at him, listened to his tales, envied him. Ginge felt he would like that. Coming back bronzed and rich from across the world. He daydreamed Angela's big blue eyes fixed adoringly on his.

That would make a change, he thought bitterly, for when he had plucked up courage to ask her out, emboldened by her friendliness on that impromptu walk home, she had refused with scarcely concealed rudeness. He had shrunk from further contact, hurt to an extent that shocked even himself. Squashed – and by the Sea Coal Man's daughter! He could hardly remember what she had looked like as a kid, although they had grown up together and he had jeered and teased her and her mates in raucous childhood. But suddenly he met her and she was wonderful – a new and sparkling creature who obsessed him, and who treated him like the muck with which they were surrounded.

At times like this, he despised himself most. Collarless and greasy, shuffling down to the Pothouse for a dinner-time jar, as drab as his surroundings. Why didn't he up and off, the way Geoff did? Sign on one of those Aussie trips, come back with a wad of money. He hated The Street, his work, even his mates, at times like this.

Yet The Street held him, in spite of his longing and his dreams. He would never have the guts to fight his way out. But if there was a war ... he didn't know, had no idea, Geography extended only to the sands and the pier, the rest was the world, and he knew nothing about that. But people said there was going to be a war. They were always arguing about it these days. At work, in the Pothouse.

He dreamed, standing by the empty grate in the shabby room, staring unseeingly through the grimy curtains across at the Sea Coal Man's door.

... Captain Arthur Clay was today awarded a bar to his DSC after leading his men in a spirited counter-attack which saved literally thousands of British lives. In spite of murderous machine-gun fire, he

leapt over the top and charged at the enemy trenches, armed only with his revolver. Captain Clay, the youngest officer in the army, comes from a surprisingly humble background....

The Sea Coal Man's door was open and Angela was out and moving down the street before Ginge could drag himself back from Buckingham Palace and leap to his own front door. At an undignified half run he clopped after her, cursing his work boots and grubby shirt. Truthfully, he acknowledged that she, too, did not look her best, clad as she was in an old grey coat with some sort of check on it, which engulfed her slim figure, for which it had not been cut. Her sleek golden hair was hidden in a red scarf and her blue slippers were split at heel and badly scuffed.

Ginge was breathless when he came alongside her, partly through the nervousness that made his heart thunder and his freckles fade under a rosy blush. ' 'Ow do,' he said, with clumsily feigned casualness. 'Not a bad day now, is it?'

After a swift half glance at him, she looked ahead again. It seemed to him that she had taken in everything about him in that split second, and had not liked what she had seen. He didn't wait for her to answer his inane question but blundered on with another, equally stupid. 'Goin' out then? Fancy a tab?'

She shook her head. Even in this street, young girls didn't smoke on the street. He felt his colour heighten. Another twenty yards and they were at the Pothouse. He couldn't trail after her. ' 'Aven't seen yer about much lately. Mind you, ah'm on nights now, like, so ah'm not up before dinner-time.' He laughed in embarrassed fashion, knowing how stupid he sounded. He cleared his throat hawkingly, but remembered just in time not to spit. Though why bother not to? Was she going to leave him without even having said hello?

'The's a Cary Grant filum on on Thursday. D'yer fancy goin', like? Ah'll pay ye in,' he blurted desperately.

'Aye, ah'd like ter see it,' she said shortly. 'What time shall ah see yer outside?'

Ginge nearly stopped in his astonishment. His heart would surely burst. If he jumped now, he'd soar ten foot. He accepted as entirely natural the convention that they should not meet in the street itself. 'The six o'clock show, eh? See yer about quarter to. Well, ah'm off for a jar. Tara well.'

'Tara.' He forced himself not to stand watching her as she set off down the road. His insides felt weak and unsteady. He could still hardly believe it as he pushed open the squeaking door of the Pothouse.

The bar was not too full. It was early yet. He noticed his dad talking to some cronies at one end of the ring-pocked counter. Mr Clay saw his son and called out, 'Come on, ye bugger. Gerrus a bloody gill in. Thowt ye'd never come in.'

Sourly, Ginge ordered two halves. Only on Thursdays would you find everyone drinking pints. Dole day or pay day, people pushed the boat out then. And on Saturdays, too, maybe. The rest of the week they were forced to count their coins and sup halves.

'Now, Ginge? 'Ow's Stewart's, then? Not gone bust yet?' Alf Foster smiled thinly at his regular joke, wiping his small moustache with the back of a crooked finger. It was a habit which added to Ginge's dislike of him. One Saturday night, Alf had reminded him in front of his mates that he was under age and shouldn't be drinking. Still took his money though, the get.

Mrs Foster came in, wafting a powerful scent that did not mix well with the pungent smoke and stale beer smell. She patted her brass blonde pile of hair absently, though the look with which she surveyed her half-dozen customers failed to disguise her contempt for them. 'Yer chips are in the oven,' she rasped at Alf, who disappeared without a word. Love's young dream, Ginge thought, with bored amusement. He looked round for a mate to talk to, standing and taking a long pull at his glass, fighting not to shudder. To his private mortification, he hated the taste of the draught bitter. Any more than three pints and he felt like a bilious football.

The door squeaked again, and Old Jonson came in, the strange navy cap with the shiny peak pulled well down over his white hair. Behind him came the round-shouldered, stupidly smiling Ellis. They stood at the bar beside Ginge. Ellis maintained a diplomatic silence while Old Jonson ordered two halves and paid for them.

'Been down town, Mrs Foster?' Old Jonson asked. He took a sip of his drink, the suds clinging to his moustache. 'Dey gettin' ready for de var, yessir. Dey puttin' sandbags around, and dere's shelters down by de rec.' He chortled, his good humour increased by the obvious unease of his listeners. 'Yesus! Lotta good dat shelter gonna be when de bomb drop on it. Poof!' He waved his hands expressively. Mrs Foster clicked her tongue in disgust.

'Now don't you go talkin' like that, Mr Jonson. Some of us 'ave got a lot of years left. And we don't want to hear talk like that, ah'll have you know.' Especially not by a bloody foreigner, either, she thought, dismissing the fact that he had been a customer for all the eleven years she had kept the Pothouse. 'It was just sayin' on the wireless,' she added grandly, proud to be able to display her economic and social superiority, 'that Foreign Minister chap 'as bin 'avin' talks with 'em again. An' they assured 'im they 'ad no 'ostile hintentions against Britain.' Put that in your foul pipe and smoke it.

The Sea Coal Man came in and diverted the old man's attention. 'Vus dat de po-lice at your door dis mornin'?' he asked with wicked innocence. The Sea Coal Man rested an aggrieved sea boot on the worn brass rail.

'Aye. Persecution, that's what it is. Accusin' our Eli of pinchin' summat outa school. Where's the bloody proof, that's what ah wanna know?'

'Vere is de boy?' Old Jonson probed. 'I don't see him from de school at dinner-time.' The Sea Coal Man grunted and buried himself in his glass.

'Bloody p'lice,' Ellis offered ingratiatingly. 'Pity the've got nowt better ter do than chase after bairns at school.'

In the ensuing discussion the law came off badly, quite a number of those present having at some time or other experienced being on the wrong side of it, either directly or by association. But a startling revelation disrupted their grumblings. It came in the person of a slick and smarmy young man, the Fosters' nephew, who was a clerk with the local authority, and who was said to have 'prospects'. 'The prospect of a belt in the gob,' the Sea Coal Man had wittily informed his companions after a particularly galling instance of young Oswald's insufferableness. The remark was of course made *sotto voce* for fear of the redoubtable landlady.

Now young Oswald nervously fingered his tie – the only one in the bar – at being the centre of attention, but he was helped by his aunt's stentorian voice acting as a relay for the listeners.

'Gerraway! Go on, Oswald pet. What else?' The gist of the
news was that gas masks had arrived at the Town Hall and
were to be issued to the populace. Food rationing books were
also ready, bundled in their thousands, against the day when
Armageddon struck, or, as the Sea Coal Man more prosaically
put it, 'the shit flew off the shovel'.

There was an excited hubbub of voices on all sides. Old
Jonson, in his delight at the scarce concealed look of horror on
Ellis's face, bought Oswald a drink. Alf Foster came down to
see what 'all the bloody row' was about. Fumbling down the
dark staircase, he had fondly hoped that his missus had
collapsed, ticker stopped like a clock. But by the time he
reached the passage at the foot of the stairs he was all too
aware, from her rasping tone, that she was very much alive,
even though she seemed afraid that that state might not
continue for very long if Herr Hitler had anything to do with it.
'Eeh, my God! Well, ah've told Alf, we're not stoppin' 'ere an'
that's a fact. The towns'll be the first ter go. An' we're the first
thing the' come to once the're across the sea. Eeh, our Oswald!
Are ye sure, 'oney?'

'The're all in cardboard boxes, Aunty Flo. An' the's Micky
Mouse uns for the bairns, like.' He took an important swig.
Two halves in one dinner hour. He'd best be careful. 'Aye. Mr
Wright was sayin' it could be any day now. 'E's been diggin'
one o' those – what is it – Anderson shelters, in his back
garden. The' reckon the'll save a lorra lives, will those.'

The Sea Coal Man spat noisily and successfully into the
spittoon, not even noticing Mrs Foster's shuddering grimace.
'S'all right for them bastards up be'ind the Park wi' the' bloody
shelters an' the' back gardens. What about us poor buggers,
then? The' don't give a shite!'

'Aye, yer right, lad.' There were loud choruses of agreement,
Ellis's being among the loudest. His hand shook as he lifted his
glass. His heart knocked against his shiny waistcoat. The
palpitations again. Oh God! Just let an army doctor hear that
then. Burst his eardrums right through his stethoscope, it
would. The Sea Coal Man was right. Nobody cared about them.
One good bomb and The Street would be gone. Fallen like a
pack of cards. A horribly clear vision swam before his eyes of a
night bright with flames, of bricks tumbling and white

explosions. Women and children screaming, himself drowning them with his terror....

Old Jonson jabbed him in the chest with a plug-stained thumb. 'You get in de army, boy. I tell you. You got more chance on de land dan on de sea.' Ellis's biting wit for once deserted him. He could only stare, his eyes wide and watery behind his thick glasses.

August passed by with remarkably unEnglish weather, even for that windy corner of England. Elisha made ten shillings from his theft and spent it the same day. It was worth probation, which was what he got from the magistrate, though in those days the techniques for handling errant youth were not so enlightened, the officer assigned to watch over Elisha's welfare giving him a solid cuff around his blond head the first time the lad reported to him.

Ellis, indeed, most of the street's unemployed, got jobs at Stewart's or in the shipyards, to prove that an impending war does wonders for the unemployment figures. Someone had stated that those on the dole would be the first to be called up, and the new, magic formula, Reserved Occupation, was on everyone's lips.

Mrs Foster postponed her evacuation from day to day as the street's pay packets brought back the days of the pints and the money rolled in. She made Alf spend some of it on illicit ale and spirits, against the evil day of rationing, God forbid. A smoothly dressed feller brought some crates round long after closing time, Mrs Foster keeping a sharp look out while Alf grumblingly helped the supplier to unload them from his van and passed snide comment on the miracle which had allowed the contents to 'fall from the back of a lorry' whilst remaining fortuitously intact. Towards the end of the month, Hitler, with blatant disregard of Ellis's prognostications, signed a non-aggression pact with the Russians. But life ticked on.

Angela Victoria condescended for the second time in a month to walk out with Ginge Clay, and even to let him clasp her rough little hand in his sweaty palm in the darkness of the Lex, or Bughutch as it was fondly known. Ginge lashed out, paying 9d. for the 'courting seats', plush chairs at the back with an arm that could be lifted into a hollow rest, so that couples could achieve even closer proximity. A dark curtain hid these love nests from the central aisle and many were the lewd tales of conquest to be told after occupation, tales taller than the epics that thundered across the off-white screen.

Ginge worried considerably as he went to meet Angela, his red hair even more glowing from his attempts to brilliantine it into some semblance of smooth order, his best collar cutting into his pink and pimpled neck, the stud digging into his bobbing Adam's apple. Dare he take her into the courting seats? If he did, would she think that he was letting her know that … that he wanted … that he was hoping … somehow he found the nerve, though his face burnt. 'Two ninepennies, please.'

Old Mrs Shaw grunted from the tiny pay box into which she somehow fitted her bulk. For her, the world had virtually ended some years previously, when those dreadful talkies had ousted her from her rightful place down front at the keyboard, under the flickering projector light. They said Hitler was coming to drop bombs on them all, and it didn't surprise her one bit, oh no. Not since the day they'd trundled the piano up the red carpeted, white canvassed aisle.

'Packet o' Maltesers?' asked Ginge gallantly, once they were in the small, alley-like foyer with its worn lino squares. He invested another tuppence and handed her the dark-brown paper packet. He hoped she'd be generous with them. He loved Maltesers. For a swift second, he wished he was on his own, him and his Maltesers, and admonished himself for his cowardice.

It was just because they were going in the courting seats that he was panicking. He must get a grip. Be suave, man-about-town-like. He stubbed his toe as they went through the curtain into the gloom of the auditorium, and cannoned into Angela's back. 'Bit eager, aren't yer?' she snapped, loud enough for the usher, known more commonly to the patrons of the 'woodies' (the benches down the front) as the 'chucker out', to snigger. The collar dampened.

As they sat through the crackling music waiting for the lights to go out, Ginge wondered miserably what he should do. Hold her hand? Put an arm round her shoulders? Let his knee press suggestively against hers? The very thought made him quiver. What would she be expecting him to do? Summat, he was sure.

He thought of his mates. 'Ah tell ye, kidder. She was pantin' for it. 'Ad it outa me trousers before the news was ower!' And here he was, unable even to think of anything to say. His mind raced desperately, acknowledging bitterly how far short of his mental image of himself the reality was. Angela's sharp face looked bored. Or was she scowling? The paper crinkled as she opened the bag of sweets. Ripped it open? Why don't they put the bloody lights out, let's get started. Even Hitler 'ud be better than this. Ah! At last.

Somehow, after the first interval, Ginge found the courage to grope across. For one awful split second his hand hit the softness of a thigh and he positively grabbed for her hand in fright as he felt her stiffen beside him. She surrendered it, but it lay passive in his grip, as though it had nothing to do with the wrist and arm and shoulder, and all the rest of her. Ginge sweated and hated her. Two bob down the drain and she hadn't the list to speak hardly. Recklessly, he let his free hand fall across her shoulders. They felt quite hard under the plain green jumper. Delicate was the word that sprang to Ginge's mind, and he felt ashamed of his anger with her. He exerted tentative pressure, to draw her into him and, after a brief resistance, she gave, and leaned against him, her head pressing into his cheek, her glorious hair tickling his ear and mouth and her hip and thigh resting snugly against his.

He smelt her cheap scent, and it smelt wonderfully fresh and clean and feminine, and he was inarticulate with her beauty, the lump in his throat refusing to be swallowed, his eyes smarting. His left hand on her shoulder tightened. He squeezed her happily to him. All the time, their eyes remained on the screen, their bodies uncomfortably twisted together, but Ginge was soaring with happiness. He had no idea what the giant images were doing, their words were a sea of noise that beat senselessly about his happy ears. Who the hell cared?

Drop a bomb right now, and it couldn't be a better way to go. This lovely creature was actually in his arms. Well, in one of them, anyway. Oh, darling Angela, I love you, Ginge screamed silently inside himself. Aloud, he stirred and with his lips inches from that marvel of an ear hidden behind the golden tresses, whispered unsteadily, 'Fancy a tab?'

Only minutes before the baddy bit the final dust, Ginge turned against the blonde head and his lips nuzzled at the sweet neck. Again he felt her stiffen, but she did nothing to make him desist, and it occurred to him that her new rigidity did not spring from repulsion. He nibbled ecstatically, and her shoulders twitched under his almost numb arm.

Jesus, Angela thought, trying not to squirm, stop that. A wet mouth on your neck and you weren't supposed to shiver. But he wasn't a bad lad really. Not like some that she'd wrestled with in this very spot. And had the bruises afterwards to show for it. He was quite sweet.

But he was from The Street. No good even thinking about him in *that* way. Stewart's all his life. And never get to wear a collar and tie to work in a million years. But still. A nice kid. Shy. Better let him have something for his ninepence. And she turned with a convincing moan, mouth open, smearing her lipstick over his startled face before they were sealed teeth to teeth, tongues twirling, for timeless seconds, chests heaving and breathing noisily when they broke.

'Gosh!' Ginge breathed, staring at the dark silhouette of her head. 'Ange, ah think – ah mean you're a smashin' lass. Y'are, really!'

He didn't see the quick half smile flick over her lips before his mouth found hers again. Then she was fighting. For breath and for something else. A strange, stirring, deep excitement that made her angry with her trembling body. No! Stop it! Stop feeling like that! It's disgusting. And it's dangerous. Just a few kisses. And then … not with a lad from The Street. Suddenly she wanted to cry.

On the way home, he was chattering, over the moon, holding her hand, arms swinging, unable to believe life could be so good. Along Park Road and round the corner into Stockton Street, the gas lamps strange against the almost pale, not quite dark summer night in which you could actually see stars twinkling, undeterred by the gas works, and the steel works, and the shipyards, and Stewart's and the rest. The breeze was almost warm, the shunting engines sounded lazy, muted. There was a smell of land instead of the damp salt sea. Of fern, of heather, of fresh mown grass. It was exotic and not at all like the town. Summer warmth didn't sit easily on it. It was embarrassed, waiting for the grey and the cold and the driving rain, and the nightly sea fret haloing the lamp posts.

To Ginge the night was magic. He wanted the length of Stockton Street to be infinite, time to stretch for ever, walking, hand clasped, in the warm night. But it wasn't. As they drew near The Street, he sensed the strain, the popping of the fragrant, fragile bubble, and, almost in desperation, he stopped in the lane that ran by the brewery and came out near the school at the top end of the street.

A wooden fence ran along one side. Although Ginge couldn't see it, he knew the Sandeman Port advert was there – the black-cloaked, big-hatted figure that had been there for years, and that had so terrified him when he was a kid, making him run the lane's cobbled length with head averted and heart pounding.

He felt a touch of nostalgic tenderness that was a part of this night's magic that he so wanted to cling on to, and that he knew must fade, was already slipping from his grasp. Although Angela was only inches away, still beside him, he had released her hand and there was a gulf between them.

Nobody from the street ever went 'serious' with each other. It wasn't done. He didn't know why. Perhaps it was because they knew too much about each other. There couldn't be any magic. But that was nonsense, and the proof of it was beside him. This fair, golden, well-named Angel. She had grown and blossomed yards from him and all the magic in the world was in her blue eyes and her little nose, and he didn't know how to tell her, couldn't begin to, couldn't even shape his thoughts for his own understanding. He cleared his throat, he growled, he shuffled in the grit, and tried. But his rough voice, his harsh accent, stumbled clumsily against the unfamiliar softness of love.

'Ah've right enjoyed meself. 'Onest.' As though she should even think he had not. 'It's bin grand. Ah – ah think ye're grand. Ah mean – ye looks an' everythin' – grand. Would ye – ah mean can ah – would ye go out again wi' me? Some time?'

The throb of longing, the intensity that couldn't be expressed, was clear to Angela, and her sixteen-year-old heart was moved, deeply, and saddened. Life seemed a sad affair to her, its reality The Street, grim and inescapable unless you devoted every ounce of yourself to the struggle.

She mustn't weaken. She would get out. It was a vow,

solemn like the nuns. She wouldn't weaken, not even for a nice lad like this, for he was of the street, though amazingly good and gentle.

She pressed against him, squashing her small breasts, leaning into him, giving him her mouth eagerly, angry with herself, and wild, torturing herself. See! He's a nice lad. You like him. Feel him against you. You could do it with him. He'd love you. You could make him.

When she broke, gasping, her head on his shoulder, he couldn't see the tears sparkling like miniature stars. She blinked them from her lashes. 'Ah'll 'ave ter go,' she whispered.

'Can ah see ye again?' A wealth of pleading in his unsteady voice. She was tempted. It swept over her with weakening sweetness. What else did she want? This lad would be good to her. Her mouth tightened.

'Aye,' she said, forcing the lightness. 'Ah 'spec so, eh? Ah'll see yer around. Not far away, are we? Thanks, Ginge. Tara.'

'Ange!' His cry of dumb pain spoke volumes. She fought to be cruel, hurting both of them.

'Look, ah've gorra go, all right? Been a good night an' ah've said thanks. What ye want? Ah don' want a reg'lar boyfriend, see. Safety in numbers.' She tried a laugh, but it didn't come out. 'Mebbe we'll do it again some time. But don't push us like. OK? Ah'll see ye. Tara.'

She turned and hurried out of the lane, crossing the road. He saw her under the lamp at the end of the street. Its light silvered her hair. She looked very slender in the skirt and jumper. Her slim, unstockinged legs gleamed palely. He thought how frail she looked. And how desirable. He stood in the shadows of the lane, making no move to follow. Aching, every inch of him, with sadness and loss.

At home, Angela was glad to find that her father and mother were still at the Pothouse. Elisha was sitting leafing through a ragged comic under the naked bulb. The younger children were asleep. He squinted up through his tousled thatch. 'Been wi' that Ginge Clay, then? The pictures, eh?'

'Shurrup,' she said tiredly. Attack, attack. All the time. You had to. That was life. Elisha gave an unpleasant laugh.

'Give 'im a bit, did yer? 'Ope you 'aven't got one—'

'Shut yer filthy trap!' He was astonished at the vehemence with which she flew screeching at him, a hooked hand tearing his cheek before he could catch her wrists. She twisted. They wrestled briefly before she tore herself free, to sink in the one battered armchair and bend forward, her head on her knees. The long blonde hair hung down to the dirty floor. Her shoulders heaved with the volume of her sobbing.

Elisha watched her with wary puzzlement. 'Bloody 'ell! What you got yer knicks in a twist for? On'y a bit of a joke.' He went back to the comic, undisturbed by the noise of her weeping, which was swiftly brought under control.

'Ah'm off ter bed.' He maintained a diplomatic silence, contenting himself with a grimace at her departing back. All of them except the baby shared a room and Angela undressed in the dark, crawling into a space at the edge of the wide, lumpy bed. Next to her was Little Jimmy, then Terence. And at the other end was Elisha. At sixteen, she couldn't ever remember a night when she had slept in a bed by herself. And the Sea Coal Man couldn't understand why she wanted to get away.

Downstairs, Elisha yawned hugely and went through to the back of the tiny kitchen, to an even smaller room, the 'back-kitchen'. In the musty pantry, he cut a thick slice of bread, not even noticing the scurrying black beetles. A dish of cold dripping stood on the shelf and he smeared the bread's surface thickly, and sprinkled salt from a yellow cardboard drum.

Munching noisily, he went back to the room and sat in the creaking armchair. He'd finish this and go to bed. Must be late, his mam and dad had been out hours. Ma Foster must be letting them stay on. That young bobby was probably in the back supping free pints. Be just as well to be out of the way when Dad came back with a bellyful. Mind, Angie seemed to be in a right state with herself tonight. Still, she'll be asleep now. Probably got the rags up. Never knew where you were with lasses. If only Little Jimmy and daft Terence weren't in the way, he'd show Ange a thing or two. Probably knew all about it by now. Most lasses over twelve did round The Street. With casual thoughts of incest, he brushed off the crumbs and went upstairs.

* * *

The Sea Coal Man's Doris was in Sam's one dinner-time chatting to Mrs Clay and the other women when Sam told the assembled company, 'The've called up the Terriers. Was on the wireless at twelve. Mrs Everett from Combe Terrace was in jus' now. 'Er Brian's in the navy, like. Bin ordered ter report back to 'is ship, 'e 'as.' Sam's red face shone with sweat and importance. 'Gonna come any day now, mark my words. An' a right bloody state we'll be in an' all.'

Sam's wife came through, bearing a tray of floured fillets of cod. Normally taciturn, she was sufficiently moved by the crisis of the times to nod a dour hello to Doris and the others. She sounded near to tears. 'It can't 'appen. They won't let it. Eeh, our Joe's doin' so well an' all.' Joe was their son, at eighteen an apprentice electrician serving his time in the shipyard.

'It'll 'appen all right,' pronounced Mrs Clay, with grim satisfaction. 'An' your Joe'll be all right with 'is trade. The' won't take 'im for the army. Not like our Arthur,' she added bitterly. 'The' don' give a damn about labourers. Good enough ter go off an' be shot, they are.'

The discussion was entirely personal, as always. World events were only ever examined in the light of how they affected The Street. Otherwise, they were rarely mentioned or even known. But now the women chewed over the unpleasant fact of war, now that it thrust itself under their startled noses. Blame for steadfastly ignoring its growing menace through many months could be laid at much more imposing and illustrious doors than The Street's.

'We're not ready,' Sam declared, his gloom in no way affecting the swift skill with which he dispatched the fish and chips over his greasy counter. 'Bloody criminal it is. Make mincemeat of us inside a fortnight.'

'Hey! Do them Germans eat fish an' chips?' asked the Sea Coal Man's Doris with wicked innocence, and was rewarded with a new wail from Sam's wife out the back.

Four

Though only four of the forty-odd houses of the street possessed wirelesses, and one of those was Tojo the sweep's, the announcement of September 3rd, in the apologetically solemn tones of Mr Chamberlain, spread with the speed of fire, and with a similar dramatic excitement. Ellis was one of the first to come tumbling through the door into the smoky morning air, having crouched at Old Jonson's elbow by the fizzing set only long enough to gather the essential fact of war, then racing for the street, forgetting his 'delicate chest' and issuing forth in his shirt-sleeves.

He pounded on his neighbour's door, the despised Sea Coal Man, in his anxiety to be the bearer of disaster. And all his hopes were realized, for, when an irritable and suspicious Doris yanked open the door and eventually made sense of Ellis's garbled account, she let out a piercing scream that made doors clatter all round them.

'What the bloody 'ell?' The Sea Coal Man appeared, bare and hairy to the waist, fists doubling when he saw Ellis, though he could hardly believe that that daft streak would tap up Doris.

'It's war! It's war!' she screamed in his startled face, her penetrating shriek informing four more households immediately.

'Effin' 'ell!' The Sea Coal Man looked as if he were about to join her in a fit of weeping. Little Jimmy did. People spilled out on to the pavement in the nippy but sunny Sunday morning. There were shouts and sobbing, for it was a shock, in spite of the fact that it had been expected daily for some time and for the last two days almost hourly, though Ellis had said desperately, 'We won' go ter war fer a bunch o' bloody Poles!'

After an hour or so, the inhabitants of The Street began to

41

think ahead to dinner-time, relieved to find themselves alive still. Some even wondered if the Pothouse would be open. Their throats were tight. Thirsty work, this fear. People began to drift back indoors to get on with the business of living. Though there was still an end-of-the-world weirdness about even the most mundane actions, like putting the kettle on, which Peg was now doing for the umpteenth time.

Ellis had taken the medicine bottle of brandy from the sideboard and was liberally lacing his mug of tea. 'It's me 'eart, Peg,' he told her mournfully. 'Palpitations again. Feels like it's gonna jump right up in me mouth.'

With a snort, Old Jonson pushed his mug towards Ellis. 'Maybe ve all be dead in vun hour. Give me a brandy. For my last drink, dere's a good boy.'

With malevolent thoughts of the old man, Ellis tipped the bottle, righting it swiftly. That old bugger was as strong as an ox. Be dancing a hornpipe on Ellis's grave. That's if they can find a bit big enough to bury.

Next door, the Sea Coal Man was earnestly assuring his family of his desire to fight for King and country. 'Aye. Ah'd be off like a shot,' he told them, 'if the'd 'ave me. But too old, ye see. That's me trouble. Thirty-six. The'll not tek men my age. Pity,' he added bravely, thinking, by Christ, Harry you bugger, you'd better be right. 'Still, we can all do our bit, eh?' He glared around him patriotically and poked the grate with a sea boot. 'Keep the 'ome fires burnin', eh?' He laughed at his cleverness and Terence brayed uncomprehendingly.

'Ah'll join the Raff, me,' Elisha vowed fiercely, 'if it lasts till ah'm old enough.'

'Eeh, our Eli. God fergive yer,' wailed his mam. Her eyes were red and puffy, slit-like through the smoke.

Angela sat there with an empty, fluttering feeling in her stomach. Must be what they call butterflies. Sort of wanting to go to the lav all the time. She was ashamed to acknowledge an element of excited pleasure.

She hated the smothering, sordid nothingness of life in The Street. Well, now that would all change. She was sixteen. She had heard talk that it wouldn't be just the men who'd have to go. They'd be calling up women as well, for all kinds of jobs. Her da couldn't stop her going then, could he? Not if it was on the orders of the King. She sipped at the chipped cup and smiled a secret smile.

The first siren sent them all panicking, running about like headless chickens. It was just on dinner-time, a few days later, and many of the menfolk were away at work. Mrs Clay's screams were louder than the warning blast, and Ginge, still on nights, leapt out of bed in his drawers, groggily expecting to see a Hun (whatever they looked like) on the stairs. 'The're 'ere,' she wept. 'An' yer da's out. What'll we do?'

'Now, Mam, calm down,' said Ginge, pale and fearful. He began to pull on shirt and trousers. Embarrassing, being bombed in your underpants.

'The stairs!' Mrs Clay bawled. 'The' said under the stairs. Ah told yer da 'e should've got that bloody cupboard ready. Serve the bugger right when 'e finds us dead an' gone. Ah told 'im!'

Richer folks in more prosperous areas had already dug out their Anderson shelters, cosy with their bunks and lamps and primuses, and even plants and shrubs thriving on the hump of earth beneath which these solid citizens snuggled. Others had invested in the reinforced sturdiness of a Morrison shelter, under whose table you nestled while the house tumbled harmlessly about you. The Street had to make do with the tiny cubbyholes under the narrow stairs which housed the meters, or run the gauntlet of the rain of fire, bowel-movingly imagined by many in these initial stages of the conflict, to the long concrete slab of a communal shelter over a distant furlong away, past the school and at the bottom of Inkerman Street.

Mrs Clay's head was already buried in the small, black hole, burrowing determinedly through the assorted rubbish which she flung cavalierly back over her shoulder. "Oway, our Arthur. Ye'll 'ave ter squeeze in.' Ginge dutifully eased himself in after his mother's wide bulk. He fell to his hands and knees over brooms and boots, pressed against Mrs Clay, who managed somehow to turn and pull the door closed, sealing them in impenetrable blackness.

Mrs Clay broke wind noisily. 'Dear me,' she moaned. 'Ah want ter go.'

It was bad enough without that, Ginge thought, screwing up his nose. Rather be bombed than suffocated. Phew!

How long they sat there, neither of them knew. Their ears strained for explosions. Ginge sniffed. He could smell smoke. Burning. Yet they'd heard nothing. A silence, total and terrifying. Suddenly, there was a thunderous knocking at the front door. Mrs Clay screamed, and a beefy arm caught Ginge on the jaw. 'It's them parachutist things! My God!'

Ginge was shaken. The knocking went on and on, echoing in their black tomb. And definitely the sharp smell of burning was stronger. 'Don' go, son,' sobbed Mrs Clay. Ginge groped for the door, ready for anything, though, in all his fright, a tiny part of him laughed at the idea of a German parachutist knocking to be let in.

He crawled out and thrust the door closed instinctively. The passage was full of smoke! On his eyes, his mouth. Coughing, doubled up, he made for the front door less than two yards away, ignobly leaving Mam to burn. Must be a direct hit.

He pulled the door open and fell thankfully to the pavement among several legs, the smoke billowing out around him.

For a while, he didn't know much, though he was aware of his head resting on the moss-green kerb and hands pulling him about. "E's fainted, 'as 'e?'

'Must've choked in all the smoke.'

Suddenly, Angela's beautiful face was inches from his, her blonde hair framing her pale, anxious features. 'Ginge! Are yer all right?'

He smiled. The wounded war hero. Captain Clay seen here with his lovely fiancée, the vivacious Lady Angela. 'Aye. Ah'm fine.' Mam! Good God! He pushed through the little knot of onlookers. The Street – the house. It was still there. No flames. And the smoke had thinned out. The front door stood wide open and there were more people in the passage. He thrust against the backs, shouting desperately, 'Mam! Mam!'

And there she stood, in the kitchen, looking somewhat sheepish. She held out a charred and stinking frying pan. 'Eeh, ah fergot all about it when I 'eard that bloody sireen go,' she confessed. 'Ah left the bloody fish on the stove!'

They soon got used to the banshee wail, and came to ignore its strident call. For it became manifestly obvious that Hitler had had second thoughts about dropping bombs on England. There were more serious problems to contend with. Rationing was to become a reality, and the buff-coloured books with the bits of coupons in them became all-important. Most of The Street's families felt little extra pinch. They had known nothing other than scraping uncertainly by, and, besides, most of them could muster six books or more per family and were the world's best at making do and eking out.

For the men, their chief worry was conscription, and how to beat the Medical Board. Ellis cycled downtown and shut himself in the reference library, under the stern portrait of Councillor Ward and behind a two-foot pile of medical tomes, and came back feeling awful. He was fairly certain he had any of a dozen serious if not killer diseases to choose from, but could he rely on the unprincipled butchers who worked for the Forces finding any of them?

He had suddenly become keen at work, volunteering for overtime, sycophantically bowing and scraping to all his superiors, and there were many of them. How he envied the fitters and turners, safely hiding behind their skilled trades, the bastards. One day he noticed Sam the Fish Shop Man walking down The Street, magisterially wearing a circular tin helmet and an armband, with the letters ARP on both. An idea crossed his mind and he went over to Sam with almost sprightly eagerness.

Next day, he was at the local headquarters, his cap respectfully in his hands as he assured the middle-aged woman in her draughty office, 'Ye see, ma'am, me 'ealth's not good like, but ah want ter do me bit, see.' He became a warden. Maybe it would be enough to save him. He lived in terror of the postman, superstitiously averting his gaze should he catch sight of him, loathing the rare sound of the letter-box rattling.

Although, as the year tailed off into winter, he sometimes thought nature might save the Germans a job, when Sam officiously knocked him up for a cold night's duty patrolling the pitch dark streets, or sitting on Stewart's roof, waiting for the bombs to rain down on them. Save Stewart's from burning, Ellis reflected sourly. Not bloody likely! Still, he dodged as many nights as he could with his 'chest', and His Majesty's Forces hadn't got him yet – much to Old Jonson's disgust.

But it was happening to others. The net was spreading wider

– and nearer as familiar names got the summons. Going into the Pothouse at midday, he was surprised to see Sam at the bar, with his son, Joe.

"Ello, gaffer,' Ellis said. He felt Sam liked being called that, and a bit of respect did no harm, especially in a place like this, when a free pint might be had for a touch of politeness. 'Don' often see you in 'ere. Are ye not open then?'

'Nay, lad,' said Sam philosophically. 'On'y been open three days a week this past month. Where've yer been? 'Ave ye not seen them stickers up everywhere? "Dig for Victory". The' give me one fer me shop. Ah told 'em, the nearest bloody bit o' grass is at the Park, an' ah can't see 'em diggin' that lot up fer tatties like.'

At last the blessed words. ' 'Ave a jar, will yer? Got summat ter celebrate,' said Sam importantly, nodding towards Joe. Sam's son was a dark-haired, athletic-looking youngster, quiet and well mannered. He was serving his time in the shipyard, and had another two years to go, so that Ellis was surprised, and alarmed, to hear Sam say, 'Aye. Our Joe 'ere got his call-up papers today like. Fer the navy an' all.'

Sam actually sounded proud. The silly old fool. He sounded as though Joe had won something. Ellis's heart fluttered uncomfortably. 'But ah thowt ye were an apprentice. The' couldn't touch yer!'

'Seems the've got ower many leckies as it is. Any road, the've called me up,' Joe told him. 'Ah've got ter report ter Chatham barracks on Mond'y mornin'. The've sent us a warrant fer the railway.'

The silly young bugger was smiling. Ellis stared at him, his eyes wide behind his glasses, as though Joe had just confessed to bubonic plague. Ellis had to steel himself not to edge away along the bar. The taint might rub off.

'Chatham. That's down London way,' Sam announced proudly. Ellis took a disbelieving sip of ale. This was weird. Like celebrating a death sentence.

'Well, all the best, kidder,' he said solemnly. 'The Senior Service, eh? Ye're a lucky bugger.' Politeness always pays, you lying twat, Ellis told himself. London. It was hours away on the train. Hundreds of miles. They were funny down there. Southerners. A different breed. Don't let it happen to me, Lord, he prayed earnestly. I'll not go sick for the firewatching tomorrow night. And that's a solemn promise.

Five

Ginge swallowed nervously and faced the clerk behind the counter. This individual needed a shave. And his collar was dirty. 'Yes?' he growled impatiently. Ginge drew a deep breath.

'Ah want te volunteer. For the RAF. The' told me ter come 'ere.'

The clerk sucked his teeth, utterly bored, and tossed a form down. 'Fill this in. An' bring it back ter me.'

And there's the first obstacle, Ginge thought. Filling in a form. A pen was not a familiar instrument. But he must struggle through. Here he was, laying down his life, and nobody wanted it. They couldn't care less. Ginge was hurt. It had not been an easy decision. He had lain awake for a number of nights, dithering, trying to pluck up the nerve, seeing himself dying in a dozen horribly bizarre ways. All very vague, for aeroplanes had never been closer than distant, buzzing dots in the sky. But he had seen at the pictures a newsreel of the young pilots of a fighter squadron. It had shown them training, flinging Spitfires around with breathtaking skill. They were laughing, good-looking young men, dashing and modern, and not weighted down by bags of 'bullshit' – a word much favoured by his dad when on the subject of military life.

So the RAF it would be, or so he hoped, but they didn't appear eager to have him. He chewed the pen, dipping it into the inkpot repeatedly, but failing to transfer the ink to paper, until the clerk resignedly filled it in for him, and all Ginge had to do, laboriously, was write his name. He had hesitated long over the space beside religion, but the clerk confidently scribbled C of E. 'Looks good,' he explained. 'They like it. Patriotic, see?'

'Oh, aye.' Ginge nodded, at a loss. He was given a card, and sent to another building across the road where, to his intense embarrassment, he was ordered to strip naked for a medical examination. There were other lads sitting about in various stages of undress, but Ginge was too shy to ask whether their experiences had been similar to his. But the elderly doctor couldn't have been anything else but a queer, for he actually hefted Ginge's balls for a long second, saying something ridiculous like, 'Cough.' And the chap who was his assistant wasn't much better, for he gave Ginge a little glass flask-like thing, and said, calm as anything, 'Piss in that.' If these were medicals, Ginge was glad he'd never endured one before.

In yet another office, thankfully dressed once more, he was given some test papers, in a room with desks, just like at school. He had done his best, but some of the questions had seemed crazy. He couldn't make head nor tail of them. Finally, he had been asked to state his preference, and, with a deep breath, and a sudden pounding of the heart, he had indicated 'Air Crew'.

When he emerged into the five·o'clock dusk, he felt exhausted. It had taken him all day, and even then they had told him, 'We'll let you know.' He felt a sense of anticlimax. He wanted to talk to someone. Not someone: Angela. There was no anticipation of joy in telling his parents. His dad would call him a 'daft beggar' and his mam would have a fit of weeping.

But Angela ran a mile every time she saw him. He just couldn't understand. That night at the Lex. The kisses. And in Brewery Lane, when she had pressed herself against him like that. And ever since, she had avoided him like the plague.

In desperation, he had stood at the window for hours, watching for a glimpse of her, rushing out to waylay her into conversation. But she wouldn't look at him, hissing at him, 'Not 'ere. Me dad'll see us. Leave us alone, will yer?'

She couldn't realize what she was doing to him, how he felt. What would she say now that he was going away? Perhaps for ever. For a second or two, he toyed with the idea of saying nothing. He would just be gone. She'd realize he wasn't around any more. Then she'd hear what had happened. She'd go across to his mam, ignoring the wicked, curious gossip, tears rolling down her beautiful face. 'Mrs Clay, please. Ah must write to 'im.' Then she'd read it.

Squadron Leader Arthur Clay, Britain's youngest RAF officer, gave his life for his comrades, driving his flaming Spitfire into a wall of enemy aircraft, thus saving the lives....

She'd cut his picture out of the *Mail* and she'd keep it on her mantelpiece the rest of her life. A lonely, beautiful virgin.

Whoa hey! Steady on, ye daft bastard. How do you know she's ... Ginge cut off his ignoble thought by breaking into a run. He could see two dim pools of light as a rare car crawled past. This bloody black-out. They put the lamps out, but the bastards didn't take the posts away. Hospitals were doing a roaring trade stitching split heads. Probably on piece work, like they all were at Stewart's.

Ginge thought of his workmates. All raking in the money. Overtime, Sundays in. Laughing all the way to the Pothouse. They'd call him a mug as well. Until he got his DFC of course. Then they'd all want to buy him a pint.

What if he didn't get in? Keying himself up for nothing, for a letter saying, 'Dear Sir, We are sorry....' They said he'd know within a week. Suppose it was no? He'd better say nowt until he found out. If it was no, he'd have to stay. In The Street. With Angela across twenty-five feet of potholed roadway. What the hell *do* you want? he asked himself fiercely and just missed another lamp post.

Ginge's besetting sin was not arrogance, and, after several days of brooding, he had convinced himself that he would be rejected. As with the rest of The Street, letters arrived rarely, so that when Ginge came home after a night shift, his mother met him with the news as he came through the door. 'Letter for yer,' she announced solemnly, ready to cry at the rip of an envelope.

It stood on the black mantelpiece propped against the imitation marble clock that had belonged to Mr Clay's father. Its buff length, with the OHMS stamped on one corner, looked sinister. Mrs Clay was building up to a good cry. 'If it's the Forces it's a mistake. The' can't take yer. Ye're not eighteen yet, our Arthur.'

Ginge put down his bait bag and wiped his dirty hands on his dungarees, postponing the moment of truth, irritated by a gruff, 'Come on then, ye bugger!' from his father, who was installed in front of the fire, 'on the sick'.

'If that bloody Ellis 'asn't got 'is papers, ah'm not lettin' you go, an' that's that,' worried Mrs Clay.

Ginge flushed under Stewart's grime. They were all looking at him, and he felt momentary panic. He would have to tell them. And it would be worse, with the answer being no. See Mam, I tried to join up in the RAF and they wouldn't take me.

Nervously, he clawed at the flap and clumsily extracted the folded paper. There seemed a lot of it. It didn't take that much to say no. There were several sheets of correspondence and, with wildly beating heart, Ginge opened them, his eyes darting over the first sheet in an effort to absorb the meaning of the unfamiliar print, and taking in disjointed phrases. 'Pleased to inform you.' 'Will proceed by train.' 'Railway Warrant (third class) enclosed.' 'Should bring the following articles.'

His head swam. He was in! His parents were spluttering, his dad had left his chair and was peering uncomprehendingly over his shoulder, muttering, 'What the bloody 'ell?'

'Is it yer call up? Is it?' his mam asked, twisting her pinny in her red hands. Ginge nodded, his eyes still flicking over the page. He looked at the top again. The Royal Air Force Regiment. Didn't sound like Air Crew. Why 'Regiment'?

Mrs Clay was working the pinny into a tiny, crumpled mass. 'The' can't!' She rounded on Mr Clay as though he were King George himself. 'Ah tell yer, the' can't take 'im. It's against the law!'

'Hold yer bloody tongue!' shouted Mr Clay, accepting her outburst as a personal attack upon himself. 'What am ah supposed ter do about it, like?'

Ginge joined in, shouting in unison, and for some seconds uproar reigned until his words registered, and the noise faltered away like air from a bagpipe. Mr Clay was the first to regain the use of his vocal cords. 'Ye – ye what?' he asked disbelievingly, dark, unshaven jaw hanging open.

'Ah volunteered,' Ginge asserted, with a truculence he did not feel. 'Ah'd be called up any road in a few month,' he continued, with a desperate rush of words, trying to stem the avalanche of his mother's hysteria before it engulfed them. 'An' ah'll be better off in the RAF than the army.' Mrs Clay was sinking into a protesting wooden chair. She moaned, rocking her large body back and forth.

'Our Geoff out there wi' them torpedoes, an' now you. Both me sons! Gone!' She wept noisily, seeing their names on the marble scroll. The Last Post and Poppy Day.

With some bitterness, Ginge dropped the letter on the table. 'Don' worry, Mam. It's not air crew, look. It's the RAF Regiment. On the ground. Prob'ly never leave bloody England.'

'An' a bloody good job an' all,' his father asserted. 'Upsettin' us like that.'

And then the recriminations started. Ginge endured them in martyr-like silence. A fine reward for answering the call. Mrs Clay shook her head. 'Volunteered,' she wailed yet again, making it sound as though he had been hauled up before the magistrate. The one who was always on about The Street being an eyesore. 'Volunteered! What'll the neighbours say?'

They had quite a lot to say when the news of Ginge's action leaked out, as it was bound to do, within hours of the postman's visit. Indeed, the chief source was the aggrieved mother herself, who, finding that her husband left much to be desired in his role of responsive confidant, pulled on the gent's mac over her pinny and sallied forth to spread the sad tidings.

By lunch-time, the subject was put forward for general discussion in the dingy bar of the Pothouse, mercifully, in Ginge's absence, though not his father's, who was one of his loudest critics.

Alf Foster shook his head with a contented grumble. 'Bloody daft, ah reckon. Eeh, these youngsters!' He wiped half-heartedly at the soaking counter. But Ellis was much more deeply moved. He couldn't suppress a shudder at this crass example of man's stupidity. It upset him. Its fearful insanity disturbed the tenor of street life, revealed a chink in the smotheringly warm cocoon. Ellis didn't like to be disturbed.

'Well now, ah don' know,' he observed philosophically. 'Young lad like Ginge. 'E's got the spirit of adventure, like. Look at 'em in the First War. Went off in the' thousands, the' did. All volunteers. An' women 'andin' out them white feathers in matchboxes if the' saw a bloke in civvies.'

Old Jonson snorted. 'By Yesus, dey need a lot of feaders if dey come in here yust now, hey?' There were indignant protests all round. The old man chuckled happily.

'Naw,' Ellis was saying earnestly, 'if it wasn't fer me chest an' that, ah'd be tempted. Aye, ah would. Bit of action. Excitement. Chance of a lifetime.'

'Ye effin' liar!' observed the Sea Coal Man, and Ellis was disinclined to argue the point further. 'People got more sense nowadays,' the Sea Coal Man went on. 'What's the sense o' volunteerin' ter get yer arse shot off? Jus' ter keep the world right fer the toffs ter live in. Serve 'em bloody right if 'Itler *did* come over 'ere, ah tell yer stright!'

Unfortunately, Mrs Foster came through into the bar on this last remark. Her bosom billowed like a hearts-of-oak figurehead, for she secretly prided herself on belonging to that very class of 'toffs' that the Sea Coal Man was so deriding. 'Mister Thompson,' she said grandly, giving each syllable a slow, deliberate emphasis, 'that is not only foul language, but also treason. That sort of talk can get you stood' up against a wall and shot.' And bloody good riddance, too, the little nowt. 'And I'll not have it in my bar, thank you very much.'

She gave her duchess's smile to the startled Mr Clay. 'Ah think what young Arthur has done deserves the 'ighest praise. If we all thought like *some* round 'ere,' and her eye swept her customers like an accusing machine gun, 'Hitler certainly *would* be over 'ere, and nobody ter stop 'im. Thank God there are some brave souls like young Arthur still left in this land, I say.' The ample breasts quivered with patriotic pride. The eyes glinted challengingly, and the men buried themselves in their pint pots.

' 'Ere-'ere,' Ellis said stoutly, thinking silly old cow.

Alf struggled out into the passage with a crate of empty brown ales and thought that maybe facing Jerry mightn't be so bad. Certainly the lads in khaki weren't exactly defying death, if the news was anything to go by. The worst thing they had to worry about in France was the weather, now that winter was coming in.

Hitler was obviously content to leave things as they were as far as the western front was concerned. Poland had given him enough to worry about. And the Russians messing about with Finland. Be a damn sight better off chasing a few mam'selles than facing Flo day and night. Yes, he'd have beaten Ginge in the queue if he'd been a bit younger and no mistake.

* * *

Ginge was The Street's second departure for King George, though Joe Morley, Sam's son, had at least been conscripted, not like 'yon daft bugger', which was how the inhabitants, with the exception of Mrs Foster, referred to Ginge, as they frequently did in the few days before his going.

Angela Victoria was examining her pale face for blackheads when the Sea Coal Man brought the news, and her fingertips ceased their exploration at once. She came shuffling in her slippers from the kitchen. Her golden hair was tied and pinned in rags and curlers and an old, once white shawl clung to her shoulders. "E 'asn't!' she said, at a loss.

' 'E 'as!' her father assured them with a smirk. 'The silly bugger's gone an' volunteered fer the raff. 'E goes off on Mond'y. Somewhere down Nottingham way, ah think ould Clay said. 'Oppin' mad, 'e was.' He shook his head and eased himself into the battered, newspaper-lined armchair. 'That's kids for yer. Ungrateful buggers. Just when 'e was startin' te bring in some good money at Stewart's an' all. Bloody disgraceful.'

Angela flushed. 'Oh aye! Money! That's all you think about. 'E might be killed fer all you know, an' all you can do is call 'im ungrateful.' She was almost as surprised at her vehement outburst as the rest of the family. Elisha grinned, sensing a row.

' 'Oo the bloody 'ell d'ye think yer talkin' to, my girl? All ah think about! An' what the 'ell d'ye think would 'appen if ah didn' think about it?' Scandalized, he appealed to his wife. 'D'ye 'ear that, Doris? All ah bloody think about! You're gettin' a bit too big fer yer boots these days. Ye'll get the back o' my 'and if ye don't shut yer mouth. Ye're still a bairn, remember. Thirty bob from the bloody fruit market doesn't give ye the right ter lay the law down 'ere. Yer want ter do that, ye'll 'ave ter bugger off out of it, me lass. Pronto!' His dark eyes shone with fury.

But the blue of Angela's blazed back, then misted with tears. 'Ah will an' all!' she stormed. 'An' bloody good riddance!' She raced for the door and sprang up the protesting stairs, crying loudly. The Sea Coal Man was up and roaring, yelling up the stairs, his hand instinctively fumbling with the buckle of his broad belt.

Doris pressed her scrawny frame against him in the narrow passageway, thrusting him against the damp wall, and pandemonium reigned. 'Ye can't take yer belt to 'er,' she panted, grabbing his wrists. Her husband shook with rage.

'You shut yer mouth an' all. Too many people tryin' ter tell me what ter do in me own 'ouse. Geroff!' With a determined heave, he escaped from her restraining grip.

' 'Arry!' his wife yelled. 'She's sixteen. Ye can't belt 'er any more.'

The Sea Coal Man stared back at her wildly, but his anger was controllable again. With a guttural sound of disgust, he contented himself with a final yell up the stairs. 'Don't you show yer face down 'ere, yer little bitch or ah'll tan the arse off yer.' He swept back to his chair and Elisha quickly hid his grin. Pity his dad didn't carry out his threat though. Ange was altogether too much these days. It just didn't pay to speak to her.

Tea that night was a very strained affair. Nobody spoke, but simply wolfed and left the table hurriedly, and Little Jimmy got his ear clipped twice in as many minutes for misdemeanours that remained a complete mystery to him. But then, that was life, and Little Jimmy, bawling and smearing jam across his chin, crawled stoically for the blessed obscurity under the table.

Angela was not of course present. She was still lying face down on the bed, her head throbbing and face swollen from her weeping. She could feel the sheet wet under her cheek and her nose was blocked, necessitating a loud, crackling sniff in order to breathe again.

She would take her father at his word, she vowed, and sneak away that very night. She relished their frantic worry, their remorse, fitting dialogue to the scene. She pictured her own, vaguely rosy future. Found in London, taken in by a rich and concerned family. Robert the handsome young son. With Daddy in the family business. Falling madly in love. Angela, one of nature's ladies. Back to The Street in a Rolls and furs. How her dad would grovel.

She shattered the fantasy, and wiped her face on the dirty sheet. No you won't, she told herself bitterly. You won't go anywhere. You've got five bob in your bag, no clothes, and you're frightened to death of being five miles away. Not like Ginge. He'd done it. Got away. Escaped.

Volunteering. She felt a surge of admiration. Such a quiet little lad. With his carrot hair and his freckles. And that awful mother of his. But he was stuck on herself, she knew. Had been for months. And that time, when she'd let him kiss her in the Lex, and afterwards, in Brewery Lane, she could feel him shaking. So shy and afraid.

Not like the others. Freddy Barraclough and that lot. Come on then, lass. What you got hidden away there? I've got summat that'd fit that nicely. Foul tongues and foul minds. Four-lettered words that didn't include Love. Ginge was different. Not enough go though. Not enough fight. Happy even in The Street.

But now he was leaving. Going far away, perhaps abroad. Perhaps he'd fly one of those Spitfires, or a bomber, over Germany. She shied away from the thought of a violently broken body. Of flames, burning flesh. A crashed plane. What was left when a plane crashed out of the sky?

But no, death wouldn't touch him. He was close to her, Angela Victoria. Her heart suddenly gave a strange jump. She would be his girl. Yes! He could write to her. A lad in the Forces! Yes! He was nice really. A fine lad. She loved him. Liar! Shurrup, she argued with herself. I *could* love him. The new Ginge. Formed by danger and the world. Gentle and assured. She would love him. Anyway, be fond of him. Not permanently. But this was war. Nobody could think forever. But for now, definitely.

It was cold and dark in the back bedroom. Little Jimmy came up and crawled under the covers, filth and all. She heard her parents go out and came sure-footed down the pitch black staircase. The room was empty. Elisha must be out, too. And Terence.

She peeped through the ragged blackout curtain. Stupid. What could she see but blackness? She had looked across the street towards the Clays. How could she see Ginge? Talk to him? She felt a second's sharp fear that he might have gone. But her father had only mentioned it today. He must have just heard. But it could have been days ago when Ginge had actually done it.

She stood in an agony of indecision, then spun impulsively on her heel and groped her way back upstairs. She found her best dress, and finest stockings, holed though they were, and changed in the dark. She tried to guess the time. It couldn't be very late. He wouldn't have gone to work yet. What time did the night shift start? Ten? But he wouldn't still be working, would he? She felt a fresh surge of hatred for her father. Why hadn't he told her exactly when Ginge was going? He would probably be out with the other lads, maybe down town at the Rink or somewhere, celebrating. Aye, even going away to war was something to celebrate if you were leaving The Street.

She went through to the kitchen and splashed cold water on her face, then worked with her cheap make-up, carefully, and with hurried concentration. She frowned critically at her dim reflection and pulled a grimace. 'Ye'll 'ave ter do.' She tugged on her best grey coat and was out into the cold night before she hesitated. What bloody time was it? With this damn blackout you couldn't see a thing. She avoided the lamp post, groping along the house walls until her eyes became accustomed to the dark.

She found the gutter and crossed the road, peering in front of her, one hand forward to encounter any obstructions. She couldn't even be certain of getting the right door. And if she did, had she the nerve to knock on it? Five minutes later, she was fairly sure she was there. She ran her cold fingers over the worn wood, sick and frightened, and despising herself. With sudden ferocity, she rapped painfully.

After some seconds, she heard cautious movement, and Mrs Clay's fearful voice. ' 'Oo's that? What ye want?' Mrs Clay was still under the misapprehension that Hun parachutists would knock before entering.

Angela coughed nervously. 'It's me.' Then, realizing that this might not be considered adequate identification, added, 'Angela Thompson.'

There was a startled exclamation and the bolts were drawn back. The door opened a fraction, and light spilled through a crack in the living-room door a few feet behind Mrs Clay. "Ello, 'oney,' she said. 'What's amatter?'

Angela took the plunge. 'Is Gin – er – Arthur – in, Mrs Clay?'

'Arthur? Ye want our Arthur?'

Angela's face burned. 'Yes. Could I 'ave a word with 'im?' Even in the blackness, Angela could sense Mrs Clay's hostile curiosity. Subtlety was not Mrs Clay's strong point.

'Wot yer want?' she asked bluntly.

Determined, blushing furiously, Angela refused to be beaten. 'Ah just want a word wi' 'im,' she maintained obstinately.

The little slut. What a family. Like her mam and dad, this little madam. That Doris, with a tongue on her like a dirty razor. With an explosive grunt of disgust, Mrs Clay turned and shouted into the darkness. 'Arthur! Our Arthur! Someone ter see yer. The Thompson lass!'

Angela, in the midst of her mortification, felt a surge of relief. At least she hadn't endured this for nothing. He was in. Shame made her bitter. She wouldn't ask me in of course. Oh no. Might contaminate her place if I set foot across the door. Then Ginge was there, peering wide eyed around his mother's bulk. Astonished. His voice shrill.

'Ange!' He could say no more, only gawp. And Mrs Clay looked as though she would go on standing there for ever, ears flapping.

' 'Ello,' Angela said, with nervous gameness. 'Ah just wanted to 'ave a word with yer like. If yer not busy.'

'Naw. 'Ang on.' Trembling, Ginge grabbed his coat from the hooks in the small lobby, almost tearing it in his eagerness, unmindful that it was the stained, workaday Stewart's outfit. Struggling into it, he forced his way round his mam and into the cold street.

'Where ye goin'?' she demanded.

Ginge was uninformative. And brusque. 'Out!'

The door clashed echoingly. His eyes never left the pale sheen of Angela's hair as they moved side by side down the uneven pavement. Angela's voice was small and unsteady. She sounded as though she'd been running. 'Ah just 'eard from me dad. About yer goin' away like. In the Air Force. When d'yer go?'

Ginge's voice was no steadier. 'Mond'y. Two days,' he added unnecessarily.

'Ah wanted ter see yer before ye go,' she said simply. She put her cold hand into the crook of his arm, and he patted the knuckles awkwardly.

His heart was racing. He still could not believe it. She had broken the taboo. Come looking for him, knocking on his door.

Facing his mam even. 'Ah'm right glad. Ah was meanin' ter see yer anyways before ah went. Ah just didn't know whether ye'd – well, want us to, like.'

She returned his squeeze, and Ginge felt his tentative question had been answered. He felt strange, in a state of shock still. One minute reading the *Mail* in the fug of the kitchen, the next in the cold blackness with Angela on his arm. An Angela who had come to seek him out. He was frighteningly happy, and sad, too. He was going away in two days' time. Just when....

He pushed Monday away from him with determination. They walked carefully across the road, past the school, to the darker entrance to Brewery Lane. 'Where'd ye want ter go?' he asked gallantly, aware of his old work coat, shabby and smelling of paint.

She hugged his arm. 'Anywhere. Ah just wanted ter see yer. Talk te yer.'

They walked into the malt-smelling obscurity, and his arm moved around her waist. Fifteen panting minutes later, Angela tore her stinging lips away from his to gulp in air. Disloyally, she wondered how her coat was faring, pressed up as she was against the wooden fence. Fleetingly, she reflected on the difficulties stacked against them in this winter's night. There was nowhere to go.

While Ginge eagerly thrust against her, she fantasized a warm, flickering fire, a thickly carpeted room to themselves. No chance. Up against a fence in Brewery Lane. Ankle deep in dog muck and broken bottles. And that black you could hardly see the face that was kissing you.

She was suddenly swept by a desire to be wicked, to make love with Ginge, to lose her fought-for virginity now that he was escaping The Street. She could feel faint sparks of excitement even in the breath-fogging chill. But this was certainly no place to lose one's guarded honour. Not for the first time.

Ginge seemed content to stand all night, knees touching, noisily kissing. But, in a break, she said, dodging his mouth, 'What yer doin' temorrer night?' It was blatant, a naked invitation, and she blushed in the dark.

'Ah was just 'avin' a few jars with me mates. Listen, why

don't yer come? We can 'ave a drink an' then push off. Ah
promised like. In the Black 'Orse.'

A swift refusal sprang to her lips. His mates would be lads
she knew. Like Freddy Barraclough. It would be out in the
open then, an acknowledged liaison, and, naturally, she shied
away from it. Then suddenly thought, what the hell? Why not?
She didn't mind any more. Ginge Clay's girlfriend. He was
going off to war. She pressed against him. 'Aye, all right. Ah'll
meet yer 'ere, eh? What time?'

Six

The pub was Saturday night crowded. Beer was not scarce, and the air in the appropriately named Snug was blue. Newcomers brought in the smell of the cold night, but it was lost in the gas-fired, packed heat. When Ginge walked in with a shyly proud hand on Angela's arm, a roar went up that made the drinkers look at the blushing lad with brief curiosity. Freddy Barraclough, from nearby Sevastopol Street, pantomimed astonishment. 'Well, well, well! Looker 'oo's 'ere. 'Ello, Angie, luv. 'Aven't seen you fer a while. Keepin' the conquerin' 'ero company, are yer?'

Her young, cheaply made-up face took on its accustomed hardness as she squeezed past the knees and the table. 'Aye,' she said coolly, not looking at him. 'Shift yer arse, will yer?' Ginge, with a silly, embarrassed grin on his face, had little to say, enduring the taunts with burning ears, but Angela returned all the fire with interest, and was the centre of attention, the lads vying with one another to appear the most witty. She handled them with great aplomb.

'Eeh, it's amazin',' sighed Freddy, with crafty innocence. 'Ah don' know 'ow yer do it, Ginge lad. Ah've been chasin' this lass fer months, an' she winnat even look at us. An' you've been seein' 'er on the sly all the time, yer crafty get. 'Ow long yer been goin' out now?'

'Ages,' Angela answered. 'Some of us just don't go round broadcastin' what we do, like.'

'By God, that's true an' all.' He nudged Ginge. 'Ye've come te the right pub, you. Talk about a dark 'orse.' He leaned towards Angela and put a heavy, mauling hand on her shoulder, speaking out of the side of his mouth to the uncomfortable Ginge. 'Ye'll want someone ter keep an eye on yer lass for yer while yer away. Keep 'er out o' mischief like.'

There was a burst of laughter, which doubled when Angela sent his hand flying with a harsh, 'Piss off!' Though Ginge laughed with the rest, inwardly he winced. Angela, his Angela, didn't use those kinds of words. Still, it was his own fault bringing her in here. He should have had more sense. He might have known what it would be like. Angie could be no other way with this lot.

Although he didn't know it, Ginge's view of his forthcoming departure was very similar to Angela's. He, too, saw it as an escape, a road to who knew what. Away from The Street. And then....

Vaguely, he pictured a rosy life with Angela, literally rosy, a cottage dotted with them. And angelic, chubby infants. Mentally, he blushed again, recalling Freddy's revolting words when they stood side by side out back, peeing. He had used that sly elbow. 'Ye'll be all right ternight, kidder, eh? Bet she can't drop 'em quick enough for yer. An' she's a bloody 'ot piece if yer can get 'er goin'.' He chuckled and stepped back. 'Yer can take it from me. One 'oo knows.'

Ginge had stood there, smarting and shaking. He should have smashed him. He wanted to, he was all white-hot rage, his fists balled. But he had done nothing, just stood staring with loathing at the broad back, hearing the dirty laughter.

Watching tough little Angela dealing with them in their own recognizable way, he had felt proud of her, and a bit sad. When they managed, not without difficulty, to escape on their own and were walking slowly along the dark streets arm in arm, he remembered Freddy's words again. And, though disgusted at himself, he wondered. Was Freddy just teasing him or had he meant it when he said he knew? And how should he go about ... about....

He didn't even know how to put it to himself, without employing the lavatory wall basics, and that didn't apply. Not to Angela. Rather leave the sex side alone altogether than spoil it. He would anyway, even if the impossible happened and she offered herself.

He didn't know what to do. He imagined Freddy's knowledgeable hoot of laughter and quickly qualified it. Of course he knew what to do. Only he'd never done it. Anyway, what's the point of these dirty little conjectures? The question won't arise.

' 'Ere,' she said at his shoulder. ' 'Ang on. Don't be in such a rush.' In his agitation, he had actually begun to stride ahead quite quickly.

They walked almost three miles, to the near deserted coastline, misty and hissing, then pounding as the ocean beat against the iron-railinged sea-wall. They laughed, kids again, dodging the white spray that jumped out of the darkness at them. Its noise was all round them. She put her arms on his shoulders and drew his head down to her open mouth. 'Ah wish yer weren't goin',' she whispered, after their long kiss. A voice mocked her. You wouldn't be here kissing him if he wasn't, you little bitch.

'So do I,' affirmed Ginge, and searched her face again.

'Mebbe it'll be over soon,' she offered. She was aware of her ignorance. She had no idea about it. And did she care? If it was over, it would be The Street again, for both of them. Could she go back on her own vow? A picture of her, like her mam, in the years to come, came into her mind. Woodbine dangling, putting up bait for her husband to take to Stewart's. Shocked at her own wickedness, she hoped the war wouldn't end too soon.

'P'raps ah'll be able ter join up an' all,' she murmured. 'Ah'm seventeen in January. Ah could go in the what'sits. The women's raff.' She sighed, and added fervently, 'Ah wouldn't mind. Gettin' away from 'ere.'

Ginge stammered, 'Ah know. Ah mean – if it wasn't fer – ye know – leavin' you an' that – ah think ah'd be lookin' forward to it. Yer know what ah mean?' he asked anxiously.

She pulled him down fiercely to her. 'Aye. Ah do. Ah really do.' Her lips were rawly sexual, passionate, somehow defiant, and she took one of his hands from her hip and placed it inside her coat, over her young breast. It stroked apologetically at the slight, exciting roundness under the wool of her jumper. Her legs moved, and her thighs clutched at one of his.

'D'ye love me?' she panted fiercely.

'Aye. Ah do – ah love yer.' He sounded as though he were sobbing.

'Right then! Come on!' She had made a momentous decision. She clasped his hand tightly and led him along in the cold mist.

Beside the pier the sea-front boasted two levels, and, after some searching, they found the slope that led to the lower promenade. Further along, stout wooden posts had been erected, joined by vicious swirls of barbed wire, decorated with notices covered in black deaths' heads and warning people to keep out by order of the War Department. Solid concrete blocks had been constructed down on the beach itself, with more notices declaring, 'Danger – mines'.

Angela's brother, Elisha, and others of a curious frame of mind, had spent considerable time trying to squirm or dig a way through the defences. Painfully defeated by the vigilance of the soldiery stationed at the neighbouring battery, and the local constabulary, who had clipped ears with fine abandon, the youths had resorted to flinging missiles as far into the alleged minefield as their strength allowed, hoping for a resounding and spectacular success which had so far eluded them.

However, the wooden benched shelters, enclosed on three sides, the open side facing the sea, were still accessible. Ginge and Angela stumbled on until they had passed a number of them, all apparently deserted, though it was impossible to see into their deepest recesses. Angela all at once veered to the right, pushing him towards the deeper blackness. ' 'Ere. This'll do. Strike a match.'

Its wavering light showed the discarded cigarette packets, the dried up peel, the green wooden benches with initials gouged into them, the rough-cast walls with their obscenities. But more important, it showed the shelter's emptiness.

The light died away. 'Come on,' she said bravely. 'Let's get cosy.' Gently, she took charge. 'Take yer coat off. An' we can use mine ter cover us – like a blanket.' She was glad he couldn't see her. She grunted. 'It's a bit – 'ard like. An' not much room. Ah could – sit on yer knee.'

She settled him down, and herself on his trembling knee, and pulled her coat over the two pairs of legs. 'Yer'll 'ave ter keep me warm,' she whispered, and let her cold nose touch his. 'See?'

She laughed nervously; then, for long minutes, they kissed, gasping and clutching at each other in mounting excitement. She guided his hand under her jumper. Timidly, he felt her breasts under the silky cover of petticoat and brassiere. She tingled. His rapturous hands grew a little bolder. Soon he could feel the suggested hardness of a nipple in the centre of each rise.

She sighed breathily, 'Ginge – ah've never – never – ye know.' They were both blushing furiously.

'Neither 'ave I,' he whispered, and immediately thought, you bloody idiot. You should be the experienced one. It's the girl who's supposed to be the virgin. One of you's got to know how to go on.

But he couldn't see Angela's little smile as she sat up from his arms. 'Ah love you. An' yer goin' off ter war. God knows what'll 'appen. Ah want us ter do it. You'll be the first, that's the truth.'

Ginge felt the lump rise in his throat, and his eyes stung. This girl was beautiful. He must prove worthy, deserve her. He felt her wriggling on his knee, then her voice, small and shivery. 'Ooh, quick, Ginge.' 'Old me.'

When he did as he was bidden, he discovered that she had bared herself above the waist. The small breasts were delightfully soft to his touch. The tiny, invisible nipples were puckered and hard against his fingers, though whether from passion or cold he knew not. Faint almost with the novelty, and with longing, he felt their sweetness in his mouth.

Angela's slim body twisted under him. 'Ginge! Ginge!' she breathed, at once urgent and frightened. She was up and off his knee. 'Wait! Wait!' He heard clothing rustling, felt her slight movement. 'Right, Ginge. Come on, love. Be careful, won't yer?'

He realized she was crying, as he allowed her to pull him on top of her on the narrow bench. He opened his flies and their flesh touched. He was startled to feel rough coils of hair. He stabbed inexpertly, unable to enter her, his hands grasping the rough wood underneath her shoulders. He gasped as her freezingly cold hands fumbled between their bellies. Suddenly he felt her wet softness. She guided him.

'Push,' she urged and Ginge felt a hysterical urge to laughter. He thrust, desperately, praying and cursing. Oh God! Oh Christ! This was wrong. Don't spoil it. This clumsiness, this cold, wet, dark groping. It wasn't love, it was ludicrous. Her hands were on him, sending fire, then he felt her giving. She cried out, a sharp cry, and he was in.

It was hurting, the tightness clinging. But he thrust against her and felt himself entering her more deeply, thrusting harder, unable to help himself, even though he was tearing cries of pain from her and he could feel her face wet with tears. She moved her loins to accommodate him. Her drawn-up legs seized him. Still weeping, she urged him, 'Come on. That's it, love. Oh. Come on.'

He pumped up and down, he, too, sobbing, and wincing with pain. But then pounding, blood-racing excitement, and swiftly, with a silent scream, he exploded, felt himself gush inside her, and his rigid frame relaxed, heavily pinning her into the hard wood. She sobbed violently, her hands gentle on the back of his head, her lips against his ear. 'Yes, oh yes, oh my darling.' The forbidden word, the word of another world, the word of soft endearment that would have made her blush at any other time. She had never said it to anyone before.

He lay like the dead, crushing her. She felt him quiver, and she was aware all at once of how much she hurt, of the wood cutting into her back, of the muscles of her legs, and of the soreness of her loins, the roughness of his clothing on her bare skin. She squirmed slightly, and they both were consumed with embarrassment as he messily slipped out of her.

' 'Ave yer got yer 'ankie?' she murmured, fighting against her sobbing, and sitting up stiffly, aware of the indignity. Ginge was standing. She could just see his dark shape against the darkness of sea and sky.

'Oh – er – aye.' She found it and wiped herself. More than ever she was glad of the night's blackness. She was awfully sticky and wet. Had she bled much? She mustn't let him see the handkerchief.

She was shivering violently, and no wonder, for she had taken off practically everything. She sniffed. 'Ginge. Could ye strike a match? Ah can't find me clothes.' She gave a brave little, tremulous giggle. 'But don't look at us. Please.'

He did as she asked and she found the bundled stockings and underwear. 'OK. Ta.' He shook the match out and had the sense not to strike another. With hasty clumsiness, she groped into her clothing, glad that he couldn't see the shabby knickers, with the elastic showing at the waistband. There was a dull ache. She felt uncomfortable and stiff and cold. And close to new tears.

Ginge had hastily buttoned himself up and stared out to sea, embarrassed and confused. Guilt and shame tortured him. He could only vaguely recall the mindless, ecstatic release of the climax. Now he thought of the consequences of what they had done, the seed that he had injected into her, that even now might be determinedly fighting to start another life. He should have been prepared. Carried a johnnie the way the lads did, like the Boy Scouts, be prepared. Blushingly, he thought about the act itself. The discomfort, the pain, the brief joy.

More guilt as he thought about the penetration. It had been difficult. At first. But when she had helped him – it had not been as he had imagined. A wall, to be bloodily battered. She had been tight, gripping him tightly, but ... he was miserably aware of his ignorance. And the fact of what he had done. With Angie. Why were his eyes full of tears? I love her, I love her, he bellowed silently.

He coughed. 'Angie.' He groped for and found her shivering form. He sat quickly and pulled her into him, kissing the side of her head. 'Ah'm sorry. Are yer all right?' He felt her turn towards him. He put both arms around her. Their lips touched, with a new, gentle awareness.

'Ah wanted to,' she whispered, crying quietly. 'Ah love you, Ginge, an' ah wanted to. Ah'm glad. Ah belong te yer prop'ly now.' And you shurrup, she told herself defiantly. I do love him. I *do!*

It seemed to Ginge that he had spent an age smothered in wet cheeks by the time the train, with a blessed jerk, pulled away from the black walls and girders of the station. 'Tara well. Write to us. Look after yerself.'

His mother, bulky and dressed in her best coat, as dark as the soot on the bricks, with the bold, vulgar spray of the glass brooch at her throat. His dad, face half hidden under the voluminous check of his best cap, white muffler neatly tied at his neck. Gruff, embarrassed at this public scene, shuffling his polished boots, though he had wept the night before, his paternal instincts stirred by nine heavy pints of the local bitter,

Ginge's last fling with the wealth of his final pay packet from Stewart's. And thank God for it, Ginge thought, glancing up at the small, new, shiny blue cardboard suitcase on the rack. Otherwise, he'd have been setting off clutching a carrier bag under his arm.

He sat fidgeting with his tie, feeling that the other occupants of the full compartment must be staring at him, after his mam's noisy grief on the platform. He was aware of his stomach's discomfort, for he had taken a great deal of ale himself yesterday, both at dinner-time and again in the evening. Even Ma Foster had grandly stood him two pints. One or two of the more decent folks had wanted to buy him a drink, though he felt as he muttered an embarrassed thanks that they secretly thought he was a bit of a pillock.

Nevertheless, he had naively basked in the spotlight, aware of a glamour hitherto unknown, distinguished as he was from his fellows by the fact of his going away. That he might be going to danger or even death scarcely bothered him. The RAF Regiment didn't sound like death-or-glory stuff. In fact, he had kept it very quiet, and had allowed people to assume, and they mostly did, that he would, in a matter of weeks, be tearing across the sky, with cannon blazing against the foe. He suppressed a belch, and wished briefly that people had not been so generous.

Angela's face, shining with tears, came into view as he closed his eyes. She had never been very far from the front of his mind since unbelievable Saturday night. He had seen her to say farewell the previous evening. They both agreed that she couldn't come to the station, even though she wasn't working on Monday.

Time had run against them. Ginge had to look in at the Pothouse again by nine at the latest, and Angela's mam was not out boozing with the Sea Coal Man on a Sunday. They'd had less than two hours, with what seemed a lifetime's talk to squeeze in, though Ginge found himself sadly inarticulate when it came to the language of love. Characteristically, it was Angie who was the first to refer to the previous night.

Blushing, looking at the ground in the dark, clinging to his hand painfully, she said, 'Listen, Ginge. Don't you worry about last night. About me bein' – ah've got me time due next week. So ah couldn' be – well, yer know.'

Ginge, too, was blushing furiously. That sea-front shelter was certainly an epoch in his young life. He squeezed in reply, a loving squeeze. He couldn't think of anything to say.

'You *do* know you're the first?' She faced him in her anxiety, and Ginge felt a guilt that kept the colour in his features for his wondering.

'Of course, love.' He said it firmly. He laughed in an embarrassed fashion. 'An' ah guess ye know it was fer me. Ah was that – 'opeless,' he finished, with a gusty sigh.

They were walking aimlessly along the dark length of Oxford Street. Though cold, the night was, for once, clear, and they could see dim shapes, shop fronts, the edge of the gutter. In response to her, 'What d'yer want ter do?' he replied miserably, 'Ah've got te pop in the Pot'ouse – me dad's there. An' a few of the lads. Yer know.'

For a brief second, she was speared with jealousy. Oh aye. Da and the lads. And a pint or two. Mustn't let anything come before that, least of all Angela Thompson, who dropped her knickers for the first frightening time last night. She felt suddenly alarmingly adult, and very much akin to her mam and all the women of The Street, stranded across an impassable gulf from the freedom of the beer-swilling menfolk.

She pushed her ignoble thoughts away. They would say their sweet, tearful goodbyes now, without prolonging the agony. And then she could savour it, hug it to herself, warm and fragrant against the harshness of the street. Already she was learning that the capitalled Love she held in her breast, the passionate images she saw in her mind, were a little greater than the reality.

The giving of herself was endowed with much more romance when she relived it in the darkness of the stuffy bedroom than the shelter itself had been. Without the colour of romance, it had been cold, uncomfortable, and briefly agonizing. Then wetly disappointing. The excitement had been there, true, but buried, distant, only starting to spark in the seconds before the final collapse. It needed Love to invest it with any positive sort of quality at all. And yet out of those awkward moments could come motherhood. She had been scared and worried, part of her mind anyway, from the second she had felt him discharge inside her. If that was God's universal plan, He was a bit of a joker.

At her side, Ginge was haltingly talking about going somewhere. Where? The Rec. Oh aye. The railinged-sports ground, only it wasn't any more. Railinged, that is. The council had taken them all away. As they had from the top of the school wall, and from the front gardens of those posh houses up Westbrook. Something about making shells. What they had done was make it easier for courting couples. No more risk of doing yourself a nasty injury on those spikes.

Once again, to her dismay, her first reaction was a flash of bitter resentment, and a feeling again of the unfathomable divide of the sexes. The voices of universal womanhood rang in her brain. All they think about. Never had it out of his trousers before last night, now he can't get enough. Ashamed, she conjured up the memory of his clumsy, shy ineptness, his rough tenderness. 'Aye. All right.'

They marched off purposefully, Angela thinking how horrified he would be if he knew of her reluctance. How even more horrified at the sudden, unbidden thought that entered her head that she could, alone, using her own fingers and her fertile mind, make much more stunning, perfect love on his behalf.

The wall was low, and they stepped easily into the row of ragged, level bushes bordering the grass. Lovers had a hard time of it in England in winter, she reflected, and no mistake. A few minutes later they were ensconced in the frosty atmosphere behind a goal post. Angela put aside her disturbing abstractions and gave Ginge a lesson in the techniques of making love to her that made the experience at least meaningful physically for both of them. She was amazed at her own temerity, and found time, as her excitement began to build towards its enveloping frenzy, to wonder ashamedly what he would think of her display of knowledge and the increasing urgency of her gasping encouragement.

She lay back, clutching him, shuddering under his weight and crying, but murmuring, 'Ooh, Ginge. That was good. Really, love – marvellous.' And Ginge, out of breath, elbows driven into the tufty grass, felt ten feet tall.

But not when, finally, just beside Sam the Fish Shop Man's Sunday-dark wall, out of sight of the Pothouse door, he held her as she shook fiercely with her weeping. Abandoned, ugly grief, that channelled her make-up, and made her seem to an aching, tender Ginge, like a little girl. Lost. The pain had gone on, until she had to tear herself almost literally from him and stumble at a clicking run into the blackness. And Ginge had to gouge his eyes with thumb and forefinger and take many deep breaths before he dared face the smoky bonhomie of the public bar.

He felt tested, older, something of a warrior already as he sat in the smoke-smelling train. For hours. The war had affected everything and railway timetable was almost a contradiction in terms. With a deep gut feeling of cold unreality, he climbed, with thirty others, stiffly, over the tail-board of the truck that collected them from Nottingham station.

Nobody was doing much talking. It was all too new. And to arrive in the middle of a pitch-black night so that you had no idea what your surroundings were like added to the unrealness. Ginge still hadn't got used to the blackout, this black absence of light. The dark was different now. Before, the dark had been full of twinkling lamps, the flickering gas of the street lights, the blazing friendliness of the shop windows, downtown the garish gaiety of the advertisements. Not so much in *his* town, of course, but he *had* travelled as far afield as the neighbouring city in his time.

'All right then! 'Ere we are. Out ye get!' The speaker was a peak-capped individual with two stripes on his sleeve. He shone a dim torch into the back of the lorry. 'Come on, let's 'ave ye. 'Ome sweet 'ome. An' tea an' biscuits laid on for yer.'

He led them through a curtained doorway into a large dining-hall, with row after row of wooden tables flanked by benches. All empty. But a hatch was open. Beside it stood a steaming urn and a wooden baker's tray, heaped with thick cheese sandwiches. Tasting a week old, as Ginge discovered when he eagerly bit into one. 'Don't worry,' the corporal smiled grimly. 'Soon get used to the bromide. Right! Mugs on the counter there and foller me.'

Clutching bags and cases, they stumbled in rough order along a dark pathway, following the narrow spot of light made by a torch. They paused before a low, dimly seen, rounded shape. 'This is where you lot live. Get inside and grab a bed. Shit'ouse is there.' The torch arced briefly. 'And the ablutions for them as is particular. In you get, and get your 'eads down. No sky larkin'. You'll be up bright and early in the mornin' that's for sure.'

There was a push through the doorway and a scramble for the narrow beds that stood in two rows, heads to the strangely curving, iron walls of the long hut. "Ere,' someone called out in a shocked voice. 'There's no sheets.'

The corporal's sarcastic tones floated in from the door. 'Oh dear! Ain't that a shame? Where the 'ell d'you think you are? Buck Palace? You'll get your sheets issued in the mornin' with the rest of your kit. Meanwhile, you'll have to make do with blankets. All right? If you don't like it, you shouldn't 've joined.'

There was a howl of protest, for, of the whole batch, only Ginge and two others had not been conscripted. Not that this gave them much advantage, even of pay. In fact, their 'regular' status earned them naught but opprobrium from both their fellow recruits and their instructors.

'Ah. Where's our three 'eroes? There we are. Real Brylcreem boys these are. Death-or-glory fly boys, that's what we got 'ere. Well lads, want ter serve your country, do yer? Grab 'old o' those buckets then. See this floor? Filthy, ain't it? So come on, lads, put yer backs into it. Sweat fer King George!'

Seven

The new recruits were on a genuine airfield, they discovered, when they had a chance to examine their surroundings. But they were not allowed within two miles of a runway or an aeroplane. In RAF Apsley, the Regiment had its own camp within a camp. Even their own NAAFI, so that the bomber squadrons stationed at Apsley remained distant, somewhat mythical figures. The planes were no more than distant, squat shapes, or disturbingly loud noises in the night.

Ginge soon learnt, with his mates, that in the hierarchy of the Air Force, they, the Regiment, were regarded as the lowest of the low. At the top were the real glamour boys, the air crews. The magic wing on the battledress jacket made you a king on the ground. Of course, they were largely officers, who were a different breed anyway, but there was an increasing number of young flight sergeants, who served as gunners, some even who were training as bomb aimers or pilots. They had their own mess, put on a tremendous amount of side, and ignored all but the most basic rules of discipline.

They had the pick of the WAAFs, of whom, again, more and more were in daily evidence as the war machine stretched forth its demanding tentacles. Though their uniform was designed, some said deliberately, to ignore their femininity, witness the long, elastic-legged knickers which the girls themselves were quick to name passion-killers, even the thick serge of a tunic could not entirely disguise the mammary bulges, and, as sex objects, the girls were much sought after. And those who were clever or who could afford it had ways of making the regulation dress look more alluring.

But they quickly adopted their brothers'-in-arms contempt for the lads of the Regiment, and the nearest the new recruits came to their female charms, apart from official encounters with the clerks and other operatives of various stores and offices, was the nightly guard duty they were required to undertake on the female quarters. With blancoed belt and gaiters, swathed in greatcoats, they were required to patrol in pairs, two hours on and two off, armed with torches and whistles.

The first time Ginge was detailed for this, only a few days after his arrival, his companion, a tall and impressively broad young man by the name of Ronald Jackson, from the wilds of Somerset, with a rolling accent that earned him the name of the Yokel, asked the corporal, 'What do we do if we see anybody sneakin' in, Corp?' He was referring to the fact that they were given no weapon of any kind.

'Scratch their eyes out or scream for help,' the corporal replied unhelpfully, then added sourly, with a nod in the direction of the WAAFs' huts, 'it's them buggers gettin' out you wanna watch out for. And you really will need to scream if they get to grips.'

His opinion seemed to be verified by the behaviour of the groups of women returning from the NAAFI or the camp cinema before Lights Out. Ginge thought they needed little protection as he blushingly tried to ignore their gibes. 'Gotcher whistle, 'ave yer, sonny? Bet it's a tiny one, yours. Gonna get it out an' give us a look? Disappear to nuthin' in this cold weather.' And they pushed each other, screaming with laughter.

And Angie talked about joining up in that lot. Uncomfortably, he admitted she would probably be able to hold her own in the crude banter. He remembered her efficient dealing with Freddy Barraclough and his mates. A girl couldn't grow up in The Street and not be familiar with all the effing and blinding, and all the rest. Angela had taken charge in the shelter that night.

That night! Only twelve days. A lifetime ago. She had known what to do. More than he had, anyway. She had got it in, first time or not. He clenched his teeth at his constant disloyalty. Why should he doubt her? How the hell did he know what it should be like? She had chosen him to be the first.

The magic word Love. It was just all so unbelievable, that a beautiful girl like that should make a gift of herself to him. He was no Clark Gable. But she had. He wished he could remember more of it, picture it more clearly. He hadn't ever seen her nakedness, for in the shelter it had been too dark. And at the Rec she had kept her clothes on. Except ... he blushed hotly in the cold night at the memory of her guiding his hand, his fingers, up under her skirt, to the strange, soft wetness. Her moaning little cries, her wriggling under him.

She loved him. She had said so. She would have his painfully written note by now. He hoped she would write back. He waited with pounding heart for the mail every day. She must be his, he thought wonderingly, after what had happened. He turned away from the shrill screams of laughter.

But thoughts of women disturbed Ginge and his contemporaries less and less in the days that followed. Parade ground and assault course. Exercising, marching, running through the winter frosts of the flat countryside. Lectures. The history of the Regiment. Perimeter defence of an airfield. Weaponry. It went on long after the November dark had fallen and the flimsy looking Wellingtons had pulled away into the night, for friendly French 'dromes, or distant Germany, carrying, unbelievably, leaflets explaining how misguided the *herrenvolk* were to give their support to Herr Hitler.

The corporal of Ginge's section had delivered his private opinion of this propaganda in very certain terms. 'Bloody toilet paper, that's all it's good for. Riskin' blokes' lives and good kites, just so Jerry can wipe 'is arse!'

To Ginge and his mates in their ignorance, even the dangerous dark over Germany seemed attractive compared with their harsh lot. In the hut, as they pulled their muddy boots off their damp and smelly feet, and, groaning, set about restoring person, uniform and equipment to spotless cleanliness, so that they could muddy all again crawling under wire and over sandbags on the morrow, they had little sympathy or even thought for any other plight than their own.

Ginge's 'oppo', the Yokel, his impressive length stretched along the neighbouring bed, moaned, 'Chroist. They dun need ter put bromide in our tea, me ould fruit.' He banged the squeaking iron bedstead beneath him. 'If Hedy Lamarr wus in

'ere besoide me, oi'd say, not ternoight, luv. Oi gotter get some
kip.' Though there was a howl of protest at this somewhat
drastic illustration of the rigours of their new life, there was an
element of truth under its brash unlikelihood. For almost all of
them, the physical exercise to which they were subjected was
entirely unaccustomed. The exhaustion of their aching bodies
when Lights Out sounded ensured a deep sleep untroubled by
thoughts and fantasies which are normally the prerogative of
youthful minds.

Ginge's memory of the eventful Night of the Shelter grew
woolier and less bothersome with each passing day, though
Angela was very much in his thoughts after the midday meal,
when the mail was dumped on the table by the stove. And his
gloom deepened each time he turned away empty handed. It
was so noticeable that the Yokel soon remarked on it. 'Cheer
up, Ginge,' he consoled. 'Lot o' people don' really reckon ter
letter wroitin', see.' He grinned. 'Look at me. Gotter smashin'
piece back 'ome, oi 'ave. But never sent 'er a loine since oi come
'ere. Can't 'ardly wroite my bloody name, an' oi reckon she ain'
no better. 'Soides, wroitin's no bloody good. Don' make up fer
what she's missin' whoile oi'm away, do it?' He gave a
rumbling, lecherous laugh. 'We'm gonner finish the basic
trainin' boy mid December, ould fruit. Then we gets leave.
'Ome fer Christmas boy-oh, 'ow's that suit 'ee?'

But, at last, one dinner-time, it came. A blue envelope. In a
large, childish hand. His hands shaking, unmindful of the
noise around him, Ginge bore it to his bed and looked at it for a
second, delaying the delicious moment of opening. It was, of
course, from her. Neatly written on very thin blue paper, which
offered a faint but wonderful suggestion of her perfume. Ginge
held it under his nostrils, sniffing longingly, and forgetting
where he was for a few seconds until, blushing fiercely, he
lowered it and began to read.

My Darling Ginge,

*I hope you don't mind me calling you that. Ginge I mean. It
sounds better than Arthur. Thanks very much for your letter
recieved some time ago and Im sorry for not writting sooner but
you know how it is with one thing and another. I was very glad to*

*hear from you that you are all right and they are keeping you
bussy. Don't worry about me I mean evrythings all right with me
you know what I mean. I miss you very much and think about
you evry night and wish I could be with you anywere at all it
wouldent matter.*

    *Things are just the same here dad went mad when your letter
came tho its got nowt to do with him and I told him. I have to hide
it. Keep writting as I want to hear all about you. I must go now
and get this in the post. Look after yourself and sorry this isent
longer. Im not very good at writting but I love you very much.*

                          Your own Angela.

A row of Xs followed. Ginge devoured it again slowly,
mouthing the words silently.

Angela had spent a long, draughty time struggling with the
agonies of composition, tearful at her severely limited ability to
express herself on paper, once again resentful at The Street for
her lack of education. Yet she would have been comforted if
she could have seen the effect of her letter on Ginge.

He was transformed. He carried it in the pocket of his tunic
until it was in danger of falling to pieces, and that very night, in
spite of his throbbing weariness, sat down with much pen
chewing, to begin his reply. Christmas became the light at the
end of the tunnel, the magic goal towards which his spare-time
thoughts were directed. Just let me get on leave, he vowed,
through all the unfamiliar discomfort of training, and you can
send me to hell and back. Mercifully, he little knew how close
to truth his sanguinary bargain was to come.

That first Christmas in The Street, the war made itself felt in the
shortage of festive fare, although this was no great hardship for
most of the inhabitants, used all their lives to going without or
making do. They grumbled of course, for they had money now,
more than they had ever known, with Stewart's and the
shipyards and the steelworks going night and day. It was
comforting to help the war effort and to get a fat wage packet
for doing it. And even more important to people like Ellis, and
there were quite a number, the Home Front was a damned
sight better place to be than the Forces, for this was still the

phoney war and Britain had yet to face a bomb dropped in anger.

It was only on the high seas that the war was being fought at all, it seemed, with the torpedoing of the liner *Athenia* on the very first day, to be followed two weeks later by the loss of the aircraft carrier *Courageous*, again by a U-boat. Over 500 of her crew went to the bottom of the Atlantic. Already, it was becoming clear just how deadly an enemy the *Untersee* craft were. By November, the Battle of the Atlantic was bloodily under way, and the menace came from the surface as well as below it, witness the blasting out of the cold, northern waters of the converted P. & O. boat, *Rawalpindi*, by the *Scharnhorst*.

To The Street, these were distant newspaper and wireless events, dimly comprehended if at all. Only Old Jonson seemed to get excited. And Mrs Clay, whose eldest, Geoff, was aboard a tramp steamer from a neighbouring north-eastern port, which was plying her trade in Australia and the Far East at the outbreak of hostilities. They had heard nothing from him since August.

'Don' worry, Mary,' Mr Clay told his wife philosophically. 'The'd soon be in touch if 'owt 'appened to 'im. We're 'is next of kin.' The last words brought forth fresh wails of grief, sounding, as they did, so officially ominous.

Her fears for Arthur were temporarily allayed, as RAF Apsley seemed in no imminent danger of falling into Hun hands, though, of course, there were still the dangers of the nearby city of Nottingham to worry about. Anything south of Darlington was foreign and unknown, the natives categorized as 'funny'. Ginge had already received an urgent, indecipherable and misspelt warning from his mam. But now fresh trouble fell on her substantial shoulders. It came one cold, wet morning, when mist and rain combined to make the wetness underfoot gritty, each footstep marked on the pavement in liquid blackness.

Mrs Clay was leaving Wilson's, the corner shop, with a basket over her arm, when she was surprised to find herself addressed by the diminutive, headscarved figure of the Sea Coal Man's wife. 'Ah'd like a word with yer.'

Mrs Clay stopped and sniffed to indicate her disapproval. Her feud with the Thompsons was of long standing, so long that its origins were now vague. Basically, it stemmed from Mrs Clay's conviction that the Sea Coal Man and all his tribe were 'common as muck', and occupied a station on the social ladder a good many rungs below herself. In fact, there were few, if any, of the street higher than herself on that same ladder. 'We've never been in court in our life,' she was wont to say with emphasis. Some would argue that this was an example of the royal 'we', especially those who had known Mr Clay in his younger days, but there were few of Mrs Clay's neighbours who could say the same.

So now her bulk quivered with contempt as she waited for the slight, ragged woman to continue. Doris was unabashed. She began in her grating, Woodbine voice, 'Ah thowt yer ought ter know like. Our Angela's been gettin' letters from that lad o' yours. She 'ides 'em away, burrah've seen the postmarks an' the' comin' from a raff camp. Apsley or summat. That's where 'e is, isn' it?'

Mrs Clay was shocked. She remembered the night the young hussy had come bold as brass knocking at the door asking for Arthur. But Arthur had told her afterwards that she had merely wanted to know details of another lad, one of Arthur's workmates. Typical of the brazen young madam, Mrs Clay had thought, and dismissed the matter. As if her Arthur would have anything to do with a young baggage like that. She'd brought him up too particular for that, thank you.

But now she was startled. And dismayed. Not least at the advantage it seemed to give to the hard-faced, slatternly woman facing her so aggressively.

'She's on'y a bairn is our Angela. A bit daft like, the way bairns are. If 'er da finds out, 'e'll 'alf kill 'er. She's too young fer owt like that. Ah don' want 'er gettin' into any trouble. What wi' this bloody war an' all. She's on'y sixteen. P'raps yer could 'ave a word with 'im. Tell 'im ter stop pesterin' 'er.'

'Pesterin' 'er!' Mrs Clay's wide face reddened. 'She'll not come to any 'arm with our Arthur. 'E's a decent lad, an' wouldn' know owt about gettin' any girl inter trouble. Not unless 'e was led on,' she added significantly.

Doris's sharp, rodent face grew even more hostile. She knew very well Mrs Clay's superior attitude. Indeed, a considerable number of others in The Street behaved in exactly the same manner. Even the rest, the chatty ones, tolerated her and sniggered. Harry couldn't care less. Nor could she. For herself.

But Angela was different. This last year she had seen her blossoming into a good-looking lass. More than that. Beautiful. She sometimes secretly studied her, with wonder and more than a tinge of jealousy. The long gold hair. The eyes. Angie was beautiful and she must use her beauty wisely. It was one in the eye for The Street, that beauty, and Doris wasn't going to see it go to waste. Not on Ma Clay's pasty-faced drip of a lad any road. She rose to battle with grim joyousness, her voice screeching like a file on metal.

'Led on! Our Angela! She's as good as gold. Like a lamb. An' we don' want 'er gettin' spoilt, see? So just tell 'im ter pack it in, right? An' not come round botherin' 'er when 'e comes 'ome.'

Mrs Clay was almost incoherent in her anger. 'Boh – botherin'! 'E'll not *bother* 'er, mark my words. Ah'll 'ave a word with 'im all right. An' if your Angela's only a bairn, our Arthur's a babe in arms. 'E'll not see 'er again, not if ah've got owt ter do with it.' She turned and waddled indignantly away, her broad back expressing the contempt she felt.

Successfully, too, it would seem, for Doris, suddenly seething, bawled, 'Aw, shut yer gob, ye fat ould cow!'

She contemplated racing after the flabby bulk and giving her a good belt. But that would inevitably lead to the magistrates again, and the family was in enough trouble.

She was in an ugly mood by the time she reached her front door, and, unfortunately for Angela, she was there to receive the brunt of it. 'That effin' ould bitch!' Doris fumed, and Angela gazed at her blankly. Who had roused the ire this time?

'Mam,' she protested automatically. It was the cue Doris had been waiting for.

'Don't you mam me!' she spat, eyes blazing. 'What you been up to, yer little slut? Wi' that bastard Ginger Clay? What's 'e writin' te yer for, eh?' Angela flushed guiltily, then the colour drained away to leave her paler than ever. She felt as though some secret, sensitive area of herself had been brutally trampled upon, and she shrivelled up, hurt and shocked, even though she had expected it daily.

'Ah went out with 'im a couple o' times, that's all,' she replied unsteadily. "E asked if 'e could write to us. Nowt wrong with that, is the'?' She tossed her chin up defiantly, then ducked swiftly aside, as her mother's bony hand cracked across her skull. She yelped and burst into noisy tears, rubbing at the stinging spot, and backing away, expecting another blow. Her mother bent forward from the waist, thrusting her face at her daughter furiously.

'Yes, me lass. The's plenty wrong. Ah'll not 'ave you goin' about with blokes. At your age. Ye're not a bairn now. You ought to 'ave more sense. Ye know the trouble ye can get into. On'y after one thing, lads like 'im. An' ah suppose ye've been daft enough ter write back to 'im, 'ave yer? Promisin' 'im all sorts when 'e comes 'ome in 'is smart uniform. Well, it's stoppin'. Ye'll not see 'im again, ah've made sure of that!'

Angela stared at her through her tears. 'What 'ave yer done?'

'Done? Ah've told that fat ould bitch ter keep 'er precious son away from 'ere. And ter stop them daft letters. And she will.' She gestured angrily. 'She doesn' like the idea of 'er precious son bein' contaminated wi' the likes of us. An' she'll tell 'im.' She added sneeringly, 'An' 'e'll do as 'is mammy tells 'im, that one. Right bloody milksop if ever the' was. She still wipes 'is arse fer 'im. So, me lass, ye'd better get it through yer 'ead an' all. Ye're not seein' 'im an' ye're not writin' to 'im. See?'

Angela fought to control her sobbing. 'That's what *you* think!' she shrilled. 'I *am* seein' 'im! And ah'm writin' to 'im an' you're not stoppin' me.' She crossed her arms in front of her face to ward off the next blow, stumbling backwards from her hissing mother.

'Yer young slut. Ye'll do as yer told. Yer'll not leave this 'ouse. Wait till yer father gets 'ome. This time 'e can belt yer, an' ah'll not stop 'im.' She pursued her daughter round the table, delivering stinging slaps on the upraised arms. Little Jimmy drifted in unnoticed and watched wide eyed from the doorway. He was glad it wasn't him getting it, but his eyes blurred in sympathy with Angela.

Who, driven beyond endurance, screamed with all her might, 'Ah might marry 'im! Ah might 'ave to! Ah've slept with 'im. Twice!'

There was a sudden silence, Doris frozen, her head still raised. In spite of her own experience, she was momentarily shocked. 'Ye've what?' she said, dangerously quiet. Angela was frightened now, terrified. She wished she could take it back. It was so stupid. She pressed her hands to her wet face. The words were torn from her.

'Ah've slept with 'im. Before 'e went. An' ah'll marry 'im. Ah wanted to.' Her thin shoulders heaved.

Doris's fury exploded once again. 'You stupid little bugger! Are ye pregnant? Are yer?' She sprang forward and dragged Angela by her hair close to her own contorted face. She struck with her free hand, back and forth, resoundingly. 'Are ye pregnant?' she shrieked.

Angela howled. 'Ow! Ow! Mam! No, no, ah'm not!' Doris pushed her away from her, into the armchair. Angela huddled there, her face hidden again in her arms, her slim body shaken with gulping sobs. 'No – ah'm not. Ah'm sure. Ah've 'ad me period suh – since.'

Doris was shaken, too, her throat sore, and her hands stinging. She fumbled out a Woodbine and lit it. The match trembled in her hand. 'Thank God for that,' she said bitterly. For a few seconds she was stirred with pity for the bent form.

It was the sex that caused women all the trouble. And what a fuss over nothing. She remembered her own youth, a lifetime away – a hard, ugly, slaving lifetime away. She had thought it was an escape then. Maybe it was. She'd forgotten. But at fourteen, she'd let a big lad take her in the prop yards. For a shilling. One lousy bob.

After that, it wasn't so important. Until you were caught. Then it mattered all right. You had to have a feller quick. Any feller. It wasn't going to happen to Angela. She hardened, staring down at her.

'Ah'm tellin' yer da. 'e'll mebbe knock some sense inte yer. Gerrouta my sight!' She didn't even see the red marks on the pale, tear-grimed cheeks, or on the thin forearms, as Angela hurried up the damp stairs.

But in fact, the Sea Coal Man's anger was not as great as either mother or daughter anticipated. Though he blustered and raged when Doris, with a fine sense of crisis, eventually, after an opening tirade, disclosed the fact of Angela's lost virginity, his wrath was largely assumed. Secretly, like his son, Elisha, who was an interested onlooker, he was not really surprised.

Had, moreover, speculated already in an unfatherly way over Angela's emerging beauty these past months. Girl looking like that. Somebody bound to give it to her. Sooner than later.

However, he roared, played up to his wife's notions of disaster. Certainly, the kid was a bit young to go getting one up the spout, though at least she'd had enough sense to avoid that. Or someone had. That bastard young Ginge. Couldn't blame him for fancying Ange. Everybody did. But he'd still knock shit out of him, and no mistake.

He felt a swell of pride. Angela was a smasher, and the lad that got her would have to be somebody decent. And he'd have to wait till they were wed proper before he got his end away. Doris was standing there fidgeting with her bloody fag, looking like the day of judgement. What did she want? He was going to give the lass a belting.

With grim pleasure, he stood up and unfastened his belt. Elisha's eyes shone. 'Angela!' The Sea Coal Man stood in the tiny, square lobby, shouting up into the darkness.

After a long pause, there was a muffled, 'What?'

'Come down 'ere now!'

The voice floated down, sullen but afraid. 'Ah'm in bed.'

'Well, get yer bloody self outa bed an' bloody quick.' He was working himself up into a genuine fury, his stocky frame bouncing restlessly, pulling the wide leather from the straps around his trousers.

'Not in front of the bairns,' Doris cautioned, and her husband turned on her, his dander up, the head of the house, bristling.

'What the fuck you on about? Get the bairns out the way then!'

Elisha was conscious of a keen disappointment. Angie had been asking for this for weeks. He was excited, a knifing, sexual excitement that throbbed. But his mother was shepherding Terence and Little Jimmy towards the doorway. 'Come on. Gerrupstairs.' She nodded at Elisha.

The Sea Coal Man was still standing at the foot of the stairs, a menacing figure half in shadow. 'You comin' or do I 'ave ter come an' drag yer down?'

She appeared, coming slowly down, wrapped in her old grey coat, barefoot. She was afraid. She knew her father's wild temper. The Sea Coal Man recognized her fear, and a primitive excitement stirred in him, too. He cleared his throat noisily. 'Get through there, yer ma's tellt me all about it, ye little hoor!'

Silently she edged past him, pathetically attempting to hold her head high. She clung to her noble feeling. She loved him. How could they understand? But a minute later, she was howling, raw, ugly cries as the wicked leather cut into her tender skin. Skin shamefully bared as her father forced her down across the chair and clawed the ragged petticoat up.

Elisha and Little Jimmy and a whimpering Terence huddled in the doorway, forgotten, peeping round the tense figure of their mother, who stared mesmerized at the milky flesh of her child, suddenly and cruelly streaked with livid red. The squirming buttocks, the backs of the kicking thighs, until the screams forced her to leap across and grab the upraised arm. She had to struggle with all her strength against her husband, his face wild and possessed. She was fiercely ashamed, identifying suddenly and totally with the young girl and the outrage to her frail beauty. She, too, was yelling.

'That's enough! For God's sake, 'arry!' He thrust her away, still savage, but she stood in front of Angela, who, with gulping sobs, managed to push herself to her feet and cover her burning skin. Her blonde hair hung in streaks across her face, which was already stained and swollen from hours of crying in the cold bedroom. Her cheeks shone in the harsh light with her tears. But her slim body was rigid with hate, for her pride and dignity throbbed worse than the raised welts. Her words were fought out against the racking sobs.

'You bastard! You ever touch me again and ah'll go ter the p'lice. Ah mean it.' The Sea Coal Man gave an animal growl and did indeed start forward, the belt still clenched at his side, but Doris faced him squarely.

'That's enough, 'arry,' she said again, firmly. Angela, trembling, stood her ground, and the Sea Coal Man turned away, in control, aggrieved, but, underneath it all, ashamed as well. He saw the intent faces in the doorway and was glad of the diversion.

'You lot get out of it. Shift yersels.' He was comforted by the clattering, jammed effort to escape up the stairs. He avoided looking at Angela, whose body still shook with her weeping. It was the only noise he could hear and he said with gruff defensiveness, 'Ah'm away down the Pot'ouse,' and turned quickly away, with the grime of the shipyard still on him, relieved to be out of it.

No need to feel guilty was there? A good belting. That was what Doris had wanted him to do. And the kid deserved it, opening her legs for that young Clay twat. He pushed the uncomfortable sensation away with the anticipation of the first cool draught.

When he had gone, Angela's weeping redoubled. Her mother was awkward, for gentleness was foreign to their lives, but she tried to show sympathy. And Angela again allowed herself to be bent forward, her lower body bared, while Doris dabbed gingerly at the ridges across the buttocks and the thighs. The outline of the belt was there in hard bars, the angry welts darkening from red to almost black, the blood close to the surface. Doris winced as her daughter tightened, pulling instinctively away from even her light touch. Finally, she rubbed some margarine over them, and Angela straightened stiffly, letting the old pink garment fall to cover her. She hobbled towards the door, but her mother's cry stopped her.

'It's fer yer own good, Ange. Ye can't go lettin' lads 'ave everythin', love.'

Angela's breast heaved with the effort to stop crying. ''E's the first,' she answered scornfully. 'And we did it twice. Once at the Rec and once on the promenade. It was a few minutes. And ah didn't enjoy it.' She went on quickly, over her mother's interruption. 'But it was my idea. 'E didn' ask fer it. Ah know yer can make it sound real dirty. But it wasn't. Ah love 'im.'

Doris managed to bite off the contemptuous sound that sprang to her throat. Love! That was for the filums and *True Confessions*. It was something a sixteen-year-old lass thought should be true. 'Ye're too young,' she said reasonably. 'Ye've got ter wait, our Angie. Ah want summat better for yer. Than this.' Her wrinkled, chapped hand gestured around her, and Angela knew exactly what she meant. Oh, Mam, she cried inside herself, so do I. So do I.

But aloud, she said, 'Ah'm gonner see 'im. Ah don' care what you or me da do ter me. Ah'm gonner write to 'im, and ah'm gonner see 'im when 'e's 'ome. An' ah won't be goin' out with any other lad. You'll see.'

The tenderness that was almost always buried, forgotten, welled up as Doris felt all the pathos, the hope of youth in Angela's cry. 'Aye, all right, pet. If yer will, yer will. But don' talk about it again. An' don't let yer da know, will yer? Let's try an' 'ave a bit o' peace, fer God's sake. The's enough fightin' in the world just now.' She felt tears prick her eyes. Her voice even more hoarse, she murmured, 'An' ah'm sorry fer tellin' 'im. Ah didn' think—' She gestured towards her daughter. Angela nodded. She walked with slow painfulness towards the stairs. Doris watched her go, deeply stirred, wanting suddenly to run after her and hug her.

Angela gritted her teeth climbing the wooden stairs. She felt suddenly close to her mam again, felt like going up to her and cuddling her like when she was a little girl. But that would be daft. She wasn't little any more. She was grown up. And a bloody miserable time it was, too.

Eight

For many of The Street, '39 went out better than a good many of its predecessors, in spite of the shortages. The Fosters did a roaring trade. Sam's son was also home, and Flo made a big fuss of the two somewhat embarrassed heroes in the dark and light blue of their respective services. Joe was almost accepted as part of the street, even though Sam and his wife no longer lived over the chip shop but had a neat little bungalow near the distant sea-front, in a newly exclusive estate that was still not completed. And wouldn't be now for some years.

A sort of unofficial welcome home occurred in the bar, just three days before Christmas Day and one day after Joe's return. Ginge had preceded him by about thirty-six hours. Secretly, he was rather envious of Joe's exotic square rig. The blue jean collar, the gold cap tally. Especially as the country, even The Street, was buzzing with the news of the River Plate and the destruction of the *Graf Spee*. The Navy was everybody's hero, and Ginge felt that his Air Force blue serge with the Regiment across the shoulder tabs was somewhat drab in comparison.

But already, it was a different Ginge, a leaner, harder young man, weathered and toughened. A quiet, more confident air if you studied him closely. The spotty Street youth was gone, and no one rejoiced more than Angela, who managed to be the first to greet him, even before his parents, who had not been informed of the exact time of his arrival.

Angela was alone on the grimy platform when the train came in. Nervously shuffling in her best clothes, cold and anxious. Until he was there, out of the clatter of doors, self-conscious in his uniform, the huge coat enveloping him, and, characteristically, it was she who rushed forward and flung herself at him, kissing him wetly and noisily. His blushing, simple face beamed, and Angela felt noble again, comforting the warrior home from the wars. To her, Nottingham was distant and dangerous enough.

Awkwardly refusing to relinquish each other, they squeezed through the barrier, and made their way across the cobbled forecourt to the Stanton Tearooms, secluded among the steaming, gurgling urns and the yellow-white net curtains. He sat devouring her across the narrow table, their knees touching.

She sipped lady-like at her tea, staring back at him over the chipped cup, aware of the effect of her eyes. She thought suddenly of the stripes across her bottom. Yellow now, but still faintly visible. Would he see them? She giggled nervously, and he smiled, at a loss.

She reached forward and placed her hand over his. 'Eeh, it's good ter see yer, Ginge.'

He nodded. She had told him enough in her letters for him to know that they must keep their association secret. Besides, he had had the indignant epistle from his mam describing in great detail her encounter with the redoubtable Doris, and giving him a colourful account of the history and character of the entire Thompson clan, ending with a solemn warning to him never to give them the time of day.

He sighed and squeezed her hand. Yes, they would keep it secret. There were plenty of opportunities to meet away from The Street. No need to flaunt it. Ginge was not the most rebellious of youths, and Angela was far too practical to call down her da's wrath on her blonde head again. Or on any other equally tender part of her anatomy. Not until she was able to do something about it.

But they were reduced to cinemas or cafés, or the bleak outdoors. As they watched the line of waves breaking out of the mist, Ginge looked longingly at the Lower Promenade. But there were work gangs down there at the water's edge, setting up more of the great square concrete blocks. And at night the LDV, the newly formed Home Guard, patrolled the whole area with righteous zeal.

As if anyone would want to land here, Ginge mused morosely, even Jerry. He thought of the rubbers collected from the medical orderly before going on leave, and carried ever hopefully next to his heart. He looked to Angie for a lead, but it was as though the Night of the Shelter had never happened except in his fevered brain. She seemed content to walk. And talk. And kiss. By God, but it was cold. Even in uniform. He noticed her nose shining, and she sniffed. She must be nithered. He dismissed his evil thoughts and squeezed her more tightly, striding out along the pavement.

He was apprehensive about meeting the Sea Coal Man and managed to avoid doing so until the day after Joe Morley came home. Ginge had already been to the Pothouse, and received a warm welcome from Flo Foster. So warm that it occasioned several aye-ayes and guffaws, for she was still an impressive figure of a woman and could inspire lecherous longings in most men. When she wasn't trying to act like the Duchess of Sutherland Street, of course, and that wasn't too often.

It was Ginge's dad who informed his son of the evening gathering. 'So don' go fixin' up owt wi' them mates o' yours,' he warned, referring to the alibi already much used in the brief time he had been home. Somewhat nervously, Ginge surmised that the Sea Coal Man must surely be present, for festive celebrations were well under way. He was right.

"Ow do,' he said, blushing, when he found himself facing the stocky, sea-booted figure in the crowded fug. The Sea Coal Man growled, an indeterminate sort of noise that could at a stretch be interpreted as a greeting. He turned away with his glass.

Both Ginge and Joe were modest enough youths and their ears burned with the attention paid them, while their bellies struggled with unaccustomed quantities of ale. Ginge forgot all about his personal problems until, as he buttoned up out back after one of the increasingly frequent trips to ease his bladder, he became aware of the Sea Coal Man menacingly blocking the passageway back to the bar. If Ginge was bloated with ale, the Sea Coal Man was awash in it. His speech was thick, his jaw slack. But his belligerence was unmistakable. 'You bin seein' our Angela?'

Discretion was definitely the better part, thought Ginge. 'No, Mr Thompson,' he asserted, though unable to look above the Sea Coal Man's collarless, unwashed neck.

'Aye, well don't, thassall. Stay way from 'er. Ah know what

ye've been up to. Don' think ah don't. Yer dirty young bastard.'
He swayed alarmingly, and his anger increased. 'In fact, ah
said ah'd belt yer, and ah will. Jus' lerrit be a lesson—'

The old Ginge would have stood petrified. Or at best
hollered and ran. But this was Airman Clay. In the King's
uniform. He had learnt a lot. He backed away so that the Sea
Coal Man's unsteady punch whistled past his chest, then drove
his fist hard into the unprotected belly as his opponent was still
staggering forward under the momentum of his swing. To his
own dismay, Ginge found himself reflexively bringing up his
knee and just prevented himself from smashing it into the face
that was heading rapidly for the lino-ed floor.

The Sea Coal Man made spluttering, drowning noises as he
folded up. He began to vomit and Ginge grabbed the collar of
his donkey jacket and pulled him the couple of yards to the
gents'. The figure knelt there spewing large quantities of
recently imbibed beer all round him. Ginge's face twitched in
disgust. He discovered he was shaking, his breath coming
quickly, his voice unsteady.

'Don't try that again,' he panted. 'An' don't take it out on
Angela either or ah'll kill yer!' And he went back to the noisy
bar, where no one had noticed his absence.

The Sea Coal Man told nobody about his little contretemps, and
Ginge said nothing, not even to Angela. Though he was
tougher and more worldly-wise in the two months he had
spent away from The Street, he soon found himself slipping
into the same baffled, subservient role with his beloved,
waiting for her to suggest, to make the moves, afraid to take
any initiative.

He thought of the precious days ticking over. Heaven knew
when he would get any leave again, and here he was with this
lovely creature. The girl who had already given herself to him,
and whom he wanted desperately. Yet his words stuck in his
throat, refusing to be expressed, and all they'd done was kiss
passionately over and over again.

If only there was somewhere for them to go, apart from a
shelter on the prom. Even the rec was dodgy now they had that
barrage balloon installed there. Huts and guards and
everything. He dreamed of a room, a bed of their own. He felt

weak at the thought. But it was wishing for the moon. He even dreamed of booking a room. The Grand Hotel. He'd never been in a hotel in his life. Besides, he only had a few bob to his name. But oh, she had never looked so good. He was aching for her. Why couldn't he speak?

Oh, why doesn't *he* suggest something for a change, thought Angela irritably, feeling the cold striking up through her thin soles and silk-stockinged legs. They were walking down Bright Street, one of the main shopping thoroughfares. It was Thursday afternoon, only two days of the old year left, and the next day Ginge was to catch his train back to the war. They would not even be able to see the year out together on Saturday night.

She felt perverse, at odds with herself, not knowing what she wanted. The spark of irritation she felt with him dismayed her, but she could not disperse it. How quickly the eight days had slipped by. And what a fool she'd been for not letting him have it, getting all worked up with the kissing and the feeling. But why should she have to make all the running? Why for God's sake, didn't he just take her somewhere and do it?

Before he had come home, she had decided that she would let him have her, again and again, until she was pregnant. And what could her da do about it then? But then she'd got scared. She didn't really want a kid. A millstone that would tie her to The Street in spite of the war. Wherever Ginge was, she'd be stuck at home, figure ruined by a squalling brat, old before she'd had a chance to grow up. She'd seen too much of that.

And besides, she wasn't a hoor, as her da had called her. She wasn't going to give herself just like that. Even if he did say he loved her. And that she had to extract from him, like a dentist pulling teeth. Though he did end every letter with it and write SWALK across the envelope. She'd wondered what the hell it was at first.

She was quiet as they wandered aimlessly through the considerable crowds. 'Fancy a cuppa?' Blimey, she thought uncharitably, it speaks. And a real idea all on his own. They turned into Merigo's. Eyeties, someone said, in with the enemy. Didn't seem to matter here, people still thronged in for tea and coffee and the ice-cream.

The babel of voices, the damp smell of clothing, the coffee

vapours, hit them. With difficulty, they squeezed into a narrow, pew-like stall occupied by a fat woman and her brood. There were one or two cloth-capped, scrubbed men among the customers. Only a few. Men in this town rarely shopped or drank tea with their wives in public. Some things even Hitler couldn't change. And a bloody bad job, too. Though servicemen and women were becoming a more familiar sight, Ginge was still the only man there in uniform, and Angela derived some satisfaction from that. He had sensed her withdrawn mood, and she felt an affection for his worried young face. Sternly she admonished herself. Snap out of it. Got to make his last day pleasant.

After an age, a tired waitress took their order. People left and they edged along until they were next to the wall, their feet touching under the narrow table. She held his hand, strove hard to be nice to him. 'Ah wish yer weren't goin'. Ah'll miss yer.' Her blue eyes held him. 'Ah never go out, ye know. When ye're not 'ere.'

He coloured with pleasure and pressed her cold hand. 'Yer should. Ah don't want ye stoppin' in. Ye should get out. With yer mates.' Her blonde hair swung across her face as she shook her head emphatically.

'Naw. Daft lot. All the' think about is lads. Diff'rent one every Sat'dy.'

He sighed and flushed again. 'Ah wish – ah wish the' was somewhere we could go like.' He paused, awkward and embarrassed. 'Ye know. On our own.'

She twined her legs about his, pressing her knees against him, open, loving. 'Ah know.' Their hands clung. 'But—' She, too, was hesitant, struggling to express herself. 'The'll be time. We will.' She made it sound like a promise. 'Ah love yer. Ye know that. Ah want it ter be more – than a – a few minutes on a bench. Or be'ind a bush. Ye know what ah mean?'

'Aye.' He did, too. But it didn't make the wanting any easier. Or maybe it did, talking about it. He wasn't sure. Certainly he loved her. He was sure of that.

This time, they said their goodbyes as they had met, on the station platform. Ginge's parents had not braved the bitter night but bidden him farewell by a carefully banked fire at home. Ginge wondered privately if it was a good idea, as he watched Angela trying not to cry, without much success. They were both tongue tied, and the train seemed prepared to stand there forever. But at last the guard shouted and blew his whistle and Ginge bent awkwardly from the window and they kissed fiercely. With a jerk, and a crazy chatter of skidding wheels, they began to move. He swallowed the rising lump. 'Tara,' he croaked.

'Ah love you,' she called, crying unashamedly now. His own eyes dancing with tears, he watched her white, blurred face recede, then pulled up the thick leather strap of the window and drew down the blind. Christ, he felt as though he had been doing this all his life. His first leave. How many more partings would he have to endure before it was all over?

As he settled into his seat in the dim lighting, he felt sad and tender and comforted by the thought of Angela. It hurt, but it was a strange, sweet kind of hurting that he hugged to himself.

'Now then, wings. Good leave? It's a bugger going back though, eh?' The speaker was a soldier, and Ginge felt a sudden identity. He nodded, glancing condescendingly at the drab civilians. He undid the top button of his tunic and settled down in the manner of an old stager.

'Aye. It's a bugger all right.'

On her way home through the windy darkness. Angela tried to sort out her whirling thoughts. Why are you snivelling? You're not that fond of him, are you? You just think you ought to be. You're in love with Love, that's what's wrong with you. Better start growing up a bit. You'll be seventeen next week. There's plenty of fish in the sea. Why not do what Ginge says? Get out. Enjoy yourself. You can do better than an airman.

Hating herself for these whispers, she walked on, pulling her coat round her. As she neared The Street, she hurried, half running, remembering the latest sensation. A man they called Sandshoe Charlie, who accosted women, grabbing them from the darkness, and fleeing on plimsolled feet with their handbags. One woman had been half throttled just at the end of Brewery Lane. No joke that.

She was coming up to the Pothouse. Across the road and into The Street. There! She was puffing. Suddenly, she gave a squeak of fright as a figure seemed to appear from nowhere, in her path. She stood shivering. A torch came up, and shone on her frightened face. 'What the—'

'Oh, 'ow do, Ange. Ah wondered 'oo it was.' She recognized Ellis's whining voice. She fought to get her breath back.

'Fer Christ's sake! Don' do that, man. Yer'll give somebody a 'eart attack comin' on them like that. Ah thowt ye were San'shoe Charlie.'

Ellis laughed. He tapped his tin hat. He was proud of it. It made him feel very martial, part of the war effort. 'Firewatchin',' he said importantly. 'The' bound ter start comin' over soon like. What you doin' out this time o' night?'

She moved round him, ignoring his question. 'Aye well. Ah'd better get in then. Tara well.'

'Tara.'

She hesitated at her front door. Her da would be in. It was after chucking-out time. She blinked against the light. It was plain that she had been crying, but the Sea Coal Man was not very observant. 'Where've yer been?' he growled, anticipating a row. But his wife was quick.

'She's been at the pictures with Mavis Carslake. 'Er pal from the fruit market. Ah tellt yer. Did ye enjoy it, pet?'

'Aye. It was all right.'

'D'ye want some supper? The's some beans ter warm up.'

'No thanks, Mam. Ah've gorra bit of an 'eadache. Ah think ah'll go up.'

She smiled to herself as she climbed the dark stairs. Her mam still felt guilty over the belting her dad had given her. And it was just as well. She'd helped a lot covering up while Ginge was home. She sighed with dissatisfaction. There'd be no need now.

She pulled off her clothes quickly in the freezing cold and slipped into the bed. One thing, it was always warm in bed. No bloody wonder with all these bodies. She cuddled into Little Jimmy's sleeping form, glad to hear Elisha's snoring, deep slumber breaths in the darkness. She was not in the mood for his crude goading right now.

She wondered what it would be like to sleep with Ginge. Properly. Wake up beside him. Well, no one could call her a hoor now. Eight days and he hadn't touched her. Well, hardly. Funny. Her dad hadn't said much at all about Ginge being home. And all that carry on a few weeks back. Taking his belt off to her. The dirty old bastard!

Seventeen in three weeks. She must do something. Find out about getting away. Joining those waffs. She might even get sent to Apsley. With Ginge. She thought about it, cosy in the darkness, until she drifted off to sleep.

The old year went out on a tide of beery sentiment. There were the usual fights, of course, but nothing serious. The Pothouse had a special licence to stay open until eleven and several households had laid bottles in, so there was a great deal of noisy first footing, slapping and tickling in darkened lobbies. The ARP warden, neither Sam nor Ellis that night, did his best for a while to stop the lights spilling from open doorways or carelessly drawn blackout curtains, but he soon realized he was having no success; indeed, was making himself unpopular, and with The Street starting on various bottles of hard stuff, that was an unwise thing to do. When the young bobby walked in from a well-lit pavement into a crowded front room, he saw the warden playfully trying to sup brown ale from his brimming tin helmet. 'Th' won't come ternight,' he informed the young bobby gaily. 'It's New Year's Eve.'

Few were sober enough to give serious thought to the future. In fact, in many cases, the drunkenness was reinforced by a strong determination not to do so. Feuds were temporarily forgotten in a drunken no-man's-land of booze and mince pies. Ellis, with more than half a bottle of sherry inside him resting, for the moment happily, on several pints of bitter, met up with the Sea Coal Man while they waited for the midnight buzzers.

Both had lumps of coal, and salt and bread, and the Sea Coal Man was further encumbered with a medicine bottle of dark liquid which, in an excess of bonhomie, he offered Ellis. Bravely, Ellis swigged. His watery eyes swam behind the thick spectacles. He doubled over, his mouth opening and closing silently, then, gradually, a hoarse, rasping sort of gulp emerged. The buzzers were sounding before he found his voice. 'Bluh – bloody good,' he croaked, wiping away the tears. ''Appy New Year.' In an alcoholic rush of emotion, he invited his neighbour in. 'Aye, bring the fam'ly,' he coughed happily.

Old Jonson was drunk on rum. Fortunately, he was still at the merry stage, and welcomed the new arrivals quite cordially, especially when the Sea Coal Man passed him his bottle. Ellis reluctantly admired the old fellow's iron constitution, as he watched the Adam's apple bobbing in the scrawny neck. Old Jonson took a lengthy pull, withdrew the bottle and wiped his long moustache approvingly. His face glowed. 'Ya,' he pronounced. 'Dat bloody good stuff, Sea Coal. Bloody good!' Some minutes later, he produced his concertina, and a sing-song began.

'Where's your Angie?' Ellis asked. On learning that she was in the house, Ellis insisted on going to fetch her. The dashing blade. Fine bit o' stuff, young Ange. Whoops. The pavement lurched beneath him. He drew himself up. 'Ange! Ange! 'Oway out, pet. Come an' 'ave a New Year's drink.' Eventually she appeared.

'All right. Ah'm 'ere.' Inwardly, she groaned. But what the heck? It was easier to go than say no. Besides, she'd help Mam keep an eye on her da. He'd had a real bellyful and now with that firewater he'd got off some sailor mate of his down the docks, anything could happen. Probably end up punching Ellis on his stupid conk. Despite her gloom, she almost smiled at the prospect.

The singing was loud and spirited. Old Jonson was standing somewhat unsteadily on a chair, with the Sea Coal Man beneath him vigorously acting as choir master.

'We'll build a sweet, little ne-e-e-st,
Some – a – where out in 'a we-e-e-st....'

She returned Peggy's friendly greeting, and accepted a glass of sherry from Ellis, who was making a bit of a meal of guiding her into the circle, his hand clutching her soft, upper arm greedily. The silly get! He'd certainly had a drop too much. 'Come on,' he spouted suddenly a few minutes later, pushing through the bodies and dragging her to her feet. 'Le's 'ave a dance.'

She laughed. 'Aye. Right-oh. If yer can stand on yer feet.' She winked at the plump Peg, who was looking concernedly at her husband.

"Oway, Grandad!' Ellis yelled, blinking owlishly at Angela and gripping her hands tightly. 'Play summat nice an' slow.' They launched out unsteadily in company with several other

couples which included her mam and dad. She was aware of
Ellis's hand pressing in her back tighter than need be, then his
knee nudging hers, and again, suggestively. She was half
amused, half indignant. His hand slid down her back. The dirty
old bugger. He was having a feel. He leered at her foolishly, his
eyes magnified by his pebble lenses. A mood of devilment
seized her and she suddenly leaned in to him, pressing her
breasts against his chest, her face on his neck.

'Why, Ellis,' she whispered seductively. 'I 'ad no idea ye
were – so … ye know.' She pushed her leg between his, their
thighs and bellies rubbing together. She caught a whiff of his
beer breath as he shot up rigid, backing off from her, horrified.
His glance went over to Peggy.

'Er – just a minute, pet. Must go. Won' be a tick.' And he was
off like a shot, beetroot red for the toilet at the back of the
kitchen. She shook with suppressed laughter as she squeezed
back to her place near the sideboard.

In the kitchen, Ellis thrust a finger in his collar and eased it
from his sweating neck. Phew! The brazen little bitch.
Plastering herself up against him like that. In front of Peg and
everyone.

In the stuffy little packed room, Angela yawned and thought
about making her escape. She couldn't see a clock but guessed
it must be two, at least. She wondered what Ginge was doing
right at this minute. Whatever it was, it couldn't be more boring
than this. She sidled towards the front door and, in reply to a
shout, waved and slipped quickly out.

The air dried the sweat on her, and she stood for a moment
in its pleasant cold. The clouds had cleared and the stars were
sharp. The roadway shimmered a faint pale with the
beginnings of a frost. A new year. She was resolved about one
thing. Terrible though it might be, it was going to bring her
escape from all this. She turned and went into the strangely
silent house.

Ginge had fallen. With a bump. At that moment, he was filled
with unutterable self-loathing, thinking of Angela and weeping
bitterly at his unworthiness.

The evening had started out innocently enough. Only the
third night back in camp. New Year's Eve, and the whole

section decided on a binge. Sample the delights of Nottingham. And Ginge had gone along with the oppos, the Yokel and the others. Enjoyed being one of the lads. Drinking pints. And nips from a half bottle someone had. More pubs. More chasers. Spewing, decorously in a toilet. Then back in and more booze. Drunk, all drunk, he drunker than ever.

He and the Yokel, sitting in the corner of a bar, while the lads sang round a piano. Ginge talking, thick tongued, but talking. About Angela. About the sex. About the contraceptives still in the back of his pay-book. 'Never touched 'er,' he reaffirmed, sadly and solemnly. He stared ahead of him, lost in introspection. The Yokel, hugely sprawled and equally drunk, suddenly pulled his limbs together and leaned forward decisively.

'Got the bug, me ould fruit. Very bad fer 'ee, that is. Know what you need, boy-oh. You need your end away, 's a fact. Stick with yer old matey. Oi'll see you a'roight, Ginge, C'm on. Leave they darft bastards.'

And, foolishly, Ginge had gone with him. To another rowdy pub, full of airmen and soldiers. And tarts. Old, young, fat, thin, blonde, black. A whores' convention. A piano thumping, tarts screeching, men punching. More drinks. Bravado. Secret envy of the Yokel, who was suddenly a very worldly sort of bloke, a real airman with all the patter. Trying to follow suit.

Suddenly there were two birds with them. Ginge didn't know where they'd come from, but they were there, and drinking ports. He and the Yokel paying for them. The dark one sitting next to him. She looked old to him. Not bad though. Her hand was on his leg, stroking, moving up. Her sweet wine breath warm on his ear.

'Don't spend it all, airman. Save a couple quid for Eileen, eh?'

'Sure.' He chuckled drunkenly. Then they were outside and he couldn't walk. The road was tossing him about, Eileen clinging determinedly to him. 'Not far, love.'

He was alone with her in the dark. Where? Walking, miles and miles it seemed. Then into a block of flats. Smelling of dirt and urine. Still black, stumbling up some stairs, and, at last, thank God, a light and a bed. Across which he fell face forward, greatcoat still buttoned. Boots still laced.

Someone pulling him, tugging him about, hauling off his

clothes. 'Hey!' Cold. Cold hands on him, crawling under blankets, head swimming, stomach heaving, bed rocking. Pee, want a pee. Feel sick. Black sleep before he could do either. Troubled, fearful sleep, something wrong, something holding him, trapping him.

He came to consciousness painfully, aware of a number of strange things all at once. The pain in his head, the sickness still clutching at his stomach, made worse by a cloying perfume that seemed to be everywhere. It was black. He didn't know where he was, but he knew it wasn't home, and it wasn't camp.

It was a big bed, and the blankets were heavy. And in the same split second, he was aware of his nakedness and a hot female nakedness pressed to him, a hand pulling at his limp penis urgently and breath on his face.

'Don' go ter sleep on me, love.' Eileen sounded petulant. 'Come on, fer Christ's sake. I thought you wanted to.'

What Ginge wanted was to pee, to vomit, to run. It was a dream, wet, and nightmarish, and he was lost. How had he landed here? But she was pulling him roughly, rolling him on to her ample, smooth, rubbery flesh. And she succeeded.

His face was buried in a large breast, the nipple poking his eye, and, with a heave, she got him on top of her. Sturdy legs gripped him, the hand still held his penis, rubbing it against her moist genitals, and Ginge, frightened, lost, felt his sex react, stir and harden, and now both her hands ferreted between their bellies, peeling on a contraceptive over his hardness.

'You tol' me you 'ad these,' she whispered. She wriggled and took him inside. 'Come on,' she urged and dug her heels in as though he were a reluctant mount. She heaved him up on her wide belly. Ginge felt bile in his throat. Tears stung his eyes. Her hair tickled his nose, he could smell the heavy scent on her neck.

She grunted, tossing him up again. 'Come on, love. You gotter do *some* of the work. It was your idea, yer know.'

Savagely, he jerked up and down, thrusting at her, grimly satisfied when she exclaimed, 'Ow! Steady on! Ouf! Take it easy!' Thoughtlessly, animal-like he plunged and plunged until he ground his teeth, shuddered and exploded safe inside the sheath.

He could feel her breasts and stomach slippery with sweat,

which trickled between their glued bodies. He lay on her until she stirred and gasped in protest, then he tore himself from her and lay in the damp sheets. She broke the silence. 'There! That better, love? Reckon you needed that.' Her foot scraped his leg. She groaned and laughed. 'Cor, You've 'urt me, you 'ave. Mr Big!'

Ginge pressed his face into the pillow, biting it to hide his tears. Her hand moved playfully down his sweaty back. 'Better get some sleep now, love. You can do it when you wake up. Before you go, eh?' Ginge lay there, feeling the wetness on his cheeks, listening to her beside him. He wanted to run. And never wanted to move again. To die. In this smelly bed. With this smelly tart. He could make out a square of window, very faintly.

She was asleep. He was careful not to touch her. What time was it? How far was he from the camp? God, he felt lousy. He thought of Angie and it was like a searing, white-hot iron. He shied away from her. Probably he'd picked up the pox. The clap, as the lads called it. Well, he was one of the lads now all right. The Riff Raff. He lay until he could stand it no longer, then quietly eased his feet out to the floor. Christ! He couldn't see his clothes, daren't move. The bed creaked as his partner flung herself over, came snortingly awake. 'Wha – whassup? That you?'

'Yeah,' he murmured. 'Think ah'd better go.'

'Eh?' She sat up and groped. A lamp at the side of the bed cast a dim glow. She leaned on one elbow. Her black hair was short and spiky, her face creased with sleep. She was big. He couldn't help noticing her large, full breasts hanging down. The nipples and their surrounding circles were dark, a browny colour. Her mouth gaped in an unlovely yawn. She ferreted on top of the locker. 'Christ! It's only bloody four o'clock. Get back to bed. You'll find nuthin' runnin' this time o' mornin'.'

Embarrassed, he sat with the sheet over his loins, his curved back to her. 'Naw. Ah'd best be off. 'Onest. Gotta get back ter camp.'

'Your mate said you didn' 'ave ter be in till seven. Why'nt you wait an' get a taxi back?' She tried to put an invitation in her voice, and failed miserably. 'Come on, love. Come an' cuddle in. We got some unfinished business in the mornin'.'

Acutely aware of his nudity, he stood and grabbed his clothing. It was heaped on the floor. He staggered as he pulled on his underpants. She lay back on the pillow.

'Suit yerself, love. Still the two quid though, like we said. This is an all-nighters.' He saw his wallet with pay-book. It had been removed from his tunic. She hadn't taken the money, but had left it sticking out, an unmistakable reminder. He put the two pound notes on the crumpled bed.

'Ta,' he said awkwardly. 'It was – I—' He sat down and pulled on his boots. She yawned again.

'Yer know where te find me. Thanks, Ginge. Ye're a good un.'

He was ready and faced her, buttoning up his heavy coat. "Ow do ah get back te camp?'

She grinned, only her head above the bedclothes. 'Turn left an' keep goin' until yer get te the first main road. Can't miss it. Used ter be all lit up,' she said wistfully. 'Turn right on the main road an' keep walkin'. 'Bout a mile or more an' ye're at the station. Know the way from there, doncha?'

'Yeah. Well, tara then.'

'So long, Ginge. See yer around, eh?'

'Yeah. Tara.' Down the stairs and out into the cold night. His steps rang out on the frosty air. He was stopped only once, by a policeman.

'Oh. Apsley, is it? Aye, keep on this road. Bloody long way, though. 'Night.'

Ginge walked on in the unfamiliar darkness, listening to his footsteps. The tears rolled down his cheeks and his chest heaved. You big tough airman. Your first action. VD and Scar. And you posted a letter before you left camp. My darling. I love you. All the kisses. You dirty bastard.

Nine

The Street was growing blasé about the war. Washing on the Siegfried Line. Bless 'em all. A lot of fuss about nothing was the general feeling. The Lex still ran its old newsreels of the Führer, speeded up, looking more like Charlie Chaplin than the great comedian himself. They had had a few air-raid warnings, all in the daytime, the first one or two causing some panic – the shelter next to the school was jam packed the first time – but no action followed. The nearest guns to be fired in anger had been so far up the coast that they had not even been heard, and in any case the enemy planes had stayed well out at sea, taking a distant and circumspect look at the shipping going in and out of the Tyne and Wear.

The Sea Coal Man was working regularly. His favourite stretch of beach had been barbed wired and tank trapped, with War Office notices telling him to keep out. It meant cycling nearly eight miles now to reach Blackwell Rocks, where the black harvest washed up on to the sand could be safely gathered. Worse still, eight weary miles back, on foot, pushing the bike weighed down with the heavy, wet sacks. It was not worth the few extra bob, especially as the yard was offering all the overtime anyone could handle.

Privately, he wouldn't mind if the Jerries went on chucking their weight about for the next ten years. Regular work wasn't that bad, once you got used to it. And not having to worry where the next pint was coming from was a rare luxury, even if old Duchess Foster did look down her nose, as if your money was contaminated. Fine-looking woman, he often thought when he was well down his third pint. Lovely pair of tits on it. All wasted on poor old Alf. He hadn't got a good one in him. No wonder she was so bloody sharp. Could do her a good turn or two if only she wasn't so hoity-toity. Well, her loss, and no mistake.

Ellis's fear of the rattling letter-box was a little less acute. The way things were going, those buggers in France would be Chelsea Pensioners before shots were fired. He could wax patriotically indignant in the Pothouse. 'Sittin' on their arses. Gonner be like the last lot all over again. Why don' the' gerrin there an' do summat?'

Old Jonson smiled and nodded. 'Dat's right, boy. You go over dere an' show dem how to do it, hey?'

Angela Victoria was seventeen, though the event passed by almost unnoticed, for funds were temporarily low in the Thompson household only a week after the excesses of the festive season. Still got enough to go swilling down the Pothouse, Angela brooded darkly. She was not in a happy mood. Three weeks and still not a word from Ginge. She was there every morning, waiting for the post, just to make sure the Sea Coal Man didn't try any rotten tricks. She wouldn't put anything past him. I'll go downtown Monday morning, she vowed. To that recruiting office. Find out about the WAAFs.

Flo Foster was as patriotic as ever, as well she might be, for the war was doing wonders for their trade, beer rationing or no. Her grand manner and caustic tongue made her customers chary of airing their views too loudly. Alf, wiping and polishing and humping crates out back, listened sourly to her pontificating, and sometimes cursed Adolph for his non-belligerent attitude. A few of them dive bombers screamin' down and then we'll see who's for King and country. He smiled crookedly.

The winter was the worst hardship they faced. Snow came and stayed. Biting winds, frozen water-pipes. Life was a misery, and even Old Jonson had to give up his constitutionals in the worst of the weather. Ellis was forced to risk going on the sick, when turning out of the warm cocoon beside Peg's cosy form into the icy blackness of early morn became too much for his sensitive nature to bear.

Only the youngsters seemed to endure its harshness with undiminished enthusiasm. School was curtailed, to save on the heating, and, on the bitterest days, they were sent screaming with joy back home again. Doris made Little Jimmy a pair of thick trousers from Elisha's cast offs, and a kind of combination undergarment from one of Angela's old vests, which effectively sealed in the warmth, but engendered some intriguing contortions when he wanted to relieve himself.

Elisha and his cronies had transferred their interest from the coastal defences to the site of the barrage balloon and neighbouring searchlight station on the Rec. One strong reason for this, apart from the cruel weather, which made the shoreline a particularly inhospitable region, was that there had been a recent influx of ATS to 'man' the post. Elisha, and his mates, approaching the ripe old age of fourteen, already inveterate smokers and ready to leave the innocent pleasures of childhood far behind, were deeply involved in the study of this new and intriguing species of military life. The more knowledgeable made some sensational claims, gleaned from older brothers, concerning the depth and range of these girls' sexual expertise. The boys hung about the single bar of the barrier and the three-stranded perimeter fence ever hopefully.

Elisha's blond thatch was easily recognizable, and the girls were soon chatting boldly to him, amused by his air of worldly bravado. He ran errands for them, fetching fags and chips, watching and waiting, the eternal opportunist. There was one girl in particular who fascinated him. Her raven-black hair escaped with unruly attraction beneath the ridiculous khaki cap, and her laughing eyes flashed almost as darkly as her hair. Two upper front teeth protruded just slightly in the middle of her mouth, adding to the impression that she was pushing her cute lips forward in teasing motion.

She was tall and thin. Once he had seen her in baggy overalls; the rest of the time, she was enveloped in a huge greatcoat that came down to her ankles, or festooned in so many layers of sweaters beneath her straining battledress that she appeared to be impersonating the vast, inflated balloon they were tending. But Elisha's fertile imagination supplied details of her figure which fermented his voluptuous fantasies. Besides, he was working on improving his first hand knowledge of the subject under study.

He and his friends had maintained a careful watch, and they were aware now which end of the long, wooden hut in which the female soldiers were quartered contained the ablutions.

Elisha was in the process of devising a method of penetrating the defences in this target area under cover of darkness, and drilling a small hole, or series of holes, in the wall at an appropriate level, in order to advance their investigations significantly.

The dark-haired girl's name was Annie. Another notable feature of her character was her voice. The exotic London accent captivated the youths. Most of the girls were from the south, and it was clear that they in turn found the local dialect equally strange. There was a great deal of good-natured banter on both sides. The newcomers had swiftly become acquainted with certain aspects of local history which did not figure in the text books. Whenever they saw the group of lads congregating on the other side of the wire, they would call out challengingly, 'Who 'ung the monkey, then?'

It was a remark which could, in other circumstances, create strife and mayhem, for it referred to an episode in the town's past about which its normally robust natives were particularly sensitive. The legend had it that, during the Napoleonic Wars, when the port was no more than the fishing village clustered around its headland, an ape was washed ashore from a shipwreck. Whether it was actually French or no remains uncertain, but one thing that was never in doubt was that it failed to give a reasonable account of itself, whereupon it was arrested, and, after a trial at which it still stubbornly refused to communicate intelligibly, it was duly condemned and executed as a spy.

It was one of Old Jonson's favourite stories. For years he had delighted in bringing it up on suitable occasions, and had come dangerously close to a broken head on several of them. It was lucky, Elisha and his gang vowed, that it was a bunch of girls who thus taunted them with this ancient corporate skeleton, but it would serve to make their planned revenge all the sweeter.

Meanwhile, Elisha was in imminent danger of becoming captivated by the lively-eyed Annie, who began to single him out with ever bolder, friendlier approaches. They were on first-name terms. His ears glowed a bit at her sniggers on learning he was called Elisha. 'Blimey! That's a right 'andle, innit? 'Ow come?'

'Me dad's the bloody Archbishop o' Canterbury!' Elisha answered roundly. 'Yer can call me Eli,' he offered shortly, and Annie gladly accepted. She was off duty one morning, and actually walked down to the shops in Musgrove Street with him. Her nose was cherry red in the biting wind, and she sniffled with a streaming cold, but he thought her enchanting. He began to have some doubts about his planned peeping-tom activities, struggling with the novelties of a conscience, and nearly came to blows with Billy Limbert over his sudden reluctance.

Preoccupied as she was with her own troubled affairs, Angela could not help but notice a change in her brother. He no longer needled her, was actually pleasant on occasion, and even intervened on her behalf in one of the numerous threatened clashes with their da, at some considerable risk to his own person. It prompted Angela to ask speculatively of her mother, 'Ma. Is our Eli all right, d'yer think? 'E's not sickenin' fer summat, is he?'

It was April of a blustery spring before the ripples of war directly ruffled the even tenor of Street life, and their disturbance had an unexpected, and, in one instance, tragic effect on a number of the inhabitants. The month began with excitement, when a lone enemy plane was sighted, flying close to the shoreline, below the low cloud cover. A stubby Heinkel 111, investigating sea traffic in and out of Teesmouth. News spread like wildfire. People around the harbour and the sea-front in the old town had seen it clearly. Elisha and his buddies were drawn back to their old haunts, his passion for the raven-haired Annie pushed temporarily from the forefront of his mind.

Thus, they were on hand two days later when an excited little crowd gathered in the vicinity of the coastguard station, a crowd which rapidly expanded as rumour flew back and forth. A Spitfire had engaged and destroyed an enemy plane just off the coast a little to the south – one of the aforementioned Heinkels – and then had to ditch in the sea itself after a malevolently lucky burst from the doomed bomber's rear gunner had caused it to sink seawards, smoke trailing in a thin but increasing cloud from its engine.

By good fortune, one of the port's inshore fishing boats had been on hand, and picked up the gallant pilot from the water, when he managed, not without difficulty, to extract himself from the cockpit of the rapidly disappearing fighter. How the news got to the coastguard and then to those outside so quickly was not clear, but there was a cheering throng to herald the arrival of the rolling craft back past the pier-head and to her berth. Elisha and his mates squirmed and forced their way to the front.

'By 'eck, 'e looks rough,' Billy Limbert commented, impressed by the ashen hue of the frail looking figure who was the centre of attention. Almost hidden in a borrowed jersey and high oilskins, the modest hero did indeed look pale and stricken, as well he might after such an ordeal. But, magically, as he made his back-slapping way through the cheering well-wishers, complexion and enthusiasm for life flowed back almost instantaneously, and it emerged that his wan appearance had been caused by nothing worse than a fearsome bout of seasickness on the return trip.

Elisha returned to The Street something of a hero himself at having been witness to these stirring events, and told and retold the tale graphically to young and old. The next harbinger of momentous happenings was Ellis, who equally relished his role as he shuffled about, risking the brisk wind, to impart the news.

'The buggers 've invaded Norway,' he told anyone who cared to listen. Old Jonson, chewing on his stained moustache, for once had little to say. Mention of places he discovered he had not forgotten stirred him deeply. He suffered a great deal in the next weeks.

'We'll soon run the buggers out of there,' Ellis predicted confidently at the news of the allied landings. Two weeks later, the first of the British troops were withdrawing again and people shook their heads unbelievingly. Were we to lose the first round on land so easily?

The Navy had, since the outbreak of hostilities, rather hogged the headlines, and they did so again in the Norwegian campaign. As a prelude, the *Cossack* had pursued the *Altmark* into a fiord, boarded her, and returned home with 300 British seamen who had been imprisoned in her hold. Now came the

Battle of Narvik, and Captain Warburton-Lee's brave attack, during which he was killed aboard his destroyer, *Hardy*, which ran aground. Another destroyer, *Hunter*, was sunk in the same attack.

In Sam's fish shop, the usually smiling face of its owner took on an unwonted seriousness. He still had Joe's excitedly scrawled letter – he had all of them – telling his parents of his draft to HMS *Hurricane*, a Hunt-class destroyer, attached to the 10th Flotilla and based in Rosyth.

'Our Joe's stationed up north. On one o' them 'Unt-class destroyers, yer know. 'E's bound ter be mixed up in that lot, ah reckon.'

Mrs Clay shifted her bulk, and made sounds of conventional sympathy. Eeh, thank God our Arthur's no further than Nottingham, she reflected comfortably, as she picked up the hot newspaper bundle. Sam was of The Street if not in it, having fed them for a number of years, and it was through him that the first tragedy touched them.

The Street still clung to routine, even in wartime, and the fact that on a Friday dinner-time Sam's fish shop was mysteriously closed aroused amazed and truculent comment. ' 'E 'ad loads o' tatties,' Doris exclaimed to a crony as, with arms folded across shabby coats, they stared at the green, padlocked door. 'What the bloody 'ell is 'e playin' at? Ah tell yer – some folk don' give a bugger, eh, kidder?'

The telegram had come to the neat little bungalow that very morning, while Sam and his wife were sitting at breakfast. They had listened to the eight o'clock news, but learnt nothing fresh. The bulletin was the same as that read by Alvar Liddell the night before.

'... *naval engagement preceding the landing of allied troops at the port of Narvik, during which a large number of enemy vessels were destroyed by units of the British Fleet.*'

Sam felt sure that *Hurricane* must be mixed up in that lot somewhere, for Joe had written of patrols in the bleak waters of the North Sea. The missus didn't try to hide her fears. She had wept last night, and Sam had jovially teased her. 'Nay, lass, it's a big place out there. The's loads of ships about. Bet our Joe's sittin' in a pub in Edinburgh or summat. Any road, it's Jerry what's got the pastin'. Howay, love, don't be so daft.' He tried the same technique on himself, endeavouring to dismiss his uneasiness, to no avail.

When they heard the dying splutter of the motor bike, they stared at each other, his wife's face chalky and rigid with terror. Sam felt choked. His heart thudded. He tore his eyes away from hers. 'Ah'll see what that is,' he murmured, desperately clinging to normality.

It'll be all right, it'll be all right. The words hammered like a prayer in his brain, his hands shook so violently he fumbled and fumbled before he could get the envelope open. He had seen the official lettering. Just wounded, just wounded, he begged the God he wasn't sure was there. And yet, all the time, in the age between pushing himself up from his chair, and this instant when he held the paper tremblingly, he had known somehow it was no good.

Something vital in the lives of Sam and his missus died too. As he had grown, Joe had become more and more the chief element in their existence. Their only child, a lovely bairn, a happy, promising youth, a young man they thrilled with pride to. They never fully recovered from his loss. Neither of them could let him go. The wound never healed. His clothes were kept, his books, his models. His photographs stood on the sideboard, and on the mantelpiece.

The citation was framed and their eyes sought it every day. The captain of *Hurricane* wrote a personal letter, sorrowing and sympathetic. Nine lives had been lost. Four more had suffered serious wounds, the ship herself scarred. Narvik was added to the battle honours, would remain for all the ships that would bear the name, *Hurricane*. Honour and Glory. Supreme Sacrifice.

Sam and his wife were a little proud. They ought to be, for Joe's sake. Yet mostly they were bitter and uncomprehending. Their life went on, but it was never the same. After a couple of weeks, they opened the shop again.

It was painfully awkward at first. The Street did not know how to express its sympathy. Any efforts that were made were cut off abruptly by Sam. His sweating, red-faced humour was gone. He responded dully to conversations, so that, gradually, apart from the initial ' 'owdo,' his customers virtually ignored him.

The trade didn't suffer. The Street was not particularly

thin-skinned, and his fish and chips were good. Sam's fish shop stayed open until the end of the war, then they sold the business and disappeared, without telling anyone, to their seaside bungalow. They had plenty of money and no reason now for having it. They became more and more withdrawn, silent with each other, and with no friends; going abroad, when things settled down, for long, expensive holidays, which they failed to enjoy. Eventually, the new owner of the fish shop gave up trying to stop The Street calling it 'Sam's'.

Ten

Ginge was racked with remorse after his New Year's Eve fall. He screamed almost hysterical abuse at the Yokel, (who came within an ace of giving him a good thumping) then lapsed into silent isolation. A fresh torture was his fear of disease. His stomach churned when he thought of the night's rutting. For two weeks, he couldn't write to Angela. Many letters were started, then torn from the pad and crumpled in self-loathing. He was almost glad that Angie was not much of a hand at letter-writing.

But one dinner-time, he saw the envelope with the familiar, laboured script, on the table at the end of the mess hut. Slipping off his gaiters and boots, he lay back on the bed, oblivious to the usual, cheery babel around him. His hand shook a little as he lit a cigarette.

My Darling,

I havent had a letter from you for ever so long Ive been dead werried I do hope you are all right. Please let me know if anythings wrong. You know I love you I hope you havent gone of me or anything. I went to that raf office in Church Street but they said i have to be 18 so Ill have to wait. I wish I could be sent to were you are that would be good.

It seems a long time since I was with you I miss you very much things are just the same here. Take care of yourself and write soon.

All my love

Angela xxxxx

He scrambled determinedly in his locker, and propped his pad on his knee. He chewed the end of his pencil, seeking inspiration. However badly he had let her down, he *did* love her, and wanted to be worthy of her. He would never again behave as he had on New Year's Eve. Would she still love him if she knew? How would he feel if he discovered that Angie had done the same thing? With Barraclough or one of that crowd.

He felt terribly hurt just imagining her infidelity, then lashed himself afresh for his inconsistency. *He* had. Why shouldn't she? Clenching his teeth, he began to struggle to put down on paper this love that was the most important thing in his life to him, mercifully unaware of the sniggers his missive would call forth from the censor officer.

However, Ginge did not have too much leisure in which to brood over his secret lapse. Through the snow and sleet and slush of the severe winter, the training continued, its pace more and more demanding. They grumbled incessantly, yet, though they would never admit it, there was a growing pride in their increasing skill.

Occasionally, they wondered if they would ever get the chance to put their warlike accomplishments into practice. They now stood regular guard at the airfield. The ugly and curiously frail bombers were their link with the war. Daylight raids had quickly become a thing of the past. The attack on Wilhelmshaven had been a severe lesson. Half the Wellingtons sent out had failed to return. At Apsley there had been more aircraft lost through the hazards of winter flying than through enemy action.

Still, dead was dead, Ginge mused, staring at the brown and green camouflaged fuselages and the powerful engines, the props standing out high and black against the grey sky. He thought of them far away in a black night full of violence, facing death over a hostile, unseen land. He had watched them returning from night raids, noticing the gathering cluster of mechanics, WAAFs, all kinds of erks, who would stand looking eastward, hands over eyes, straining to see the black dots, to hear the labouring engines. The buzz quickly spread round the camp when planes were missing.

One morning, a Wellington hung back, firing a flare, circling the field until its companions had landed. An undercarriage had been damaged and the bomber had to come in on its belly. Ginge was on guard and helped to keep the crowds back beyond the perimeter track. It seemed the whole station was there to witness the drama.

The fire tenders raced out, the crews ready by the hoses. Although the pilot throttled back as much as he dared, the dark bulk seemed to come on at a terrifying speed. There was a sickening screech of metal as the plane hit the runway, then bounced high in the air. It smacked down again, another giant bounce, then skidded along the ground, hidden in a cloud of brown dust.

The terrible noise died away, the dust settled, and the bomber was there, slewed across the grass, the hoses already playing on the smoking engines. The crew, distant, bulky figures, scrambled out and into the open truck. Ginge saw the plane at close quarters, and the great scars it had made on the runway. Apart from the damage caused by the crash landing, there was a series of holes punched through the fuselage, near the tail. The edges of the holes were ragged, the canvas flapping in the bitter wind. Enemy shells had made those holes. Ginge and the others gazed at them with something of awe.

The gentler days of spring found them still at Apsley, their training completed. The passing-out parade was conducted with a real band, before a fierce-looking air commodore, though all Ginge saw of him at close quarters was a blur that crossed his rigidly fixed, watery eyes, For once, the Regiment was the chief attraction, and a respectable crowd gathered behind the roped-off enclosure to watch the brief ceremony.

'This is sweet FA,' Flight Sergeant Crabbe, their ageing, regular instructor told them dismissively. 'Nuthin' compared ter peace time.' But they were nervous enough, and buffed and blancoed late into the night. Crabbe's expression resembled that of an early Christian martyr as he lined them up on the wet tarmac outside the hut, in the windy early morning.

'An' don't let's 'ave anybody droppin' 'is bloody rifle,' Crabby growled, glaring at the red-faced unfortunate who had done just that at the previous day's rehearsal. 'If you do that today, my lad, you might as well take that bayonet an' cut your fuckin' throat. Save me the job of doin' it myself.' With those comforting words, he moved on to the next squad, leaving the worried corporal to march them off to the parade ground beside No. 1 Hangar.

In fact, all went well. Their moment of glory passed, and they were back to guard duties, exercises, and Saturday night trips to Nottingham to the dance hall, where they drank and glowered at the wearers of flashier and more successful uniforms. 'Us orlwus gets the doggo wuns,' the Yokel observed mournfully.

'As old boots,' a mate confirmed. Ginge, his resolve never firmer, stayed at the crowded bar.

They were in action briefly, when the Yokel thumped a corporal from armaments who spoke contemptuously of their role in military affairs. The victim was catapulted over a table, knocking down four soldiers and, more seriously, many more pints. In a second, the area around the bar was a struggling mass, fists and boots flying with fine impartiality, but, though fierce, the fun was brief. Military police, both red and white capped, were swiftly on hand, and their violence was more efficient and organized. Order was restored and names and numbers taken. The Yokel, Ginge, and a number of cronies, were confined to camp and their pay docked.

'Supposed to be fighting the bloody Germans, not each other,' the wingco remarked sourly, but no mere Hun roused the Yokel's ire as did the glib-mouthed armaments corporal.

' 'E better not go down no alleys, Oi'll 'ave 'ee.'

That incident, too, passed into history, and still they stayed at Apsley.

With the Norwegian campaign started, a buzz immediately spread through the camp that they were on twenty-four hours stand-by for the land of fiords and the midnight sun. Then it was the Far East. Cold beer and hot women. Everyone was excited for a couple of days. When nothing happened, they reverted to their bitter cynicism.

Ginge was reminded that there *was* a war on when he got a letter from Angie, giving him the news of Joe Morley's death at Narvik. Tall. Dark hair. Good-looking, Ginge conceded. He remembered the night in the Pothouse at Christmas, and his own feeling of jealousy at what he considered the more glamorous uniform. He was a hero now all right, poor bugger. His name would go on the Cenotaph downtown, with all the others from the last lot. He tried unsuccessfully to feel the reality of Joe's death. That he no longer walked and breathed, at twenty or twenty-one. Yes, he'd got the glamour now. His name on everyone's lips. The Street's tears for him. But how long would it take to forget him?

Two weeks later, the British Army was on its way back from Norway, and Britain had a new Prime Minister. The phoney war was over. In five days, Holland was overrun, and the victorious German army headed for France.

At last, Apsley's Regiment was off. One sunny May morning, the ennui vanished dramatically, with the word, official this time, that one and two squadrons were to embark for France in four days. 'Fighter 'drome just outside a place called Arras,' Flight informed them. 'North of France somewhere. Now we'll see who's all mouth and no trousers, eh?'

That afternoon, after the midday meal, Ginge and the others sat around in the mess hut, discussing their future. 'It'll be like the First War,' one sage announced. 'The Frenchies 've got this Maggy-summat line, see. The Jerries'll not get through that lot, no way. It'll be the trenches again, you mark my words.' Most did, for they were not particularly well informed, but one quiet Scots lad surprised them by speaking up.

'Aye, but if they're already in Holland, the' just need tae come down through Belgium. Yon line winnae stop them.' Ginge nodded wisely, having no idea of the geography of Europe. Jock sounded pretty sure of himself. The Yokel reduced the argument on strategy to the usual mess level.

'Well,' he chuckled, 'oi dunno 'bout Maggy's loine or that Siegried loine an' all that, but oi do know a bit about them French birds an' oi reckon we'm be all roight fer a bit of the ould oo-la-la, me ould fruit.' He punched Ginge on the upper arm and leered. Ginge smiled in superior fashion.

The corporal clomped in and stood between the rows of beds. 'Right! Embarkation leave for one an' two Flight starts at oh seven 'undred termorrer. Passes an' warrants and leave pay this afternoon. Fill these bastards in an' take 'em down the office at fourteen 'undred.' He gazed at their faces, some of which were still blank, others dawning with delight. 'All right for some,' he muttered, and clattered out.

Uproar broke out. Ginge flung himself at the Yokel with a wild yell. 'Ye bugger! We're goin' 'ome, you janner bastard! 'Ome temorrer.'

The jubilation was universal. Similar cries came from the next hut. That they might within days be at grips with the enemy, facing terrifyingly efficient weapons of death, did not sober them. They didn't think about it. For them, the future was hours away, a train ride, and home and loved ones.

No time to write. Just turn up out of the blue. Angie 'll have a fit. His weekend case packed, his best uniform pressed, Ginge lay and chatted in the darkness. Voices called out, old jokes were retold, everyone laughed. The banter was good humoured, taken in good part. Ginge, in his innocence, could almost have blessed Jerry for getting him so unexpectedly back to Angie. For thirty-six hours. And by God, he'd try to spend every one of them with her.

'Ah's sorry, pet, but yer'll 'ave ter finish next week. Nowt ah can do about it. It's just not worth keepin' yer on fer the stuff we gettin' now.' Mr Moore stared at Angela lugubriously, and her eyes fastened, as they were wont to, on his broad, purpled nose. She had been expecting to be finished any day. She imagined the fuss that would be made at home. Even though the Sea Coal Man was bringing in a good wage every week, Angie's thirty bob would be missed. A large proportion of her father's pay packet was reserved for his own private entertainment, which meant that it came to rest in the Pothouse till. Her mam relied to a considerable extent on Angela's contribution to keep the household supplied with foodstuffs. There was a grim, selfish satisfaction in Angela's reflection that her da would have to cough up a bit more for other people's throats from now on.

She stiffened as Mr Moore laid a thick, calloused, red hand on her sleeve. 'Ah'll slip yer a bit extra next week,' he murmured, glancing back furtively to make sure his wife was out of earshot. 'You understand 'ow it is, pet, don't yer?'

Not a bad old stick, Moore. She remembered how, when she had first started there eighteen months ago, he had come up behind her when she was stacking the empty boxes out the back and grabbed her. His beery breath hot on her neck. His hand cupping her behind, the other clutching at her breast. She had sworn, pushing him away violently, trembling and near to tears, sure that she was going to be sacked after only a couple of days.

But he had lurched away, muttering, and had never tried to touch her again. He hadn't even referred to the incident. Mind you, Helen Revell wouldn't be sacked. Angie was sure of that. The tall, dark-haired girl certainly hadn't pushed him away. In her mid-twenties, married, with two kids, Helen viewed her adultery with the tubby, ageing greengrocer as a commercial proposition. Though cynical and knowledgeable even at fifteen, Angela had secretly wondered how Helen could even bear to let the lecherous old boozer touch her, let alone have sex with him on the floor of the tiny cubicle that served as office, as she did two evenings a week, when Mrs Moore had safely departed with the beloved day's takings close to her sagging bosom.

Well, Angela thought determinedly, as she shifted the trays of vegetables on the sloping trestles of the stall, it would certainly accelerate her own plans. The prospect of having to wait eight whole months before she could join the WAAFs was like a life sentence. And even then, they were not forced to take her. Doreen Meadowes reckoned she had tried to volunteer for the Wrens and they wouldn't have her. And yet they were conscripting girls for the Army. They were even forming a Women's Land Army, to work on farms. She didn't fancy that, thank you very much. She'd once gone up to Dalby on a day out with the school and been frightened nearly out of her wits when a herd of massive cows had come into the field.

She'd rather go into a factory than be stuck out in the country somewhere. She'd even heard that they were starting to train girls for work in the shipyard, riveting and welding, not that she'd fancy that very much, either. Guiltily, she acknowledged that the greatest priority for her was to get away from home and The Street, and see something of the world she could only imagine existed beyond her narrow confines.

Ginge had sent her a photograph of himself and his mates on the day of his passing-out parade. They were standing rigidly to attention, their rifles sloping on their shoulders, their caps with their shiny peaks pressed down on their noses. She had hardly recognized the bit of Ginge's face that could be seen. He was staring fixedly ahead. Fierce, almost scowling, ready to take on the whole of Hitler's army there and then. A different person from the timid lad who had sweated into her palm in the Lex, or fumbled his way into her on the prom shelter bench.

Getting away could do just as much for her. She must get into the Air Force. She must. Her stomach fluttered as she contemplated going further afield, say to Newcastle, and trying again, lying about her age. How would they know? Newcastle was the furthest she had ever been. It had seemed a frighteningly big place, such huge buildings, so many people, so much traffic.

He would be so proud of her. She always felt like blushing when she thought of Ginge. A little guilty. Confused and angry with herself. It was always the same. A furious argument going on inside her head. You don't love him. I do. Don't. Not really. You're just playing at it. In Love. But it wasn't playing at it in the shelter. Or on the Rec. He was the only one, the only one she'd ever done it with. She belonged to him. Didn't she? Beautiful blond, handsome war hero.

' 'Ere! Give us a 'and with these sprouts, Angie.' Helen's husky voice roused her, and she pushed a lock of golden hair back under the turban with a grubby finger.

At five o'clock, she was sweeping up the dust and cabbage stalks, with the sun still beaming through the glass roof of the market, when she heard Ginge say, "Ello, Angie.' Red-faced, smiling adoringly, he was there, across the caulies and carrots, sweating in his thick uniform. She gawped at him, unmindful of her hanging mouth, her stained pinny and ragged headscarf.

'Ginge!' She gasped out his name. At last she could move again. She sped round the stall and into his arms, hungrily searching for his mouth. Shoppers stared briefly as they brushed past.

Ginge grew even redder. 'I 'adn't time te let yer know,' he panted, when they broke off the kiss. 'Ah've got till temorrer night. We're off te France Frid'y.' She clung to him again, her heart thumping wildly. France. The war. Suddenly she was near to weeping.

She introduced him proudly to her boss. 'Go on, haddaway

home,' Mr Moore told her kindly. 'We're all right 'ere. Away ye go with the lad.'

The spring evening was still warm. They walked arm in arm the mile or so back to Sutherland Street, Ginge clutching the small case in his left hand, Angie on his right. She felt proud, at the same time conscious of her own unglamorous appearance, old check coat pulled round her, hair tied up in a blue scarf. She had thought of taking it off, but the image of her hair, unkempt, lank and greasy, deterred her. 'Ye should've let me know,' she chided, squeezing his arm. Patiently, lovingly, Ginge explained again.

Both felt the momentousness of the occasion. This time he was really going off to war. They might never see each other again. Angela's eyes blurred, a lump rose in her throat. The nasty inner voice started again. Ooh, how romantic! Just like the pictures, eh?

She clung to his arm with tight defiance, even when they reached the corner of The Street. 'Can ah see yer tonight?' she asked simply.

'Why, of course. Ah'll see yer in an hour.' He paused uncomfortably. 'Er – over in the lane, eh?'

She nodded, then closed her eyes and pursed her lips, raised her face expectantly. Ginge's face flamed. The back of his neck prickled. So blatant. How many eyes were watching, tongues ready to wag? Bravely, he darted forward and fleetingly kissed her. 'Love yer. Tara.'

As Ginge had anticipated, Mrs Clay collapsed in watery hysteria, which required Mr Clay to reach grumblingly for the medicine bottle of brandy hidden away at the back of the top shelf in the pantry. She had not long been restored to comparative calmness when Ginge's announcement that he was 'off out' threatened a further outburst. 'Ah'll walk down wi' yer,' declared his father, to Ginge's alarm. 'Ah could do with a gill meself.'

'Well – ah'm not goin' te see the lads,' Ginge blundered on. 'Ah was – er – ah'm just goin' fer a stroll like.'

His mother's voice rose. 'Are ye seein' that Thompson lass? Ah've told yer about 'er.' Ginge admitted it. His mother wailed on. 'A bad lot they are. All tarred wi' the same brush. Ye want nowt te do with them, our Arthur. The's not an ounce o' decency in any of them. Pinchin' an' thievin' an' drinkin'. An' God knows what else. Ye'll rue it, ah'm warnin' yer.'

'Aye. Right-oh. Ye've told us.' Ginge felt close to tears himself. He straightened his grey-blue battledress blouse and squared off his forage cap in the mirror over the fireplace. His mother's voice pursued him out into the dark lobby.

'An' she's no better than she should be an' all. Like 'er mam, that one. The little slut, settin' 'er cap at anythin' in trousers—'

Ginge clashed the front door shut. Thank God for the light nights. He tried to push his mother's unpleasantness away. Angie a slut. Ridiculous. Too daft even to get mad about. He ached with fervent longing as he walked along the uneven pavement towards Brewery Lane. Why couldn't they be left alone? He wished they were married. Together, in their own house. Their own bed.

Sexual excitement flared as he passed the railingless brick wall of the school. He wanted to make love with her, properly, with time to be gentle, to do everything right. Not propped on elbows in a spit-ridden shelter, or among the dog muck behind a goal post on the Rec. He flicked his cigarette into the gutter. One thing about the winter, it was at least dark, even if it was freezing cold. Now where could they go?

He saw her hurrying towards him. She had a light, flowered summer dress on, with short, puffed sleeves. Her arms were thin and white. Her yellow hair gleamed and hung in a luxuriant wall of pale gold. They kissed, then walked hand in hand down the cobbled lane, past the fence and the Sandeman Port man, to the high, sooty wall and towering brick chimney of the brewery, the air still flavoured with the malty smell. He saw her narrow feet, the toes poking through cheap, open sandals. The nails were painted a vivid red. She's beautiful, Ginge thought.

They walked through the town, and along the road that led to the sea-front. They couldn't see the sea, for, on their right, was the high wooden fence of the prop yards. There was no sign of the squared piles of timbers that had towered over the fence in pre-war days. But finally the fence ended, and they climbed the iron steps of the footbridge over the railway lines, and there it was, bluey-grey, like Ginge's uniform, with lively white caps and a stiff breeze blowing in from the ocean. Ginge breathed in rapturously and turned to Angie with a wide grin. Coming to the sands always thrilled him, just as it had every summer when he was a lad.

The tide was low. They walked along the wet edge of the shore, Angela carrying her sandals, letting the water lap over her feet, then scampering out, squealing at its icy touch. Landward, the sun was low, ready for setting. The sky was dappled pink. Stanton church tower was black against the glow, and the chimneys of the steelworks, with their dark plumes of smoke streamed out like flags in the yellow light of evening.

Angela did all the talking, chattering on gaily about work, The Street, her uncertain future. Ginge listened enraptured, glad to be there, holding her moist hand, watching her thin legs and white feet as she scampered about, leaving prints on the glistening sand. Glancing back to the town, Ginge saw a new silhouette, the almost comic shape of a barrage balloon rising in the fading sky. Its intrusion on the evening's beauty was a sharp reminder to Ginge.

'Angie,' he stammered forlornly, 'Ah wish the' was somewhere we could go. Ye know – ah've gotter go back temorrer night. Eight o'clock train. Ah wish – ah wanna be with you. Tonight.'

Serious, her eyes wide and intent on his face, she stopped and stepped in closer to him. They gazed at each other. 'We can,' she almost whispered. 'Stay together.' She jerked her head, pointing behind her. 'The's the dunes. Be'ind the guns. Yer can't stay down on the prom. It's all wired off now. But the's the dunes. Couples still go along there. Courtin' like. We could stay there. It won't be too cold. If yer want to.' He pulled her to him and kissed her.

Deep in a hollow of soft sand, Ginge spread out his blouse and Angela's cardigan and made a nest for them under the darkening wide blue of the sky, in which one or two stars were already showing. 'What about yer mam an' dad?' Ginge had asked, as they stumbled hand in hand over the low hillocks.

Angela had turned to him, lifting her hand to his mouth. 'Shurrup,' she pleaded. 'Don' spoil it. We've gotter ferget about them all. Just us. We'll worry about them again after.'

Now, aching with love, he gathered her to him, holding her tightly, his desire already roused by her soft body moulded to him. She slipped her bare legs between his, shivering slightly, although they were snugly protected from the sea breeze. They lay kissing, while the spiky tufts of long grass swayed and whispered and grew darker, until only their black outline moved against the night sky.

Her flesh was cold and puckered in goose bumps when he clumsily helped her out of the thin frock. She was breathless with embarrassment, for there was still light enough for him to see her pale body and the cheap white underwear. But at least it was clean and not threadbare. The excitement was mounting in her, too, and, though she blushed, and the tears hovered on the lids of her tightly closed eyes, she dug her heels in the sand, lifting her buttocks to allow him to pull her panties down her trembling legs. Her hands flew to cover the startlingly dark patch of hair at the apex of her thighs. Her voice was shaky and tearful. 'Don' look at us. It's not fair. You've gotter get undressed an' all.'

Ginge was gazing in rapture at her slim beauty. He roused himself and struggled out of his trousers, dropping them beside the discarded boots. Hastily, he fumbled on the contraceptive and made to fall on top of her, but she gasped, 'No!' Her hands pushed against his shoulders. 'Just hold me fer a bit, Ginge. Please.'

Their mouths scarcely parting for many long minutes, she guided his rough hand to the soft roundness and moist opening of her eager frame, until she pulled at him and clasped him between her thighs. It was soon over.

Angie sobbed quietly as they lay limply together, her face buried in Ginge's shirt. She waited for the torment in her loins to subside, for a few minutes lost in a bitter desolation all the more painful because she had been so near orgasm when Ginge finally spent himself. Her cries had matched his own explosive groan, and she had bucked furiously under him, so that he now lay in blissful, exhausted unawareness, believing her tears to be part of the gushing release of emotion.

She fought to control herself, deeply ashamed. At last, she stirred, and reached up to kiss the red neck showing above his collarless blue shirt. 'Ooh, that was good. But ah wish yer didn'' 'ave ter use them – things.' She shivered and clung to him. 'Eh, ah'm freezin' wi' nowt on. Come on, warm us up again.'

The world that Angela had tried so desperately to shun was with them when they walked back through the town. The clock on Stanton church tower was no longer illumined, but an elderly police constable, who shone his torch on them and relaxed when he saw the air-force blue, told them it was quarter past one. 'Ye'll cop it off yer da when ye get 'ome,' he shouted laughingly. Neither Ginge nor Angela smiled.

She was afraid now, though she sought hard to be brave, to cling to the magic of their love. 'Ah can always go round ter me gran's if the've locked us out,' she said. She squeezed his arm and giggled. 'Eh, ah've got sand everywhere. Ah'm goin' mad.'

Eleven

Summer came early to England that year. The latter half of May was mostly cloudless and sunny, and with the blue summer skies came the war. The Street heard about the bombing raids on the south coast. A squadron of Hurricanes arrived at Elton, an RAF airfield a few miles up the coast, and yet more AA batteries were set up along the front. 'Any day now. You mark my words.'

It was impossible to ignore world events any longer, even in The Street. Sam, a new, grim-faced, suddenly old Sam, came round with the broad sticking tape that had to be criss-crossed over the windows. Old Jonson came back from his daily walk, apple cheeks glowing and a malicious twinkle in his eye. 'Dey callin' up de under twenty-fives now, ya. Soon be your turn, my boy.' He knew it upset Peg, who chewed her lip nervously, but he couldn't help it. He couldn't resist the look of fright in Ellis's eyes, staring huge and watery through his glasses.

The Sea Coal Man joined the Defence Volunteers, the Home Guard as they were called, even though it seriously interfered with his drinking habits, as he was required for duty on the front by the prop yards two or three nights a week. Still, he reflected morosely, won't matter much soon. They were talking about bringing beer rationing in any road. Have to take your coupons along for a pint next! He sat in the shelter, gazing out to the blackness seaward, and drew on a surreptitious cigarette. He almost wished Jerry *would* appear. He'd give him what for. Though Christ knows how he was supposed to repel an attack, with a whistle and a pick handle for his total armament.

Even Sunday was no longer sacrosanct. If he wasn't in at the yard, he was drilling, under a sergeant who was as wide as a barrage balloon and couldn't see his boots, or a captain who was so ancient he must have fought the Fuzzy-Wuzzies, and who talked as though he had a mouthful of marbles.

One day, they were practising street defence and the Sea Coal Man found himself, to his intense mortification, running about Sutherland Street itself, his face blackened, and a wreath of greenery stuck in his helmet. To add to the unreality, he was carrying a broom handle, there not being enough rifles to arm even one platoon, and he was dressed in baggy overalls, the uniforms having failed to arrive.

He and three others ran, bent low as instructed, then turned and flung themselves on their stomachs, pressed against the walls, their broom handles pointed menacingly down the narrow roadway, in the direction of the imaginary enemy. The Sea Coal Man was opposite his own front door. Old Ma Ashton came waddling in her slippers towards the corner shop. She gave no sign of being surprised at his strange behaviour. 'Mornin, 'Arry,' she called cheerfully.

' 'Ello,' he replied, squinting up at her and grinning foolishly. Then the door opened and Doris appeared. He groaned. She let out a startled shriek at seeing her husband stretched on the ground, with a face like the chocolate-coloured coon, but quickly ascertained that he was all right. 'Bugger off!' he hissed. 'We're on manoeuvres.'

'Stop buggerin' about an' gerrup off that mucky floor. Yer'll catch yer death. 'Oway in. Ah've just put the kettle on.' Five minutes later, the four-man squad was crowded in the Thompsons' front room, sipping tea that you could stand the spoon up in, and the rotund sergeant was breathing heavily as he combed the area for the mysteriously Lost Patrol.

Then came the first night air-raid warning. It was after eleven, and most of The Street were abed, the Pothouse having closed an hour earlier. The rising and falling metallic tones sent panic darting through them, fanned into epic proportions by the cacophony of crashes made by the AA batteries on the nearby shore. Doors banged, kids and women screamed, men swore.

Families, clad in all stages of dress and undress, fumbled and fought their way down the steps of the long, concrete shelter in the corner of the school yard. It smelt stale and raw and earthy, but its rows of green wooden benches were soon crammed with bodies. Mrs Clay appeared, wild and Wagnerian, in a white cotton nightie over which she had flung Ginge's old work coat. To her bosom, she clutched the black pillared clock. She stared about her abstractedly.

Ellis, wearing his ARP helmet, pushed her aside and squirmed into the throng, cannoning into the Sea Coal Man, and too caught up in his fear to enjoy the sight of a wide-eyed, tousled-haired Angela, clutching her old check coat about her slim figure. ' 'Old 'ard.' The Sea Coal Man thrust him away vigorously.

'Wharra noise,' Ellis moaned. His shaking hands were clasped in front of him, the fingers writhing constantly. 'Sounds like 'undreds of them. The'll be nowt left.'

'Where's Peg an' the ould man?' Doris asked sharply. Ellis stared at her with the fixity of a rabbit before a stoat.

'Jonson wouldn' come. 'E's got 'imself in the cupboard under the stairs. Ah told 'im, the stupid old bugger. An' Peg wouldn' leave 'im.' He became aware of the women staring contemptuously at him, and he floundered, feebly trying to master the hysteria in his whining tones. 'Ah said – ah'd just come – ter see what was goin' on an' that. Yer know.' He glanced at his feet.

'Shouldn't you be out on the street? Bein' a warden an' all?' the Sea Coal Man asked nastily, and in his mind Ellis screamed abuse.

'Ah'm norron ternight. Ah've been bad. Wi' me chest.'

No bombs fell on The Street, or on the town, but it was the beginning of a new way of life. For almost four years, the sirens would sound almost nightly, as waves of enemy planes crossed the coast for more alluring targets inland, the all clear ringing out in the early hours, after the bombers had passed over once more on their way home. People roped off their own corners of the shelter, took along mattresses and spirit stoves and other comforts. Card schools would run on through the long hours of darkness, the men squatting under the flickering light of a lantern, ignoring the crack and thump of the guns, quarrelling over pennies, while death weaved and flickered and sparked in the night sky.

But that was in the future. It took them a long while to grow indifferent to the chilling night wail. There were some who never did. Who even today would feel their stomachs jelly at that distinctive sound.

And hard on the heels of their own tribulation, came news of gathering disaster on the continent. The Expeditionary Force was being driven back relentlessly, rolled up by that new and devastating weapon of war, the Panzer division. Nowadays, at the Lex, only the very young hooted when a ranting Adolph appeared on the screen. Faces were drawn and more serious. More than one of The Street's older members slipped furtively but with determination away to church or chapel on a Sunday morning. There was a God in His heaven all right, and better late than never. You never knew.

People stopped sneering at the Home Guard, who marched and drilled and flourished their brooms belligerently. 'An' a lot o' effin' good this'll do,' the Sea Coal Man reasoned, going through the motions of thrust and parry with less than wholehearted enthusiasm. 'The bastards land 'ere an' ah'm burnin' this soddin' uniform. Right off! Bloody King'll be 'alf-way to America by then. Too bloody true!'

'Give 'em 'ell, lads!' the fat-gutted sergeant roared, and the Sea Coal Man raised his eyes eloquently to the ceiling.

One day, Mrs Clay was in Wilson's, the corner shop, when the bell jangled and in came Doris, eyes screwed against the Woodbine that hung from her lip. They eyed each other with wary hostility before turning away. Doris noted the lines of haggard worry etched deeply into the pale, fleshy face. She cleared her throat noisily, dragging away the cigarette with her brown-yellow fingers. ' 'Ow's your Arthur? 'Ave you 'eard owt yet?'

Mrs Clay turned. For one scandalized second, Doris thought she was going to hurl this monumental flag of truce back at her. But the jowls quivered and the puffy eyes swam with tears. 'No, I 'aven't. Not a thing fer three weeks. 'E was still at that French place.' She hesitated. The name sounded so rude. 'Arras or summat. But we don' know what's 'appenin'. We're worried sick, we are.'

Doris shook her head in sympathy. 'Well, the'll just 'ave te get them all back over 'ere, that's all. Should never 'ave sent them in the first place. Bloody daft. What's them Froggies done fer us? Nowt.' She cleared her throat, and continued awkwardly, 'Ah do 'ope 'e's all right. Our Angie's goin' daft.' There. It was at last in the open between them.

Mrs Clay picked up her carrier-bag, and fought against the rising lump in her throat. 'Aye. Well, thanks anyway. Thanks very much.'

'That's all right, kidder. Tara well.'

When she got home, Mrs Clay dumped her bag on the kitchen table and sat down. She burst into tears. Mr Clay, who was on the two till ten shift, groaned. 'Now what, fer God's sake?'

'Our Arthur,' she sobbed. 'It's our Arthur.' Her massive body shook with grief, and she buried her head on her folded arms.

Mr Clay looked at her hopelessly, then moved and patted her almost timidly on one heaving shoulder. 'There there, lass. Don't fret. Don't fret.'

'Get down! Get down!' The corporal's voice broke in an urgent scream, and they leapt off the dusty road and pressed their faces into the short, spiky grass of the bank. Ginge's fingers dug frantically into the dry earth, to which he pressed himself in a lover's embrace, his eyes screwed tightly shut, his teeth grinding together to keep the fear inside him as the scream of the plane became a thunder through every fibre. Then the mad clatter of the machine guns and the crump of bullets stitching the road, flinging up straight mushrooms of dust and stones.

Dimly, he realized that the Messerschmitt had swept over, and he raised his head. He saw its black, square-winged shape clearly as it climbed up the almost clear sky. He prayed that it wouldn't bank and come down again, the bile rising in his throat when he saw it turning.

'Stay down! Stay down!' In spite of the frantic cries, people were picking themselves up, starting to run. To his right, Ginge saw a boy of about eight or nine, gypsy dark, with ragged clothes, push himself up. He was sobbing, his eyes wild, and he smeared the tears over his dust-caked face. Ginge flung himself across the grass, clawing the child down, under him, gaining a strange comfort from the feel of the frail, trembling body. The nightmare whipped over them again, followed by the dwindling whine of the engine.

At least I didn't piss myself this time, Ginge thought grimly, getting to his feet. The boy rushed over to a tall peasant woman and her husband, and clung tightly to her shabby black dress. Figures began stepping on to the pock-marked road, and a group gathered round an inert bundle of flapping black cloth. Ginge stared at the startling white round of a buttock and white thigh above a dusty black stocking. The bullet had passed through the woman's back. Above the waist was a bloody mess of bone and flesh and tattered black ribbons of dress.

'Come on, get fell in. Get a move on.' The corporal herded them like a sheep dog. Ginge stepped out beside the Yokel, their heads turning to stare at the corpse. Ginge was shocked to see thin, greying hair stirring in the darkening spread about the still form. The flesh had looked firm and young, obscenely alluring. They marched on, silent and appalled, often having to break step, or move off the road altogether to get through the jammed flow of refugees.

Dizzily, Ginge tried to assemble his thoughts, to understand what had led to this unreal horror. It seemed a lifetime ago that they had embarked, clumsy in their full kit, including rifle and ammunition, in the shuddering, noisy transports, for the freezing trip to northern France, sitting on the hard floor with knees drawn up to their chins, their backs against the curving frame of the fuselage. They had shouted laughingly at one another above the stupendous noise, to allay the secret fear of their first flight, though they soon forgot the churning stomach in the physical agony of cramped limbs and jarring spine.

Ginge had taken the photo of Angie from his pay-book. It was a talisman for him. He gazed at it longingly, clinging to this reminder from another world, their world where all was special and safe. She stared back at him, a small, self-conscious smile about her carefully painted lips, her blonde hair immaculately waved, lit by the studio bulb.

She had given it to him the day after their night in the dunes, soon after he had met her in an exotically sunny Brewery Lane. He had half expected she might not turn up, that he would have to go over and hammer on the Sea Coal Man's door, like St George at the dragon's lair. But Angela had looked as lovely as ever, smiling dazzlingly at him as she approached. She sounded astonished still herself as she told him how Elisha had sneaked down after everyone had gone to bed, and left the door off the latch for her.

She was wearing her workaday clothes, with her best dress carefully rolled inside a carrier bag. As she had hoped, old Moore had given her the day off, and a ten bob note in advance of her final wages. She changed in a Ladies' toilet, then they caught a bus out to Eden Dale, ten miles into the green, hilly countryside. Angela insisted that Ginge take the ten bob to cover expenses, and they had a sandwich and a beer in the village pub, sitting close together on a high-backed, polished pew in a dim corner of the bar.

Afterwards, they climbed up the steeply sloping, wooded bank of the river, to the waterfall, and found a cosy and private nook among the flat rocks at the top. They clung and kissed and Angela enjoyed his newly bold hands under her thin dress, rousing her until she was giddy and breathless and secretly damp. Lovingly, she admonished him, and finally struggled free, smoothing the creased material down over her thighs, but she felt meltingly warm and tingling, and there was none of the tension or weeping frustration of the previous night.

As the day wore on, the sadness of the imminent parting overtook them. Angela, her head on his shoulder, began to weep quietly as they sat on the back seat of an almost empty bus in the brilliantly sunny afternoon. 'Ah won't come ter the station.' She gulped and, unmindful of the conductress, pulled him fiercely down to her demanding mouth, striving to let him know the love and fear welling inside her.

Ooh, just like the pictures, her other self mocked. Sweethearts and wives. The girl he left behind.

The airfield was only three miles from the town of Arras. There was a picnic atmosphere about their first days, for they were living in bell tents close to the parked Spitfires, housed in their sand-bagged, camouflage-netted shelters. The weather was fine and, when they were not on duty, they lay about on the grass in underpants, or joined in impromptu games of soccer, with battledress blouses for goal posts. On the other side of the field, the young pilots played cricket, or sat outside a wooden hut in deck chairs, until the shrilling telephone sent them sprinting for their planes.

The local populace afforded them a hero's welcome. They seemed unable to distinguish between the various ranks or branches, much to the delight of the Regiment boys, who lorded it in the cafés, ogling the girls and accepting the free wine until their stomachs rebelled. But the holiday atmosphere was brief. Columns of marching, khaki figures swung by, moving westwards, their heads bent, their uniforms dusty and unkempt. Rumours of defeat poured in. Arras was out of bounds. They were set to digging a series of sandbagged trenches and machine-gun emplacements around the airfield.

The first air attack came while they were still digging in. There was a scramble and the Spitfire engines set the blue morning shimmering. Three were still lined up to take off when the bombers came over, high specks, remote until the bombs shrieked down, blasting craters that flung up great gouts of earth, clods raining down on the helmeted figures in the trenches.

Two of the Spitfires made an undignified but successful run into the air, but a bomb burst directly in front of the third, slewing it round on the very edge of the hole. The engine stalled, the pilot clambered out and leapt on to the wing, then dashed across the grass to land in a heap beside Ginge. 'Right up my bloody nose!' he gasped, fighting for breath. Unmindful of the explosions, he stood up and yelled encouragement to the Spitfires, who were already engaging the enemy. Ginge was amazed to learn that the attack had lasted seven minutes.

He was one of the squad detailed to fill in the holes left by the bombs on the grassy track. Stripped to the waist, they worked frantically so that the fighters could get back down. Within an hour there was another alert. For the first time, Ginge and his friends witnessed the terrible effectiveness of the dive bomber.

Thin, sinister shapes hurtled down in vertical, screaming dives that struck terror into all who heard them. The bombs skittered and bounced before bursting. Soon the buildings were all blazing, and the damaged fighter exploded in a brilliant ball. A machine-gun post thirty yards from Ginge received a direct hit, which he did not see, for he was pressed to the bottom of the trench, with his arms over his head in a futile attempt to blot out the nightmare.

The blast rocked the ground beneath him. Earth spattered

the curved backs of the cowering men. When Ginge raised his head, he stared disbelievingly. There was no trace of the three men who had been manning the gun. Just a smouldering black heap of bags and bits of twisted metal. Until they got closer, and realized that some of the black, stinking lumps were not sandbags after all.

The roads were becoming jammed with vehicles. Army lorries, staff cars, the beginning of the endless stream flowing westward. The planes came again, and again, and the Spitfires did not return. The precious fighters had been moved towards the coast. An infantry unit marched into the camp, the weary soldiers glaring with hatred at the RAF boys, who were ordered to fall in with full marching packs. 'Fuckin' Brylcreem boys,' an angry soldier called out, from a group who were sprawled around the lip of a trench. 'Fuck off out of it while we stay an' do your fightin' for you.'

Too ashamed and too relieved to reply, they moved off through the gap in the hedgerow, on to a dusty lane, the derisive cries growing faint. ' 'Ere, listen,' the Yokel commanded, as he and Ginge marched along the gravel road. He turned and nodded behind them. There was a distant rumble, like thunder, except that now and then sharp, distinct booms could be heard.

The corporal in charge of their section was walking in the middle of the road, on their left. 'Them's artillery,' he informed them. 'That's where Jerry is. Right up our arses, so step out, lads.' No one spoke, and they trudged on, until they came to a wider, main road, running north-west to Bethune and the coast. A stream of pedestrians and vehicles of all shapes and sizes filed past the halted column.

'Oright. Fall out,' ordered the corporal, and they eased the packs off their shoulders, carefully laying down the heavy service rifles, before they stretched out on the grass. The NCOs were conferring with the squadron leader, who looked extremely irritated.

'Damn transport should be at the crossroads. Send someone to scout around, will you, Flight? Could be anywhere in this chaos. Looks like every Frog and his grandmother are doing a bunk, what?' Why not? We are, thought the flight sergeant, but, wisely, kept this observation to himself.

They found the four canvas-covered trucks in a farmyard half a mile away, and the men marched through the throng of civilians to the low, grey farmhouse, where they scrambled over the tailboards. 'Daren't leave 'em on the road, sir,' one of the drivers explained. He jerked his head towards the distant files of people. 'Might've been mobbed. As it is, I don't know how we'll get through. It's all choc-a-block from here to the Channel.'

They travelled by country lanes whenever they could, but were forced back time and time again on to the major road, where they crawled at snail's pace, with blaring horns, through a motley collection of fugitives, fleeing by car, by bicycle, or on foot. Donkeys pulled carts high with swaying piles of possessions. Once Ginge and the Yokel gazed over the tailboard at two teenage girls, who managed to blush and giggle as they sprawled on an open mattress balanced atop a heap of household items. They waved and grinned and gestured for ten minutes until the convoy pulled ahead. Soon afterwards came the first attack.

There were only seconds of warning. The truck suddenly swerved off the road and jolted across the shallow ditch on to the grassy verge, the occupants tossed together in a tangle of limbs and equipment. Above the curses, an urgent voice called, 'Git out! Planes!' Figures spilled out and threw themselves prone. A lone Messerschmitt flew low along the road, spraying bullets in a brief pass, then climbed steeply away.

After a few minutes, they picked themselves up and gathered around the undamaged vehicles. The flight sergeant, normally a pleasant enough individual if you played it by the book, came up, eyes blazing from his brick-red face. 'Any man I catch without his rifle will be on a charge. Don't leave your effing gear in the trucks. You'll be needing it before long!'

The next attack was by two Stukas. The lorries were trapped in a seething tide and couldn't move off the road. This time they needed no warning, for the tortured scream of engines drowned any human cries, and the men flung themselves out and rolled into the grass.

Ginge and the Yokel together raced for a pile of logs beside a low, straggly hedge. To Ginge, it seemed as if the terrifying roar was for him alone, and he flung himself over the wood, to crash painfully into the hedge headfirst. At the same instant, the world exploded in a white-hot blast that sucked away the air and thumped his breathless frame like a massive fist. Unbelievably, he discovered that he was alive. He was face down, with bits of the flattened hedge around him, his body half buried in the carelessly flung logs. He felt a cooling wetness between his legs and knew that he had urinated, but accepted it as a fact, glad only to identify it, without feeling any shame.

A loud crackling drove into his consciousness, together with a pungent smell of burning. He had difficulty in willing himself to move, but he scrambled on to hands and knees, and turned towards the truck. It was still standing, but was ablaze, palls of black smoke billowing upwards. An explosion down the roadway seemed miles away, divorced from the scene around him.

Beneath the truck, lay four or five still figures in air-force blue. One of them moved an arm, and Ginge heard a thin cry above the roar of the flames. The Yokel, face streaked with dirt and sweat, or tears, tugged at his arm. 'C'm on, Ginge. That lot'll go up any second.'

A quick check was made for casualties, someone (thankfully, not Ginge) going back to the burning truck to identify the bodies. The names were murmured back and forth. Freddy Stubbs. A Geordie lad. Ginge had talked to him and given him a cigarette when they had fallen out at the side of the main road, before they found their transport. A happy, loud, alive character. He called Ginge 'the monkey-hanger', relating the legend to a delighted Yokel and his messmates. Now he seemed to Ginge like some dimly recalled friend, not seen for years.

They crammed into the remaining trucks, and flowed along with the refugees, hour after dusty hour. A Messerschmitt returned, and this time they sat with their bent legs splayed and fired at the skimming shape in a futile gesture of defiance. When the plane had gone, bundles of clothing stirred with life. People rose and dusted themselves down, here and there an anguished wailing announcing a private tragedy. Others shifted round the stricken group, with eyes averted, ashamed of the welling feeling of relief that sprang up.

In a tiny hamlet whose few deserted cottages clustered round the road, the convoy was stopped by a Red Cap. The trucks pulled over and the men scrambled out, stretching cramped limbs and lighting up cigarettes. An army van drew up alongside, a signaller crouched in the back, talking urgently into a portable transmitter.

The flight sergeant led them between two grey stone buildings into an enclosure of hard earth. He stood them to attention while the NCOs took a roll call, then told them to stand down. They squatted in the dust, silent, waiting. 'We're gonna have to leg it, boys,' he announced calmly. 'The trucks are wanted to shift some more units. Any road, we can go faster on foot than we can in that bleeding lot. There's a right cock-up and Jerry's knocking everything for six. Our orders are to make for Bethune. We should get there by morning. Get something to eat now from your iron rations, and we'll set off in half an hour. There's a pump over there for water. Have a good drink and make sure your canteens are full.'

Where possible, they marched in twos in the ditch close to the hedgerows. 'Oi notice Willis 'as pissed off,' observed the Yokel, referring to their squadron leader, who had not been seen since they had left the trucks. Dive bombers and Messerschmitts continued to attack the slow-moving columns, their primary targets being motor vehicles, so that the men felt less angry at losing their transport.

After they filed past the body of the woman on the roadway, the Yokel swore viciously. 'Where the fuck are our lot? Not a soign of them. These Jerries are doin' jus' what they want an' not a Spitfire or Hurricane ter be seen.'

The Scots lad trudging along behind them answered. 'Jerry's got us beaten. And he's no gonna stop. They'll need all the Spitfires they can get back home. And more.'

'Wot the 'ell's gonner 'appen to us then?' a voice squealed, with almost comic indignation, but no one laughed.

'I s'pose we'll 'ave ter make a stand at the coast,' their corporal mused. 'We got nowhere else ter go unless we bloody swim 'ome.'

'What about the Navy?' put in Ginge.

The corporal gave a derisive laugh and jerked his head at the blue sky. 'You think them Jerry planes are gonna let the Navy stop an' pick us up? They'll bomb everythin' that moves. Any road, we gotta stop 'em this side otherwise the buggers 'll be across the water in no time.'

Ginge felt the hollow queasiness, the helpless feeling of tears that contemplation of their plight brought. This might be my last day alive. He tried to shy away from the awful thought, but it leapt to the forefront of his mind, tormenting him. No, he mustn't think that. He'd heard about blokes in the last lot getting that sort of feeling, and it could make all the difference. If you thought like that, chances were you'd buy it. He couldn't imagine not being alive.

Angela! That's it. Think about her. Us. He felt guilty as he realized he hadn't thought about her for hours. But even that led back to death. He visualized her receiving the news of his death. Her grief. His eyes smarted and sadness for them both welled up.

And he had brought all this on himself, with his foolish, romantic notions. There was nothing romantic about war. It was terror and violent death. He thought of the corpses under the truck, the woman in the roadway, her behind bared in the last savage mockery. And the stillness. The finality of it. He could have been at home, with Angela, with others whom his mother mentioned bitterly in her letters.

He had had only one letter from Angela since they had left Apsley, and he carried it carefully folded inside his pay-book next to her photo, reading the stilted words over and over with wondrous delight.

I werry about you all the time and think about you evry night so please be carful darling. I think about the sands and I wish you hadent used one of them things I would love to have your baby.

He felt a painfully fierce desire to live and to get back to her. Never again would he complain about Sutherland Street, if only he could walk again down the cracked pavement and see the shabby, peeling door from which she emerged. He prayed fervently as they trudged wearily through the mellow evening sunlight.

Twelve

For once, The Street, like the rest of the country, was hungry for news. They stood in Wilson's, or in Sam's, and discussed the situation, shaking their heads and clicking their tongues like a Greek chorus at the awfulness of fate. 'Be no better under Winnie,' opined Ellis, the student of History. ' 'E made a right cock-up of the last lot, didn' 'e? Look at them Dardanelles.'

'Ah see the've put posts up in the park,' Elisha informed anyone who cared to listen. His eyes glowed with excitement. 'It's ter stop them glider things landin' with all them troops in.'

But Mrs Clay was not concerned with the broad aspects of current events. Arthur was in France, and France was in a state of chaos. And her eldest son was across the other side of the world, facing the sea war, with its own attendant horrors. Grim and ill with anxiety, she had little to say to her neighbours, except Old Jonson, who would ask her in to listen to the latest bulletin, saying nothing, but setting before her a mug of steaming, powerful tea, and sitting back, wreathing his head in pungent fumes.

One day, as she was leaving after the one o'clock news, she came face to face with Angela, who was coming out of her own door. Instinctively, Mrs Clay drew herself up, pursing her lips. Then she saw the almost pleading, cowed look on the young face, the worried question in her eyes. After an embarrassed instant, Angela blurted, ' 'Ave you 'eard owt, Mrs Clay?'

'No, nothin'.' Mrs Clay's voice was stiff with awkwardness. 'Burrit sez on the wireless that the' makin' plans ter bring the Army back. The guv'ment's takin' over all the small boats – private like. The' reckon the' can shift 'em all if they 'ave to. That's what the' said, any'ow.'

Angela smiled timidly. 'Well, 'e might be 'ome soon then, eh?

The'll prob'ly fly them back, with them bein' raff.'

Mrs Clay coloured, and the frown crept back over her features. ' 'Ave you 'ad a letter from 'im? Recent like, ah mean?'

Angela returned the blush. 'No. Only the one when 'e first got ower there. 'E wouldn' write ter me without one ter you an' all,' she offered.

Mrs Clay was mollified. 'Aye, well. Right-oh then. Ah'll let yer know as soon as we 'ear owt. Tara.'

Angela watched her pad off in the broad, worn slippers. How'd you like that for a ma-in-law? mocked her inner voice. Probably have to live with them, in the back bedroom, you and Ginge. Never get a place of your own, not for ages. 'I'd love to have your baby'. She smarted at the mockery of her thoughts. What a mess you'd be in if you did. Then you really *would* be stuck here for the rest of your life. Out like a house end, and the talk of The Street for getting caught. Until the next one.

She saw her dad coming towards her, from the Pothouse. He was on nights this week, which didn't help matters. 'Get yersel' outa bloody bed at last, then? 'Ave yer done owt about a bloody job yet? Think we're runnin' a 'otel, d'yer? Lyin' in bed all day, buggerin' off down town with a load o' muck on yer gob. Yer can start earnin' yer bloody keep fer a change.'

She felt herself shrinking inside, an angry, violated sensation, almost as though he had physically abused her. Mouth closed thinly, she walked off, blinking back the tears of frustration. She would get away somehow. She would even muck out pigsties or milk cows, terrified as she was of them. Anything, as long as it was miles and miles from here.

Bitterly, she remembered that she hadn't even a penny for a paper. The purse inside her cheap handbag was empty. And then she thought of Mrs Clay's ravaged face, and of Ginge. What would he be doing right now, at this minute? She was disgusted at her preoccupation with herself. He might be ... she didn't want even to think it, but, unbidden, came an image of her beautiful, pale face, framed by its golden halo, noble in grief. Her slim frame, proud and silent. In black.

As she crossed from Brewery Lane into Stockton Street, Freddy Barraclough skidded up beside her and swung off his bike, falling into step. He was in his greasy work clothes, with his gas mask across his shoulder. She wouldn't be seen dead carrying one of those ugly things. ' 'Ow do,' he leered. He jiggled the gleaming handlebars. 'Wha'd yer think o' this then, eh? Saves a lorra bloody bootleather, does this. Gorrit las' week.' He stared boldly at her. 'Course, the money we makin' nowadays, ah reckon ah'll 'ave a motor bike afore long.' She increased her speed, remaining pointedly silent.

' 'Ow'd yer fancy 'elpin' us spend some of it? Fancy the Rink Satd'y night? An' we'll 'ave a few pints in the Black 'Orse first. Wha'd yer say, kid?'

'No thanks.' She tried to inject sufficient ice into her tones. He laughed jeeringly.

'No good savin' all yer charms fer yon daft bugger, Ginge. 'Ave you 'eard the news? The buggers are gettin' pushed right inter the sea. The nazzies 'll be across 'ere any day now. Better enjoy yersel' while yer can, lass.' He winked and nudged her arm. 'Better get used to it, pet. Them Jerries won' be too partic'lar.'

She reddened with anger. 'One thing. *You* don't 'ave ter worry. Yer can jump on yer posh bike an' piss off!' His laughter mocked her as he rode off, and again the waves of self-pity engulfed her. Why should Barraclough and that lot be lording it in dancehalls and pubs, pockets full of money, while Ginge was out there fighting for his life?

She should have accepted the loathsome Freddy's offer. Taken some of his lousy money, made him spend on her. Plenty of girls did. And let the lads take them on the dunes, or the Rec, to pay for the night's entertainment. But she was Ginge's girl and she would be loyal to him, especially as he might never come back. She hurried even more, as though to outrun the thought itself.

'That water boiled yet?' Ginge moved the mess tin on the glowing embers, swearing as he burnt his fingers. They had built a makeshift windshield of bits of charred wood, and squatted in the hollow of the sand dunes, thinking luxuriantly of the scalding tea from their enamel mugs. It would help to soak some of the weariness from their aching, filthy bodies.

They seemed to have marched for weeks. A lifetime of nomadic tramping, of falling exhausted on the ground whenever they halted, of diving for cover from the stuttering of machine guns, or the crash of bombs. After Bethune, they had slogged on, still part of a choked mass of civilians and troops, fleeing for the coast. Boulogne. Then news that Jerry was cutting them off from the south. Swing north. Up the coast. Snatch a few hours, under hedgerows. Once, in the luxury of piles of straw, in a barn.

They had woken to see the eastern sky lit with flashes, and the thunder came clearly to them in the still darkness. To their dismay, they set off in the early hours, their tramping feet loud in the moonlight. The following morning, the sky seemed full of enemy planes. They had dug themselves in, on the edge of a small coppice, a safe distance from the road, and tried to sleep, marching again as the sun went down on a rich, violet and crimson sky whose beauty shrieked out man's insanity.

The nearer they got to the beaches, the more organized they found the evacuation. Military policemen, even some of their own White Caps, whom, for once, they barracked good naturedly, grasping at a familiar straw in the chaos. They were amazed, when they approached the little coastal town of Dunkirk, to see the remnants of an army camped out on the long beaches.

'Jesus!' the Yokel muttered, wiping his sweaty, grimy face. 'They'll never shift this lot. Must be 'undreds of the barstards.'

They were assigned an area of beach in the grassy dunes. The two machine guns were set up in makeshift emplacements, and slit trenches dug against the ceaseless attacks of the Messerschmitts and Stukas and Junkers 88s. Squadron Leader Willis reappeared, and even had the brass neck to joke about his deserting them on the long march to the sea. 'Now it looks as though Jerry's got it all his own way for the moment. There are plans under way to evacuate almost everyone, except for a rear guard, who'll have the duty, and the honour, to stand firm and stop the Germans as long as possible. Until every man has been taken off the beach.'

On the word 'honour' there was a hard and derisive bark of laughter. The flight sergeant's face flashed fury. 'Silence in the ranks!' he bellowed. The men quailed under his fierce, roving gaze, which said clearly that a little thing like death and destruction was not going to threaten the frame of discipline by which he lived. When an officer spoke, you were silent, and paid attention. Even if he *was* talking a load of shit.

Occasionally, a fighter would skim low over them, strafing the dunes, but, more often, they concentrated their attacks on the destroyers, and smaller boats that raced about close to the shore. After their first night on the beach, the RAF boys glowed with proprietory pride as they watched three Hurricanes disperse a gaggle of bombers. One of the enemy planes sank gracefully into the sea, trailing a plume of smoke which gradually thickened. Two parachutes blossomed before the aircraft disappeared into the distant, hazy grey. 'Wish they fuckers were in range,' mused the Yokel, fingering his rifle.

Ginge was shocked. Those two drifting dots were lads, same as them. Or maybe married, with photos of kids. And they had been dropping bombs, had perhaps killed God knows how many. Civilians on the crowded roads. It took some sorting, this lot.

'Eh! Look at this lot!'

They stood in astonished silence, watching a squad of about fifty men marching in ramrod unison down the beach. A large, moustached individual roared in a voice loud enough to make hundreds of heads pop out of burrows. ' 'Oo the 'ell's that then? Playin' effin' soldiers!'

The word buzzed around. 'The Grenadier Guards, mate. Still think they're in Buckingham Palace.' But behind the banter was an unexpressed admiration, the glimpse of unshakeable discipline a tonic to the motley collection who huddled in groups up and down the sandy strip.

More and more boats began to gather offshore, a strange collection of craft, old and new, sizeable and small. Seaward of them, destroyers raced back and forth, angry black puffs spotting the pale sky as they fought off the droves of enemy aircraft. The evacuation went on at night, queues of troops standing for hours on the flat sand, then in the breaking shallows, waiting for the dinghies and small boats to ferry them out to the larger vessels. But there were too many men still clinging to the dunes. The rescue went on during daylight hours, with the consequent rise in casualties.

No one talked at the time of miracles. Men cursed and lived like animals on the beach, defecating in the hollows yards from where they slept, and snatched makeshift meals from emergency rations. Some men from the Leicesters occupied the sandy patch next to the Regiment. They became friendly, after the first, bitter resentment at the absence of RAF planes.

'Nuthin' ter do with us, mate,' the Yokel told a group of shirt-sleeved soldiers. 'We jus' march about same's yew lot.'

'Left our A and B companies up north,' one of the pongoes told them. 'Poor buggers will 'ave 'ad it by now. We lost 'alf of our lot up in Belgium. Jerry tanks jus' wiped us up. And they shift their infantry along with 'em. Sod all you can do to stop them.'

On the afternoon of the third day, an MP came along the beach with a megaphone. 'Two Squadron RAF Regiment. Fall in. Fall in.' He moved on. 'Second Battalion, D Company Leicesters.' Squadron Leader Willis came walking from the direction of the town. He looked freshly shaven, his uniform neatly pressed. The Yokel began a vitriolic denunciation in harsh whispers, until the flight called them to attention.

They were told they would move up the beach and occupy a new area, already marked with strips of tape, much nearer the lifting-off points. 'Be ready to move out tonight or tomorrow morning. Every man will carry his weapon and all rounds of ammunition. Anyone who fails to bring these across with him will face a court martial. We're going to need every bullet we can lay our hands on. Now do what the beach marshals tell you. Move when they say so, and not before. Good luck! See you all in Blighty.'

'Not if oi see 'ee first,' the Yokel muttered as they were fallen out.

They watched the myriad little craft, black silhouettes against the setting sun, the long snakes of men winding up the flat beach to the dunes, the columns writhing and changing shape when the planes roared in to strafe the beach. A two-funnelled destroyer had settled close inshore, gutted by the fires the bombs had started. Her upperworks stood out above the water. Several small boats were using her as a makeshift pier, before their final dash into the breaking shallows. The buzz of planes, the whistle and crump of explosions, the staccato bark of the AA guns, did not die away until the last grey twilight had gone. Over the town, the scarcely moving pillars of black smoke reared pointer-like to their plight.

Ginge had just made another wet of lukewarm tea. 'Told 'ee ter wait till the water boiled,' the Yokel grumbled, spitting out the leaves floating in the scum at the top of his mug. Ginge grunted, and sipped appreciatively. He scratched at his crotch, trying unsuccessfully to calculate when he had last undressed. A red stubble covered his weatherbeaten face. The lack of sleep made his eyes burn.

They stared as a dispatch rider fought his machine through the hillocks, and asked for the senior NCO. A hooded torch shone, while the flight conferred briefly with the soldier. To sea, flashes lit the sky. Deep thumps told of the return of the enemy, the night bombers dropping clusters of bombs into the crowded flotillas.

'Right, you lucky people! Flights One an' Two prepare to move out. All aboard the skylark. Get your rifles an' packs an' follow Sarnt Davies. You're off home, boys. And don't forget to have the kettle on when we follow on!'

Hasty farewells were exchanged. There was a touching embarrassment about the leave takings. 'See yer over the other side,' Ginge called to an oppo from another flight. He and Yokel stood side by side while a quick roll call was taken.

'Where the eff is 'Arrison?' the agitated corporal hissed.

' 'Ere, Corp.' The missing figure emerged from the dunes, still fastening his trousers.

'Yer'd shit yerself all right if yer missed the boat!' the corporal growled, relieved to have his squad all correct.

They set off along the beach, walking a surprising distance before they veered down the gentle slope towards the softly breaking tide. They joined the end of a vast line of men, standing patiently in the warm night. NCOs and a couple of officers hurried up and down the lines, worrying like industrious sheep dogs. Slowly, the lines edged closer to the water.

Someone cannoned into Ginge as he paused instinctively at the water's edge. 'What's wrong?' a voice said sourly. 'Afraid to get your feet wet?'

'Ah can't swim,' Ginge quipped, his grin hiding a sudden nervousness, for the line snaked on, well out into the gentle swell. 'Eh, ah bloody can't!' he murmured, more seriously, to the Yokel, who grinned down at him.

'It's all roit. Oi'll 'old 'ee up, yer short-arsed bugger.'

They stood in the cold sea for hours, until their arms and shoulders ached abominably from the effort of holding up the precious rifles and ammunition to keep them dry, and they could feel nothing below the waist. The swell lapped up to Ginge's armpits, and his teeth wouldn't stop chattering. At long last, they were at the head of the queue, where a tiny inflatable dinghy was manned by two life-jacketed sailors.

There was a lengthy pause, without any further boats appearing, though, mercifully, the attacks from the air seemed to have abated, and all they could hear was the muted rumble of firing from the land. Suddenly, a larger wave came sweeping in, sending the dinghy bobbing wildly, and knocking Ginge backwards off his feet. His head ducked under, and he clutched panic stricken at the Yokel, who stood there, rock solid. Ginge coughed and spluttered and swore volubly. His rifle and pack were soaking.

'Oh, you'm a bad lad,' the Yokel chuckled. 'Prob'ly won't let 'ee on board now.'

Two open boats approached nose to stern and turned broadside on to the column of waiting men. 'Come on, you lot. Look lively.' Ginge couldn't pull himself up over the gunwale, even when willing hands had relieved him of his equipment, but he reached up his arms and two sturdy fellows grabbed them and plucked him with ease out of the water. He fell, a sodden, grateful bundle, among the crowded limbs and bodies, and others fell on top of him, and he didn't care.

He had thought in the numbing cold of the long wait that he would never feel anything again, but within minutes he discovered how wrong he was in that assumption. The swaying and bobbing of the shallow, open craft, which was nothing more than a converted fishing coble, set off a most unpleasant sensation in his gut, which rapidly became a new kind of misery. He suddenly found he could move again as he managed to fling his head and shoulders outboard in the nick of time before vomiting violently into the sea.

He was tearfully glad when the comforting bulk of a destroyer loomed at them out of the darkness, for he had been afraid that they were going to make the trip across the Channel in this overgrown rowing boat. Somehow, he managed to claw and fight his way up the netting draped over the side, encumbered with pack and a rifle whose strap lodged itself in a stranglehold round his neck. Desperation drove him onward and upward, and he fell, sobbing with relief, on to the warm, trembling metal of the deck plates, and lay there luxuriating in the feeling of solidity beneath him.

There was no room below decks. The upper deck itself was crammed with slumped shapes. 'That's it, Number One,' a voice called from somewhere high above them. 'No more this trip. Let's get the show on the road.' The trembling increased, there was a clanging of bells, purposeful orders barked, and they were off, moving cautiously through the crowds of vessels.

They had almost got clear when the bombers caught them. The fine weather, which had been so helpful in getting the thousands off the beaches, displayed its impartiality by allowing the raiders an unimpeded view of their target in the clear night. Ginge had recovered sufficiently to sit up and take note of his surroundings. 'We made it, you janner bastard!' he exclaimed jubilantly, then the rapid clatter of the AA guns and the spitting tracer cut off his words.

The figures on the overcrowded deck slid and tumbled as the destroyer turned with savage desperation, away from the first stick of bombs, which sent high spouts of water palely up into the night, to fall in a fine rain on the backs of the cowering men. They were not so lucky with the second cluster. One bomb penetrated the foredeck and exploded below the water-line, wreaking fatal havoc in the packed messdecks, and starting a raging fire. A second hit the superstructure a glancing blow, strong enough to detonate it, so that those on the upper deck in front of the bridge, as well as those of the crew on the bridge itself, took the full impact.

Ginge's world erupted in a white roar that transformed everything. It was like being in the middle of a whirlpool. He was swept along by its force. The noise went on, it didn't die away as it should have done, and things turned even crazier as Angie screamed, then moaned in ecstasy under him, and she was naked, pale and lovely, with that startling patch of hair at her belly, and he tried desperately to cover her, to tell her, painfully aware of the Yokel's burning gaze on her flesh, and all the others. But he couldn't speak. Something had clamped his jaw down, it ached terribly, his ears, too. and he couldn't move to help her. His arm, his left arm was useless, like it had gone to sleep, he couldn't feel his hand at all. Jesus. Angie. Don't go. Wait for me.

Now his arm was burning, in fire up to the shoulder, and he was screaming, and crying at the same time, trying to apologize for his weakness in making such an unearthly row, but he couldn't stop screaming with the pain of it. And the water again, freezing, but it didn't stop the burning in his arm, which was crazy. He was bobbing about, not that bloody little rowing boat again? Was time moving backwards? Somebody was cradling his head, he could feel a lap beneath him. Angie?

But she was wearing trousers, thick, rough, wet. And a face bent over him, murmuring, wiping his brow and cheeks, but it was a black face, a big face with cracked lips, and it was weeping, too. He was moving now, fast, being lifted up by something, and he suddenly knew with absolute clarity that he was dying, that he had been hit somehow, somewhere, he didn't know where. Had he dreamt about the beach, standing in the water, climbing into the boat?

He didn't mind, though, that terrible, burning pain was going, only a faint echo of it now in his shoulder, and this drifting movement was quite pleasant, and he could see the beach again, only this time he recognized the dunes, and, yes, she was there, she'd got her dress on, thank goodness, the pretty flowered one with those puffed sleeves. He grinned at her beautiful smiling face, and tried to run to meet her.

Thirteen

Although Angela had known for some time she was attractive, witness the lewd pantings of Barraclough and his ilk which she had aroused since before her fifteenth birthday, she was only just beginning to realize the true effect of her dawning beauty on men of most ages. It shocked her, as well as giving her a secret frisson of pleasure in its power. She had gone into the Labour Exchange more out of desperation than for any other reason, after her da had driven her frantic, going on about her idleness and general uselessness.

Frazer's factory. Good money to be made there soon, with government contracts to be awarded. There was a scheme to train girls in the shipyard, though you were supposed to be eighteen. Both those jobs sounded dirty and unpleasant, and neither would enable her to escape from the atmosphere of home. It would just mean more money to be swallowed up in the kitty, getting her dad off the hook so he could spend even more swilling ale.

Then she'd noticed for the first time the sly way the middle-aged clerk's eyes behind his round little glasses were sliding over her. She fluttered her eyelids a little. 'Ah was hopin' fer the forces or somethin',' she sighed wistfully. 'Ter get away from home, like.' She had already given details of her age, and he shook his head regretfully.

'No good applying till you're eighteen.' After another reddening glance at her gracefully rounded bosom in the flowered dress, he went back to his box of cards. 'There *is* something here that might be interesting. They're looking for staff up at Dalby Hall. They're very short now, what with the war. They need a maid.'

A scornful dismissal of this proposal almost sprang to her

lips, until the clerk added the magic words, 'They're offering accommodation, of course. And Miss Guy, the housekeeper, was saying they're looking for someone to train. Might be a good opportunity.' He smiled, as he thought, winningly. 'And you don't have to be eighteen.'

Service. She didn't know the first thing about it. Except no doubt she could skivvy with the best of them, and that's what it would be. She knew Dalby Hall was the home of the Marston-Greenes, Sir Roger and Lady Agatha, big nobs. The biggest. She had a vague idea that he was the owner of the Green Funnel Line, a shipping company which traded out of the port, mostly coastal stuff around the British Isles and across the North Sea. She didn't know that his forbears had made their fortune from coal, and that he still had shares in several mines in the north-east. She only knew that they were filthy rich and she couldn't help giggling at the notion of her having anything to do with the likes of them.

She expressed her doubts as to her suitability, all the time feeling a rising sense of excitement at the very thought of such an escape from The Street. The clerk leaned forward now, really close, his eyes twinkling, his grin ear to ear. If he comes any closer he'll have his nose between my tits, Angela thought, without any real malice. 'I know Miss Guy personally,' he assured her. 'I could give you a good recommendation. Have you any references?'

She thought of Old Moore. He was a lecher, too, only a bit more honest about it than this creep. 'Ah can get one,' she answered confidently. It would be a glowing one, too, and she wouldn't have to stretch out on the floor of the cubby hole for it, only let him have a quick kiss maybe, if she had to. She arranged to return on the morrow, when the clerk would give her a letter of introduction, and set up an interview. Angela gave a little skip as soon as she was safely through the door. She wanted to run and shout, and was suddenly consumed with guilt as she remembered Ginge and the dangers he was surely caught up in.

As she had anticipated, there was nothing but fierce opposition on the home front. 'Go an' be a skivvy fer that bloody lot? Not on yer nelly!' the Sea Coal Man announced dismissively. 'What's the wages?' he added, suggesting that his dismissiveness was not as final as his opening remark had indicated.

'Ah dunno,' she muttered defensively. 'I 'aven't got the job yet. Ah've gorra go an' see about an interview temorrer. Ould Moore's gonna give us a reference, though.'

'Ah should bloody well think 'e is, givin' yer the sack like that. Ah should've gone down an' knocked 'is 'ead off!'

Her da continued to be against the idea of her going into service but, somewhat to her surprise, her mam was almost enthusiastic in her support. She seemed to think it was a great step up, would lead to who knew what opportunities. 'An' it's on'y a few miles up the road, pet. Yer'll be able to get 'ome on yer days off.' Big deal, Angela thought, but said nothing.

She was nervously excited when the roving-eyed clerk got on the telephone while she waited, and came back glowing with self-importance. 'Now make sure you look your best,' he grinned. He held on to her hand, rubbing his thumb curiously back and forth across the backs of her knuckles. She waited patiently for him to surrender it to her once more. 'Don't forget to wash behind your ears.' He chortled, squeezed her hand hard, making a meal of it. The tips of his own ears burned red. 'You've got an excellent reference. I told Miss Guy I was sure you'd be just the girl she was looking for. Clean and bright. Don't let me down now.' He laughed and reached out awkwardly, patting her shoulder. She beamed a simpering smile at him, and clicked away rapidly in her heeled shoes, aware of his eyes fastened hungrily on her behind under her flowered dress, and aware, too, that that was where he would far rather be patting her if he had the guts. Dirty old sod. Old enough to be her da. Not that that stopped them.

Nevertheless, she was careful to take his advice before catching the bus to take her out to the distant village of Dalby and the imposing residence of the Marston-Greenes. She not only washed behind her ears but every other part of her anatomy, choosing her time so that she had the room free and could linger, knees drawn up in the small zinc bathtub, in front of the fire, with the curtains safely drawn. With her da at work, and Eli and the others out of the way, she could perform her ablutions in a leisurely fashion, and even spend enough time on her long hair, which she bound up in a towel.

'Ye're a bonny lass,' Doris declared simply, as Angela rose, gleaming, and she handed her the rough towel to dry herself. 'Make the most of it, love.'

She knew she looked good in her best dress and flimsily neat shoes, but her knees were shaking when she walked up the long, gravelled drive of Dalby Hall a few hours later. A row of tall, thick conifers formed a solid hedge on her left. On her right was a wide sweep of newly cropped lawn, and beds of early blooming rose bushes, in front of the weathered face of the house itself. Ivy covered the majority of the frontage. The leaded windows, framed in their grey-stoned sills, shone elegantly in the sunlight. How many rooms, Angela wondered dizzily? Four or five mellow steps led up to the imposingly pillared front door, before which she paused in quaking doubt. Surely, there must be a back door for the likes of her? Too late. She tugged bravely at the bell pull and tried to conquer her churning stomach.

A tall woman with dark, attractively waved short hair, and a slimly erect carriage, answered the bell's summons. Angela's mouth felt awkward suddenly, dry. She stammered with nerves. 'Ah'd like ter see Mrs Guy, please. About the job. As maid.'

'*Miss* Guy.'

Angela blushed. 'Oh, aye. Sorry. Anyway, ah'd like te see 'er. She's expectin' me.'

'That's right. I am,' the woman replied, startling Angela, who had expected someone much older, more homely, and – ordinary. She didn't know why. She had half assumed that this impressive, smart stranger was Lady Agatha herself. Good start, Angela thought miserably, as she followed her into the wide hall. Angela was concentrating too hard on getting things right, making the right impression, to take much notice of her surroundings. Only later was she able to acknowledge her dazed wonder at the splendour and vastness of the mansion itself.

The interview was conducted in a small room along a dark passageway that was near the kitchen, the housekeeper's sitting-room, Angela discovered afterwards, though, as she sat that first time on the hard-backed chair, plucking at her fingers, it seemed the height of comfort and delicacy. Miss Guy's

magnificent dark eyes had a disconcerting way of gazing so
directly, they made Angela feel uncomfortably that they could
see right through to her skin, maybe even to the thoughts
inside her head. Which were topsy turvy enough in those
hectic minutes. Her voice, too, was special. Quiet, but deep,
arresting. The kind that made you listen carefully to what it
said.

The blushing girl blurted out her confession of her ignorance
of domestic service. 'Ah've never – ah've worked in the fruit
market, that's all. But I 'elp me mam, mother, with the cleanin'
an' that. Ah know 'ow to—' Her voice trailed away. She
thought dismally of the dirt and chaos, the smells and
confusion of the tiny, overcrowded space of her home,
contrasting it with the airy splendour with which she was
presently surrounded. A deep gloom settled over her.
Perversely, as her hopes of gaining employment faded, her
desire for the job flared.

'What about boyfriends? You won't get much free time, I'm
afraid. Wednesday afternoon, Sunday after ten-thirty.'

Angela blushed anew. She started to shake her head, about
to give a virtuous denial of any interest in boys, then said
impulsively, 'There is *one* lad. We've just started goin' out, like.
'E's away though, in the raff.' Her voice quavered. To her
dismay, her eyes filled, brimmed with unavoidable tears. 'Ah
don' know if – 'e's in France. Ah don' know what's 'appened to
'im.'

'Don't upset yourself.' The rich voice was warmer now, no
longer so detached. 'Things are chaotic, I know. But I
understand they've brought thousands back. And they're still
picking them up. Some of Sir Roger's boats have been busy all
this past week.' She reached over and took Angela's clenched
fist firmly in her hand.

Angela sniffed noisily. 'Ah've never bothered with any other
lads. Only 'im. And ah don' know when—' She shook her
head, and the fingers patted her hand comfortingly again.

'We're very short staffed,' Miss Guy told her. 'Mr Gordon
has already gone, and our two parlour maids have both gone
off to a factory in Sunderland. That's why we're having to
consider taking on people with no experience. You've been
given a fine reference from your employer. He says you're

thoroughly honest and reliable. And quick to learn, too. I hope so, Angela. How soon can you start?'

Angela gazed at her open mouthed. Her blue eyes still sparkled with tears as the incredulous delight spread over her young features. 'Yer mean ah – temorrer. Ah can come temorrer. Ah've nothin' – that's lovely. Thank you!'

Miss Guy laughed softly. 'You haven't even asked about wages. And let me show you where you'll be sleeping. It's up at the top of the house, of course. Normally, you'd share, but I'm afraid you'll have to be on your own. At least for the moment.'

Angela almost laughed aloud. Miss Guy made a room of your own sound like a punishment. If only she knew. Her head was spinning. She'd got the job! And tomorrow, she'd be here, in all this luxury. Twenty-five bob a week and her board. She'd have done it for nowt, and glad of it to make her escape from The Street.

She was pulled up once more in her delirious happiness by her searingly guilty thought of Ginge. Just let him be safe, she prayed beseechingly. God was on her side for once, she'd got the job, the last thing in the world she'd expected. Just let him be safe, that was the only other favour she'd ask, then everything would be perfect.

Angela wondered quite a lot in the weeks and months that followed whether God had answered her prayer or not. Once more, she suffered pangs of guilt at the way she could forget completely about Ginge, for hours at a stretch, as she became so totally involved in the tremendous change in her circumstances, trying to adjust to what was an entirely new life for her. She even had her own bathroom! A bathroom, all to herself, and Miss Guy sounded half apologetic when she showed her it, tucked away in the attics, with a sloping roof with a large skylight in it.

'It's rather poky, I'm afraid, but with Beatrice and Margaret leaving like they have, it's all yours. Mrs Cullingford doesn't live in, so she never gets up here. And I've got my own, of course, on the landing below. The geyser's a bit temperamental, but I'll show you how to light it. You'll soon get used to it.'

There was a lavatory, too, squeezed in beside a hand basin in the small room. It was the height of luxury, heaven, to Angela, and she was wise enough to fight hard to hide her ecstasy in front of this elegant woman. She'd think her a right savage if she knew just how wild with joy she was feeling right now, and so she managed to murmur her pleasure with all the living arrangements in suitably subdued tones.

Mind you, there was a head-spinning lot to remember, and a lot of hard, grinding work that kept her going twelve hours a day. It was an enormous place, and the family's living areas were of a degree of richness and comfort that left her dazzled with wonder. The huge drawing-room, the morning-room, the panelled dining-room – even a library, bigger than a whole house in Sutherland Street. Imagine, a vast room just for keeping books in. Her voice, when she struggled to convey the splendours she lived among to her own family on her first day off, was still tinged with incredulous awe. 'Ah still don' know me way around the place. Ah get lost sometimes, 'specially upstairs. The's that many rooms, ye wouldn' believe it. Sir Roger an' Lady Agatha – the've each got their own bedroom an' another room the' call the' dressin'-room an' all.' The Sea Coal Man tried hard not to be impressed, but failed. The others were agog.

Angela discovered that she was the only live-in maid. Mrs Cullingford was the cook, but she lived locally, and Miss Guy had succeeded in finding two other local girls, both fifteen year olds not long out of school, to come in daily and help with the cleaning. Miss Guy herself got stuck in with them on many occasions though Angela was quick to sense that this was not part of her normal duties at all. She also had to be prepared to look after the family at meal-times, now that the butler, Mr Gordon, had left. 'You'll have to help me, Angela. That's why I want to show you the ropes as soon as possible. It might stand you in good stead later.'

'Yes, Miss Guy.' She loved the way the housekeeper pronounced her name. It sounded so different, pretty, on her tongue. Angela. No one called her that. Not even Ginge. Ange. Angie. She'd never been anything else.

The idea of serving the family at meal-times, the idea of meeting them at all, made her stomach hollow with nerves again, but in her first week, no one put in an appearance. There was only Miss Guy and her in the whole mansion. It was quite scary if you thought about it, but the village constable always did a tour of the grounds just before dark, and knocked at the house to see that everything was all right. And the local Home Guard unit frequently sent a patrol round as an additional check.

'I don't think we'll see very much of the family at all,' Miss Guy told her, at the end of her first day. 'Sir Roger's working for the Admiralty now. An important job in London – he hardly ever gets up here these days. And now Lady Agatha's got something down there as well, something to do with Red Cross. Master Tony's finishing his course at college this term. He's hoping to get into the Navy. He spends all his time in London, too.' Angela detected a subtle change of tone, a coolness, perhaps even a hint of disapproval, disguised though it was. 'They've got a flat down there. So really, I think that apart from the odd weekend, we'll be more caretakers than anything. Still, it gives us a chance to get you used to things, eh?'

Angela had found some things laid out on her bed. Overalls and head scarves, towels and soap. Miss Guy had shown her how to light the geyser and, at the expense of a blistered finger end, and a few seconds of breathless terror until it tardily and noisily ignited, she was able to enjoy the unimaginable delight of her first bath in a proper bathroom, with a bolted door to ensure privacy, and a white enamel tub that she could stretch out almost full length in.

Five inches, they said, was all you should use in these dangerous times. My God, they were even trying to ration water now. Feeling gloriously wicked, she ignored the authorities and filled the bath so full that when she climbed in, the water rose nearly to her chin. She lay there and studied her pale body and limbs shimmering in the clear water. She felt decadent and sensuously aroused as she slowly washed herself. Her own touch stirred her and, all at once, her face was hot as she thought of Ginge. She wanted him, fiercely, sexually. Her body blazed and she couldn't leave herself alone.

Afterwards, she cried a little, and repeated the short litany of her prayer. Please let him be safe, let him be safe. What was the date today? The 4th June? Miss Guy said they'd got them nearly all home now. She'd invited Angela down to her room to listen to the nine o'clock news. 'Just pop your dressing-gown on. We'll have a cup of tea.'

Dressing-gown! That was a laugh. As if she'd ever have one of those things. And Miss Guy had said it so ordinary like, as though it was the most natural thing in the world for people to go round popping on their dressing-gowns. It was a different world she was in now, all right, and she was going to make the most of it. One of the first things she'd buy when she had a bit of money was a dressing-gown.

She dressed in her floral dress again, and carefully arranged her hair, before going down the narrow stairs from the top floor to the more comfortably appointed landing below, where the housekeeper had her room. Miss Guy looked surprised to see her fully dressed. The older woman was wearing a full-length, plain brown robe tied with a cord around her waist, and her feet were encased in neat, multicoloured carpet slippers. 'You shouldn't have bothered dressing again,' Miss Guy began.

Suddenly, Angela didn't want to lie to this woman, who had turned out to be so different from the grim martinet she had been expecting. Though she blushed crimson, Angela murmured, 'Ah don't 'ave a dressin'-gown. We not – at 'ome—' She sank into miserable, embarrassed silence. How could she tell this wonderful looking figure what it was like back in The Street?

Miss Guy answered quickly, lightly, to ease the tension. 'That's all right. If you don't mind, there's one of mine you can have. It's no good for winter, it's only a thin thing but it'll do for now. It's quite pretty. We can take it up for you if you like. That reminds me. There's a couple of Margaret's uniforms here. I should be able to alter them to fit you.' She grinned at her. 'Beatrice was a bit too hefty. Hers would swamp you. Here, let's see how much we'll need to take in. Slip your dress off.'

Angela blushed again. She was embarrassed anew. 'Ah didn' bother with a petticoat,' she mumbled, somewhat reluctantly unfastening the light dress. 'With just comin' down 'ere like.' She was wearing a bodice, fastened with hooks and eyes at the front, and there was a gap of bare flesh before the elastic waistband of her panties. She was glad she'd put her best ones on, for there were no holes or elastic hanging out, and they were clean. She still couldn't help feeling embarrassed, though, at standing there half naked before Miss Guy.

'You've got a lovely little figure,' the housekeeper said easily. 'So slim. That's what all the girls want nowadays, eh?'

Not as good as yours, Angela thought, but didn't say so, in case it sounded cheeky. She slipped on the black dresses, which needed taking up just an inch or two. They were a little loose around the bust though not enough to matter. She was relieved to get back into her own frock again, and settle down with a cup of tea beside the wireless set. Her expression grew serious as they waited for the news bulletin.

As the very first item, the solemn announcer declared that the last of the troops had been safely embarked from the beaches and that the port of Dunkirk was now in enemy hands. Angela was not feigning the anguish which settled on her young features at the end of the broadcast. She might have some private doubts as to the exact depth of her feelings for Ginge, but that he occupied some kind of special place in her affections was not in any doubt at all.

She answered Miss Guy's gentle questions as best she could, glad to talk to someone so quietly but clearly sympathetic. She was surprised herself at how ready she was to open up to this warm-hearted stranger. There was something about her, a special tenderness, a concern, and a gentle strength, too, that made the young girl feel as though she was a lot closer to her than most of the folks she had known for years. She found herself opening up more, volunteering information she would not have disclosed normally.

'The folks aren't keen on us bein' serious like. Yer know – courtin' proper like. Specially me dad.' Her frown deepened. 'And 'is mam. Dead against it, she is. Mind you, ah feel sorry fer 'er now, though. Dead worried, she is. I 'ope 'e's all right,' she added, with such pathetic simplicity that Miss Guy rose swiftly and came over to sit beside her on the small, high-backed settle. She slipped her arm around the slender shoulders, and gently hugged her. The hand came up to smooth the yellow hair at her brow.

In other, more usual circumstances, Angela would have shied away from such a demonstrative gesture, especially from someone she had scarcely met. She *was* embarrassed, though more startled than anything. Then she became aware of how comforting it was, to feel the closeness of the tall figure, the reassurance of the enfolding arm, and she leaned her head in shyly towards the fragrant neck. Miss Guy released her after a few seconds, but remained sitting close beside her.

'Is there anyone at home you can contact? Anyone with a telephone? You could find out if they've heard—'

Angela shook her head with a little smile. Once again, she marvelled at the gulf between The Street and this softly cultured woman. 'Well, I'll tell you what,' Miss Guy offered. 'As the family aren't going to be around this weekend, you can go off home Saturday afternoon and come back Sunday night. How's that?'

Angela's lip quivered and her eyes filled with her gratitude. 'Thanks, miss,' she murmured, wondering if she had enough for the bus fare there and back. Well, she could always try and hitch a lift once she got on the coast road.

'But I'm going to work you to death before then to make up for it,' said Miss Guy, smiling broadly. She brushed her fingers very lightly and swiftly along Angela's cheek. 'So run along to bed now. I want you down in the kitchen for breakfast at seven sharp. Don't be late.'

She did not have to wait until the weekend for news. On the Friday morning, she was busy cleaning in the awesome elegance of the dining-room when one of the young local girls, Madge, came bustling through. 'Eh, Angie! The's someone ter see yer, in the kitchen. Yer brother, ah think. Eli, is it?'

Angela raced through the corridor, her mind travelling faster than her hurrying legs. She felt a keen embarrassment at Elisha turning up like this, bringing the aura of The Street into this new and alien world, but she also knew it must be something serious for him to have come all this way. She was breathless with anxiety when she burst through the swing doors, her face red, to see him sitting at ease at the long table where they took their meals, a half-drunk glass of milk in front of him.

'It's Arthur Clay – Ginge,' he stated without preamble. 'Mam sent us.'

Angela's knees were rubbery. She leaned on the dresser, feeling giddy. He's dead. She could see it in Eli's face. She nodded as though he had already pronounced it.

' 'E's been found. 'E's in hospital. Somewhere down south. 'E's bad. 'E's lost an arm.'

She gave a little scream. Mrs Cullingford, a chubby, fussy little woman, moved and grabbed her, assisting her to sit at the table, opposite her brother. She began to cry, shrilly, spluttering, almost a hysterical giggle. Daft thoughts flew through her head. Lost an arm! How can you lose an arm? Anybody seen an arm round here? She put her head forward on her arms and sobbed loudly, rawly, her shoulders heaving, all the pent-up emotion of the past days, not only to do with Ginge, but the change in her own situation, overwhelming her.

The attack was quickly over. Miss Guy came in in the middle of things, and for a few brief, shameful seconds, Angela felt anger at her brother being there, at Ginge for disrupting her life like this. She didn't want this mess paraded before this wonderful person who was giving her the greatest chance of her young life. Then she was tormented by the wickedness of her thoughts.

Miss Guy put her hand on her shoulder. Immediately, Angela felt that sense of strength, of comfort and tenderness flowing into her. The housekeeper waited until she had recovered from the violence of her grief, and was able to sip at a cup of strong tea. Elisha, with a dramatic sense of his importance, filled in some details for his attentive audience. 'Apparently, the boat 'e was comin' 'ome on was bombed an' they 'ad ter gerroff inter the water. 'E was picked up by another boat. 'E'd been badly wounded. The' told his mam the'd tried ter save 'is arm, the left un, burrit was too bad like. 'E's bad wi' other things – like shell shock or summat.' He hesitated. 'The' not sure 'ow 'e'll come on. It's still serious.' He looked across at his sister. 'Ma Clay came over special ter tell us. She's in a bad way 'ersel'.'

'Why don't you take your brother up to your room?' Miss Guy said kindly. 'You'll want to be on your own a while. Come and see me after lunch.'

'She seems quite canny,' Elisha observed, as they climbed the three flights of stairs to the top floor. He whistled appreciatively when he saw the sloping roof with its large window, the neatly made narrow bed. 'By 'eck, this is a bit of all right, eh? Yer in 'ere on yer own?'

She flung herself down on the blue-checked counterpane and gave way to another noisy outburst of tears, while Elisha

looked on awkwardly, unable to offer any solace. Her eyes and
face were red when she sat up. The blonde hair escaped in
untidy tendrils from the generous blue scarf knotted about her
head. The faded floral overall came down nearly to her ankles.
Elisha noticed she was wearing an old, scuffed pair of shoes
which he recognized, and her legs were bare. 'Is 'e gonner be
all right?' she asked frantically.

Elisha shrugged. 'Ah don' know any more, Ange. Ma Clay
was in 'ysterics. She didn' even know where 'e was. Ah mean
she knew the name of the 'ospital but she doesn' know where it
is. She can't even get down ter see 'im. It's right down south.
Past London somewhere.' He made it sound like the ends of
the earth. It might as well be, for Mrs Clay and for Angela.

She said as much to Miss Guy when she went to see her in
her sitting-room off the corridor leading through to the kitchen.
The housekeeper frowned. 'I'm sure you're entitled to some
sort of help in those circumstances. I'll telephone Mr Briggs.
He's a friend of Sir Roger's. He'll know what to do.'

Later that afternoon, Miss Guy came to seek her out as she
was working on the second-floor landing, taking all the folded
linen out of the huge laundry cupboard before sweeping down
the walls with a feather duster, then washing down the slatted
wooden shelves. They were so deep Angela had to heave
herself up and scramble on her stomach, feet waving in the air,
to reach the things at the back.

'When you go home tomorrow, find out where the young
man is, the name of the hospital. I'll give you a note to see Mr
Gibson, the clerk at the Labour Exchange who fixed up the
interview. He'll help you. Certainly your young man's mother
should be able to travel down to see him. You, too, I should
think. We'll manage something.'

'Oh, miss!' Angela breathed, the tears spilling over again.
'Ah'm sorry – fer all this. Yer so good—' Briskly Miss Guy cut
off her thanks. She nodded at the piles of white linen and the
gaping doors of the cupboard.

'It might help to take your mind off things. Hard work and
cups of tea, that's the answer.' Angela gazed at the retreating
back with a fervour bordering on worship.

Miss Guy's note and her own youthful charm worked
wonders on the ogling Mr Gibson. He wallowed in his role of

benefactor. By the Tuesday morning, he had organized travel
warrants for Mrs Clay and Angela. 'You are his fiancée, aren't
you?' he purred, his tongue darting across his lips. Angela
nodded firmly.

Mrs Clay's opposition to her had crumbled. The poor woman
was in a daze of grief anyway, and she now looked on Angie as
some sort of miracle-working angel indeed. Mr Clay did not
seem upset that he would not travel with them. His chief
feeling was one of relief, though he did not express it. 'Yer'll be
a'right with Angie,' he assured his wife. Angela had to
suppress a smile at the sudden elevation of her status. Quite a
promotion for the 'little tart' of just a few weeks ago.

She was excited, and of course guilty at feeling so. She had
never been further than the thirty-odd miles to the city of
Newcastle. Now she was about to travel practically the length
of England, all the way to the south coast itself, and the distant
town of Southampton. Or at least Netley, which was only a few
miles outside, and the site of a large military hospital where
they had taken Ginge.

She felt very grown up and responsible, especially as Mrs
Clay was pathetically helpless, like a huge child, half hysterical
with worry over Ginge, and fear of what might happen to them
on this monumental journey. Doris dashed about the street
borrowing here and there, so that Angie had a few decent
things to take with her. And a case to carry them in. She even
had a cotton dressing-gown, which Miss Guy had brought to
her room, freshly washed and pressed, the day before she was
to set off.

'I'm afraid I haven't had time to take it up yet, so it'll sweep
the floor rather.' She added with a little rush of uncharacteristic
embarrassment, 'Oh, there's a few other things you might find
useful, or you can pass them on, if you like.' She gave Angela
that little, fingered caress on the cheek. 'We'll expect you back
on Friday some time, all being well. I hope you find Arthur
starting to recover. Safe journey.'

Angela's eyes filled with tears yet again, when she inspected
the little pile of neatly folded things. There was a soft, clearly
new towel and face cloth, some scented soap and a bottle of
shampoo. Also, hidden away inside the gown, was some
beautiful silken underwear. Two pairs of lace-trimmed panties,

and a delicate camisole, also edged with fine lace. Angela rubbed their fragrant sheen caressingly across her nose and lips. She had never seen anything so beautiful. She couldn't wait. Hastily, she peeled off her clothes, pulled on a pair of the panties, shivering with joy at the smooth, whispering feel of them on her skin. She tugged the camisole over her head, smoothed the silk to her breasts, felt her nipples respond to the lightness of the satin touch. She turned and crouched in front of the dressing-table mirror.

My God! She looked like a film star. Wait till Ginge saw ... her cheeks burned, she felt the hot rush of shame. How dare she? She thought of her oft repeated prayer. Let him be safe, let him be safe. He was, wasn't he? Terribly hurt. It hadn't really sunk in yet, the idea of him without an arm. She shuddered. She didn't want to think about it. But he was alive. God couldn't let him die now. Not after all this. Suddenly deeply ashamed, she quickly stripped off the silk underwear and dragged on her old cotton nightie.

Fourteen

The epic journey to Southampton took Angela and Mrs Clay nearly two days. Angela felt by the end of it she had spent a lifetime lugging their two battered cases on and off trains, fighting for seats in crowded compartments. They didn't touch fabled London. Place names were just soot-ridden stations of blackened brick, with chilly, paint-peeling waiting-rooms.

Once more, she was powerfully aware of the importance of her fresh young looks, her long yellow hair, the slim allure of her body. It served them on many occasions; she used it almost shamelessly. Soldiers, sailors, airmen, hefted their bags on to luggage racks or reached them down for her, bodies squeezed up to make room for them, railway officials went out of their way to guide them to the right platform, the correct train. They were decent lads, most of them, content with a grateful smile and a bit of conversation.

She was generally glad of that, for Mrs Clay had very little, apart from oft repeated worries about whether they were on the right train, and admonitions to keep an eye on their cases. She stared with wide-eyed suspicion at everyone they came into contact with, seeing them as a potential thief. Angela tried to be patient with her, kept reminding herself that she was Ginge's mam, and of the ordeal she was going through, but, despite her guilt at her private reflections, Angela found her woefully lacking as a travelling companion. She began to resent the obesely glowering figure, and to be embarrassed by her. There was even a hint of defiance in the coquetry of her manner with some of the young servicemen, for she could sense the disapproval of the older woman's tight-lipped silence.

York, Birmingham, Reading. They crossed station bridges,

tried to doze in the dimly lit sanctuaries of the Ladies'
Waiting-Rooms, on the hard wooden benches. Khaki everywhere. In the bleary brightness of a sunny morning, at a
wayside halt near Oxford, they saw a horde of unshaven men,
in an odd assortment of military clothing, herded the length of
a narrow wooden platform. Windows rattled open, there was
shouting back and forth, and suddenly a great cheer went up
from all along the carriages, and the men on the platform lifted
their heads and arms and smiled. Packets of cigarettes
showered out at them, like confetti. Angela saw at once how
weary they were. Eyes dark, and something stamped on their
features, indefinable, but clearly shared.

'Picked up off the beaches. One of the last lot.' The word flew
up and down the train, and Angela was brought back, her
stomach churning sickeningly once more, to the object of their
journey. What would he be like? Would he be the same Ginge
with whom she had shared the Night of the Dunes, and, for
her, the more magical day out at Eden Dale, the last hours they
had spent together?

The station at Southampton seemed more like a military
encampment. Light and dark blue and khaki everywhere. It
was already late evening. Angela was bone weary, sticky with
grimy sweat, and close to tears of exhaustion and appre-
hension. The added responsibility of Mrs Clay, whose bulk had
subsided into a trance-like state, was perilously close to tipping
her over the edge.

The Salvation Army lady who accosted them as they stood
outside the barrier was a ministering angel. After procuring for
them tea and sandwiches from a mobile stall set up in the
station forecourt, and listening to Angela's tremblingly
unsteady tale, she got a girl who looked younger than Angela
to take them to a Women's Refuge, where clean beds,
bathroom, soap and towels awaited. The kid was ever so posh,
with her 'Would yew like a barth?' but she meant well. Got a
bathroom of my own where I live, kidder, Angela thought, not
without a glow of pride, but she said nothing.

They even arranged for them to use the accommodation at
the hostel the following day, if necessary, until their train left at
night, and gave them directions for the lengthy, two-bus
journey out to the hospital at Netley, on the shores of

Southampton Water. It was after midday by the time the green and white coach deposited them at the gates, and it took them a further half-hour before they found the building which housed Ginge's ward.

It was obvious that there had been a sudden influx of patients. Ambulances moved in and out, staff and inmates thronged the grounds. Men on crutches, men with limbs or heads swathed in bandages. Angela fought against her rebellious stomach and prayed she wouldn't make a fool of herself.

They were shown to an office, where they stood in silence until a formidably impressive figure hurried in. She wore a sparkling white head-dress which fanned out in a nun-like billow from the tight binding at her brow. Over her blue uniform dress, she was wearing a short, dark-blue cloak with a rich scarlet lining. What a fantastic get-up, Angela thought distractedly, trying to hold in her emotion.

'Where is 'e?' Mrs Clay asked pathetically, and the sister offered her a seat. Angela put out a hand, motioning for her to sit, and the fat frame lowered itself precariously on to the creaking wooden chair.

'He's suffered a severe trauma,' the sister began, while they stared at her blankly. 'Fortunately, we think he'll make a good recovery. The arm is healing well, already. The damage to his ear-drums may not be as bad as we first thought, though he's still quite deaf at the moment.' She paused. 'Mentally, though, I'm afraid there are some complications. We're not sure of the degree of damage, or how permanent it will be. But try not to show how upset you are, even though you'll be shocked.' Again a pause, even lengthier. 'We're hoping he'll recognize you. That might have a beneficial effect, jar something in his consciousness.' Angela couldn't really take in what this impressive woman was saying. Recognize them? What on earth was she on about?

They went through the double doors into a long ward. Every bed was occupied. The sickly combination of ether and disinfectant set Angela off. She swallowed hard, struggling not to gag. She could never be a nurse. She was terrified, hated this. No matter how glamorous the uniform. The sister's rubber-shod feet squeaked softly, their own clacked sharply as they followed her down the stretch of polished wooden flooring. And then they were there, at his bed, half-way down on the left, and she was crying at the sight of his chalk-white face, the freckles standing out vividly, the bareness of the shorn sides of his red head. His eyes were dark shadows. Closed as they were at the moment, they looked made up, like some old-fashioned film star. His left arm was held in a frame affair, out to the side. Its obscene shortness ballooned out into a beehive swelling of bandages.

'Arthur! Someone to see you.' The sister touched him lightly on the shoulder, and he started up immediately, with a plaintive, whimpering cry. He stared dully at the two shapes at the bottom of his bed. Suddenly, his eyes widened.

'Mam!' he croaked. His mouth twisted, the lower lip curved into a parody of childish sulk. The face crumpled and he let out a loud bawl of misery and need. His mother cried out his name as she rushed forward, bent and smothered him in her embrace. He sobbed loudly, harshly, without any restraint, his right arm came up over her bulky shoulder, the contraption holding the stump shook at his instinctive effort to embrace her with that hand also.

Angela stood there, appalled, forgotten, the tears coursing silently down her cheeks. It seemed an age before the darkly enveloping mass moved, releasing the figure beneath, and Mrs Clay dabbed at his face, and then at her own. His one hand stretched out to her imploringly, and he made that whimpering sound again, terrified that she would leave him. They clenched hands fiercely as Mrs Clay lowered herself into the chair which a nurse quickly brought forward. Ginge's eyes held his mother. He stared at her intently, the tears still flowing.

'There's someone else to see you, Arthur. Do you know who this is?' Angela felt utterly without strength as the sister's firm hands grasped her shoulders and propelled her forward, closer to him. She could smell that sickly bandage smell, it nauseated her.

The blankness of his watery gaze directly on to her was like a body blow. She tried to smile, grimaced, tried to speak. Couldn't. She saw his freckled brow crease in a furrow of doubt or query. He turned away, with a guttural cry, tried to lift himself back into his mother's bosom. Mrs Clay leaned forward once more, with a huge sob, enveloping him.

Angela turned away, frightened she would collapse, and the sister's arm was swiftly about her. 'Don't worry. We didn't even know if he'd recognize his mother. It's a good sign. Something may come back. These things take time.'

'Ah feel sick,' Angela managed, her face a parchment colour, and the sister hastily summoned a young nurse, who steered Angela down the ward to a toilet. She hung over the lavatory bowl and retched. She splashed water on her face at the basin. 'Sorry,' she murmured to the hovering girl. 'Ah'm fine now. Ah'll just use the toilet.' When she was alone, she sat and hunched forward, elbows on knees and sobbed uncontrollably, for long minutes. When the violence of her grief had passed, her eyes were swollen and red, but some of the shock had been absorbed.

She had been prepared for anything but this. A weird desire to giggle hysterically all at once flickered into being. After all this, the suffering, the prayers, the upheaval of this great journey, he didn't even know her. The blue eyes were empty, totally devoid of recognition. It was ridiculous really.

Eventually, she got her make-up out of her handbag and dabbed away at herself, trying to repair the damage of her weeping. She left the ward quietly, went outside for a while. Across the road was a stretch of grass, and a line of tall, dark conifers through which she could see the sparkling sea. It was a lovely spot for a hospital. Ginge must be able to look out to sea from the windows of the ward.

She went back in, drew a deep breath, and again passed through the double doors. Mrs Clay was still sitting there, hunched forward, holding Ginge's hand. There was a smile on his young, pain-marked face, a child's smile, and Angela felt a deep shame at her own feelings of betrayal. ' 'Ello,' she said bravely. ' 'Ow is 'e now? All right?'

'It's Angie, pet. Ye remember Angie Thompson!' The use of her surname by Mrs Clay cut Angela like the lash from a whip.

' 'Ello, Ar – Ginge. Yer feelin' better?' She felt the muscles pulling her mouth into the smile, held it. He gazed at her questioningly, the furrow folding into place again.

' 'E's gonner be all right now, aren't yer, Son?' At the sound of his mother's voice, he turned back to her, the smile again appearing. Angela sat there, further back, on a second chair, numbly, her mind wandering disconnectedly through a thousand fleeting thoughts, while Mrs Clay sat on, crooning to her son.

When they finally had to make their tearful farewells, Angela saw Ginge looking at her with even deeper concentration, as though her presence worried him. The sister led the weeping Mrs Clay to her office, quietly suggesting that Angela should stay with Ginge on her own for a minute or two, to say a private goodbye. 'It might help him to remember something,' she urged.

Angela couldn't help registering the hurt she experienced when she saw his eyes flicker miserably and anxiously in the direction of the departing Mrs Clay, but she pushed aside the emotion. She moved close to him, cupped her palm along the side of his cheek, leaned in close so that her hair hung down, brushing against his skin. Her lips moved even closer, against his ear. 'Ah love you,' she whispered. 'Ah'm glad yer all right. Yer've gotta get better, Ginge. Ye'll soon be 'ome.'

The lines on his brow were etched deeply now. Her nearness, the scent of her, her beauty flowed over him. He was making small guttural sounds in his throat. She kissed him, very softly, on his dry lips. She saw a light flame up, magically, in his eyes, an eager animation transform his face. He grabbed her hand so tightly it hurt her. Before she realized what he was doing, he dragged it under the blankets. She felt the heat of his pyjama-clad body as he thrust her palm eagerly against the hard, swelling rise of his beating, blossoming erection. She tore herself free, ran, open-mouthed, sobbing, crashed through the double doors, stumbled blindly into the bright sunlight.

Angela endured the equally drawn-out and tedious nature of the return journey almost numbly. There was a notable difference now between the two of them. To Angela, it seemed that there was a smugness, a grim sense of triumph, about Mrs Clay which gave her a new strength, to counterbalance the defeated weakness of her youthful rival. For that's what they had been in reality, that's how they had both seen it, Angela knew. 'The' said the'll transfer 'im up ter Shotley Bridge as soon as the' can. 'E'll be all right as soon as 'e's 'ome with 'is mam again.'

Angela heard the ringing triumph of the victor in Mrs Clay's words, and wearily acknowledged it. She wished Ginge well, she still prayed that he would recover his wits. Yes, she did, she insisted to herself. But that furtive fumbling under the bedclothes, the spark in the poor lad's crazy eyes in the only instant of recognition for her, had told her what she was worth. What their Love was really worth, and she would never be able to forget it. Divine justice. She didn't know the phrase, but she felt she had been punished, and rightly so, for she had fooled herself and fooled Ginge, trying to make something noble and grand out of what they had shared when she had known all along that she was fooling both of them. It served her right. The truism echoed and echoed in her brain, through all the discomfort of the night and day of their trip back up north.

Angela had never felt so hurt and alone in her young life. After watching the dawn come filtering greyly through the smoky dreariness of Thornaby Station, they got their last train and arrived back home in the already bustling early morning. 'We'll gerra taxi up 'ome,' declared Mrs Clay grandly, delving into the purse she had been so reluctant to open during the various stages of their long trip. 'Yer'll not manage the cases on the bus. Any road, yer never know when the' runnin' these days.'

She was still horrified when the driver told them what the fare would be. His was the only cab parked in the cobbled area in front of the station, but there were no other customers waiting. 'We on'y want ter go ter Sutherland Street,' she protested loudly. 'We don' wan' ter buy yer car!'

'The's a war on, missus,' the driver said offhandedly, using the formula that was coming to be popular for all kinds of inconvenience, from whooping cough to the weather. 'An' it's not my car,' he added more feelingly.

Angela would have preferred to go straight out to Dalby and her new existence. She dreaded the questions. And then the knowing looks, the snickers behind her back and behind hands as the word spread, as it doubtless would, knowing Ma Clay, about what had happened down at Netley. 'Didn' even know the little tart. 'Er with 'er big ideas, the little madam!'

She could not avoid the questions. They bombarded her as

soon as she got inside the door, before even, as a delegation which seemed to represent the whole street gathered at the significant event of a taxi in their midst. Once inside, her family crowded round her. She was glad her da had already gone off to work, but her mam and Elisha were bad enough. Her brother, especially, pressed for details so enthusiastically, that her stretched nerves broke and she almost screamed at him. 'Ah've told yer, fer God's sake! 'E didn' even bloody know us. 'E's like a bairn.' In her extremity, she gestured cruelly at the grinning Terence. 'Like 'im!'

She washed her hands and face at the sink in the kitchen, then escaped to the bedroom she shared with her three brothers. 'Ah'll 'ave to 'ave a lie down. Ah'm all in. An' ah'd better get out ter Dalby ternight. Ah told Miss Guy ah'd be back ter work on Frid'y.'

She was surprised herself at the feeling of relief and anticipation she felt as she walked up the curving drive and saw the imposing façade of the house once more. Now more than ever, she was glad of this opportunity that had come so fortuitously to her. She felt oddly as though she had been away for months, that she was returning a much older, and more worldly-wise figure.

She was grown up now. She'd travelled the length of England, could look after herself. It was the end of one era in her life, she thought. She had forgiven Ginge. How could she blame him for whatever had gone on in that crazy, bomb-shattered mind and broken body? It was her own romantic notions she found it hard to forgive. Especially as she had only half been taken in by them, had willed herself into believing them, trying to ignore that deep-down feeling of distrust.

Believed them enough to make surrender of her body, the milestone which, more clearly than any other, delineated the crossing over from childhood. She had cheated them both. As for Ginge, God knows what he had thought. First time for him, too, she knew that for sure. Not that it was such a world-shattering event for lads. They couldn't wait to get rid of their virginity, and to brag about it to all their mates. A deep, smarting shame stabbed like a toothache as she wondered if Ginge had told Barraclough and that lot about it. Before her visit to Netley, she would have confidently declared the answer to be no, but now....

She still had Ginge's letters, his laboured hand with the 'I love you' above the signature, but in the mixed-up, tormented mind his ordeal had reduced him to, her memory was merely a hot, furtive hard-on under the covers and a hand to bring him animal relief.

But so what? If it was no big deal for a boy, was it so different for a girl? Certainly, physically, it had been far below what her fevered imagination had dreamt it to be. Glimmers of the dream had been there, she had glimpsed how it could be. But the first time was not the heart-throbbing violins, the soaring eruption of firework bliss you were led to anticipate. No, and there's no Santa Claus, either, she thought, with a twisted little smile of self-mockery.

Next time, she wouldn't be so foolish. Wouldn't be so easy. She wouldn't get caught by her heart again. The wound would heal, was already healing, it would harden over, and that was a good thing. She was truly away from The Street now. Ginge had been of The Street, that was her mistake, and she should have known it, had known it if only she'd listened to herself, her nasty self. Her real self, it would be from now on. She walked around the side of the house, through the door in the wall surrounding the kitchen garden, already with an eager sense of belonging.

Miss Guy didn't press her for details. She smiled warmly, beautifully, when she saw her. 'I didn't expect you back till tomorrow or the day after. You must be worn out. Why don't you go up and have a nice hot bath and I'll bring you up a tray? There'll be something in the kitchen. And you can talk if you want to, or just have a really early night. You can borrow a book if you like. I've got quite a few novels. I'm sure you'll find something you'd enjoy.' *True Confessions* and the *News of the World*. That was the extent of her reading and even then she soon grew tired. Once again, she vowed that from now on things were going to be different. She would learn to read, proper books, and enjoy them, too. It was all up to her.

She *did* talk. Miss Guy's warm, tender concern was so different from the rabid curiosity of The Street, from her own family, that she found herself again opening up to this comparative stranger. Except that, oddly, she felt wonderfully closer to her than anyone she had known. She didn't hold back anything of the pain, of her feeling of humiliation at what had taken place.

' 'E cried like a bairn with 'is mam. But 'e just didn' know me at all. 'E looked at us as if 'e'd never seen us before.'

'I'm sure, when he recovers fully—' the gentle voice suggested.

Angela shook her head with new resolve. 'Naw,' she said, with quiet finality. 'It's over like. Like ah said, we'd never really got serious. Ah mean ah'm fond of 'im, don' gerrus wrong. But all 'e needs is 'is mam now and 'ome.' There was an awkward pause, then she added with unintentional force, 'An' all ah want is ter be away out o' there for good and all. Ah want summat better out of life than that.' She blushed, deeply, glancing away shyly, but forced herself to go on. 'Ah know nothin'. Ah'm ashamed of the way ah speak, of 'ow ah go on. Ah want' – she shrugged hopelessly – 'ter be diff'rent. Ter talk proper an' everythin'.'

She was crying quietly again, though she wasn't aware of it. She sat in the too long dressing-gown, her fingers twisting in the lap, her toes curling on the worn rug. They bore faint, flaky fragments of the nail polish, most of which had come off during her soak in the tub.

Miss Guy got up off the bed and came to her, taking her hands in hers and holding on to them. 'My dear,' she said, giving her that beautiful, tender smile. 'It will all come right for you, I'm sure of it. You *do* know how lovely you are, don't you? I want you to know I'll help you all I can, if you'll let me. I think you and I will be great friends, and I know you won't let me down. Come on. You hop into bed now.'

Blushing with embarrassment, Angie let her slip off the gown, glad she had put on her cotton nightie, even though it was short and skimpy, and tight across her modest bust. After all, she'd been wearing it since she was about twelve. She felt about twelve as she snuggled down under the cold, crisp sheet and Miss Guy tucked her in, one hand smoothing the hair at her brow. But she didn't mind. Far from it, it was a nice warm feeling, and the tears that threatened now were nice tears, at being cared for, and protected.

'Yer've been ever so kind ter me,' Angela murmured shyly. 'Ah don't deserve it. Ah've been nowt but trouble since ah got 'ere. Here. Ah can't thank yer—'

'Yes you can. Work hard, stay here. And let me be your friend. I'm already very fond of you.' Miss Guy's wonderful face was pink, too, now. She bent forward, and kissed Angela softly on the lips. She kept her mouth there, their lips remained in contact, gentle, sweet. 'Night-night, Angela.'

Angela's head was spinning. Almost literally. She was giddy, with so many racing emotions. The trauma of the past few eventful days washed over her. But most of all, her mind was racing with the stunning wonder of that kiss, the taste, the soft imprint of it, which she could still feel, savoured. Her heart was thudding, her body quivering like a taut wire. It was so wonderful, to be able to share that with someone like Miss Guy. She had never met anyone like her, she was thrilled by her. All at once it struck her, with all the suddenness of a blow, what it was that so astounded her. That kiss, impressed so sweetly upon her lips, was the very stuff of her childish dreams – the fabled love of True Romance that her short experience of life had shown her could never be.

Fifteen

Elisha had put the challenge to Annie Bartlett more in hope than expectation, so that when she agreed to go over to the Headland with him, he could not believe that she meant it. He suspected that she had something planned, some devious way of making him look a right fool, and vowed to himself to be on the alert. But her crooked-toothed little grin looked sunnily innocent. 'Righty-oh, Eli, me ol' china. 'Alf parst ten termorrer mornin' unless it's chuckin' it. An' I'll 'ave me bathin' suit ready an' all ter give you a real eyeful. Origh'?'

He ran home from the Rec, leaping and whooping aloud, bursting to tell the lads, tell anybody. So he was only fourteen! He was going out with an AT. She fancied him, God knows what they'd get up to, once he got her on the South Sands and up in the dunes. Where was Limbert? The bastard would do his nut when he heard. Hold hard though. There was no way he was going to tell him. Or anyone else for that matter. He could just see the whole mob of them, dug in there from dawn, waiting for them to arrive. No way! He wasn't going to say anything to anyone about this.

All at once, he wished that Ange was still at home. He could at least have told her. Even though she would have had something dead sarky to say about it, she wouldn't have blabbed about it. Or tried to put him off. He'd already mentioned Annie to her, told her how friendly she was, and she made a few jokes about it, took the micky out of him, but not in a really nasty way.

He felt uncomfortable as he remembered the secret, evil thoughts he'd had about his sister. Filthy thoughts. And how he'd lain at nights, on the other side of the bed, tormented by his lust, body burning up with it. The turning, sighing, pretending to be asleep, peeping through slit eyes when she got up early in the morning, to try and catch a glimpse of her dressing.

He used to hate her for making him feel like that, for looking the way she did, getting him excited. She was a stunner all right; no lad could look at her and not feel himself rising. But he was ashamed of being like that now. He knew it wasn't right. He felt different about her as well now. Sorry for her, especially over this business with Ginge Clay. She was hurt badly, really badly, though she pretended she wasn't, that she was all right. He wanted to talk to her, to let her know how he felt, but there had been no chance. He was glad for her that she had got this job out at Dalby. She wanted to get away, he knew how desperate she was. Who wasn't? God, he hoped the war would last a year or two longer.

When he met Annie at the edge of the Rec the next morning, she had another girl with her, a short, darkly gipsyish sort of girl he also knew. Her name was Rachel. He was put out at first, and was almost sulky, until Annie, perhaps sensing his mood, said to her friend, ' 'Ere, Raich, don' you go gittin' any ideas 'bout this young feller, mind. 'E's my date, so don't ferget. Yore only along as chaperone. You'll 'ave ter find yer own young man if yer wanna walk out. Origh'?'

Elisha grinned. 'Origh'?' he mimicked, his good humour fully restored.

' 'Gercha, bloody old monkey-'anger!' she retorted, aiming a swipe at him with her khaki haversack.

The two giggling girls made Elisha keep watch while they crouched in a shallow dip and scrabbled out of their clothes and into bathing costumes. ' 'Oy! Yore s'posed ter be lookin' the other way, cheeky blighter!' Annie called, but she was laughing, and everything was decently hidden behind towels anyway.

He reminded her so much of her brothers, that was why she had got friendly with him in the first place, it made her feel less lonely, and closer somehow to home. She had never dreamt she would miss the crowded little East End terraced house so much. He was a good kid, and she knew how rough it was for them at that age, looking back with all the lofty wisdom of her nineteen years.

She was a bit too lanky and skinny, and her chest was embarrassingly flat, but she couldn't help but be flattered by his wide-eyed, sideways glances (which he thought she couldn't notice) at her in her black woollen bathing suit. Mind you, to be honest, Rachel was copping a few stares as well, and, to be even more painfully honest, Rachel's well-rounded little figure deserved them. But Annie was aware of how Eli felt, and it gave her a kind of half-innocent, half-wicked thrill to see it, even though he *was* just a kid.

He was interested in her, too, as a person, fascinated by the way she talked, by the fact of her coming from far away London. 'They're gonna get it bad soon, I reckon,' she said seriously, when the three of them were lying on towels, drying off after a quick plunge into the icy sea. Eli dragged his eyes off a large, dark bruise high on Annie's thigh, and his ignoble speculations as to how she had acquired it. 'Nothin' ter stop Adolph now, is there? Now 'e's got France, 'e'll be able ter send 'is bombers over in 'undreds. Flatten us, 'e will.'

'Not now 'e's got you ter contend with,' Rachel chuckled teasingly, and at Elisha's look of enquiry, she went on to explain. 'Our Annie's got 'erself transferred ter the gunners. Ack-Ack. Yer know them mobile guns we've got now, on the backs of the lorries? She's on one o' them. Nearly finished yer trainin', 'aven't yer?'

'So when Jerry starts comin' over, yer might see me down yore street, Eli,' Annie laughed. 'Not that 'Itler would dream of tacklin' you lot. Not when 'e 'ears wot yer do ter bleedin' monkeys, eh?'

Angela was confused rather than ashamed of her private feelings over Miss Guy. She couldn't understand them, they didn't make sense to her, yet she couldn't deny them. She never questioned Miss Guy's innocence in all this. It was not the sweet kiss, it was her own reaction to it which shocked Angie. Miss Guy was as lovely and warm as ever to her the following day, and as easy and friendly as before. Angela guessed that the effects of the news about Ginge, his terrible injuries, and then all the upheaval of the epic journey and what had happened to her there, had a lot to do with her strange and confused emotions. It was only natural, after all, that she should feel so deeply for someone who from the very first had been so kind towards her. Anyway, shocking or not, it was a good feeling she had about the older woman; she hugged it to herself and tried to express it only in the wholehearted devotion she showed in performing her menial tasks as well as she could.

A few days after her return from Netley, Angela was sitting at the long kitchen table with Mrs Cullingford and the two young local girls. They had just finished their dinner, and Madge and Ruth were about to carry the few dishes over to the sink to wash them, when Miss Guy came in. She stood behind Angela and put her hand lightly on her shoulder. 'I've altered those other uniforms. Come up when you've finished and we'll see if they fit all right.'

As soon as she had gone out again, Madge and Ruth burst into a fit of giggles as they stood at the sink. Their sniggers so clearly had something to do with Miss Guy that Angela felt a burst of irritation, though normally she got on well enough with the two youngsters.

'What's wrong wi' you two?' she asked abruptly, but they continued to dig each other with elbows and double up with increased laughter.

Madge, the prettier of the two, turned to her, her brown eyes dancing with gossip. 'Eh, yer wanna be careful with that one, Ange. Ah wouldn't let 'er within a mile of me like. And ah certainly wouldn' be tekkin' any o' me clo'es off with 'er around.'

Angela felt a sudden deep rush of emotion she could not define. Her face was hot. 'Wha'd yer mean by that?'

The girls were still giggling salaciously. 'Wait till yer get down the village. The lasses 'll all tell yer, man. The' were all talkin' about it.'

Angela had learned already that the 'Big 'Ouse', as Dalby Hall was familiarly known to the villagers, as well as providing a large number with employment, had also through the generations provided the small population with a large proportion of their conversational topics. 'Talkin' about what?' she asked. The sniggering girls were oblivious to the tension in her voice.

'Why about Miss Queery Guy of course! And ah mean

queer!' The scandalized laughter exploded through Madge's nose, as Ruth jostled her and they clung to each other, their merriment heightened by the look of outrage on Angela's blushing features. Madge reached forward, put her hand on Angie's arm in an unconscious gesture of intimacy. 'She's one o' them – yer know. What fancies other women.'

'Converts, is it?' put in Ruth, and her partner shrieked with helpless laughter.

'Perverts, ye daft bugger!' Madge corrected, pushing at her. 'Beattie Wallace, one o' the lasses that worked 'ere, used ter come in the Mitre an' she used ter say apparently 'ow Miss Guy was always comin' up te the' room, walkin' in on them when the' were gettin' dressed an' that.' Her face alive with mischief, she leaned in close to Angie, totally unaware of her listener's peculiar stillness, or the paleness which had replaced that hectic flush. 'So, ah'm just warnin' yer, Ange. Y'oughter be very careful with that—'

The vicious slap to the side of her face caught Madge entirely by surprise. She was still yelping in astonished pain when Angie seized a handful of her dark hair and yanked it vigorously, almost lifting her off her feet. She screamed, belatedly trying to fight back. Ruth, frightened at the sudden violence, stepped back, leaving her friend to her fate.

Madge put up some resistance. Her hands came up, tried to claw at her attacker, sought a grip, but Angela, brought up in the hard school of The Street, was more than a match for this village lass. Another cruel slap to the face sent her reeling, and now Angie dug both hands deep into the scalp and held her victim mercilessly. She forced the head down, over the sink, thrust it into the still hot, greasy water, dunking the face and cutting off abruptly the piercing scream as the hapless girl bubbled and choked. Swiftly, Angie released one hand and turned the cold tap full on. Its icy jet hit the back of the bent head, splashed out over both of them. Madge's wild struggles ceased and she slumped, struggling only to keep her nose and mouth clear of the water, half drowned and terrified out of her wits.

By the time an amazed Mrs Cullingford had made her way to them from her end of the kitchen, Angela had released Madge, who folded to the floor, sobbing hysterically. Her hair was plastered blackly like seaweed all over her face. Her shoulders and the bodice of her work dress were soaking. She lay there, gulping and coughing while Angela stood over her. 'If I 'ear any more filthy talk like that from you, kidder, ah'll do more than wash yer mucky neck for yer. Ah'll cut yer lyin' tongue out! Ye hear?'

Angela was dreading meeting Miss Guy. She did not go to the housekeeper's room to try on her uniforms, but carried on working in the first-floor bedrooms throughout the long afternoon. Her mind was a whirl of dismal and conflicting thoughts as she went over again and again what that wicked little bitch had told her. It mustn't, it couldn't be true. Evil, malicious gossip. She hated all of them, hated the whole world, which seemed so set on dirtying and twisting every wonderful, special thing it came across. Well, she wouldn't let it. Not this time.

She thought of Love as she had tried to construct it with Ginge, how even her own ignoble thoughts had tried to pull at it, knock it down. And the sex itself had been so painfully and messily short of what it should have been, the way she had built it in her own mind.

With a jarring shock that made her actually pause in her task, the thought came to her that maybe she was one of those women, those what's-its, she didn't know the proper term for them, that those two sniggering little cows had been on about. After all, all Miss Guy had done had been to kiss her. She had been the one to get herself into such a tortuous state over it, to feel those strange, hot depths of emotion that had so shaken her. The idea scared her. But it also gave her a sense of trembling defiance. It wasn't mucky, fit for dirty little guffaws like those two had reduced it to. She relived with grim satisfaction the beating she had given to Madge. Like a drownded cat she was, lying there spluttering and coughing her guts up. She'd be a bit more careful who she spread her lies round to in future.

Angela brazened it out, going down to the kitchen for her afternoon tea as usual, despite the crackling atmosphere. Ruth and a still-sniffing Madge, the imprint of Angela's palm vividly outlined on her cheek, sat heads together at the far end of the table, whispering. An uneasy Mrs Cullingford made stilted conversation with Angie, and tried unsuccessfully to bring the two youngsters into the talk.

Although Miss Guy usually ate alone in her room, she had for the past few evenings come down to eat in the kitchen with Angela. It was cosy, just the two of them, even in the large, silent room, and Angela looked forward eagerly to it. Not tonight, though. She half expected that Miss Guy would not show up at all. She had not appeared during the afternoon to supervise her, nor had she joined them in the kitchen at four for a cup of tea. Which had been just as well, considering the icicle-forming atmosphere.

Angela warmed the food Mrs Cullingford had prepared. She was hesitating over setting out the cutlery when Miss Guy came in. Her fine features were grave, and, Angela thought, just a little flushed with embarrassment, though she seemed as poised as ever. 'I gather there was quite a scene here at lunch-time,' she said quietly.

Angela's blushes were altogether more evident. 'Oh – she told yer, did she? Little cow couldn' wait ter drop me in it, ah s'pose?'

'As a matter of fact, it was Mrs Cullingford who told me. Madge never said a word. Not that she needed to. I could see you'd left your mark on her.'

'Ah'm sorry,' Angela muttered, all at once choked with misery, and a feeling of hopelessness, 'but she – she was sayin' some – some rotten things. Ah just lost me temper with 'er. Ah'm sorry, miss.'

'You can't go round slapping people just because you don't like what they say.'

'You wouldn've liked it, miss!' Angela blurted, her eyes wide. Then she blushed crimson and hung her head, muttering like a child. 'Ah won' do it again, ah promise.'

There was the slightest pause, before Miss Guy's deep, soft voice went on. 'No, I don't suppose I would have liked it much. You're right.' She finished laying the table, then smiled across at Angie, whose blue eyes filled with tears at the beauty of that smile. 'Now. Look. See how I've set that table? That would be for the soup, that for the fish. Those at the top are for the sweet.'

They ate the simple meal, the comfort of their companionable chat settling over them. Then Miss Guy said rather suddenly, 'Oh, Master Tony's coming up for a couple of days tomorrow. On his own. You know his room? Give it a good clean first thing. And the bathroom at that end of the landing. I shouldn't think he'll get here before afternoon, but you never know.'

There was another hesitation. The rich tones were tuned to a careful neutrality when next she spoke. 'Master Tony's – well, he's twenty-one. You probably know a bit what young men are like. He can be a bit too, er, friendly, at times. Be polite of course, but be on the lookout. Let me know if he tries – if he upsets you in any way.'

Angela had to suppress a smile at the awkwardness of Miss Guy's manner. What she was trying to say was that he might get fresh with her. The idea quite excited her. It certainly didn't disturb her. A young toff chatting her up. She'd know how to handle him all right, make no mistake. The private smile faded at Miss Guy's next words, however.

'I've left those uniforms on your bed. Try them on and let me know if they don't fit. You can tell me in the morning. I don't think I'll bother listening to the news tonight. I'll have a really early night. After all, the Germans might arrive at any time. And somehow I don't think we'll need to listen to the news to find out about it.'

Angela's meeting with Tony Marston-Greene could hardly have been less formal. She was up early as usual and chatted to the cook over breakfast. Ruth and Madge did not start until eight o' clock, so she collected her cleaning things and headed for the first floor and Master Tony's room. She decided she would do the big, old-fashioned bathroom at the east end of the corridor first. Get the mucky job out of the way first, then she could concentrate on the bedroom, which shouldn't need much more than a swift dusting and freshening up. The bed was already made up.

She was into the high-ceilinged room, crossing the black and white tiles of the floor towards the high-sided, claw-footed bathtub, when a cheery voice called out behind her, 'Hello. You're new here, aren't you? And a helluvan improvement, if you don't mind my saying so. Good morning. I'm young Tony, by the way.'

She jumped and gasped with fright. Then stared goggle-eyed, too astounded to be embarrassed. There, sitting on the lavatory pedestal, striped pyjamas around his knees, lean bare thighs showing below flapping coat tails (she hastened to glance away lest she see anything else more interesting flapping) was a politely smiling, fair-haired young man. That much she took in before, face blazing beacon red, she averted her gaze and raced for the door. 'Hey, don't dash off,' the pleasant voice continued, astonishing her further. 'Not on my account, anyhow. You haven't introduced yourself.'

She stopped, holding the brass handle, half-way through, keeping her face turned away from him. 'Yer should've locked the door!' she squeaked, outraged.

His easy laugh floated after her as she pulled it to behind her. 'Mother always told us we should never lock bathroom doors,' he called out. 'What if we slip on the soap and break our necks?' But she was gone, hot-faced, fleeing down the corridor.

She almost collided with Miss Guy near the stairhead. 'I see you've met Master Tony,' the housekeeper observed drily, before she could speak. 'Apparently, he came back in the middle of the night. I must find out how on earth he got in. Probably through a window, knowing him. I didn't know anything about it until just now when I saw his bed had been slept in and found his clothes in a heap.'

As Angela gasped out brief, shocked details of the circumstances of their meeting, a smile tugged at the corners of Miss Guy's mouth. 'I told you he can be a little too familiar at times.'

Angela had several opportunities to further verify this statement during the next few days. He seemed to pop up disconcertingly wherever she was working, usually closely followed by a watchful Miss Guy, in front of whom Angela felt a guilty embarrassment. 'Ah don't encourage 'im, miss,' she asserted plaintively.

'I know, Angela. Better keep your door locked though, while he's home. He's not a bad young man really, but there *is* a war on.'

He told Angela he was hoping to go into the Navy. 'Just

waiting to hear from King Alfred. You might never see me again. We can't afford to be the way we were in peacetime. Things are happening too fast. You're absolutely captivating, you gorgeous little thing. Come on, just a kiss, eh? To carry with me into battle.'

He *did* grab one, and she pushed him away rather half heartedly. He was a good-looking lad, in a posh sort of way, and very jolly. There was no real harm in it, and she wouldn't let him take any real liberties. 'Ah'll tell Miss Guy,' she threatened, again half-heartedly.

He laughed. 'Old Pennifer? She's all right, really. Just needs a good man herself. No chance though, with gorgeous little you around to drive us wild.'

'Be'ave yerself! Pennifer?'

'Yes. You know. Penny for the Guy. I've called her that since she first came. Years ago. Now look, Angie. I'm perfectly serious. These are dangerous times we live in. What about it? Let's nip out for a drink somewhere tonight. I've got to go back down to London tomorrow. I know you won't last five minutes here. You'll be off to become a glamour puss in the Wrens or something. What do you say? Let's do like Old Winnie said yesterday and make this our finest hour. Yes?'

She didn't go, was gigglingly scandalized by the very idea of going out with such a toff. Yet all at once, when she thought about it, it didn't seem so wild after all. Times *were* changing, and anything could happen, any day.

He caught her next day, in the hallway, where she was lingeringly polishing, knowing he was about to depart, and hustled her through into the deserted library, where he clasped her tightly to his arms. She struggled, then gave up. 'All right,' she panted, primly turning her cheek. 'Anythin' for peace.'

'Perish the thought!' He pulled her face round; his mouth closed hard, searchingly over hers, teeth pressing, tongue searching, a raw, blazing embrace of passion. She broke gasping, breasts heaving, her lips smarting, unable to speak. He was grinning brightly, infuriatingly. 'That's more like it,' he preened. 'When you take your bath tonight, look up and think of me, my angel!' A light laugh and he was gone, leaving her gawping after him.

She remembered his words as she was in her tub, and

instinctively did as he had bidden. She squinted through the steam, then gasped. A square of paper was stuck by a drawing pin to the frame of the skylight window, just below the blackout blind. Dripping wet, she fetched the cork-tipped stool and stood, reaching up to retrieve it.

I'll always think of you this way, Angelic Angela. It will always be my favourite view of you, my sweet. You really should get these windows cleaned, though. I look forward so much to our getting acquainted. Don't go off and join the Wrens just yet. You'll drive all the sailors to despair. Till we meet again,
Yours, Tony.

She gasped, standing there, dripping, a hand to her mouth. She looked down at her gleaming body, gasped again and let out a shocked giggle. He couldn't have! How could he ... of course not! It was just his way of taking the micky, the cheeky thing. Miss Guy was right, he was quite a lad. Till we meet again, eh? Well, let's see, shall we, Master Tony?

The raid came only five days after Churchill's speech had hurled defiance at the might of the enemy poised across the Channel. Bombers from the Scandinavian 'dromes joined in, as a large force assembled to hit the north-eastern coastal targets, part of the softening-up process before the grand invasion itself. The siren went about 1 a.m., lifting people from sleep into a heart-racing reality of fear. Few people were blasé about this one. Everyone in the land was living in daily, if not hourly, dread of something like this.

The panic was not the first, but it was just as nerve-racking, as people grabbed at their clothing, and treasured possessions, and stumbled for dubious protection. This time the town did not escape. There were other, more famous, targets, to north and south. Several bombs were dumped on nearby fields by planes who had failed to find or even try for their original targets, but the sticks of high explosive that fell through the night, and landed on Sevastopol Street, and Inkerman Street were part of those intended to dispose of the steelworks, and they were not far away.

Most of the windows of The Street were blown out. Old Jonson and Peggy, hugging each other in the dark cubbyhole under the stairs, felt the rattling blast, and were sure their hour had come. Ellis, on duty, was lying in the mess of someone's back yard, pressed into the angle of the wall, his arms hooked over his helmeted head, screaming and sobbing wild obscenities, his version of fervent prayer. The folks packed into the long shelter felt the whole edifice quiver at the thud of the nearby bombs. An acrid dust billowed in through the vents and the doorway, along with a pungent smell that convinced many that they were in the midst of the dreaded gas attack, and they clawed on the rubber masks, creating a ripple of secondary panic.

Afterwards, they talked of it as something of a miracle that so few casualties had occurred. The vast majority of injuries were minor, caused by flying or broken glass. The inhabitants of the streets where the bombs had fallen were practically all in the communal shelter. One old lady was found dead, crouched in a chair in the usual cupboard under the stairs, which were intact among the rubble. There were no visible signs to account for her death, and it was established that she had suffered a heart attack.

The family who lived at the end of Inkerman Street, husband, wife and three children, were feared dead, for their house was a heaped pyramid of bricks and charred wood, the whole lot surrounded by shattered slates, which littered crunchingly the entire street. They had not bothered to go along to the shelter. But, in the early morning sunlight which filtered through the hanging dust and smoke, when the air-raid squad moved in to survey damage, they heard a faint but clear yelling, and began feverishly to pull and scrabble at the ruin with such enthusiasm that they almost threatened to do more damage than the bomb itself had achieved.

The family were there, all of them safe, including the baby. Black, filthy, scared nearly witless. The wife had a badly bruised back, for she had thrown herself over the baby, but even that had been caused by a heavy shelf full of boots and shoes and other odds and ends, put up by her husband in happier times, being shaken loose and falling across her. More than half the houses had been destroyed, and of the others many were not safe enough to move back in, but there was almost a festive air about the dazed survivors as they stood and gazed at the gaping dwellings, the jagged walls, the rooms opened up like stage sets, with faded, bug-marked wallpapers peeling off for all to see, pictures still hanging at crazy angles, floors tilting madly, with beds poised over cliff edges, chests of drawers teetering into space.

There was another fatality: a young lass in army overalls and tin hat was found at the corner of Sevastopol and Inkerman, right between where the two almost straight lines of bombs had fallen. Not a mark on her, she looked as if she was lying asleep, or drunk, except for the curious way her head was tipped back, and the fact that there were two symmetrical, thin, dark lines of dried blood running from each nostril, down to her cutely bowed upper lip, pushed forward slightly as though she were blowing a kiss.

The slender neck was broken. The helmet, designed to save life, had possibly caused her death. The canvas strap was still firmly fixed under her chin. In fact, the force of the blast had embedded it deep into the softness of her throat, and the heavy helmet had whipped her head back, snapping her like a dainty flower-stalk in the wind. Annie Bartlett would not see again that little, shabby house that she found she had missed so much.

Angela had fled down to the landing below as soon as the wail of the siren disturbed her. Miss Guy appeared, the torch illuminating her tall, slender figure. 'It's probably nothing,' she assured Angela, reaching out to hold her hand, 'but we'd better go down to the cellars just in case.'

They stepped out of the front door briefly, Angela deriving great comfort from the firm handclasp. Searchlights fingered across sections of the sky, reflecting prettily from the high, pale clouds. Suddenly the distant rhythmic thuds of the coastal batteries started up, grew barkingly louder as nearer guns took up the firing. The sky was lit up, flash after flash, like summer lightning, or fireworks. Then they heard the high drone of unseen planes. Angela shivered.

All at once, there were several deep, heavy thuds, hollow booms, which they fancied they could feel faintly beneath their feet, and there was a brighter flare of light from the south. It came clearly from the ground. Angela gave a soft cry of fear. 'That's the town,' she gasped. 'The' bombin' the town!'

'We'd better go in,' Miss Guy decided. She slipped her free hand around the slim waist. 'Come on.'

They waited, shivering in the lantern-lit coldness of the thick cellar, huddled together, sharing the rugs wrapped about their lower bodies. Angela liked the feel of Miss Guy's legs pressed innocently against hers, the feel of her arm about her shoulders. She leaned towards her, laying her cheek in the crook of Miss Guy's fragrant neck, cuddling in to her. Miss Guy responded by placing her hand on Angela's brow, and smoothing the golden hair, as though she were shushing a child to sleep. Angela's anxieties for her family, for herself, faded. She dozed happily in the protecting shelter of the warm embrace.

A lone Heinkel dropped its load blindly into the darkness as it roared thankfully westwards, picking up the shimmering sea. The bombs burst in the fields between the village and the shore. Dalby Hall rocked to the blast, but took it well. Some tiles were blown off the old stables, and two upper windows on that side of the house blew in. The explosions, coming when it seemed the danger had largely passed, though the all-clear had not sounded, terrified the villagers, and the two women who clung tightly together in the damp safety of the cellar, which trembled only slightly.

Angela closed her eyes tightly and buried her head in Miss Guy's breast. The long, narrow hands held the golden hair, pressed the shivering form just as tightly, as though she would with her own body save her. As Angela realized they were not about to die, she lifted her arms and wrapped them fiercely around Miss Guy's neck. ' 'old me!' she sobbed. ' 'old me tight!'

She pressed her face drowningly in the soft, fragrant swell of warm, trembling flesh, and felt the responsive shudder from the slim frame. 'There there,' Miss Guy crooned, her lips savouring the fine, clean-smelling hair. 'It's all right. I've got you.'

A long time later, they rose, determined not to break contact, and walked awkwardly, arm in arm, into the dim lamplight of the wide hallway, up the imposingly wide staircase to the upper floor. Miss Guy steered them towards her room, and Angela never faltered, her eyes clinging imploringly to the loving gaze of the woman who held her.

Sixteen

Elisha stood in the front row, where he had squirmed and wriggled and pushed to place himself. He saw the smartly turned out, well-drilled little squad raise their rifles, he jumped with the others in the big crowd when the shots cracked out, felt his skin crawl at the piercing, high notes of the single bugle. The flag-draped coffin disappeared. The flag was folded, carried smartly away. The wreaths were placed at the grave's edge.

Her father was doing his best to hide his grief. He looked big, far younger than Elisha had imagined he would be, younger than his own dad. He looked ill-at-ease in the dark suit, the tight collar and tie. He would drag it off as soon as he could, Eli was sure. Her mam was tall, as tall as her daughter, but she looked really old. There were lines all over her face, dark as if they had been drawn with pencil, though most of the time they were hidden behind a vast, clean, white handkerchief, and her shoulders shook with her weeping.

When the ceremony was over, Elisha couldn't leave. He edged near the grave, he felt compelled to say something to them. He got right close, cleared his throat. He was directly in front of them. The mother's washed-out eyes looked directly at him without seeing him. They were dull, lifeless, but they were brown, like Annie's, and suddenly his own eyes blurred and filled, his throat choked, and he turned and ran off, blindly, appalled at the sobs shaking him. 'I 'ope this bloody war lasts a year or two,' he wept as he ran, and couldn't outdistance the pain.

'The family's coming home for the weekend,' Miss Guy announced. 'I've just received Lady Agatha's letter. So we'd better get the place looking as spick and span as we can make it. Madge and Ruth. You two can make a start on the bedrooms right away. Do the windows. And take the curtains down and give them a good shake. Outside though, eh?' She turned towards Mrs Cullingford. 'We'll have to sort out a menu. They're staying up until Monday, at least. You can start in the breakfast-room, Angela.'

When the housekeeper had left the kitchen, Madge pulled a face at her companion. Angie saw the grimace, and pinked slightly. She chose to ignore it. She was coolly civil to the two youngsters, who spoke only when it was necessary to do so. The atmosphere was not good, and Angie knew that Mrs Cullingford was distinctly uncomfortable about it, though nothing further had been said about the fight. Angie wasn't sure whether the easy-going cook had heard anything of the conversation that had led to the attack. She guessed that she probably had, for she did not question her as to the reason for her onslaught, even when, after a few days, a measure of calm had been restored.

Angie was glad of that. She was still trying to sort out her own turmoil of emotions, the ambivalent feelings which were causing her so much pleasure, and pain, since the night of the air-raid. Following Miss Guy into her bedroom, Angie's heart had been thumping, her body trembling with fear – and anticipation. What if those awful things were true? What would she do if Miss Guy ... if Miss Guy what? She didn't even know the mechanics of what might happen. She only knew the remembered, special sweetness of that kiss, her own excitement, and tenderness as she lay there afterwards.

Miss Guy turned down the sheets on the narrow bed. 'Come on,' she said simply. 'Hop in. There's no need to be scared.'

'I'm not,' Angie stated, but her voice was unsteady.

She lay stiffly on her back, though it was impossible in the confined space not to touch Miss Guy, their bodies of necessity pressed together. 'Come on.' The deep tones were warm, with honest affection, as were the arms that were held out to enfold her, and Angie turned, with a little cry, to snuggle childlike into that wonderful, soft warmth, the fragrance that enveloped her in a thrilling gentleness.

Once more, her tear-wet face rested against the swell of

silken breast. She could feel the cool skin, the delicate scratch of lace, the caress of the satin, through which the nipple pushed enticingly against her very mouth, and sent a delightful quiver through her roused frame. 'Just lie still, my dear.' The soothing, whispered tones added to the delicious feeling of wellbeing in which she was cocooned.

When Angie woke, she could see the brightness of sunshine forming a halo around the heavy blackness of the curtains. Miss Guy's warm, bare legs were wrapped intimately about hers, the arms still held her. The dark head, the dark, dancing eyes, were within inches of her own, and, as she came fully awake, the face moved, and the lips planted a slow, gentle kiss on her proffered mouth. 'Thank goodness you're awake. Your snoring was driving me mad.'

Angie blushed in dismay. 'Ah don't, do ah?'

The arms tightened, and Miss Guy gave her a friendly shake. 'Only teasing. I could listen to you all night.' She bent forward, and they kissed again. This time it was an even longer embrace, their mouths held together until Angie's heart was racing. When Miss Guy released her, she was gulping for breath. 'Do you mind me kissing you like that?'

Angie blushed deeply. Her heart was hammering even more painfully. 'No,' she answered, in the faintest of whispers. 'Ah like it. It's nice.'

Miss Guy's hand caressed her cheek, moved down to the slender neck, her fingers traced the hollow of the delicate shoulder. 'You're very beautiful,' Miss Guy murmured. Her tone was not light. The dark eyes held Angie hypnotically. All at once, she was aware of the warmth of Miss Guy's body rubbing intimately against hers, moving with slow sensuality, their breasts and bellies and thighs, in contact. Angie shivered, could scarcely breathe. She could feel her secret, pulsing excitement, hunger for fulfilment, yet, strangely, she wanted this enchanting state, this sweetly tortuous suspension, to remain. Intuitively, she sensed the borderline on which they were caught.

She was aware of a keen disappointment when Miss Guy suddenly gave a tremulous half laugh, half sob, and thrust herself away from Angela, and violently swung her legs out of the bed. Angie stared at the supple back, exquisitely revealed under the sheer silk topped with the thin band of lace. Miss Guy spoke without turning to look at her. 'I could lie all day cuddling you. But we'd better see what those beastly Jerries have done. I'll see you downstairs in a quarter of an hour. It's only six. Mrs Cullingford won't be in for another hour and a half.'

Despite her embarrassment, Angie was determined to say something about the night. As they were cleaning up the glass in the corridor where the windows had blown in, Angie forced herself to speak. 'Thanks for lettin' me sleep with yer last night. Ah was that scared. An' – an' it was lovely. Ah felt – it was wonderful!'

Miss Guy was pink, and looked slightly less poised than normal, but Angie could tell she was pleased. And relieved. 'I'm glad you don't think I'm odd.' She laughed in embarrassed fashion. 'Well, I *am*, I suppose. But as long as *you* don't think I am.' The look on Angie's face was an eloquent response.

The following night, Angie lingered in the bath, and took great pains fixing her hair, brushing it out until it gleamed, before she pulled the dressing-gown over her short, cotton nightie, and went down to Miss Guy's room, for the ritual of cocoa and the news. She blushed as she wondered whether she would be returning before morning. She was startled to discover how hurt she was when, after the nine o'clock bulletin had finished, Miss Guy rose and merely fondled her cheek with a caressing palm. 'Let's hope we're not disturbed again tonight, eh? See you in the morning. Sleep well.'

She did not sleep at all well. She almost prayed for the dreaded wail of the siren to sound, so distraught was she. She lay tossing and turning, reliving the feel of Miss Guy's arms about her, her body folded on hers, until she was weeping with a scarcely understood hunger.

By Thursday, when Miss Guy made the announcement about the Marston-Greenes' homecoming at the weekend, Angie was suffering an emotional storm. Twice, she had risen, and almost plucked up courage to go down to Miss Guy's room in the night, though she couldn't think what to say. Surely there would be no need for words? She would simply fling herself in her arms, crying out her need for her. Then what? It was that thought, that fear that drove her back to her own lonely bed, and hours of haunted sleeplessness. She lashed herself furiously. 'It's you who's the queer one, Angie Thompson! You're sick, you are! Going soppy over a woman who's probably old enough to be your ma!' Oh, but she was so beautiful, and so loving, too.

That night, when Miss Guy moved to make that chastely affectionate gesture of goodnight, Angie blurted out abruptly, 'Don' yer like me any more?'

Miss Guy was colouring up, too, as she stopped, remained tensely still. 'What do you mean?'

'That – that night. In bed, Ah thought—' Angie choked, a sob rose, and escaped. The tears came quickly. She was desolate when Miss Guy did not hasten towards her, embrace her.

'Angela, why did you have that fight with Madge?' Miss Guy faced her bravely, the dark eyes holding their contact with her.

'She said some – some bad things. About you, miss. About how you – you liked girls.' Angie was crying freely now.

Miss Guy's voice was low, trembling. 'And if it were true? Can't you see why I—'

'Ah don't care!' Angie's voice was raw, with passion and sudden, clear longing. 'Ah want to – ah want yer to be like that. With me. Ah love you!'

All at once they were together, tears mingling, crushing one another, mouths searching, sealing each other's sobs. 'Oh, miss, miss!' Angie wept, clinging frantically.

'Helen. Please. Call me Helen. Oh God, Angela, my angel. Don't hate me, will you? Don't be shocked. Please. I love you so.' Abruptly, she released the weeping figure, stepped back. The dark eyes, shining with tears, compelled Angela to meet her intense gaze. There was a second of absolute immobility, then she reached forward, plucked at the sash around Angela's waist, drew the gown off the shoulders. As it fell about the girl's feet, the older woman bent, the brown eyes never leaving the blue, and, seizing the hem of the short nightdress, drew it slowly up over the golden hair, and off the raised arms. She bent again, and, as the limp body sagged towards her, picked it clear off the floor and bore it tenderly to the bed.

'You'll be fine. Just take your time. And don't be afraid to speak if they speak to you. Lady Agatha will probably want a word with you, anyway.' Angie took comfort from Helen's warm smile. She returned it tremulously, and nodded.

It was not quite the ordeal she had anticipated. In her white apron and cap, over the readjusted black dress, she looked rather fetching, she knew, blushingly aware of Master Tony's eyes following her as she moved around the table nervously in Miss Guy's wake, serving the vegetables from the heavy tureen.

'Angela, is it? We're very glad to have you here, my dear. We hope you'll be happy with us.' Sir Roger was tall, distinguished, with immaculately groomed, wavy grey hair. It was easy to see the resemblance between father and son. Lady Agatha was large, with pale, heavy arms and plump shoulders, but she, too, had all the impressive accoutrements of wealth and privilege. Her eyes, Angie felt, were sharper, more critical, than the males', who gazed on her with benevolent, disguised lechery, though, in Master Tony's case, the disguise was somewhat thin.

She had enough on her plate, at the moment, she reflected, to absorb the dramatic turn her young life had taken in the last two days, in her passionate involvement with Helen Guy. She was still dazed by it, powerfully disturbed by the recognition of how deeply her senses could be roused, how the physical skill of her lover could send her into a blazing oblivion of thought, a splendour of animal sensation that tore her apart, left her dizzy and shattered at the force of release she knew.

It terrified her, that power. It was the stuff of hottest, most private dreams, the consuming passion of imagination, translated into a truly frightening reality. Madge had used the word pervert. And she was, too, she guessed, to experience such total consummation of desire. And she was afraid, too, of Helen Guy, for holding that power. Afraid of her, and hopelessly, completely, in love with her. And somehow, although that word, pervert, echoed again and again in her confused brain, another part of her seemed incapable of accepting it as evil at all. It was so natural, so inevitable, that only a woman should know how to unlock that secret, ultimate passion in the depths, only that knowing tenderness could finally release it.

It was still harmlessly nice, though, to be conscious of Tony's attraction to her. She was not surprised when he waylaid her as she tidied up in the drawing-room after tea on the Saturday. 'Have you cleaned that window yet?' he teased.

She blushed with pleasure. 'You *were* kiddin', I 'ope,' she admonished, trying to look efficient and competent as she gathered the tea cups and plates together. 'Anyway, ye'd break yer neck out on the roof.'

'It was well worth it for a glimpse of heaven,' he intoned, and she blushed deeper, unsure again. 'Listen. I'm starting training at King Alfred's next month. Aren't you going to give me some happy memories to carry off to sea with me? How about if I pop up to tuck you in tonight? Give you a goodnight kiss and all that?'

'Aye, it's the "all that" ah'm worried about,' she answered drily. 'And don't you dare. Ye'll get me the sack, you will.'

He was genuinely surprised when she struggled vigorously to get out of his arms, her head turned to avoid his lips. 'What? Not even a kiss to keep me going? You were kinder last time—'

'An' that was a big mistake an' all,' she panted, blinking back the sudden threat of tears. Why had his larking about upset her like that? It was only a bit of daft carry-on. She could hardly understand herself. She tried to recover herself, and laughed unsteadily. 'Any road, the's plenty more. What about Madge and Ruth? 'Ave yer not seen them? Pretty young things, they are, both of 'em.'

He made a dismissive sound. 'Ha! Kids! And how can they compare with you, angel?' His voice softened, his good-looking features were serious all at once. 'I'm not kidding, Angela. You're a beauty, really. Why don't we meet tomorrow? You've got time off—'

'Ah can't!' she replied swiftly, genuinely flustered now. 'I 'ave gorra boyfriend, ye know. And 'e's been badly injured an' all. At Dunkirk. 'E's in 'ospital down south.' She stopped, deeply ashamed of herself at the deception. She felt worse at the look of contrition on his handsome face.

'I'm sorry. Of course, I didn't know. I'm truly sorry. Let me know if there's anything I can do.'

Well, at least it had got him off her back. She felt bad about it, though, especially as, for the rest of the weekend, he was courteous and sympathetic, and behaved with perfect politeness. What's more, he didn't treat her like a maid at all, and she wasn't in awe of him, as she was with his parents.

'Young Master Tony's sweet on you,' Helen said teasingly, on the Monday evening after the family's departure, when the two of them had the house to themselves again. 'I was livid with jealousy when I saw the way he was looking at you. And he's actually volunteered to come up and see how they get on with the damage repairs, and the ploughing up of the lower meadows. He's never been the slightest bit interested in what goes on here before. It's because of you, you young minx.'

Angie blushed with pleasure. Then she felt bad again at the way she had used Ginge to deceive him and play on his sympathy. And it had worked, too. He hadn't tried to grab her at all, not even before he left. He was a nice-looking lad, she had to admit. She carried their plates to the sink and rinsed them under the tap before running the hot water into the bowl. Miss Guy came up behind her, and slipped her arms about her waist. Her hands moved up to caress the soft breasts, and Angie sighed, and leaned back into her, offering her neck to those searching lips. 'It won't do 'im any good, will it?' she murmured provocatively. 'Not when ah'm – what was it yer said we are – lesbians, is it?'

' 'Ow yer doin', Arthur? Nice enough day, eh? Long as yer wrapped up well, kidder. Keep that blanket tucked round yer, there's a good lad.' Doris grinned at the pale figure sitting out on the pavement on a wooden kitchen chair. The grey blanket covered his lower limbs. As always, her eyes were drawn helplessly to the pinned back, empty sleeve of the old cardigan. The white, freckled face was covered with a fine ginger stubble. His mam said he still couldn't shave himself, his hand shook so much. Safely inside her door again, Doris shook her head.

Poor Ginge. Poor ould Ma Clay. They got on very well now. Mrs Clay often invited her in for a cup of tea on a morning. At first, when Ginge was in hospital down south, and then when he was moved up to Shotley Bridge, Doris had felt guilty at Ange's apparent sudden callousness, the way she seemed to avoid Ma Clay, to avoid the very subject of Ginge. Then Doris had realized that Ginge's mother didn't mind, was, in fact, relieved at Ange's indifference, just as she herself was, she had to admit, at least to herself. It would have been really tragic if Angie had gone on harbouring feelings for the poor lad, now that he was crippled, and out of his senses. She had no reason now to feel anger at what she had seen as Ma Clay's feeling of superiority which had made her disapprove of their young uns' association. A blessed relief all round that Ange had come to her senses, now that Ginge had lost his.

Nevertheless, Doris was still upset, and embarrassed, by her daughter's apparent coldness, especially as she knew just how close their relationship had been, brief though it was. The girl might at least make an effort to appear concerned, if only for decency's sake. She said as much, in an indirect way, to Mrs Clay, a few days after they brought Ginge home. Oddly enough, it was his mother who made excuses for Angie's behaviour. 'Prob'ly upset 'er too much te see 'im like this. She's on'y a bit of a bairn, still.'

Shame and resentment smouldered within Doris's thin chest. They hardly saw anything of her themselves now. They were lucky if she came home once a month. True, she still sent her bit of money regular, she'd give her that, but she seemed mighty reluctant to show up in The Street at all these days. Getting too many big ideas, hanging about those fancy folk and that posh house. Silk knickers and dressing-gowns! What did they want to be giving her things like that for? Putting too many high-falutin' notions in her head for her own good. They'd even noticed she was talking different last time she was home. All correct and toffee-nosed. Too big for her boots, the little madam. Well, she'd have a hard job avoiding poor Ginge next time. He sat out there all day, staring into space, his face all screwed up and worried like. Like he was trying to remember something.

That door. Ginge gazed across the road at it for hours, observing every detail of the flaking paint, the grime-encrusted letter-box and knocker. There was something. Something special he was waiting for, but he couldn't remember. He knew Doris came out of there. And that blond lad. Something about him, too, the golden hair, but he couldn't think what it was. He liked Doris. He liked the way she was always cheerful, the fag bobbing at her lip. He always smiled at her. He liked cigarettes. He was always happy when his mam brought him the five

Woodbines, let him keep them in his pocket. She wouldn't give him matches, though.

She still cried sometimes, and that made him feel bad, because he knew somehow that he was to blame, though he couldn't tell her. He didn't talk much at all, just the odd word, never a sentence, except in his head, where he talked all the time. Odd things, too, things he couldn't understand. His own voice shouting out. 'Janner bastard'. What did it mean? He cried, too, like his mam. He'd wake up at night, sobbing, after his dream of the water, and then his arm would ache, the arm that was only a stump, and he'd weep, wondering why it had gone. And then there were the times when he forgot, and wet himself, and his mam would have to change him. He felt so bad then.

But that door. He had to sit here and wait. When the weather turned wet and autumnal, at the end of the September that forestalled any lingering German hopes of an invasion of England, and Ginge had to move inside, he protested loudly and hopelessly, then had to spend much of his day standing at the front-room window, uncomfortably staring through the curtains to the houses opposite. There was something, someone. He didn't know who, or what, only that he had to keep watching.

There was a respite after that July raid, though in the glorious summer skies further south, the battle for Britain was being well and truly engaged. Towards the end of August, the sirens began to sound regularly again, not long after darkness fell usually, as waves of bombers passed high overhead to their targets further inland, or across to Merseyside. During the last week of the month, came the terrifying devastation of Coventry, then three heavy raids on Liverpool. The north-eastern coastal defences had been greatly reinforced, and the bark of the Ack-Ack guns was almost as alarming as the sound of enemy bombs, until folks learned to tell the difference.

Broken sleep, the somnambulistic shuffle to shelter, or to the cupboard under the stairs, became a way of life; then the trudging return journey to a chilly bed, just before dawn, for the all-clear never sounded until the raiders had passed over once again on their way home. People adjusted rapidly. Those fortunate enough to possess their own shelters made more positive efforts to improve their comfort, installing bunk beds, some form of heating, and even cooking facilities. Many turned them into permanent bedrooms, not waiting for the wail of the siren to rouse them, but retiring to rest down garden paths, where they remained like moles until morning.

A few families of The Street made similar claims on staked-out portions of the public shelter beside the school, but most laid out mattresses in the cramped confines of the 'neath stairs cupboards. After all, they had their living proof of the effectiveness of such simple protection in the family from Inkerman Street, who had survived the town's baptism of fire. The gaping ruins still stood forlornly, roped off – not that that deterred the likes of Little Jimmy and his cronies from playing in the heaped rubble – and people took heart from the amazingly low number of casualties from that night.

'An' yer know that lass that was killed – the one wi' 'er neck broke?' the Sea Coal Man informed his family knowledgeably, after listening to the lunch-time gossip in the Pothouse. 'The' reckon it mightn't 'ave been a bomb at all. Could've bin the blast from that bloody mobile gun thing the' was towin' round. It was that that blew our winders in an' all, ah reckon. Useless effin' things! Oy! What's up wi' ye?' he shouted after the rapidly retreating Elisha. 'Got the trots, 'ave ye?'

A lot of folks envied the Fosters, with their nice, thick-walled cellar to retreat to. 'Should reelly open it up fer folk,' Ellis grumbled feelingly, though he did not venture to voice this opinion in Flo's presence.

'Bloody right an' all!' Sea Coal agreed, his imagination dwelling tenderly on the thought of being ensconced every night with all those barrels of ale – and a scantily clad Flo Foster to boot.

Angie came home on the Saturday at the end of the first week of September. It was a month since her last visit, and she was dreading it. She wrote regularly when she sent her money every week, and received rambling, scrawled replies from her mam, giving her the news of The Street, and, particularly lately, criticizing her for her heartlessness towards Ginge. She knew that he had been brought home recently.

'*Even if you dont want to see him,*' Doris wrote, '*you can at leest get yourself home to see your famly.*'

'I'll have to go,' Angie muttered gloomily, lying back in Helen's arms. 'It's a month now. But I 'ate it, ah reelly do!'

'Hate,' Helen corrected, leaning forward to kiss the pouting lips. 'And that's a wicked thing to say. You must go. You can have Saturday off. Come back Sunday night.'

She got off the local bus at Park Road, carrying the small, neat, overnight case Helen had lent her, feeling more and more conspicuous the nearer she came to The Street. Everything she was wearing, from her skin outward, had been provided by Miss Guy, who had insisted Angie be furnished with a complete new wardrobe. 'We'll call it a loan, then. You can pay me back at so much a week. I'll deduct it from your salary.'

That was just to make the embarrassed girl feel better, she knew. Her protests had been genuine, but not strong enough to withstand the older woman's determination, and her own youthful delight in the possession of so many wonderful things. They weren't all new. Helen had altered two of her own dresses, shortening them, and taking them in a little, and given her some silk underwear, nightdresses, and several pairs of fine stockings, whose tops she had to turn over and over to make them fit, for Helen was taller by half a head. The fact that they belonged to Helen only made them all the more special to Angie. They had managed to find some smart, new, heeled shoes, as well as more serviceable ones for working, and, even though the weather that Saturday morning was still bright and summery, Angie could not resist wearing the long, narrow-waisted grey overcoat, and the matching, wide-brimmed felt hat, which she pulled down elegantly over one eyebrow, and under which she carefully tucked her golden hair, pinned up now in a sophisticated and grown-up style which Helen showed her, and warmly declared was 'a knock out'.

Those who were out and about when Angie turned into Sutherland Street did not recognize the slim, well-groomed figure, and were startled when she greeted them. She saw the huddled, seated shape across the cobbled roadway, and felt her stomach lurch as she recognized the blazing ginger thatch. Ellis's Peggy came out from next door, exclaiming in wondrous delight, 'Eeh, Ange! Ye look marvellous! Like one o' them districk nurses in that outfit. 'Ow yer doin' then? 'Aven' seen yer fer ages!'

Her own door opened, and out tumbled Little Jimmy, followed by Terence, then Doris, and they swarmed round her, pulling and hugging, equally impressed with her transformed appearance. She glanced across at the figure opposite, distracted and apprehensive. 'Ah'll just go and say 'ello,' she muttered. 'Best get it over with.'

'Aye, go on, luv,' Doris encouraged, a hand pushing at her back to assist her. Her mam followed her, cigarette bobbing as ever. 'Look who's 'ere!' she called, with exaggerated cheerfulness. 'It's our Angie! Come ter say 'ello!'

Angela stood awkwardly in front of him, taking in the horror of the pinned-back sleeve. She noted the shadowy pouches under the faded eyes, the red stubble covering the paleness, the shabby dreariness of the collarless shirt open at the neck, the tatty cardigan carelessly misbuttoned. All at once, her eyes were drawn to the tight, bulging crotch of the old, wrinkled, grey trousers, flaked with cigarette ash, darkened with other stains, and she relived, in clarified horror, the sensation of their fierce coupling, his flesh in hers, the feel of it. She thought of the dawn awakening just a few hours previously, and Helen's touch on that same abandoned flesh, the smooth softness of their embraces, the wonderful consummation of their desire.

Her face burned. 'Hello, Ginge. It's good to see you. How are you?'

'Give 'im a kiss, fer God's sake!' Doris said heartily, with a hoarse, forced laugh, and Angie bent swiftly, and put her lips to his stubbly cheek. She straightened, tugging down the brim of her hat again.

He stared up at her in wonder, entranced at the unfamiliar fragrance that briefly enveloped him, the cool, light touch of those lips, and he wondered who she was. He was a little afraid. Was she one of the nurses? He was worried by people he didn't know, and he shuffled, turning round apprehensively to look for his mam. Who, to his great relief, made her appearance right at that instant, and came to lay her heavy, comforting hand on his shoulder, for which he reached with his own, happily reassured.

'By gum, lass, ah didn' recognize yer. Yer quite the young

lady now, isn' she?' In her hypersensitive mood, Angela was aware still of the hidden challenge, the concealed aggression in the friendly tones. She was glad to make her escape.

'Well, let's get in. What a journey! Ye never know where y'are with the buses these days. Tara. See yer later, Ginge.'

Inside the claustrophobic poverty of her home, she felt the tears welling dangerously close to the surface. 'See? Ah told yer, Mam. You goin' on an' on about me not botherin'. 'E doesn' even know us. Does 'e?'

Doris stifled the ready, caustic retort that sprang to mind. 'Aye, well. Never mind that now. Let's 'ave a look at ye. My God! Aren't you the one, eh?' She whistled appreciatively as Angie took off her hat, and the elegant coat, to reveal the flowered summer dress beneath. 'Where on earth did ye get all this from?'

Blushingly, Angie explained. 'You 'ave ter look smart. Even off duty, Mam. Miss Guy give us a loan. Ah'm payin' it back at so much a week.' She turned about slowly, enjoying the awed gaze of her young brothers. 'What d'yer reckon to me 'air like this?'

Her pleasure in their admiration was fleeting, though. Ashamed of herself though she was, she could not prevent herself from being appalled at the familiar squalor surrounding her. After three months away from The Street, she felt totally alienated from the environs she had grown up in. And, worse, from her own family.

Elisha came in, black as a sweep, at lunch-time. He had started work at the shipyard as soon as he had left the school and Bruiser for good in July. She had expected some fierce ragging from him at her changed appearance, her new clothes, but he was brusque and taciturn, almost embarrassed in her presence.

He was followed shortly by his father, in a similarly grimy condition, for he, too, had finished a half-day at Stewart's. The Sea Coal Man had plenty to say, however, largely uncomplimentary, though he acknowledged privately to himself that Angie had turned out a 'reet smashin' little piece' – and no mistake. ''Bout time yer got yesel' home te see us,' he grumbled. 'Gettin' too big fer yer boots wi' them fancy toffs ye run around after, ah reckon.'

There was recognition of her changed status, though, when Doris said, later in the afternoon, while the Sea Coal Man was still sleeping off the lunch-time session, 'Ye'll come round ter the Pot'ouse fer a drink, eh, pet?' It was a novelty to sit in the varnished, uncomfortable gloom of the Best Room, with the wives, hardly any of whom were under forty, and Angie couldn't help relishing being the centre of attention as she described her workplace and new home, and told them tales of the Marston-Greene family.

She made her excuses after a while, and returned home. Elisha was out somewhere. She played happily with Little Jimmy, but the sight of Terence's vacant grin, his slack, saliva-dribbling lips, and the sound of his braying laugh, disturbed her, forcing her to recall the pale figure she had encountered planted solidly across the street. It made the intimacy they had shared seem all the more incredible. The one man, no, boy, she painfully corrected herself, she had given herself to. And now, after all that, he no longer even remembered her. Of course, it was his terrible injury, she knew that, but, surely some spark should remain, something to stir a dim memory, a shadowy fragment, of the times they had been together? She winced inwardly at the painful admission she was forced to make of her gladness that that time was dead. For both of them, she vowed.

Seventeen

The day that Angie travelled home for her weekend visit marked the real beginning of the London blitz. Masses of bombers appeared in the still bright late afternoon, and dropped tons of incendiaries on the East End, lighting fires which acted as beacons for the later waves of planes coming over after darkness fell. Angie knew nothing of this until Helen Guy told her on the Sunday evening, when she arrived thankfully back at Dalby Hall.

'I've missed you so much, angel, even for one night.' Helen clasped her tightly to her, and they kissed passionately.

'Me too. It's awful, but ah – I felt so – out of place. It was all—.' She shrugged hopelessly, the tears shining in her eyes. 'All so horrible. Shabby like.'

Later, sharing their cocoa, propped easily side by side in Helen's narrow bed, Angie went on with her confessional. 'An' yer should've seen me mam's face when ah said ah'd sleep downstairs, in the chair. Me dad as well. I mean, look at me.' She glanced down at her graceful bosom, attractively contoured in the pink satin. 'I'm seventeen, for God's sake. And our Eli's fifteen. He's workin' now at the shipyard. And they honestly couldn't see anythin' wrong with me sleepin' in the same bed with 'im – him. I'm not wicked, Helen, am I? But the' just seem – so—' She shrugged again, defeated. 'I dunno.' She swallowed back the threatening tears. Helen slipped an arm around the thin, bare shoulders, and nuzzled the fragrant ear.

'Shush, my love. Don't upset yourself.' Her voice deepened, grew thick and rich with sensuality. Her other hand moved, slowly, under the covers, and Angela gasped, shivered. 'You belong to me now. And I've got you back again. That's it. Lie

211

down, sweet. Let me show you how much I love you.'

They began to retire earlier each evening, as the air-raid warnings became a nightly feature in their lives. Miss Guy had two camp beds set up in a corner of the large cellars, and with rugs and odd pieces of furniture created a cosier atmosphere, despite the chilly, somewhat cavernous gloom of their sur- roundings. The chastely separated beds were for form's sake. Each night, they pulled the mattresses off the beds and, fitting them side by side, made a love nest of the sheets and blankets, though, often, they did no more than lie companionably in one another's arms, sated by their earlier activity. One early evening, as soon as Mrs Cullingford had departed, Helen caught hold of Angie's hand, and, with a low chuckle and the ghost of a wink, murmured, 'We really ought to do something about saving water, angel. Why don't you share my bath, tonight?' Thus she added a new and exciting dimension to their physical passion.

Angie felt secretly ashamed that her life should be so idyllic, when so many terrible things were happening in the world. Buckingham Palace itself was bombed, and people were inspired by the pictures in the papers and the newsreels of the King and Queen bravely sticking it out in London, and visiting the worst hit areas and the homeless they produced. The summer weather broke into a wet autumn, the nights length- ened, but there was no relief from the sirens. In the middle of November, Coventry suffered its own blitzkrieg, then Birming- ham a few nights later.

Angela went home less and less frequently, claiming that the demands of her employers were too strenuous to allow her more time off. Helen released her on a weekday now, so that she could catch the earliest bus from Dalby in the morning, and return in the late evening, thus avoiding the awkwardness of the sleeping arrangements, or, rather, the lack of them, at home. The family were glad of her visits, for she came laden with gifts. Cuts of meat, fresh eggs, butter, all provided from the Dalby Hall larder. The Sea Coal Man was his usual ungracious self. 'Those toffs can afford it,' he growled, as Doris enthusiastically showed him these acquisitions. 'Ye'll soon be too grand fer us altogether,' he said accusingly to his daughter. 'Ye startin' te sound like them toffee-nosed gets. It'll cost us a tanner te talk te yer.'

'Tek no notice of 'im, pet,' Doris told her. ' 'E's on'y jealous.'

Privately, she was beginning to wonder herself. It was true that Ange was transformed. Not just the nice clothes, the silk stockings she wore. Her look was different, as well as her speech. More refined. She was a proper young lady now. Doris knew she should be pleased for her, *was* pleased, definitely. Yet it hurt, this feeling that she was losing her, even though she had always dreamt of Angie somehow escaping the drudgery she had always known. The girl was totally besotted with this Miss Guy. Helen. She went on and on, Helen this, Miss Guy that, Helen says this, Miss Guy does that. Still, if this was what the woman was doing for her, it must be for the best. It hurt though, to think that there might be some truth in Harry's denunciation that 'we're not good enough for her'.

Angie was glad that Ginge was no longer parked out there on the pavement on her infrequent trips home. She didn't volunteer to go across to see him, and Doris didn't suggest it, though she continued to mention his unchangingly helpless state in her weekly letters to the Hall. Angie preferred these visits during the week, for it meant that she spent most of the day alone with her mam, apart from the baby and Terence. The Sea Coal Man was at work, and Eli, too. Mother and daughter could talk more easily, over endless cups of tea, the air thick with the blue Woodbine fug. 'No lads on the scene then?' Doris asked teasingly, and Angie blushed.

'Nay. Ah've not spoken to a lad since – oh, ah dunno when. No time fer that. Ah never get out of the house hardly.' She wondered what on earth her mam would say if she knew the truth. She writhed inwardly at the thought. Her mother probably didn't even know such things could happen. Most of the time, she tried not to think about what she was doing. When she was with Helen, it all seemed so wonderful. And right, too. And Helen could talk so beautifully, make it all seem so good, and natural.

Alone, Angie tried to convince herself, as Helen could, but sometimes it was not easy. She would hear again the sniggers of the two youngsters, Madge's scornful classification of 'pervert'. She strove not to let it bother her, and, most of the time, with Helen's tender help, it didn't. And, even if it were true that she were perverted, there was absolutely nothing she could do about it, for the very notion of life without Helen's protective loving did not bear contemplation.

The war's second Christmas was a much more muted affair
than its predecessor. The nightly bombing raids seemed to
have been there for ever, the shortages were well and truly
biting, especially of those extra, luxury items that were part of
the festive season. Families were forced to use their skill and
ingenuity to make Santa's visit as magical as ever. Fathers vied
with one another to make the best wooden models of Spitfires
and Hurricanes and Blenheims; mothers worked on rag dolls,
and rejuvenated old teddy bears. Work, too, went on
desperately, in shipyard, and factory, and steelworks. Work
that even Ellis dared not shirk too blatantly. Better the
discomfort of long shifts and the pay packet that went with
them than the dread spectre of military service, though, as he
frequently grumblingly complained, on those nights when
ARP duties robbed him of precious and few hours of freedom,
'Them lads out in the desert 'aven' gorrit a patch on us, man.
Bloody sun and sand an' on'y a bunch of Eyeties against them.
Don' know the' born.'
   'Ya, bet you can't vait, hey? Any day now dat envelope
comin'.' And Old Jonson would chuckle wickedly.
   But to Angie, it was the most exciting Christmas she had ever
known. The family came home briefly for the holidays, and the
huge house was filled with guests. Though she worked hard,
she revelled in the sense of fun, felt a part of it, even though
she stood in cap and apron attending to their wants. She tried
to make a friendlier approach to Madge and Ruth, who were
pressed in for longer hours than normal, to cope with the
greatly increased workload.
   'You want to watch out for Master Tony,' she laughingly
warned the vivacious Madge, as they worked side by side in
the kitchen. 'He's a real devil. He's carrying his own mistletoe
round with him.'
   'Yeah, ah know,' Madge answered, then added, with daring
cattiness, 'still, won' worry you, though, eh?'
   Angela blushed, and felt the hurt deeply. But she said
nothing, let it go, and Madge sniggered spitefully, and felt
pleased with herself at scoring so tellingly. Should've clocked
her one, Angie told herself afterwards, smarting with anger

and shame. The old Angie would not have hesitated to do so, she recognized. But she was very different now, she acknowledged. Softer, quieter, ready to learn, ready to observe. Perhaps, she reflected painfully, too ready to be passive, to accept. Helen's 'little angel'. Maybe she needed a bit more of the old devil in her.

It was this disturbing thought that caused her to allow Tony Marston-Greene to catch her in the draughty first-floor corridor on Boxing Night, when she had gone up to put the gas fires on in the bedrooms, and slip the hot-water bottles under the sheets. She wasn't surprised at his silent appearance in the gloom, nor at the arms that came with only half-playful determination around her waist. 'Now, Master Tony, behave yerself,' she smilingly admonished, keeping her voice low. 'Yer a bit squiffy, ah can see.'

'Drunk only with passion for you, Angela!' he declaimed, grinning. But his hold tightened. She could feel his body touching hers, and she leaned back slightly against his restraint. 'A Yuletide kiss. That's all. Come on. Be a sport.'

'What about that Miss Barbara?' she asked teasingly. 'She's the one yer should be grabbin' by the looks of things.'

'She's the one who'll be grabbing me if I don't watch out.' He grimaced. 'She's not a patch on you, my love. That's the trouble. No one is. Oh, Angie, sweetheart, I'm serious. Can't we get together? Properly? I've got to go back on Sunday. And we'll get our postings. Most likely bloody convoy duties on some old tub. Have mercy, angel.'

She had sufficient mercy, or doubt engendered by her brief exchange with young Madge, to let him bundle her into his own room way down the corridor, and there to let him kiss her rawly, roughly, on the mouth, as he had once done several months before. He was drunk, she could smell and taste the alcohol on him, but that didn't bother her. The pure, physical passion, his desire, wasn't faked, and the excitement transferred itself, electrically, to her, when his hand came up to fondle, then squeeze, her breast, and his other slid to press furiously at her rounded haunch.

She fought strongly, after long, melting seconds, wriggling and thrusting herself free of him, gasping for air, staring wide eyed, startled more by her own reaction to the embrace. 'Pack it in!'

She saw the shame, the embarrassment, flooding over him again, his stammered apology made her feel even worse for her behaviour. She managed a shaky little laugh. 'Hey, it's all right. No harm done. But ah don' like bein' mauled, yer know. It doesn't mean anythin', does it? Ye'll be off on Sunday – and then – oh well. Merry Christmas, Master Tony.' She skipped round him, making a wide detour in case he grabbed again.

'Stop that "master" shit!' he answered, almost savagely. His face was serious. He didn't seem so drunk now. 'I'm not just an animal, you know. You're beautiful. But I'm not just trying – I wasn't – hell! I just want to get to know you.'

The encounter left her shaken a little, and feeling insecure. She found herself wishing that he and the rest of the family would depart, leave her with Helen in the sweetly exclusive sanctum they had made for each other, in the long hours when no one else existed. And yet part of her, a disturbingly elemental part at that, was powerfully stirred by Tony's attraction for her, even contemplated treacherously what it would be like to grant him his wish, and let him 'get to know' her. Pretty difficult, when she didn't even know herself!

She asked Helen, with a great deal of curiosity, about her family, when the opportunity arose. While the Marston-Greenes were home, she and Helen did not sleep together, but there was nothing wrong with sharing their night-time drink, however late it might be. Although Helen had offered to give Angie some time off during the holiday period, she had declined, agreeing to take a free day the following Tuesday, when everyone would have gone once more. It was no great sacrifice, as Helen well knew. 'You must go home,' the housekeeper insisted fondly. 'They'll think we're all ogres here, keeping you from them at this time of year.'

'Isn't there anyone *you* want to see?' Angie asked.

Helen shook her head, gave a little smile that made Angie want to fling herself at her and hug her tightly. 'No. My parents are both dead. There's a sister – she's married with two children. They live near Chester. But we don't get on too well.' She hesitated, her low voice took on a confessional touch. 'She thinks I'm odd. She knows I'm not – not interested in men. She can't understand.' She glanced at Angie, who saw the mute appeal, the tenderness, and pain, too, in those dark eyes, and this time the girl did rise and hurry to her, standing over the seated figure, and pulling the dark head into her soft bosom, holding her tightly.

'Who cares?' Angie whispered bravely. 'Who the 'ell cares? None of 'em understand, do they?'

But the small voice echoed naggingly in her mind, as she thought of Tony's mouth on hers. Do you? Do you?

She walked into a major crisis in the Thompson household that engulfed her as she stepped into the gloom of the tiny lobby. ' 'Ere! P'raps yer posh sister can talk some sense inta yer!' And Merry Christmas to you, too, Father, she thought disgustedly, putting down the small case full of carefully wrapped presents and supplements from the Dalby larder.

Elisha was sitting at the newspaper-covered table on which the breakfast mugs and plates were still littered. He had that glowering, sunken, mutinous look she knew so well. Her heart went out to its childishness, she almost welcomed it, for it was a reminder of the brother she had known, rather than the dirt-encrusted, taciturn stranger he had become.

He had apparently been to the Royal Navy recruiting office and expressed his desire to sign on in the Senior Service as a boy entrant. This of course required the written consent of both his parents, which they were steadfastly refusing to give, the Sea Coal Man rather more steadfastly than Doris.

'Ye daft bugger!' his father exclaimed, not for the first time. 'Ye've landed yersel' a job in the yard! Ye can be there fer the duration. Good money an' all.' He shook his head despairingly.

'It'll be years afore ah mek owt,' Elisha argued mulishly. 'Any road ah'll get me call up. The'll not tek me on as apprentice. Ah can gerra trade in the Navy. Ah'll go in as a stoker—'

'Shovelin' bloody coal down the boiler room! What kinda trade is that?'

'Don' be daft!' Elisha retorted scornfully. 'That went out years ago! Therall oil burnin' now. Ah'll be an engineer.'

'Don't tek that tone wi' me, ye cheeky young bugger! Ah'll tek me belt off ter ye, ah will!'

Angela suppressed a groan. The traditional solution to all life's problems. 'Well, welcome home, Angie! Merry Christmas, folks! Nice te see yer all again!' Her sarcastic tones defused the situation, at least for the time being, and she successfully diverted them by opening her case to distribute her gifts.

Her dad was on the two-till-ten shift, which necessitated his going round to the Pothouse at opening time, in order to get 'a few gills in' to sustain him through the long hours ahead. Eli was off 'sick' because he refused to go back to work, insisting that he was finished with the shipyard. Angela used the excuse of having to run an errand in town for Miss Guy to get him out of the house with her.

He trudged morosely at her side. 'If the' don't sign that form,' he threatened, 'ah'll bugger off anyway. Ah know ah could gerra job on one o' the drifters. Then ah can gerron a bigger, ocean-going boat, once ah've got some sea time in.'

Angie knew it was useless to argue with him. Not that she wanted to. She understood too well his desire, his need, to get away. 'Ah can understand them bein' worried,' she said. 'Ah mean. It *is* dangerous like, isn't it?'

He shook his blond thatch impatiently. 'Ev'rywhere's dangerous nowadays. An' it's not as dangerous as the Army 'ull be. An' the's prospecks. For after. Any road, ah wanna go!' he ended sullenly. She felt a smile tugging at the corners of her mouth.

'Well, that's it then, eh? What Eli wants....'

But she spoke earnestly to her mother, persuading her of Elisha's determination to leave home, and using his own arguments. And Doris listened. Whatever doubts she might have about the dramatic changes she could see in her daughter's attitude and behaviour, she knew the girl was bright, and was getting somewhere.

Doris knew a thing or two, as well. She waited until the following morning, when Little Jimmy and Terence could look after the Baby, and she carried two cups of tea up to where the Sea Coal Man was having his well-earned 'lie-in', being on the late shift. She was wearing her old mac, but Harry's eyes lit up when she slipped it off and climbed back under the covers beside him. That lunch-time, grunting sardonically, he signed the consent forms, and an ecstatic Elisha raced down to the recruiting office, yet another who would endorse the soubriquet 'angel' when applied to his older sister.

*   *   *

Sam the Fish Shop's heart gave a strange lurch, a little flutter that so alarmed him he actually pressed a hand momentarily to his chest, and leaned against the steamy white tiles. His red face glowed, he opened his mouth, sucked in a little gulp of air. ' 'Ow do, Sam, ev'rythin' all right, eh?'

It was simply the uniform, of course, he realized, as he sternly upbraided himself for his foolishness, but the jaunty upright young figure in the sailor's tight jumper and flaring bells, the cockily tilted round cap, had shaken him so, it was quite a while before Sam could pull himself together and recognize the wide grin of young Eli Thompson, proud as a peacock of his exotic square-rig outfit.

He was already exchanging exuberant greetings with the women in the queue, enjoying their ribald badinage. 'Aye, finished me trainin' at Guz now – Devonport,' he explained to the uninitiated, who were none the wiser. 'Junior Mechanical Engineer,' he informed them proudly. 'Be drafted when ah go back after leave. Off ter sea like.'

He was anxious to see Angie, to let her see him in his smart uniform. He had only been home once during the twelve week training period, and had missed her. 'We've 'ardly seen 'er ourselves, son,' his mam grumbled feelingly. 'Proper toff she is, now. Should 'ear the way she talks an' all. Big words like a bloody dictionary. Readin' all the time. That woman's turnin' 'er into a real lady. Ah just 'ope she doesn' get too many jumped up ideas, that's all.'

'Ah think ah'll pop up ter Dalby temorrer,' Elisha announced eagerly. 'Give 'er a bit of a surprise like.'

'Eeh, ah dunno,' Doris answered uncertainly. 'She might be a bit funny 'bout yer jus' turnin' up like that.'

'Naw,' Elisha grinned. 'She'll be pleased as punch ah bet.'

He was not quite so confident, however, as he walked up the long curve of the drive to Dalby Hall. Still, she must be allowed some time off, and a brother home from the war would surely not be frowned upon, even by the toffs. He was careful, though, to make his way round the side of the house, past the vegetable plot, to the back entrance. He recognized the pretty, dark-haired girl who was working at the sink. She stared saucer-eyed at the apparition of this fresh-faced young sailor standing on the threshold. 'Hiya. Is our Angie in? Ah'm 'er brother, Eli. Remember?'

Madge blushed. 'Oh, aye. Yes. Sure. Ah'll go an' tell 'er.' She giggled and fled, Elisha gazing approvingly at her retreating back. Not bad at all, that one. Have to see if I can't chat her up. Find out when her day off is.

Angie appeared, wearing a blue smock, her pinned-up hair hidden under a scarf of the same colour. Her face was flushed, and screwed up with worry. 'What's wrong?' she panted.

Elisha grinned at her, twirled his cap towards her. 'Nowt. Ah just wanted ter see yer, that's all. 'Aven't seen yer since Christmas. When are ye off?'

She gave him a belated hug, embarrassed under Madge's keen scrutiny, and Mrs Cullingford's interest. 'You daft lump. You terrified the life out of me. I thought something was wrong at home or something. Come on in.'

Elisha was happy to be left in the kitchen, chatting to the giggling Madge, and sipping a mug of tea, while Angie swiftly finished what she was doing and sought Helen's permission to take her brother up to her room. Miss Guy met them as the couple came up to the first floor, heading for the narrower stairs that led to the upper storeys. 'I'm glad to see you again,' she said warmly, holding out her hand to Elisha. 'Under happier circumstances this time, I'm pleased to hear. You can take the rest of the day off, Angela. It's the least we can do for the Senior Service.'

'She seems a canny soul,' Elisha observed generously when they were in Angie's room under the roof. He tossed his gold-ribboned cap on to the bed, and looked around appreciatively. 'Ye've got it cushy 'ere, though, mind. Yer own lav an' bathroom an' all. No wonder ye never come 'ome, our Ange.'

Angie unbuttoned the smock. She stood in front of the mirror and pulled off the headscarf, patting the golden locks, some of which had come loose from the pins. She grimaced at her own reflection. 'Huh! Mam been going on again about me, has she?' She began to unfasten her black dress, then paused self-consciously. She took her dressing-gown from its hook and moved into the bathroom before taking off her dress, though she left the door half open. 'It's true. Ah don't get home that much, these days.' Her voice was defensive, as though expecting some argument.

'Hey, it's okeydoke by me, kidder. Ah wouldn't come 'ome much either if I 'ad all this.' He chuckled. 'Mind you, it's funny. I actually missed the old place at first when ah was at Raleigh. Fifty of us slingin' our micks in one mess, sharin' the 'eads an' that. Ah was quite 'omesick fer a while.'

'Oh, Eli.' She came and sat by him on the bed, and put her hand on his arm. 'Yer not sorry, are ye?'

'What?' He shook his head decisively. 'No way! It'll be great now that basic trainin's done. Ah can't wait ter see what ship ah get. Prob'ly be one o' the bigguns, the' reckon. Juniors don' get small ships. Not stokers any road. Get some sea time in, eh?' He laughed again, and she joined in, warmed by his enthusiasm.

'Yer can 'ave a bath if you like,' she told him. 'There's hot water whenever ah want it.' She lit the geyser and ran the bath for him.

'Aren't ye gonna scrub me back for me?' he quipped. 'Ah feel lonely tekin' a bath all by meself. Never done it afore.'

'Well, you're a big boy now,' she replied lightly. 'We'll go for a walk along the cliff after. It's stopped raining. Be a nice night.'

Elisha had not bothered to close the door. There was the sound of his splashing and puffing about. 'Tell yer what! If you won't come in an' do me back, 'ow about sendin' that Madge up? Bit of all right she is. A cracker! What's the buzz? 'As she gorra boyfriend?'

There was a brief pause, before Angie answered, in the same light tone. 'I've no idea. She's gobby, I know that much! Got a lot to say for herself seeing that she's just a kid!'

'Hey! Just cos you're ancient! Eighteen now, eh? Seriously, Ange, why don't yer put a word in for me? Ah wouldn' mind tekin' 'er out. The pictures or summat. Be real nice.'

'Ah wouldn't trust her as far as ah could throw her!' was Angie's cool response. 'Now come on! Hurry up! Ah want ter get a wash. And then we'll get some fresh air.'

There was a damp breeze blowing, but they enjoyed the walk, Angie feeling proud and close as she linked arms with her brother. 'Yer look real grown up in uniform,' she said flatteringly. He told her about Annie Bartlett, not looking at her, staring out to sea as he spoke, and she realized intuitively his hurt, refraining from teasing him, or making light of it.

'The' was nowt soppy or daft,' he said hastily. He looked down at the empty beach, the blocks of concrete, the dark, wavy line of the sea coal that marked the edge of the tide. He remembered powerfully the day on the dunes, Annie in her black bathing suit. 'Hell, she was older'n you. Naw. She was just nice like. Didn' treat me like a kid, ye know.' Angie squeezed his arm tightly to her side. She promised to visit The Street before he went back in a week's time. Suddenly, he seemed in a rush to get off, gulping down his tea, and she guessed he had arranged to spend the evening with his mates.

Elisha waited at the bottom of the drive. He had found out that Madge Bell finished work at five. He dragged nervously on his cigarette, running over the possible opening gambits, growing more nervous with every minute. At last she appeared. He cursed as he saw her companion. He might have known. Me and my shadow. He certainly wasn't going to spend his hard-earned cash squiring two of them around. He'd better make that clear from the start.

Ruth was more than a little put out, he could tell, but eventually she left them when they reached Main Street, thanks to some pretty broad hints from her friend, which Elisha found very encouraging. It was almost dusk, and chilly. The pub didn't open until six, and there were no cafés in the village. So they walked back along the short length of sea-front to the shelter. They sat and had cigarettes, while Elisha put his long greatcoat over their shoulders. He slipped his arm around her – 'just ter keep us warm like', he assured her guilelessly.

She was an attractive girl all right. Annoying in a way, though. She had this funny, secret smile, and giggle, like something was amusing her and she wasn't letting on. Superior like. Yet she was interested, he could tell. Though she put up a bit of a struggle, when he first snatched a kiss, it wasn't serious. She soon let him pull her face round and plant his probing mouth violently against hers, felt their teeth clash as she responded forcefully. He felt himself stiffening, they clung awkwardly together, half lying, rousing each other, until she pulled her mouth away, with a frightened, excited whimper. 'That's – that's enough!' she gasped. They wrestled briefly, until he saw she was serious. He forced himself to relax.

'Sorry, Madge,' he murmured penitently. 'Yer such a smashin'-lookin' lass. An' ah've bin away that long. Ah gorra bit carried away. Ah'm sorry, love!'

She leaned her head decorously on his shoulder. 'That's all right. Long as yer know, ah'm not that sort o' lass.' She giggled shakily. 'Well, ah'll say one thing. Yer not like yer sister, that's fer sure!'

'What yer mean?' He was at a total loss. What on earth was she on about?

'Yer know. Funny. Like 'er. Ah thought yer might prefer ter – yer know – be out wi' a lad.' She sniggered smuttily, then yelped as her head bounced on Elisha's shoulder. He jerked upright.

'What the 'ell you sayin'? That ah'm a pouf?' He was incredulous. 'Yer bloody daft—'

'Well, ah thought it might run in the fam'ly. Yer know. The way your Angie on'y likes girls.'

This time, she almost toppled over, as he leapt to his feet, with a yelp of astonishment. He leaned over and caught hold of her hands. 'Just what the bloody 'ell are you tryin' ter say, lass? Now spit it out or ah'll knock yer fer six.'

She pouted, not really afraid of him, spitefully pleased at the shock she had given, as great as she had hoped it would be. 'Don't make out yer don't know yer own sister's one o' them.'

'One o' them what?'

'That go with other women! All that stuff about 'avin' a boyfriend, 'im losin' 'is arm! Tommy rot! She's been jumpin' inter bed wi' that ould dike Guy ever since she come 'ere.'

'Yer filthy-mouthed little tart!' Elisha thrust her hands away. She leaned back against the wooden boards, lifting her face provocatively.

'Aye, go on! 'It me! That's what *she* did! 'Alf killed me when ah tackled 'er about it.' She gave a vindictive bark of laughter. 'The' think the' so superior, the way they go on. So clever, keepin' it a big secret. An' the whole bloody village knows about it. Knows what goes on up there every night. Don't tell me yer didn' know! Yer own sister! Ye must've done!'

Elisha's mind was racing. He thought of how much quieter

she was, how gently she spoke. How refined and lady-like she
had become. God! She was a mirror for that Guy creature to
practise on. What had Madge called her? A dike? Was that the
name for – for one of them?

Savagely, he bent and captured Madge's thin wrist once
more. He laughed harshly. 'And you thought ah was like that?
A collar an' cuff, eh? A nancy boy?' He pulled her to her feet.
'Then what the hell did yer think ah was doin' 'ere, chasin'
after you?'

She was frightened of his fury now. And excited. She was
still roused by their kisses, his hands on her body. 'No. Ah
didn't – ah wasn't—' He hauled her into him, crushing her
against him, deliberately thrusting his loins against hers, letting
her feel the beat of his erection. He kissed her neck, biting with
savage slowness, feeling her shudder convulsively in his arms,
then he crushed his mouth over hers. She began to whimper.

'Please – Eli! Ah'm – ah like yer. A lot. Ah'm a good girl.
Ah've never – ah'm a virgin.' She was sobbing in earnest now.
He dragged her from the shelter, into the misty twilight.

'Is there a way down? To the sands?'

She nodded, shivering, and weeping audibly. 'Ah'm a virgin.
Ah've never done it before.'

'That's all right,' Elisha answered tensely. 'Neither 'ave I!' He
was still dragging her, and she let herself be led, to the worn
stone steps that led to the narrow stretch of sand. She clung to
him, stumbling as he pulled her down after him. They moved a
little way down the beach, slipping in the soft sand beside the
high sea wall. He threw his greatcoat down, dragged her down
on to it, with him.

'Someone'll see us,' she wept, lying there stiffly, shivering,
making no effort to resist. He saw the thick cardigan, the old
dress, the thick, ugly stockings, her scuffed and worn shoes.
He pushed the thin material up, over her thighs. The stocking
tops were rolled over the black elastic garters, which had made
deep red indentations in the plump whiteness of her thighs.
'Don't, Eli,' she wept, moaning softly, lifting her buttocks as he
clawed urgently at the thick, white knickers, lost suddenly to
the treachery of her young body that clamoured for him.

Eighteen

'Angela Thompson? Ah'm lookin' for yer brother. Eli, is it? Can yer tell me where ah can find 'im?' The tall police constable was middle aged, his face looked creased and rumpled with lack of sleep. She could sense the hostility despite his effort to keep his tone neutral.

'What's wrong? What's 'e done?' Her heart was hammering. She was acutely aware of Mrs Cullingford hovering behind her.

'We've 'ad a complaint of a serious sexual assault. Last night. On Marjorie Bell. She works here, doesn't she?'

'Ye what?' Angie's mind was whirling. Madge had not come in to work this morning. Ruth, looking very mysterious, had denied all knowledge of any illness, even though the pair usually came up from the village together. 'Ah don't believe it!'

' 'Er mother brought 'er into the station this mornin'. The've taken 'er into town. She'll be examined. And make a statement there. But the' need ter talk to yer brother.'

Angela was chalk-faced and weeping by the time she was alone with Helen Guy. 'Ah can't understand. 'E would never rape 'er.' Wouldn't he? Her own inner voice tormented her with doubt. He could have. She knew what he was like. What all of them were like, she thought, with sudden bitterness, recalling Ginge's desperate, rutting passion, Tony's squeezing hands, devouring kisses. She stared at the older woman, appalled. 'Ah bet she said something about us. The'll know about us! It'll all come out!'

Helen reached for her hand. 'Calm down, angel. No one knows, no one's seen anything. It's all malicious gossip.' But her thin face was strained, too, tense with anxiety.

The world had caught up with them. What had been so precious and beautiful between them was filthy and ugly when it was mercilessly exposed. Angie went home, sick at the thought of what would be waiting, and it was every bit as awful as she had imagined, yelling and curses and tears, her father raving, blaming her and her 'toffee-nosed ideas' for everything.

She knew that Elisha knew about her and Helen as soon as she looked at him. She was ashamed of her tearful relief that he had not said anything to the rest of the family. 'Thanks fer – ye know,' she muttered, as soon as she had the chance to exchange a word alone with him.

He was brutal with her, his condemnation and incomprehension was like a lash to her sensitivity. 'Ah don't bloody know! Yer bloody sick!' He told her what had happened, speaking with swift savagery. 'She was dyin' fer it. Same as me. Ah never raped 'er! She couldn' wait fer us ter – ter gerrit in 'er.' Angela shuddered at the crudity of his words, filled with a startling loathing of all of them. Yes, even of herself and Helen. After all, what were they, for all the fine words, the whispered sighs and endearments, but animals, grovelling and rutting about, only unnaturally so?

There was some doubt about proceeding with the charge. Medical evidence was inconclusive. There were no signs of physical violence, nothing to prove that the act of sex had taken place against Madge's will. 'Ah was too scared ter struggle,' the sobbing girl insisted.

'Too scared that she might be up the spout!' Angela said scathingly to Helen. 'Like y'are the first time yer do it. She wanted it all right. And like bairns, they were both too daft to do owt – take precautions. It was afterwards she got scared. Scared she was pregnant. That's why she told 'er mam 'e'd raped 'er.' Helen was staring at her, the dark eyes brilliant with tears, the features twisted with pain. 'Aye, ah know that feelin' all right!' Angie continued bitterly. 'Ah've been there.'

Elisha was allowed to return to barracks, the possibility of a charge still pending. But in the village of Dalby, the wicked tongues of Madge Bell and her family sought their revenge. Angie felt the wall of hate and condemnation that seemed to surround her, and she refused even to go down to the shop, or walk through the village. 'Ignore them,' Helen urged, with a hint of desperation in her voice. 'Don't let them spoil us.'

But it was spoiled, both of them knew. A few weeks later,

soon after the morning post had arrived, Helen sought out Angie, who could tell at once from the stricken face that something serious had happened. She stared at the letter Helen was clutching tightly. It was from Lady Agatha. Madge's parents had written to the Marston-Greenes, stating that they could not allow their daughter to go on working in such a corrupt atmosphere. They had been very specific as to the nature of that corruption. Lady Agatha was ordering Angela's immediate dismissal, with a month's wages of course. Meanwhile, Miss Guy should continue to run the house with the help of Ruth and Mrs Cullingford until Lady Agatha herself could return, and deal with the question of the housekeeper's own future with them.

Although Angie cried, she was, in a masochistic way, relieved that the situation was thus brought to a conclusion. Helen was not selfish, even though it was a personal disaster for her, too. 'I'd better start looking around for another job,' she said. 'Quite a thought. I've been with the family twelve years.' She shook her head. 'But you, angel. What will you do? Please – don't go too far. Keep in touch, wherever you are. Write to me. I promise I'll write. I'll think of you every night. And pray for you.'

Pray! Angela's young mind was shocked by the juxtaposition of religion and their abnormal relationship. But that's what had made it so special, Helen's clear resolution that there was absolutely nothing wrong with their love. Angie was bewildered by it. The last night, she did not go down to Helen's room, but sat looking round at the small space on the top floor which had become so important a piece of her. Her case was already packed. She opened immediately to the gentle tap.

She let Helen hold her, and they sat weeping quietly together on the narrow bed. 'Helen – I'm sorry – I can't – I don't want us to do anything.'

Helen nodded sadly. 'I wanted to love you just once more. The thought of not having you—' She wept desolately, and Angela almost weakened, acutely aware of their bodies lightly touching, the bed on which they sat. 'Shall we go down to the cellar?' Helen suggested presently. 'The siren's bound to go soon. At least we can be together.' She tried a brave, tearful smile. 'We can even leave the beds as they are. Please. Just let me be with you tonight.' Angie nodded.

The idea of returning home, however briefly, sickened Angie. She was determined to get into the women's services somehow, had revived her old interest in the WAAFs. Once again, Helen's help would prove invaluable. She had already spoken to Mr Briggs, who dealt with the family's legal affairs. Angie suspected that it must have been pretty embarrassing for Helen, but she had somehow succeeded in enlisting his aid, and Angie had instructions to call into the office when she got back to town, to collect a letter which she should present at the recruiting office. 'It'll still all depend on your interview,' Helen told her, 'but I know you'll make a good impression. Just look as smart as you can, and speak properly. You'll be all right.' She looked so sad as she said it that Angie's heart was full, too.

Next morning, they stood in the garden, in the May brightness, facing each other, holding hands tightly. Helen's lovely face was marked by the strain, but she was calm, brave. It was Angie who could not keep back the tears which came suddenly, in a choking flood. 'Don't forget me,' Helen said, smiling at her. 'And don't let it change. Remember what it was really like. What we had. Take care. I love you.'

'Love you,' Angie wept, and turned, blindly, following the driver to the cab Helen had insisted she should have to take her out to the bus stop on the coast road. The tears splashed down on to her gloved hands, twisting in her lap, as she sat in isolation in the rear of the taxi. She did not look back.

Not for the first time, her thoughts turned to her brother, and the act of precipitate violence that had brought down the catastrophe on so many heads. Her own misery was leaden in her breast. Even as she reflected that she would probably never make love with Helen again, she felt her body react with excitement at the very recall of their love. Their sexuality, her inner voice lashed at her. Just as Elisha had been compelled to satisfy his own instincts. And, beyond doubt, Madge, too, for all her later weeping and wailing. Why should we all be prisoners to the dictates of those bits of flesh we cover up and can't even refer to decently, she wondered miserably?

At least Eli was well out of it. He had not written to her, but her mam had told her that he had been drafted to a ship, a battle cruiser, HMS *Hood*, part of the Home Fleet and based up in Scotland, so he would probably be able to get home fairly regularly when they were in port. She grimaced. That would please him! She was going to call in to Mr Briggs' firm's office as soon as she got to town, and pick up that letter. Then straight to the recruiting office. She would even travel on to Boro if she had to. The less time she had to spend at home the better. Her da blamed her for everything that had happened, she knew. As though the fact that Eli couldn't keep his thing in his trousers was her fault! No good arguing, though. Just get away as fast as she could. Even while her heart was still breaking from the parting with Helen, her stomach was disloyally squirming with excitement at the thought of a new life in the King's uniform.

Old Jonson was one of the first in The Street to hear of the disaster, though it was not announced which ship had been lost, merely that, in an engagement at dawn, units of the Home Fleet had run into the German battleship, *Bismarck*. One British vessel had been sunk, though damage had been inflicted on the German raider, which was being pursued. 'Dey don' have de vireless next door,' he told Peggy. 'Mebbe I knock and tell dem, hey?'

His granddaughter shook her head, her plump face creased with sympathetic worry. 'Well, the's nowt ter tell them, really, Grandad. Only upset them, won' it? And prob'ly fer nothin'.' God, I hope so, she prayed.

When the telegram came the next morning, Doris was alone with the baby. Of course, her heart gave a lurch when she saw the black-capped lad, leaning on his red bike, but she immediately thought of Angie. She'd just gone off down south somewhere, started her training in the WAAFs. 'Oh God! What the 'ell's 'appened now?' She tore open the buff envelope with unsteady fingers.

She gaped at it uncomprehendingly. 'Killed in action'. Her mind seemed to be wandering. She couldn't pin it down. 'Any reply, missus?' The lad repeated his question, awkwardly, realizing now what it contained. He had not delivered many like it. He wanted to get away, quickly. She shook her head dumbly. 'Sorry,' he muttered, head down, as though it were his fault, and leapt on to his bike, pedalled off rapidly.

Doris grabbed the baby under one arm. She found herself

drifting across the cobbles, towards Ginge, who was already sitting on his chair, and had been watching the proceedings with concentrated interest. 'It's our Elisha,' she muttered dazedly. ' 'E's bin killed. At sea.'

Ginge grinned. He dug into his cardigan pocket, held out the crumpled packet. 'Tab?' he asked.

Doris took it automatically. 'Ta, pet.' She bent in close, to the flickering lighter he proudly held up for her. She dragged deeply on the Woodbine, then put the gurgling infant down carefully on the grimy pavement, before she sank on to the doorstep, and, leaning her head on her drawn-up knees, began to cry, raw, loud, ugly sobs for her lost child.

The *Hood*'s loss had overshadowed the sinking of *Bismarck*, which occurred two days later. The staggering death toll, only three survivors from a crew of hundreds, and the speed with which it happened, a mere three minutes from the moment the shell exploded in the magazine to the hull sliding beneath the waves, stunned everyone.

Angie was given forty-eight hours' leave, and then another pass of similar duration for the memorial service at the Cenotaph and at St Paul's. There had been three from the town altogether in the crew. She was glad to get back to the uncomfortable, crowded, mess-hut living, the wearying drilling and exercises of her new routine.

She had been shocked at first by the conditions, the lack of privacy, the crudity of some of her new comrades. Being with Helen had made her soft, she realized. Some of the girls thought she was toffee-nosed, posh, even, laughing at the way she spoke. It shocked her, for only then did she realize just how much of an effect Helen had had on her, on her way of thinking. But there was a whole young lifetime of The Street in her, too, and that was not forgotten. She was a survivor, and the rough and tumble of corporate service life held no terrors for her, as it undoubtedly did for some unfortunates. She knew that what Helen had taught her was valuable, and she vowed she would not lose it. She would hang on to it, cultivate it, continue to read, to try to educate herself. It would give her that polish she needed to get somewhere with her life. But the tender over-protection from the harshness of the world which

Helen had also provided was gone now. She was back in there, with a vengeance, and she would take care of herself. Polished, yes. But, underneath, hard. As nails, if need be. Elisha's death had been a cruel reminder of the harshness waiting out there. She would be ready for it, she would not let herself slip again.

That other, delicate, exclusive world she had shared was encapsulated in the long, tender letters she continued to receive every few days from Helen. It seemed a lifetime away already, though the loving, sometimes passionate, words could still make her quiver with an inward delight. Her own replies, apart from being less frequent, were also much shorter, conventionally stilted. She had only begun to grasp the merest inklings of finer things, a better, fuller appreciation of life, with Helen. Bitterly, she wished that the improvement that had already come about in her way of speaking could be reflected in her writing.

She was conscious mainly of her ignorance. She toiled over every page of her replies, laboriously checking spelling, tormenting herself over the mechanics of punctuation until she was tearfully ready to give up altogether. All too aware of her shortcomings, she tried to explain her difficulties.

Please don't stop writing, darling, Helen wrote emotionally. *Every word from you is treasured. And don't give up learning. Keep reading, that's the way. You're an intelligent girl. You can do anything, once you put your mind to it. I have faith in you.*

The mail was laid out on the table at the end of the mess hut, waiting for them when they came in for their midday break, and Angie's spirits always lifted at the sight of the beautiful handwriting. She would retire to her bed, and open the envelope eagerly, oblivious to the row going on around her.

'Hey up! There's Thompson off again! Another dose of red-hot pash from lover boy!'

Angie smiled. The girls were constantly teasing each other about their correspondence, and their love life, real and imagined.

Betty Dunn was a tall, well-built girl, with brown, tightly curled hair, and striking looks, who had, throughout the long weeks of their basic training, displayed a thinly veiled hostility towards Angie, occasioned, originally, by a simple jealousy of her beauty. 'That's a woman's writing!' Betty exclaimed now, her eyes gleaming challengingly. There were a few gasps, and the usual chorus of scornful laughter.

'Aye-aye! What's this, then, Thompson? 'Ands on yer 'apennies, girls!'

Angela was already nestled on her bed, propped up on the upended pillow. To everyone's surprise, she smiled dazzlingly at Betty Dunn, and said sugar sweetly, 'That's right, darling. How clever of you! My guilty secret's out.' The audience exploded with laughter, at the discomfited Betty's expense, who turned red, and simmered with rage.

'You ruddy little dike!' she retorted vehemently, and the others hooted, sensing the chance of a real clash.

But Angie's relaxed pose and beaming smile never wavered. 'Absolutely right, sweetheart. And you can stick your finger in me any time!'

Angie was 'a card', and became one of the squad's personalities, because of her quick wit, and her outstanding looks – in spite of them, in some cases. When their basic training was over, many were surprised when she was designated for the catering branch. She had already emerged as a section leader, and her class-mates had expected a more glamorous assignment for her. 'I keep telling you,' Angie laughed, hiding her embarrassment under a shield of flippancy. 'I'm as thick as two short planks, really. I've got no qualifications at all. I can't add up and I can hardly put two words together on paper. Cooking's all I'm good for!'

However, when she completed the second phase of her training, she was stationed at West Burton, a large bomber base in Cambridgeshire, from which both training and operational squadrons flew. She found herself on duty in the officers' mess, as both waitress and cleaner. Her CO was Squadron Officer Douglas, an ample, matronly looking woman, whose bite, her girls soon discovered, could be every bit as bad as her bark.

'No fraternizing with officers,' she warned Angie, at their first interview. 'And believe me, they'll try, with a stunner like you.' A blushing Angela tried to look suitably demure.

'No, ma'am,' she answered dutifully.

'Some of the air crews are very wound up. They're facing dangers night after night. Our losses are getting worse, not better. They can go a bit wild at times. Be discreet. And polite. But firm. Don't give them an inch, understand? Not an inch!'

A few *did* try, but mostly they were thoroughly decent, apart from the jocular suggestiveness of their talk. They reminded her of Tony Marston-Greene, with their light-hearted chaffing. Helen gave her news of him now and then. He had, as he had predicted, been posted to a corvette, spending his time on the dangerous North Atlantic convoys. She often thought of him, of his gentle concern, and the raw, snatched hunger of the kisses. Elisha's death made her afraid for Tony's safety, and she tried to pray for him, though the idea of prayer carried little conviction with her. It was more a primitive, heartfelt plea to the forces she sensed at work, far removed from the 'Our Father' of the Bible she had only stumblingly read since knowing Helen.

Helen occupied her thoughts much more than Tony. The housekeeper had been forced to leave Dalby Hall. Angie knew how much it must have hurt her to do so. Lady Agatha had found her a job in London, working with some organization like the WVS, which organized shelter for the homeless. It was work that, thankfully, was not as hectic as it had been in the first half of the year, for, about the time of Elisha's death, the nightly bombing raids on London and other cities had stopped. They were irregular and infrequent now, and people had got used to sleeping in their bedrooms again.

Congratulations on your promotion to ACW1. Sounds very grand. But when am I going to see my angel again? It's been over four months, and though I love the photo – bless you for it, it stands beside my bed and yes, you look achingly gorgeous in uniform – I'm longing to see you in, if you'll pardon the expression, the flesh. Sorry, my dear, I don't mean to sound flippant or smutty. I'm simply longing to see you. Please. Surely you can get some leave soon? Even a weekend would be marvellous. Don't let me down.

Angie's eyes misted as she read these words, and, once more, she felt herself torn with conflict. The thought of being back in Helen's arms again made her weak with pleasure. But it

was that very pleasure that she had, many tearful times since
their parting, determined to shun, to banish from her life. In
fact, had actually started, on several occasions, to pen her
resolution, as kindly as she could, only to end up screwing the
sheets of paper into a ball, hurling them savagely away. She
was so afraid of going back to that beauty, that isolated,
insulated loving. It was like being trapped in a bubble of warm,
scented water, it engulfed her, she wanted to drown in it. She
had been Helen's creature – loved, cosseted, but totally
dependent on that love. And it was wrong. Wrong. Somehow,
inescapably, Elisha's death was mixed up with it, was a
punishment for her infatuation, her perversion. It was her
responsibility. She could not convincingly persuade herself
otherwise, and it was a heavy burden to live with.

Once more, she wrote an indeterminate answer to Helen,
making excuses, putting off a meeting. Less than two weeks
later, came a letter whose writing she did not recognize. It was
from Tony Marston-Greene.

> *I tracked you down in true Sherlock Holmes' style. Got your
> address from Ma, through Pennifer, who's down here now, as
> you probably know. I've got 14 days' glorious leave and a fat
> wallet to get through. Trouble is, all the girls seem to remind me
> of you – because you're so much more beautiful than any of them.
> I'm not really so light hearted, quite the opposite, in fact.*
>
> *Any chance of seeing you? Could you get up to town for a
> weekend? Or I'll come anywhere you want me to. This is serious
> stuff, angel. I've been dreaming of you a lot in my miserable little
> bunk. At least write back. If you can get away – and I'm counting
> on it – you can get a message to me at the RAF Club, Piccadilly.
> The phone number's Grosvenor 3456.*
>
> *Please, Angie. I want to see you.*
> *Tony.*

She giggled. Her cheeks felt hot, her mind was whirling,
racing madly away. This weekend. She could swap duties and
get a forty-eight! Why not? Oh God! What for? Don't be daft,
Ange. He's a toff. No good to you. How do you know? These

days, that's all gone by the board. Anyway, he's nice. He likes me. Don't they all, Ange? And what about Helen? What would she think? You wouldn't go to see her – someone who – who what? Loves me? That's pretty sick. Isn't that the very thing you've been tormenting yourself over, all these months? The very thing you want to put behind you, for good and all?

At least Tony Marston-Greene is a feller. And a feller who thinks you're the bee's knees – 'Angel'. Isn't that the normality you've been searching to put back into your life? And now you've got a chance to do something about it. He must be really sweet on you, to go to all this trouble – finding out your address, writing to you. He's keen, Angie, you know he is.

All at once, her mind flew back to the shelter, that first night with Ginge. She recalled her fear, her discomfort, her shame. The strange mixture of pain, and embarrassment, and excitement, and promise of sweetness that their loving had brought in the brief times they had shared.

She had hated his feverish, rutting clumsiness, his brute inarticulateness, but then she had sensed the helpless honesty of his feeling for her, the tenderness that was exposed clearly beneath the red-faced floundering to express his emotion. She was the one who had not been honest, the one who had been uncertain of the truth, even though she had found it easier to murmur the 'I love yous'.

Tony would not be crippled with dumbness, she knew. She blushed hotly at the way her mind had leapt ahead to visualize them making love. He would know, in his gentlemanly way, what to do, what to say, there would be no awkwardness.

Just as there had never been with Helen, her tormenting mind mercilessly reminded her, nor any of the pain, or shrivelling embarrassment, or messy, desolate emptiness afterwards.

Grabbing her coat, she hastened across the busy roadway to the canteen and the public phone box before she lost her nerve.

Nineteen

'It's not your folks' flat, is it?' Angela glanced around the small, cluttered living-room. She unbuttoned her jacket and laid it over the back of the sofa.

There was the sound of a gushing tap. Tony laughed, calling out from the tiny kitchen. 'Good Lord, no! Not much chance of getting the place to yourself there. Not for long anyway.' He came back into the room. 'It belongs to an oppo.' He stood and gazed at her, and she thrilled to the pure joy she could discern in his beaming smile. 'I say! You *do* look marvellous in uniform. The things you do for a shirt and tie would drive an old sea dog wild.'

She pinked with pleasure, glanced down inadvertently at her rounded bosom. 'You should see some of them in my mess,' she giggled. 'Mae West isn't in it. Makes me look like Peter Pan.'

He had met her from the train, at King's Cross. She had been agonizing over how to greet him, trying to think of a smart opener, something cool and witty to set the tone for them. When she got to him, he had simply grabbed her and crushed her to him, and she had flung her arms responsively round his neck, and they had kissed until they were both breathless. 'Happy Christmas!' he gasped and, though it was a chilly October, she had known exactly what he meant.

Then the light-hearted, crazy chatter had started, all through the taxi ride, holding hands and laughing riotously. She was shocked at the strength of her delight in seeing him. Now, in the domestic intimacy of this stranger's flat, the first constraint gripped them. 'I've booked a table at the Criterion for eight. You have to get in early. Then we could go to a club. Or the Cumberland. There's a dance—'

'Don't forget I'm not one of your posh girlfriends. I haven't got a ball gown with me. Just a frock.'

'Nobody bothers dressing up nowadays!' he replied heartily. 'And you could go just as you are. You look gorgeous!'

She laughed, and eased the knot of her tie loose, widening the loop until she could slip it over her head. 'No thanks! I can't wait to get out of this lot. Look! I still haven't learned to tie my tie properly, in six months. It's murder!' She sat down and unfastened the solid shoes. She kicked them off and lifted her feet, waggling the toes luxuriously.

'Silk stockings, eh? I didn't know they issued you with those.'

She laughed again, pleased at his appreciative stare. 'They don't, yer daft 'aporth! Helen gave me—'

The name cut through the brittle jollity like a knife, and Angie crimsoned.

'Cup of tea!' Tony declared hastily, spinning round and stepping back to the little recess. 'No, it's all right, don't jump up! I'll do it. Allow me to attend on modom.'

He hesitated when he came back, and she shuffled along impatiently. 'For God's sake, park yourself down here.'

'Thank ye, ma'am.'

She sipped at her tea reflectively. Better to get the ghosts laid now. As though reading her mind, he somehow gave her an opening, by saying abruptly, 'I heard about your brother, Angie. I'm awfully sorry. I really am. It was terrible.'

She put her hand lightly on his sleeve. 'Thanks. Yeah. It was a real blow. The folks took it really bad, you know.' After a pause, she drew a deep breath, and plunged on. 'I guess you also heard about – about Helen and me.'

She could feel his embarrassment. 'Well, yes, something. Not all the sor – not all the details.' He went on swiftly, 'Look! It doesn't matter a damn. It's got nothing to do with anybody—'

She smiled sadly, kept her hand on his arm. 'I can't explain it, and I feel embarrassed as hell, but it's no good pretending it isn't there between us, so better have it out in the open. I didn't know – I mean, until I met Helen, I'd never – never felt like that, about lasses. Still don't!' She shook her blonde head, turned bravely to meet his gaze. She managed a wobbly smile, though the tears gathered brimmingly. 'But I loved her. Still do,

I suppose. But – I haven't seen her. She's asked me to – meet again. In London. I never have. I don't think I could. It—'

He stopped her then, putting his arms around her, and kissing her, slowly and gently, leaning back easily, with her in his arms, until they were both lying on the sofa's narrow length, she half on top of him, and they kissed again, and again, the passion building, until they were reaching, and pulling, and savaging one another tenderly, their hearts and blood thundering.

'Do you want to make love?' she asked breathlessly, at last. He could feel tears on her cheeks.

He groaned. 'We don't have to,' he said nobly. 'I don't want you for a quick bang. You've got to believe that. I'd rather we didn't if that's what you're going to think. I'm very fond of you. I might even be in love—'

She struggled until she was sitting up, propping herself by her hands on his chest. 'Careful now! Don't say anything rash! I don't want to make a big thing of this. But I'm feeling right randy! And besides! I've got to get out of this damn skirt. It's cutting me in two!'

They stood on either side of the double bed, their eyes on one another as they undressed. 'You look like a film star,' he murmured, staring at her silk underwear.

She stepped out of her panties, and forced herself to keep her clenched hands at her sides, letting him gaze his fill. 'You're not the first,' she said raggedly, striving for a mocking lightness. 'Let's face it. It's no big thing—'

He burst out in a yelp of spluttered laughter, and she sniggered as she realized what she had said. 'You know what I mean!' she gasped, in scandalized delight.

They leapt at each other, fell across the top of the covers, their bodies threshing deliriously together, their mouths searching. 'Come on,' she panted, soon, pulling him on to her. She felt him hesitate, felt the taut muscles in his forearms as he held himself over her.

'Are you – shall I – wear something?'

She closed her eyes. Oh God! Don't let me cry. Please. She felt as though he had struck her. The deep, beating excitement, the sheer need for his flesh, melted away. She hooked her arms tightly round his neck, arching under him, stretching her head back on the covers so that he wouldn't see her face closely. 'Oh God, yes! I don't want to – yes, get it on, quick!'

He hurt her, but it was largely her own fault, for, in the last, wild, rutting frenzy, she bucked madly, spearing herself into him, in order to get it finished with, pretending to an excitement she could feel only faintly stirring. She cried out at the final thrusts, it felt weirdly good to be punished thus.

'It was great, darling.' She found she could say that word now, just like him, without exploding with mocking laughter. But afterwards, she felt bad about her thoughts, her deceit. After all, she didn't want to get pregnant, did she? He had been thinking of her. She hoped so, anyway. And it was good to curl up in his arms, luxuriate in her nakedness, and his hard, male body wrapped around hers. They both slept deeply.

She woke to a wonderful, melting, powerful sensuality, flowing all through her, and at the same instant, was aware of his fingers moving within her, rousing her, so that she was already helpless against her desire, her need, and she groaned. She felt the cold air on her flesh as he pushed the covers back eagerly, then his lips trailed, from breasts, lingeringly, down her damp midriff, and she whimpered, unable to stop him, or herself from opening gladly to him, sobbing with her need, all at once her spinning senses swept irresistibly back to Dalby, and Helen's blazing, consuming love, until she plunged, soared, exploded in the magnificence, the death, of her climax.

She wept, curled up on her side, shivering, while he fitted himself into her back. 'Why did you do that?' she asked wonderingly, still shaken by it long minutes afterwards.

'I wanted to,' he said abruptly. 'Didn't you like it?' She turned, pulled his face down to her, curled her legs about him, reached down between their bellies for him. She felt him pause again, and shook her head.

'No,' she whispered. 'I want you. Nothing between us. I want to feel you in me.' She did, and it was wonderful, and she was deeply roused, in spite of her recent orgasm.

They didn't go out. At least, not to the Criterion. Hours later, they dressed, and, aching with their love, strolled hand in hand through the blacked-out streets, until they found a workmen's stall, and bought sandwiches to take back to the flat. 'I said you weren't the first,' she told him. 'It's true. You're the second. So don't write me off as a slut, will you?'

Next morning, late, she was making yet another pot of tea in the kitchen, when she felt him behind her, pressing into her buttocks, his hands sliding round to play with her breasts. 'Could give us both a nasty scald if you don't pack it in,' she giggled. He turned her, pressed to her in the narrow space, and hoisted her on to the cold bench top. He fitted himself between her thighs, and she stared down at him in mock alarm.

'If I get you preggers, will you marry me?' he asked, his mouth moving on hers.

'Not on your nelly!' she replied. She wiggled, moving to the very edge of the work top, manoeuvring herself, opening her thighs. She reached down and carefully took hold of his erect penis. She steered it to her entrance, then thrust forward, clutching him about the shoulders, gripping him tightly with her thighs, and he slid deep into her. She hooked her chin on to his shoulder. 'Now shuttup and get on with it, sailor boy!'

Angie sat crushed into a corner of the first-class compartment, trying gamely to join in the fun with the bunch of officers, mainly Canadian, who had dragged her in with them, despite her protests that her ticket was only third class. 'Don't worry, sweety. We'll bamboozle the old guard if he comes round. You're all right with us.'

The train was packed with RAF personnel heading back to Cambridge at the end of their weekend. In fact, she and Tony had had to put up with a great deal of good-humoured comment as they clung together at the platform gate. 'What the hell you doing with a civvy, darlin'? Traitor!' She was grateful when the group of fliers had practically hauled her into their compartment and squeezed up to fit her into the corner seat by the window. Otherwise, she would probably have had to stand all the way in the crowded corridor, and she was certainly glad to be sitting.

She ached in most places. She would have to be careful in the showers, or put up with a barrage of insults, for her body was liberally marked with the bruises of their hectic love-making. Well, he couldn't be in any doubt about her 'normality' now, could he? And could she, she wondered dismally? Why wasn't she feeling happy, the way she had told him she was when he had held her to him in that last kiss? He loved her. He had told her, over and over. He even wanted to marry her, for God's sake!

Mrs Marston-Greene. Lady Angela? She almost laughed hysterically at the absurd notion. Who were they kidding? And why did she feel an even bigger freak now, when Helen's ghost had surely been well and truly laid?

'It's only a medical. Everybody has to go through it. You'll get an exemption later.' That's what everyone assured him, that's what he assured himself, but Ellis was sick inside with worry. Well, they would know, surely, would hear for themselves his heart leaping and battering itself about inside his bony chest? He was torn with indecision. Should he not turn up for the examination, say he was too sick to make it? On the other hand, dare he take any more time off Stewart's, which was surely the reason they could not call him up, when he was engaged in such vital war work? Oh Jesus! It was enough to make a man turn to religion. He would, if he thought it would do any good.

And Old Jonson was revelling in it, the vicious old bastard! 'Dey need de men now, see.' He puffed away judiciously. 'Dey takin' a pastin' from dis Rommel now, ya. Dey needin' to build up dat desert army, for sure. Still, nice an' varm dere, hey? You miss dis bloody awful vinter!'

'Stoppit, Grandad!' Peggy begged. ' 'E's just teasin' yer, pet. Tek no notice.'

'Hm! You don't seem too fit for a man of your age, Mr Dalkin. How many cigarettes do you smoke a day?'

Ellis felt a warming ray of hope. He produced a rattling cough. 'Quite a few, doctor, ac'shly. An' ah get this pain 'ere in me chest, 'ere—'

'You seem to suffer from an alarming variety of pains,' the doctor replied drily, and Ellis's hopes took a dive. Perhaps he had overplayed his hand a little. He forced himself to keep silent, and concentrated on looking ill.

'I dunno,' he answered mournfully, to Peggy's enquiries. 'Ah think it went a' right. Ah told 'em about me nerves, like. Me palpitations. An' about me work. It should be a' right.' But he found it hard to sleep, or settle to anything.

A card came through the post. Medical category C-3. 'Yer all right, man,' the Sea Coal Man told him. 'Ye've gorra be A-1 te gerrin the forces, 'aven' ye?'

'Yeah, that's right.' Ellis nodded, his eyes big with gratitude behind his thick spectacles for these words of comfort. 'It's a bugger,' he added bravely, 'when ye not fit, eh? Yer want te do yer bit, like.'

Old Jonson was usually up, getting in the way of Peggy as she fussed over Ellis, getting him off to work. So he was the one who heard the thump on to the door mat, and brought the thick brown envelope back into the still lamplit room. 'For you, ya. OHMS.'

Ellis stared at it. 'By, they've took their time, eh? It'll be me exemption. Open it fer us, Peg, love.' His lips moved in prayer even as he told himself it could be nothing else. When he saw his wife's face, he was genuinely afraid, for the first time, that his heart might stop.

She stared at him, her mouth hanging open, her eyes fixed. 'The – the've called yer up. Army!' She let the thick pile of papers spill on to the table. He wanted to hit her. The stupid bitch!

'What the hell you on about?' He glared at her, and she nodded at the papers, her pink face pale now. He scrabbled, saw a card, a green form with 'Rail Voucher' across the top. With unsteady fingers, he found the letter. *Report to Catterick Camp. RASC Training Depot.* His lips moved, he whispered the dreaded words aloud. He looked up, horror stricken. 'The' can't!' he moaned. 'The' can't take me. Ah'm not fit.'

'Yesus! Dey mus' be gettin' desperate now, ya?' Neither of them gave any sign of hearing the old man's words, or his vindictive chuckle.

By the time Monday came around, he was feeling sicker than he had ever been. His mind had been racing for the past week with crazy ideas. Hide away somewhere in the country. Move down south. Get himself run over. Get himself injured at work. But, hopelessly, he knew that his real illness, his truly great cowardice, stood in the way of all these schemes.

In spite of his fierce, private delight, even Old Jonson tried to cheer him up. 'Army Service Corps. Ali Sloper's Cavalry! All dey do is look after de stores, man. Dey never get nowhere near de front. Bet you never leave England.' Ellis could only stare at him in dumb misery. Besides, the last thing he wanted to do now was to argue with him.

Peggy didn't go with him to the station. She knew it would be impossible for them both, that he would break down completely, would never be able to get on the train. Instead, they clung together in the dingy front room, and sobbed heartbrokenly, like children. 'Come on,' Jonson growled at last, his own eyes moist, which irritated him greatly. 'Better be off.'

It seemed as if half The Street had turned out to see him leave, and he felt like the condemned man making his last journey from his cell, as he responded to their good wishes. They had all chortled, many had felt that justice had indeed been done, but at the sight of the woebegone figure in his cap and ill-fitting suit that made him look like a black pipe cleaner, there were a good few who felt genuinely sorry for him.

Old Jonson was afraid at the station that Ellis was really going to cry again, as he hung out of the window. Certainly, his eyes were watery behind the magnifying goggles. 'Look after Peg,' he managed, the words choking him.

'Sure t'ing – Son!' Old Jonson nodded vigorously. His white head was high as he stepped with new vigour out of the station forecourt. He was only eighty-three. Or thereabouts. He wasn't too sure. Plenty of years in him yet. He would take care of Peggy all right. He always had, hadn't he? And who knows? Maybe the Army would send a real man back for her as husband.

The third Christmas brought a resurgence of the old optimism. At the beginning of November, El Alamein marked the turning point in the desert campaign. The names were already familiar to many at home – Tripoli, Tobruk. On Christmas Eve itself, came the news that the allies had recaptured Benghazi. 'An' this time, let's 'ope the buggers can 'ang on to it,' the Sea Coal Man declared. But, more important, there was the feeling of a turning tide, now that we had our new, powerful ally, America. ' 'Bout bloody time!' was the general consensus. Though Tojo had his front window put in by a drunk one night, most felt that Japan had done us a favour at Pearl Harbour. 'Just a matter of time now,' the experts at the Pothouse conferences agreed.

Twenty

A week after Angie's nineteenth birthday, Rommel's Afrika Korps took Benghazi back off the British Eighth Army once more. A group of officers were heatedly discussing the news as she stood by the coffee urn. The mess was quiet. Saturday, the end of the month. Most people not on duty would be off in town, spending up. She had volunteered to take this unpopular shift. 'You're a brick, Ange!' Maggie Philpott had gushed. By now, she'd be well into her fourth G and T – or her leading aircraftsman would be well into her, Angie thought cynically.

So, January, 1942, was about to bite the dust. A great year so far, she told herself. Angrily, she felt herself losing her constant battle against self-pity. It was going to be a bad night, in spite of her fierce resolve. Well, she couldn't win them all, could she? She'd been fighting this battle since just before Christmas, when the bombshell had fallen. It had actually arrived along with yet another of Tony's scrawled missives. There was quite a thick batch of them, that was the eighth. She kept an elastic band around them.

Not any more, though. She had shredded them, soaking them with her tears as she did so, and dumped the scraps in a stinking dustbin outside the mess hall, with the tea leaves and the empty cans. All garbage. Rubbish, to be discarded. She wished she could dump it from her mind, too.

Ironically, she had not destroyed Helen Guy's letter. That was still there, in the back of her locker drawer, even though she had never answered it.

Lady Agatha has told me about you and Tony. That he's

writing to you, is keen on you. She also knows that you and he spent a weekend together when he was on leave, that you slept with him. I'm not going to try to explain the pain you've caused her, and Sir Roger. As for me, I feel utterly sickened when I think of it. I think of us making love together, of your kisses, and your tears, the words you said. 'I love you, Helen', you said, night after night. You were mine, as I was yours, body and soul, I felt it. I can't believe it wasn't true.

So that now I think you're living a monstrous lie with Master Tony, whatever you whispered to him, and did with him in your secret little rendezvous. You must know how deeply you've hurt me. But I can't say any more of that. I'm writing to beg you to put a stop to it now, before you hurt anyone further. And most of all, him.

You must know it's impossible that there could be any decent relationship between you. Not only because of the way you truly are inside – however much you try to fool him and yourself – but because of all the other circumstances that would ruin his life. Think of your home, your background. I'm not saying this to hurt you, though I know it will. But the gulf between you and him is impossible to cross. You know it. The world is there. You can't ignore it. Where would you belong? Dalby Hall? His parents could never acknowledge you or him together. Sutherland Street? What would he really think of it?

He is a young man – scarcely more than a boy. Carried away by his first meaningful sexual experience. Whereas you – I know your history almost as well as you do. What first attracted him to you? Did he see you as I did when we first met? Do you remember the first night I took you to my bed – after the bombing? How long had we known one another? Three months almost. I lay all night with you in my arms, while you slept. That was our *love. It was you who first proffered your body sexually – and I've never been happier than that night. How long have you known Master Tony? Been with him? He saw you twice, briefly, as parlour maid. Enough to fall in love?*

Finally, if, as he has asserted, you really claim to love him, then you must *know that to persist in this affair is to destroy him, and any hope of the important future he might have.*

She had felt completely beaten when she had read it. The helpless, hysterical rage had died quickly, leaving her weaker than before. She had hidden away, sobbing, convulsed by her sense of hopelessness and grief, for Helen's words had probed like needles through to the very core of her, where all those doubts and insecurities already lay. The pain of them flared with the merciless agony of exposed nerves.

It took her days to find the courage to act, but, finally, hidden away in a corner of the Quiet Room, she had struggled with the most difficult decision of her young life, made worse by her shame at her lack of skill with the written word. Until the savage thought came that it didn't matter. Indeed, her paraded ignorance would be one of the most powerful arguments for her case. She knew the truth would not be enough. She had too much respect for Tony to believe he would accept it. This had to be a letter of rejection. It would hurt him, severely – she was angry with herself at her instinctively selfish little hope that it would – but it would save him, them, the later pain which Helen Guy had so rightly predicted.

She told him she had become deeply involved with someone else. An airman from the camp, that she had made love with him, someone of similar background to herself. *Not a toff like you.* She wished him all the luck in the world. *Keep yourself safe for some nice decent girl.*

She stamped and posted it quickly, the tears stinging in the December cold. She seemed to have spent most of the time weeping, or trying to hide the fact, since then. He had written once more, a short, final note, polite as always, accepting her decision, and it distressed her even more, for it simply reinforced Helen's point. He should have called her a tart, slag, bitch – that's how her sort would have reacted.

Now she was a career girl. She smiled in self-mockery at the chevron with the propeller at her shoulder that indicated the rank of leading aircraftswoman. Such a meteoric rise to fame! She actually got to tell girls to scrub out the lavs instead of doing it herself.

'Hi. Can I have another cup of this black mud, please? It's really swinging tonight, eh? I can hardly stand the pace.' The speaker was a slim, black-haired girl, wearing a beautifully tailored uniform with the insignia of a flight officer at the sleeve. She was a new and exotic addition to the officers' mess. Angie had noted her from her first appearance just over a week ago. Flight Officer Reece was something to do with a photographic unit, on a special assignment, making a propaganda film at the base. The males had, of course, flocked round like bees at the honey, and Angie had admired the ease with which she seemed to handle their attentions. Now she appeared glad to escape from the knot of hangers-on, and lingered by the long, white-clothed table, to chat.

'I'm Lynne Reece,' she said, smiling warmly. She held out her hand. Angie blushed self-consciously, glanced round before she tentatively accepted the greeting. No WAAF officer had ever treated her like this. 'I've noticed you before. Been waiting for a chance to speak to you. I'd like to take a few pics of you. Around the camp. You know, the usual glamour puss sort of thing. I'm sure we'd be able to use them somewhere. Boost the morale of our gallant airmen, eh?' She laughed, and pulled a comic face as she spoke, clearly indicating her cynical detachment from such sentiments, and Angie warmed to her immediately.

She was taken aback by the suggestion, and began, with embarrassed modesty, to demur. Lynne Reece cut swiftly across her protests. 'Oh, come on! You must know how dishy you are! It could do you a lot of good. Come over to the welfare office tomorrow. When are you free? We'll talk about it. You're the first ray of sunshine I've seen in this benighted spot.'

Angie did the series of pictures, enjoying the fuss and attention, the carefully casual hair dos, the elegantly styled uniform, to make the most of her slim figure. Posing in the ops room, wearing headphones, draped across a stool, Lynne interrupting the cameraman to dash in and push Angie's skirt a few vital inches higher above the knee. Outside, in slacks this time, perched atop a fuel tanker, holding the nozzle of a hose pipe, under the wing of a Blenheim. Again Lynne's last minute intervention. 'No. Not right. Just a minute.' And she had swept her off, back across the tarmac of the apron, dashing inside, racing round frantically to find a size smaller in the slacks.

'They're too tight!' Angie gasped, hauling them on in a corner of the store, under Lynne's critical eye.

'Nonsense! I want more of your bum out there, sweet. This is for King and country, remember!'

She wasn't like an officer at all, inviting Angie back to her room for a drink. 'I can't! Squadron Officer Douglas'll kill me!' Angie squealed.

'Oh knickers, sweety! I can't stand all this them an' us shit!'

They got to know one another amazingly quickly. Angie was in need of a friend. And Lynne could listen, as well as talk. 'Blokes, sweety, are nothing but trouble. Capital T!'

When she invited Angie to London for the weekend, Angie was almost certain it was a momentous choice. Lynne had not declared herself, but Angie sensed it. The seemingly casual touches, the special feeling of warmth, of intimacy between them. Her talk, leading ever more revealingly to an exclusive female bond. And Angie had to make her own decision. She felt its importance in her life.

She was fascinated by this powerfully attractive young woman. Physically excited, too. She could no longer deny it. But she clung with some desperation to her renewed resolve, her vow, that she would not be emotionally involved. Hard. She must be hard, and care only for herself. She could do it. Lynne had told her already, speaking from the wisdom of her twenty-four years. 'Your looks are your best asset, sweety. Make them work for you.' She would not allow herself to be dragged down by sentiment. No more kicks in the gut.

'Are you sure it'll be all right?' Angie stared worriedly at her companion. Lynne Reece put a hand on her elbow and steered her forward.

'Of course it will, you goose! Ray's an old friend. I often bring friends to stay. You don't mind sharing a bed, do you?'

Angie could feel herself colouring. She shook her head. She felt again that tightness in her chest, the fluttery weakness, the excitement that shamed her and that she was helpless to prevent. There was so much behind the casual words, so much unexpressed between them in the brief, hectic time they had known one another.

Lynne had a key. The flat was empty. 'Maybe he's away,' Lynne said. Was she lying, Angie wondered? Had she known all along? Was she about to seduce her?

'This is our room. Chuck your things there. Come on! Let's

make the most of it. Bath-time. Pour us a drink, sweety. In the sideboard. G and T, I think.' Lynne had left the bathroom door open. She was half lying among the bubbles, her black hair carelessly gathered up. Angie was surprised by the fullness of her breasts, the dark richness of the areolae. 'Why don't you join me?'

Angie stood there, hesitating. She had removed her jacket, but she was still in her uniform. Lynne's voice was hoarse, and unsteady. She had surrendered her air of cool amusement. 'You know I want you. I can't help myself. Since I first set eyes on you.' Her thin, aristocratic face had an expression of pleading. The dark eyes were softened, vulnerable. 'I want you to transfer to our unit. I can ask for you. An assistant. I want to use you for pictures. Films. It could be a great chance for you, sweety.' Her tone was entreating. She sat forward, her hands half raised.

Angie stood there, perfectly still, in the tense instant of silence that followed. Then she gave a small, private smile, and, putting down her drink on the basin lip behind her, began, with enticing deliberation, to undress.

Her hair was long again, flowing in a golden wave down over her shoulders, richly silkier than they had ever seen it. Her uniform was different, too, and special, beautifully moulded to her elegant figure. A military car came, complete with driver, and waited, surrounded by almost the entire gawping, child population of The Street. She was a stranger, and the Sea Coal Man and Doris stared as though she were unreal. They were dazed and awkward, could only listen uncomprehendingly, and were almost afraid to touch her when she kissed them before she left.

She looked back along the length of The Street, towards the still grimly towering block of the school, squatting like a policeman as though put there to prevent even the thought of escape. But it looked oddly vulnerable, now, the high, green railings, the barrier that had signally failed to hold Elisha's soaring spirit in check, ripped out like so many rotten teeth. She smiled at the gathered crowd of shabby individuals, appalled at how diminished they looked, her own family stood among them.

She vowed that this would be her last visit. She wouldn't desert them, of course not. She would help them, as she already had over the past months, help them to make their own break from The Street. If that was what they wanted. She had money now, plenty; it still shocked her to think how much. Smart clothes, expensive perfume, all the luxuries she hadn't known enough to even dream of when she lived here. And she was still just making a beginning. The war would not last much longer, and, afterwards, according to Lynne, their possibilities were endless.

Her mind leapt ahead, eagerly, to her own escape, the car door beckoningly open, the comfort of its interior so alien to the surroundings she was about to leave. The first-class carriage would take her away from the sooty station to the far distant capital, the quietly luxurious room in the Lansdowne Club, where Lynne Reece would be waiting for her.

She owed Lynne everything, she acknowledged, shying away as always from the painful prick of the voice that told her she was fulfilling her side of the bargain. Selling her body, and her skills as a lover, in return for the tremendous favours Lynne had conferred on her. Not much different, really, from those cleverly painted girls with the long, flashing, silk-stockinged legs, who hung on the arms of the officers in the bar of the Lansdowne or the Criterion. Or their more blatant sisters who paraded about the pubs of Piccadilly, or hung around the vicinity of the Union Jack Club.

But no, she admonished her warring self, her relationship with Lynne wasn't like that. There was nothing mercenary about the way their eager bodies came together in the blissful, crisp fragrance of the clean sheets, the tumultuous excitement their perfumed lips aroused. It was a mutual hunger which they both called love, and Angie tearfully tried to still the small, insidious voice that whispered of the old uncertainties.

Love was what she had called the frantic, tearing couplings she had experienced with Ginge. Her grandiose pretence had mocked her when she found she was obliterated from his poor, dazed memory, except for a furtive, instinctive, fumbling hand under the sticky darkness of a blanket.

And love was what she had called the isolated, encapsuled sweetness of her time with Helen Guy, whose potency even now could burn her with the hot blush of shame. Certainly, it had been a sexual awakening for her. It had shown her a wonderful, awesome depth of passion in her – and a yawning gulf that had threatened to swallow her. She had run from that gulf, fleeing to Tony's arms, and to his bed. To another 'monstrous lie', as Helen had called it, and maybe she was right. Angie liked to think she was acting from unselfish reasons in her rejection of Tony. It was true that she was undoubtedly acting in his best interest. It was painful to reflect that it was probably in hers, too.

Perhaps with Helen she had truly known what it was to love. She had believed so at the time, with all her heart, could still almost believe, when she savoured the remembrance of the all-encompassing sweetness they had shared. Why was it, then, she had tearfully but steadfastly refused to see Helen again, refused even to answer the impassioned outpourings of her letters, except in the most politely muted and detached terms? It hurt to explore her own psyche so deeply, but she recognized, with a beat of unsteady fear, the tempting dangers of that very sweetness. Danger she could sense rather than express, even to herself, from its pervasiveness, the languorous surrender of every facet of her personality to the power of the woman who had made such a mark on her.

Lynne Reece's version of 'love' – hers, too, she could admit privately – was nothing like so consuming. Physically, it exerted a power that could not be denied, that neither wished to. It was a mutual need, and they shared it as they shared their affection, as equals. Lynne might be manipulative, and selfishly clear-sighted in her goals, but then, so was Angie. She had learned to be, all over again, though the seeds had been there, had never died, from her early adolescence and the fierce determination to escape from The Street. Her looks were an accidental asset, and amazed her even more as she gazed about her at what they had sprung from, but she had a quick brain and was already learning how to use them.

Coming back here, though, scared her. It was the first time in almost a year, and it reminded her unnervingly of how close it all still was to her. It was a world she had to shake off for good. She would take nothing of it with her.

She turned on the pavement, laughing and waving at the

kids, and her pale-gold hair swung at her shoulders, and she ducked towards the sanctuary of the car.

Across the road, Ginge gave a guttural cry, the yellow hair flashed and seemed to burst like a star in his brain, and a great pain caught at his chest, as he saw and knew her. 'Angie! Angie!' He cried out in quiet agony, the great and tender ache of his love washing over him, engulfing him as he remembered all its glory, the sweetness of her body, the treasure of her gift to him. He sank back, weakened, sobbing without restraint at the loss he only now could recognize.

In the instant before she bent her gleaming head to step into the car, she looked directly at him, their eyes locked, and she saw the knowledge there, the sudden burst into life, and she recoiled as though she felt the blow, and stumbled blindly into the dark interior.

The Street watched as the car retreated, and saw, through the narrow curve of the back window, a pale, pinched face staring out, afraid; a face that blurred with the swift distance, but the face of the little girl who had dreamt longingly of just such a moment a lifetime ago.

There was still a while, and other stories, before they brought the trestle tables and the rickety chairs out, under the strings of home-made flags, and melted the tar that held the cobbles with the huge victory bonfire they lit in the middle of The Street itself, and the new generation of kids tied ropes and swung ecstatically round the relit gas lamps, while Little Jimmy, no longer little, watched disdainfully, and thought about Angela, and Elisha.

There were other ghosts at that Victory Feast, a good number, but The Street was alive. It had survived the worst that a war could do, and had triumphed. The good and the just had triumphed. The New Age, the Socialist Dream, the Welfare State, with all its limitless possibilities, beckoned, and it marched forward proudly, confidently, to its ultimate destruction, bloody but unbowed.